Everything's Fine

A NOVEL

Cecilia Rabess

Simon & Schuster
New York   London   Toronto   Sydney   New Delhi

Simon & Schuster
1230 Avenue of the Americas
New York, NY 10020

First Simon & Schuster hardcover edition June 2023

SIMON & SCHUSTER and colophon are registered trademarks of Simon & Schuster, Inc.

For information about special discounts for bulk purchases, please contact Simon & Schuster Special Sales at 1-866-506-1949 or business@simonandschuster.com.

The Simon & Schuster Speakers Bureau can bring authors to your live event. For more information or to book an event, contact the Simon & Schuster Speakers Bureau at 1-866-248-3049 or visit our website at www.simonspeakers.com.

Interior design by Carly Loman

Manufactured in the United States of America

10 9 8 7 6 5 4 3 2 1

Library of Congress Cataloging-in-Publication Data

ISBN 978-1-9821-8770-5
ISBN 978-1-9821-8771-2 (ebook)

For my mother and her mother

"Oh my god! I love Josh!"

—*Clueless*

"Love is never better than the lover."

—Toni Morrison, *The Bluest Eye*

Part One

1

Jess's first day of work, the first day of the rest of her life. Into the elevator and up to the twentieth floor, where the doors open with a little *whoosh*.

The entire building smells like money.

She receives a small plaque with her name printed in all caps: JESSICA JONES, INVESTMENT BANKING ANALYST. Then introductions—the other analysts on the team: Brad and John and Rich and Tom, or maybe it's Rich and Tom and Brad and John—and also Josh, who Jess remembers from college.

"Hey," she says, "it's you!"

He looks up from his desk—he is already installed at a workstation, looking busy and important—but his face is blank.

They had a class together last year and Jess remembers him, because he was the worst.

"Jess?" she offers. "From school?"

He blinks.

"We had a class together?" she tries again. "Supreme Court Topics?"

He just looks at her, saying nothing. Is it possible she has something on her face?

"With Smithson? Fall semes—"

"I remember you," he says. And then promptly swivels in his chair.

Cool, Jess thinks. *Nice catching up.*

She starts to go.

"You know," he says, not turning, "I knew you'd been assigned to this desk."

Jess stops. "Oh, really?"

He nods—the back of his head—"I worked with these guys when I was here last summer. And I graduated off-cycle, so I've been back since January." He pauses. "They asked me about you."

"What did you say?"

"Nothing."

"What! Why didn't you tell them I was amazing?"

"Because," he says, finally turning to look at her, "I'm not convinced you are amazing."

The first time Jess met Josh, it was fall of their freshman year. November. The night of the 2008 election. All day the campus had pulsated. History in the making. Around eleven the election was called and Jess emerged stunned and delirious onto the quad, which had erupted into something like a music festival. Students spilled out into the night cheering and hugging. Car horns honked. Someone screamed *woot woot* and, somewhere, a trombone, brimming with pathos, played a slow scale.

Jess had the feeling she had been shot out of a cannon; she was blinking into the moonlight when a couple of reporters from the school paper stopped her. They were compiling quotes from students on the eve of this historic moment. *Did she have a minute to share her feelings, and would she mind if they took her photo?* Jess said sure, even though the air was crackling and she wanted to weep.

The reporter's pencil was poised. "Whenever you're ready."

What could she possibly say? There were no words.

"I'm just . . . I'm just . . . fucking ecstatic! Is this even real? And now I'm probably going to go have, like, thirty shots—no, fifty!— because that's more patriotic!"

The student reporter looked up from his mini legal pad. "End quote?"

"Wait, no! Don't write that!"

"What do you want to say?"

Jess thought about it, collected herself. Imagined her dad reading her words. Her dad, who she'd spoken to just hours ago, and whose reaction to the early returns—Ohio and Florida were set to break for Obama—was to pour himself another Coke and say: "Well, Jessie, I'll be darned."

She started over. "I feel the weight of history tonight. To cast my very first vote for our nation's very first Black president is such an awesome privilege. A privilege that my ancestors, slaves, did not share. Standing on the shoulders of so much strength and sacrifice, I've never felt more humbled or hopeful."

"That's great," the reporter said. "Now just stand over there and we'll take your shot."

Jess took a step to the left and watched as the reporter approached another student. A sandy-haired freshman wearing chinos and a collared shirt.

The photographer said to Jess, "Look this way. On the count of three."

And the reporter said to the boy in business casual, "How are you feeling about the election?"

Jess turned to the camera and smiled.

The guy in chinos turned to the reporter and said, "Everyone seems to forget that we're in the middle of a financial crisis. The stock market is in free fall. Gas is four dollars a gallon. So I'm not convinced that now is the right time to entrust another tax-and-spend liberal with the economy," he shrugged, "but I guess I can see the appeal."

Jess, aghast, turned to give him a dirty look, her smile dropping just as the flash popped.

The next day she was on the front page of the school newspaper under a headline that read STUDENTS REACT TO OBAMA'S HISTORIC WIN.

The picture was good—the angle, the moonlight, her face radiating quiet wonder—and that, plus the gravitas of the moment, made Jess feel like this was something she would show to her children and their children one day.

There was only one problem.

The paper had spoken to ten students, a grid of two-by-two photos and quotes, names and graduation years printed below. But there were only two faces above the fold. There was Jess, but also the guy in the collared shirt, with his terrible quote. Jess's friends agreed that it was a stupid thing to say. Miky, who lived across the hall, said, "Who pissed in his Cheerios?" And Jess's roommate, Lydia, peered at the photo and declared: "He looks boring."

Still, Lydia tacked the paper to the outside of their door. With a marker, she drew a frame of hearts and stars around Jess's face. But there was no way to accordion the paper so that only her picture appeared. It cut off the text strangely and warped her smile. It was impossible to see Jess without seeing Josh. Eventually Miky took a Sharpie and drew devil ears and a weird mustache across his face, and that was better.

Eventually the tack hardened and the paper fluttered to the floor. At that point it was the spring semester and the hallway had devolved into a persistent, low-grade chaos: crushed pizza boxes, twisted extension cords, a mysterious pair of men's underwear. And when the cleaning crew cleared out the dormitory between the spring and summer sessions, they swept everything, including that momentous reminder, into the trash.

But until that happened, Jess could return to her room each day and see the newspaper, like a talisman, stuck to her door, emanating strength and inspiration, and when she looked at it, she would think: *We are standing at the precipice of a bright new world, hopeful and resolute, knocking on the door of progress, with the conviction of what's on the other side.*

And then she would slide her eyes to the right, to the photo of JOSH HILLYER '12 and his terrible quote, and she would think: *Asshole!*

Brad and John and Rich and Tom's and Josh's desks are all arranged in a tight semicircle around a dirty carpet in the center of the room. In the bullpen, they are packed like sardines, swimming in pitchbooks and gym bags and coffee cups, so there is no space for Jess.

"We've got you over here," Charles says. He is the most senior associate on the team, and Jess can tell he's in charge because he wears his tie the loosest and calls everyone by their last name. Even more senior is Blaine, the team's managing director, but he can't be bothered to meet her.

Charles leads her to a row of desks along the wall. By now, after the all-day orientation, it's after five, but the office is still buzzing. Still, the seat that Charles points to and all the ones that surround it are empty. The desks, though, are covered in equipment, telephones and Bloomberg Terminals and digital handsets.

Traders, Jess guesses.

Traders are the first ones in and the first ones out. When the market closes their day is done. Jess feels a tingle of excitement. The traders are loud and potty-mouthed and wear hideous pinstripe suits. The investment bankers, on the other hand, are nasty but humorless. Jess might have liked to be a trader but had missed the deadline to apply. Maybe this is a sign, an opportunity.

She imagines herself shouting orders into a phone, telling someone to go fuck themselves when she doesn't like a price.

"So this is where the traders sit?"

Charles blinks. "No, not exactly."

"Then what's with all the telephones?"

"Switchboard," Charles says. "Secretaries and stuff. You know, 'Goldman Sachs, how may I direct your call?' Switchboard," he repeats. "Secretaries."

"Oh."

He pauses. "Yeah."

•

By the end of her first month, Jess can say *How may I direct your call?* in four languages and she still hasn't been assigned any real work. Her back is to the bullpen, but whenever she looks over, the other analysts appear to be chained to their chairs, heads bent over their desks, doing God's work.

Jess is doing nothing.

It doesn't help that when the bankers shout for coffee orders or someone to run to the copy shop, they do it in her general direction: a secretary is a secretary, even when she's actually an analyst.

Just yesterday a harried-looking senior associate asked her to pick up a suit from the dry cleaner's downstairs.

"Oh, I'm actually an analyst."

He stared.

"So, I think maybe you should ask one of the admins?"

"I don't have time for this," he said, handing her his bright pink ticket. "Look, can you just help me out?"

She said she couldn't, but then hid in the bathroom for fifteen minutes so that he wouldn't see she had nothing else to do.

Jess begs Charles for something to do.

She reads an article about women and work. It says: "It is incumbent upon females in male-dominated workplaces to create their own opportunities for development."

She says to Charles, "It is incumbent upon females in male-dominated workplaces to create their own opportunities for development."

He squints.

"And so I was hoping you could help me. Create an opportunity? Like, give me something to work on?"

Miky sends Jess a link to a video of Nicolas Cage superimposed on a teenage girl's body, wearing white panties and a tank top, swinging from a giant cement wrecking ball.

Jess clicks on it.

Charles walks by her desk right then and says, "I see."

Later, he drops a stack of public information books on her desk.

"Jones," he says, "I need some numbers."

"Great."

"Should be pretty straightforward," he says, flipping through one of the books. "If you log in to the server, you'll see we've already got a template. I just need you to tune the model and run a few different comps. Got it?"

"Got it." Jess eyes the stack of books. "When do you need this by?"

Charles says, "Yesterday."

*   *   *

It doesn't occur to Jess that she has no idea what she's doing until it's too late to ask for help. The only person who offers is Josh, though not because he actually wants to help, but because he is her buddy.

On her second day he appeared at her desk.

"Hey, Jess."

She spun around so that she was face-to-face with his waist. "Josh, hey."

"I'm your buddy," he said.

"Excuse me?" she said, to his belt.

"Your buddy," he said.

She pumped the lever on the side of her chair and dropped three inches in her seat. Her face was still uncomfortably close to his crotch so she stood.

"So what does that mean? You're my buddy?"

"I've been assigned to help you. To answer questions if you have them," he shrugged. "They try to pair every first-year analyst with a second-year analyst, kind of like a mentor. They picked me for you. Probably because we're from the same undergrad."

"But you're not a second-year analyst."

"Close enough," he said. "Anyway, I'm here." And then he walked away.

Now every night before he leaves, if it's before she does, he asks if there is anything she needs help with. But he's always holding his phone and his bag and wearing his jacket, and his corporate badge is already in his pocket, so that Jess can tell he doesn't mean it. It's just something to say and, anyway, her desk is right next to the elevator.

Of course she needs help, has questions. How is a debt capacity model different from a credit risk analysis? How does the federal funds rate affect LIBOR? How come her key card doesn't work at the gym on the first floor?

But he is the last person she wants to ask. She can tell he thinks she's an idiot, that she doesn't belong here. She catches him sometimes, looking at her sideways. Interested but unimpressed. Like he's waiting for her to mess up.

Plus, he'd already made his feelings clear.

*   *   *

That class they'd had together senior year: Supreme Court Topics. Each week they debated a different landmark decision, and someone was always shouting. Or sharing a pointless personal anecdote. Or invoking the founding fathers to prove a stupid point. Jess hated it, but it fulfilled the undergraduate Law & Society requirement.

They sat around a big wooden table that was meant to foster "active dialogue," and the discussion was student-led, the format purposefully discursive, so that even if one day, for example, the syllabus said *Grutter v. Bollinger: Affirmative Action*, they might spend half the class arguing about basketball and standardized tests until someone groaned: "Is anyone else completely bored of this debate?"

It was the guy from Jess's door, JOSH HILLYER '12, who cared about the price of gas and hated Barack Obama. Who Jess had managed to avoid since freshman year, but who had reappeared three years later. Still with the newscaster hair and the terrible takes.

Jess had turned and glared. Not because she wasn't also bored of the debate, but because she knew he was bored for the Wrong Reasons. He'd said what he said on the front page of the school paper, but it wasn't just that: it was everything about him. His Choate sweatshirt, for example, which made Jess think of lawns and regattas and gin cocktails and haughty blondes. And there was something about his face. It had been there in the school paper, that something, but the effect was more pronounced in real life.

He looked like what a fifth grader might come up with if asked to draw a man, all even lines and uncomplicated symmetry. Square jaw, blue eyes. Like someone to whom life had been incredibly kind. Like a guy from an old sitcom who condescended to his wife.

"It's 2011," Josh had argued, "why are we still having this debate? How does throwing open the doors to elite universities fix discrimination? The problem is broken homes and blighted communities. That's where policy interventions should start. In homes, in neighborhoods, in schools."

"This is a school," Jess had pointed out.

"Whatever," another classmate said. "It's reverse racism."

And Jess had said, "If that were a thing!"

Another classmate: "People shouldn't get into college just because they're Black."

"Sure," Jess replied, "because my college application was just the words 'I'm Black' repeated one thousand times."

Someone else clarified, "I think his point is that we shouldn't take race into account at all."

"Exactly. Affirmative action isn't fair."

"It's not meritocratic."

"It's not *constitutional*."

"It *is* kind of outrageous that there's essentially a double standard based on, you know, melanin."

"What about the double standard for athletes and legacies!" Jess's heart was pounding; she felt a little wild-eyed. "Isn't *that* the outrage?" She searched the room—for what? For someone who might agree with her? That wasn't going to happen. They would make their dispassionate arguments, and when class was over they would calmly pack their textbooks away and Jess would be the only one who'd felt like she'd been kicked in the teeth repeatedly.

She took a breath. "My point is just that anyone with a squash racquet or a trust fund is automatically exempt from scrutiny. No one's asking if they're qualified. Why?"

"That's not the same thing, and you know it."

"Yes, it is."

"No, it's not."

"Yes, it—!"

The professor cleared his throat. "Let's bring it back to the case at hand. Was Grutter's claim valid? Or was the court's decision, on balance, unconstitutional?"

Jess sighed and sat back.

To her right, Josh leaned close.

He whispered, "Is that really your argument? That legacies and affirmative action are the same thing? I mean . . . really?"

Jess had ignored him and pretended to pay attention as someone prattled on about why it didn't make sense for universities to "lower the bar."

Josh slid his elbows over the table so that his clasped hands rested on Jess's notebook. So that she could smell the fabric softener on his sleeves. "Come on," he had said, his voice low. "I don't believe you believe that."

Jess had picked up her pen, drawn a series of squiggles and spirals in the upper right corner of her notebook. Avoided eye contact.

"At least you see how it's a false equivalence, right? You do see that, don't you?"

All Jess saw was his pale wrists, the titanium watch ticking silently. His father had probably given it to him on his eighteenth birthday. Along with a fifty-year-old bottle of scotch and the passwords to all the brokerage accounts.

Jess didn't reply.

He leaned closer. "So you really think relaxing admissions standards for 'underrepresented minorities' "—here he used air quotes, which confirmed for Jess that, yes, he was the worst—"is an acceptable mechanism by which to achieve"—more air quotes—" 'equality?' "

This was why Jess hated Law & Society. It was always the same story: oppressed peoples, willful misrememberings of history, a whiff of white supremacy. Unlike calculus or economics, in which the professor silently scratched out the answers at the front of the lecture hall, and in which there was rarely controversy—unless someone got started on infinity!—in these liberal arts classes people insisted on shouting out their opinions, no matter how unseemly. It was a lot to endure for a couple of college credits. Yet here she was.

And there he was. Breathing. Staring. Forcing her to engage. Emanating smug entitlement. Waiting.

"So you really believe that having a certain skin color is as good as possessing some demonstrable skill or talent?" He shook his head. "Seriously?"

Why couldn't he just go polish his watch and leave her be?

But he wouldn't let it go. He kept shaking his head, saying, "I don't believe you believe that," until Jess said: "Josh?"

He leaned toward her, expectant, and Jess tugged her notebook from under his wrists. "You're on my notes."

He seemed momentarily startled but was undeterred. "You realize you're essentially arguing that 'diversity' matters more than merit."

She was losing patience. "Well, you're arguing that swinging a squash racquet is equivalent to four hundred years of slavery and systemic inequality!"

Around the table conversation stopped.

Everyone looked over. It occurred to Jess that she wasn't exactly whispering, wasn't even really using her indoor voice anymore.

The professor frowned. "Jess? Did you have something to add?"

This always happened: She got sucked in. When she would rather say nothing, just sit quietly playing number puzzles on her phone under the table.

At the same time she accepted, begrudgingly anyway, that it was her responsibility to Say Something. This Jess had learned from her father, who, throughout her Nebraska childhood, seemed perpetually to be saying something. Demanding that the Walmart manager stock multicultural dolls while Jess stood behind him, mortified. Driving across state lines at Christmas to find the only Black Santa in the Great Plains. Pestering the principal about the lack of books about Black history in the school library.

He was doing his best, Jess knew. Compensating, probably, for the fact that her mom had died when Jess was a baby. But sometimes she wondered why he bothered. Wouldn't it have been easier to move? Instead of yelling at her teachers for fucking up the Civil War unit? Or buying knockoff Barbies? All she had wanted was to fit in, not to read another children's biography of Dr. Martin Luther King.

Not to have to whisper-fight with Josh, in his prep school sweatshirt with his newscaster hair; not to have to defend herself, her race, her right to be there.

*   *   *

Later that night, at the bar where everyone went, he tracked her down and dragged her back into the conversation. It was nine o'clock and everyone was drunk. Avenue Tavern had sticky floors and a sign above the door that said FREE BEER TOMORROW. Fifteen dollars and a fake ID bought twenty-five-cent well drinks all night long.

Jess had drunk cranberry vodkas until she ran out of quarters and when the room started spinning she found an empty booth near the bathroom. She had only been there for a minute when she felt a depression in the fabric. A body next to hers. She had opened one eye, cocked her head slightly.

"Jess, right?"—it was him—"Josh," he introduced himself, formally, sticking out his hand.

She ignored it, closed her eyes again, hoping he'd go away.

But he didn't. She could hear him rattling ice around in his drink.

"So," he said, "your argument in class today was pretty thin."

Jess said nothing, slid a little bit lower in her seat.

Josh ignored her ignoring him, pressed on. "As a direct beneficiary of affirmative action I see why you'd want to defend it. I get it, I do. But you can't really believe, I mean intellectually not emotionally, that relaxing admissions standards is an appropriate mechanism by which to address systemic inequality. Sending kids to schools that they're not qualified to attend? That's helping? Besides, it's completely unenforceable. I mean the real problem with inequality in this country has nothing to do with race, right? It has to do with class. How is it fair that a rich African American kid with mediocre grades and test scores gets preference over some poor kid from Appalachia who's had even less in life?"

"So, you're asking me, the expert"—Jess finally opened her eyes— "why we don't have affirmative action for poor white people?"

He nodded. "I mean that's fairly reductive, and I sense some sarcasm, but yes, I'd like to hear your thoughts."

"My thoughts are"—she took a sip from her drink, melted ice that tasted of metal—"fuck you."

He shook his head. "It's like pulling teeth, trying to have an honest intellectual conversation with anyone at this school."

"Maybe you'd be happier at Appalachia State."

"Funny," he said, and got up.

But then he was back.

"Here." He pushed a glass of water at her and Jess had to make an effort not to say thank you.

"So," he said, one arm slung over the banquette, "what are you doing next year?"

"What?"

"After graduation. I'm working at Goldman Sachs. You?"

"Oh." Jess shrugged. "Don't know."

"Really? You don't have anything lined up?"

Jess shrugged again. "Maybe a nonprofit that does something with kids. Or an art gallery." That was her roommate Lydia's plan. Rent an apartment in the West Village or Brownstone Brooklyn and take taxis to her full-time internship at Christie's in Rockefeller Center.

"A thing with kids? An art gallery?" Josh shook his head. "Those aren't real jobs."

"Okay, well, not everyone wants to grow up to be Gordon Gekko, yelling at their secretaries and raiding pension funds just to buy more caviar and purebred dogs. Some of us would actually like to give something back."

"Give something back? With a forty-thousand dollar salary?"

"Funny," she said, "I didn't realize everything was about money."

Jess wanted to believe this more than she actually believed it. Wanted to affect a casual relationship with money. To seem like she could take it or leave it. She didn't want to seem too hungry. Or desperate. Or striving. None of her friends wanted jobs in finance. They wanted to volunteer, to seek fulfillment, to make art. And why not? They were right. Money didn't matter.

Unless you didn't have any.

Or you wanted to be taken seriously.

He raised an eyebrow. "So what, you're going to pay rent with . . . IOUs?"

"Josh." She looked at him, exasperated. "Why do you care?"

"I'm curious, that's all. Is it because that's what your friends are doing? I thought you were different."

"Different from what?"

"From your friends."

It was true that in many ways Jess was different from her friends; from Lydia, who had attended a boarding school in the Alps where they broke at noon for cheese and chocolate and whose father was the president of a Swiss bank. Or from Miky, who wasn't a member of the Korean royal family but who seemed like she could be—she had a way of insisting that she wasn't that made it seem somehow truer. But they had been friends since freshman year and it rankled Jess to think that her efforts to obscure those differences had failed, and that some guy at a bar, in a pink shirt, would call it out.

"What do you mean *different?*"

"Not an art gallery girl."

"I'm sorry." Jess was taken aback. "Do you know me?"

"Don't be defensive," Josh said. "Some of us had to work to get here. Some of us will have to work after we leave. I'm guessing that's you too."

"You don't know anything about me. You think just because I'm Black I'm poor? How enlightened."

"Well, I mean statistically, that's the reality. It's just numbers. But that's not what I was saying. It's something else. You seem . . ." He stopped, searching for the right word.

Involuntarily, Jess leaned toward him. "I seem . . . ?"

He ran his finger around the rim of his glass. It whistled, low and melodic, like a whale. "Keen," he said finally.

Keen? *Keen?* Jess would have been less offended if he'd told her she smelled like hot garbage.

"Josh?" she pointed across his lap.

"Yeah?" he said, but didn't move.

"I'm leaving." She pushed past him out of the booth, spilling both of their drinks as she did.

At the bar, Lydia was ordering another round. "Who was that?" she asked, handing Jess a shot. "He's cute! Are you going to bone?"

Jess tipped her head back and the icy liquid burned. She let a wave of nausea pass through her and then wrinkled her nose. "You don't recognize him?"

"Should I?"

"He's the guy from the paper. Freshman year. Devil ears?"

"Oh, yeah!"

"So no, definitely not cute."

"Hmm." Lydia made a face.

"What?"

"Just," Lydia shrugged, "I don't know."

"Well, I know," Jess said, shaking her head, "and we hate him. He sucks."

"I'm heading out," Josh says. "You good?"

And because she is desperate, Jess goes off script: "Actually, I might have a question."

He looks at his watch, "What is it?"

"It's just this model Charles asked me to do. It's kind of giving me trouble?"

"You're not done with that?"

"Not exactly."

She taps her computer and it hums to life. She hopes to impress, or intimidate, him with complicated numbers and figures that appear on-screen. But he immediately recognizes what she's doing.

"A precedent transaction analysis?" He leans over Jess, pecks at her keyboard and flips through various documents on her desktop. He narrates each document as he goes: "Discounted cash flow, balance sheet, cost of capital." He looks at Jess. "So what's the problem?"

"I don't know."

He looks at her screen. Toggles back and forth between the various spreadsheets. His face is just inches from hers. He smells like store-brand soap and Altoids. "Do you even know what you're doing?"

"That depends on how you define 'know' and 'doing.' "

"Christ," he says, wheeling over the chair from the desk next to

Jess's. He sits. "Where are you calculating the discount rate?" He is keying over the cells of Jess's spreadsheet; his fingers dance over the keyboard like a pianist's.

"Here." Jess points to the screen.

"This is wrong."

Jess doesn't disagree.

"You need to take the weighted average cost of capital"—he picks up a public information book from her desk, pages through it, picks up another and turns to the appendix—"from here"—he points to a number on a page, grabs a yellow marker and highlights it—"and then use that to drive the model assumptions"—he points to the screen—"here. See?"

She nods.

"Here, scoot over." He rolls his seat toward her and pulls the keyboard into his lap. "Do you know how to set up dynamic named ranges?"

She shakes her head.

"Christ."

But he helps her.

He is a little hostile, but also patient, like a German schoolteacher. And eventually it gets done.

She sends the model to Charles first thing in the morning and immediately receives a response: "Come see me."

Jess flies over to his desk. He is leaning back in his seat, one leg crossed in a triangle over the other, bouncing a rubber band ball against the corkboard wall. The model is open on his computer.

"You rang?"

He swivels toward her. "What is this?"

"It's the model you asked for." Jess stops herself from saying more.

"Calibri?"

"Um."

"This isn't a fucking humor magazine. Next time you use Arial. Or Times New Roman if you're feeling fresh." He snaps a single rubber band just over her shoulder. "Got it?"

* * *

Jess finds Josh in an empty conference room.

"Thanks again for your help last night," she says.

He ignores her, just keeps scrolling through his phone.

Jess says, "No 'You're welcome, Jess'? No 'Happy to help, Jess'? No 'Anytime, Jess, what are buddies for'?"

"I had plans," he says, still staring at his phone.

She is trying to be friendly. To say thank you. But, fine.

"What, did you miss your Young Republicans happy hour or something?"

He finally puts his phone down, looks up, raises an eyebrow.

Jess wonders if she's offended him, wonders if she cares. Implying that someone is a Republican is not an insult, not technically. Especially not at a bank. But he definitely is, Jess is pretty sure. In their Supreme Court class he was always talking about fringy economic things, like payroll taxes and public debt. Once, she'd run into him at the school bookstore and watched him pay for a pack of gum with a hundred-dollar bill.

"Funny." He picks up his phone again.

"Well," Jess says, headed for the door, "for what it's worth, I do actually appreciate your help."

Outside, the city is teeming with new college graduates, everyone looking to have a good time. It's late August, and the hot sticky heart of the summer has passed, so it feels like spring.

It reminds Jess of college, when the entire student body emerged from the gray winter in short shorts and plastic sunglasses and dragged couches out onto front lawns. Sometimes they would cut class, Jess and Miky and Lydia, and sit on a patio drinking sun-warmed beer and spicy margaritas until their heads would spin.

But that's all over now.

Miky and Lydia make new friends, while Jess is stuck inside.

Their new friends, the Wine Girls, are sunny California optimists with trust funds and tangled hair whose parents grow grapes in the Napa Valley, who believe in free love and acupuncture and private space travel and electric cars.

Jess meets them one night, when she sneaks out of work at a reasonable hour. The bar slash restaurant is dark and loud, and in the heat of the crowd Jess feels nostalgic.

She finds them all sitting at a small table crammed with cocktails and tall glass bottles of sparkling water.

Everyone screams hello and then the Wine Girls shout over the music, "Why are you wearing a suit?"

Jess sits down and shout-explains that she works at Goldman Sachs.

They frown over their cocktails and shout back, "That sucks! Why do you work there?"

Silently Miky slides a drink in front of Jess.

The Wine Girls don't let up. "How can you work there!"

"It's not that bad," Jess shrugs.

"Not that bad! Goldman Sachs is the great vampire squid!" the Wine Girls insist, "attached to the face of the economy, sucking it dry!"

A waiter materializes.

"Ooh," Lydia lights up, "should we order the squid?"

The Wine Girls inform Jess that, given her hundred-hour workweek, she's essentially making minimum wage, less, probably, than she would slinging burgers at a fast-food place.

This is not true, obviously, and more importantly, working at McDonald's doesn't come with the imprimatur of the most powerful and important bank in the world. Or the begrudging respect of people who might otherwise write her off. Or black car rides home every night. But the Wine Girls aren't completely wrong; Jess kind of hates her job. It's boring, and no one is nice to her, and all the midweight wool makes her itch. She barely sees her friends, barely sleeps, barely eats anything that doesn't come in a take-out box. When Lydia asked, Jess complained about life on the front line.

"Lyd, it's awful. It's just a bunch of dudes, in suits, doing shit and saying shit. All day. Every day."

"Well," Lydia said, "the patriarchy wasn't dismantled in a day. At least there's no line for the ladies' room."

This was not the case in Lydia's own office, a boutique auction house, where two-thirds of the employees were women and where the toilet was always clogged with tampons and glitter.

Jess fantasizes constantly about a different job.

Like Lydia's job at the auction house, which can be demeaning, but has a decidedly glamorous air. Or like the Wine Girls: Callie, who works at a cookie dough startup, and Noree, who works at an eco-first company that makes shoes out of recycled bamboo. Even Miky, who's an account coordinator for the world's biggest creative advertising agency, is still home by six every day.

It would be nice: a fake job and a nice apartment and parents who pay the bills.

Instead: student loans, a studio that eats up half her salary, people always and forever looking at her sideways.

Jess's dad calls.

"Well," he asks, "are you giving 'em hell?"

She knows what he wants to hear. That she's showing up early and leaving late; that she's beating them at their own game. Growing up he'd said it again and again. She needed to be twice as good to get half as much. He was right, she knew, but she resented it. Why did her success have to be predicated on perfection instead of, say, a vague sense that she was someone people would like to have a beer with?

Still, she tries. To keep up, to keep her head down, to make herself useful. Even though she's not sure anyone notices. And while she's definitely better than Rich, who graduated from Harvard but still can't spell *Wednesday*, it's not clear that she's better than Josh, who can do a discounted cash flow with his eyes. She considers telling her dad the truth: that she feels like a baby sometimes, needy and helpless. That she is the only one at a loss, the only one who doesn't have a strong opinion about The Things That Matter: the price of soybeans, the nuances of Glass-Steagall, the new menu at the University Club.

But she can hear him smiling, waiting, on the other end of the line.

So instead she says, "You bet. I'm great. I'm awesome. Everything's fine."

2

They fly to Cincinnati for a series of drafting sessions with a consumer insurance company that's preparing for a public equity offering.

"Tweedledum, Tweedledee," Charles says to Josh and Jess, "pack your bags, we're going to California."

"What?" Jess asks. "Really?"

"No, just kidding," he says. "Ohio, actually. But I hear the weather is really shitty so, yeah."

First class from LaGuardia to Ohio on the earliest flight possible; before the flight attendant even offers them orange juice Jess falls asleep in her seat. From the airport they take a taxi straight to the client's office, dragging their suitcases behind them like bodies.

They are ushered into a cavernous boardroom with a conference table as long as a bowling lane.

Charles asks complicated technical questions about their actuarial models while Josh grills them about their growth strategy. Jess takes notes.

The client has a certain slick quality to him and Jess can imagine him in sepia tones, a robber baron plundering America's coffers for his own ill-gotten gains, or maybe just a common outlaw stealing copper from railroad tracks under cover of night. He goes on and on about price discrimination and profit maximization and he all but calls his customers suckers.

At some point he makes a particularly complicated argument and Charles turns to Jess and says, "You got that?"

Jess nods and in her notes she summarizes: *steal from the poor to give to the rich.*

*   *   *

After, Jess reads about a local chili chain online.

"'Come taste what made them famous,'" Jess says, reading the tagline from the website.

"No thank you," Josh says.

"Come on, we have to eat."

Charles is having lunch with the client and they are not invited.

So they cross six lanes of traffic to get to the strip mall on the other side of the highway where, at the restaurant, people are lined up for hot dogs and spaghetti.

Josh says, "Manhattan this is not."

Jess says, "You know, I'm kind of from here."

"From where?"

"Here," she says, as they are seated and the waiter pours their waters. "The Midwest. You know, 'flyover country?'"

"Chicago?"

Jess shakes her head. "Nebraska."

Josh leans forward so suddenly that his drink almost topples over. "Really?"

"Born and bred."

"I would have never guessed. You seem so"—he searches for the right word—"New York-y."

"Thank you?"

"Nebraska, huh." He sits back. "I definitely need to revise my mental model of you."

"Why do you have a mental model of me?"

Josh ignores her and orders a garden salad with grilled chicken. Jess gets the chili cheese sandwich.

"Let me guess," she says, "you're training for a marathon."

"Excuse me?"

"They're famous for their *chili*, not their, like, steamed vegetable surprise. Why don't you live a little?"

"I'm pretty sure heart disease and high cholesterol are the opposite of living."

"So what? You only eat food that's good for you?"

"Pretty much, yeah. Why would I want something if it's bad?"

"Because," Jess says, "it's good to be bad. To embrace the dark side. To give in to your most depraved appetites."

He raises an eyebrow.

"I just mean, you don't ever crave, I don't know, french fries or deep-fried Oreos or pepperoni pizza?"

"I like leafy greens."

The waiter reappears and drops two plates on the table: a mountain of chili and shredded cheddar cheese for Jess, a sad bowl of vegetables for Josh.

Jess laughs.

Josh does too. "Okay," he says, spearing a limp cauliflower floret with his fork, "you win."

Later, Jess says to Charles, "Can you believe those guys? Their whole strategy, it's like . . . inverted."

"It's hugely profitable is what it is."

"But don't you think on some level it's completely . . . upside down? It's almost predatory. Don't you think it's fucked up?"

"I think it's insurance."

"But it's so wrong!" Jess understands that this is naive, but still.

Charles shrugs. "I suppose you're right. But . . . people in glass houses, yeah?"

He christens it the Reverse Robin Hood. And then whenever someone does something especially smart or underhanded Charles crowns them the new king of Sherwood Forest.

Though the closest Jess ever gets is when one day she wears a silk blouse with a scalloped collar and Charles says, "Nice shirt, Maid Marian."

At the airport their flight to New York is delayed three hours. There is exactly one standby seat available on a flight leaving in twenty minutes and, at the check-in desk, Charles claims it. He says, "Sorry kiddos, but I need to get the fuck out of here."

Jess and Josh wait at the gate watching planes taxi through a big window. Jess thinks of the airport test, the "fit" portion of all their investment banking interviews: Would I want to be stuck in an airport with this person? Jess looks over at Josh, considering. He glances back and they make brief eye contact. She hopes he can't read her thoughts.

"So tell me about Nebraska," he finally says. "What was it like growing up there?"

Jess rolls her eyes. "It's always the same with you East Coast people. Gather round. Let me tell you all about my childhood in the heartland. I rode to school every day on a tractor and instead of a dog I had a *prairie* dog."

"That's not what I meant."

For some reason she decides to tell the truth. "Well, if you're really asking, I would say . . . it was kind of . . . lonely."

"Were there many other African American families?"

"No. Not many," Jess says. Though 'not many' feels like an understatement. At times it had felt like she and her dad were the only two Black people in the entire Lincoln metro area. The only two Black people in western Nebraska, in the Great Plains, in the universe.

It wasn't just that she barely knew any other Black families, but other than her dad, she didn't have any of her own family. Everyone was dead—her mother, her grandparents—or distant—an uncle her father never mentioned, assorted cousins Jess had never met, who sent Christmas cards from faraway places like Los Angeles and Toronto.

Everyone else seemed to have homes full of people and pets— brothers, sisters, cats, dogs—and when Jess visited them, they always seemed noisy and unkempt, which made her tiny family seem dignified, just the right size. But then it would be Christmas or Thanksgiving or Mother's Day, and there were only so many ways for two people to celebrate, and then she would feel a piercing loneliness, and remember that her family was incomplete.

Josh says, "That must have been hard."

"I thought you said that class, not race, was the real problem in America today."

"You really don't forget anything, do you? Do you have a dossier of shitty things I said when I was in college that you're going to use against me every time we talk?"

"So you think it was a shitty thing to say?"

He sighs. "I think I may have said a lot of things back then that were lacking in nuance."

"Back then? You mean last year?"

He groans. "Jess, give me a break. It's not like you were a paragon of virtue and understanding yourself."

"What are you talking about?"

"You and your friends. You were always drinking and doing drugs and turning up your noses at everyone and everything. You were always hungover in class. All those egg sandwiches and giant cups of coffee. Come on. Don't try to pretend you had the moral high ground."

Jess says, "I'd rather be drunk than a conservative constitutionalist."

He gives a small laugh.

"I got made fun of," Jess tells him. "Nothing extreme. No one, like, told me to kill myself on Facebook, but . . . I don't know. Kids can be dicks, you know?"

He nods.

Jess says, "So what was it like for you? Growing up in . . . ?"

"Connecticut."

"Oh. Right. Connecticut. Choate." Jess suddenly remembers who she's talking to. She wishes she hadn't said so much. "Don't tell me. When you were a kid you got into trouble for hitting your baseball over the fence into David Letterman's estate. During the week you wore a tie to school and on the weekend you played polo at the club."

"You really think you've got my number, don't you?" He looks at her sideways. "I do get it, you know."

"Get what?"

"Feeling like you don't fit in. I grew up without a lot of money. My parents got divorced when I was in middle school and my dad moved to California. My mom had to work. It wasn't easy."

"But you went to Choate."

"I had help."

"So were the other kids jerks? The rich kids?"

"No," Josh shakes his head, "they weren't. But I still felt different, you know?"

Jess does know but is surprised to hear him express a thought that doesn't sound like it comes from an economics textbook.

She nods at him. "Yeah, like even though the kids I went to school with *were* jerks . . . I still wanted to be like them. I wanted to be friends with them."

The boarding announcement crackles over the loudspeaker and they shuffle toward the gate.

"It's understandable," Josh says, rolling his suitcase behind him. "The desire to belong is one of the most irreducible human instincts. We're cognitively wired to want to fit in."

And there it is: the annoying Wikipedia-based theory of the world.

"Right," Jess says drily, adjusting the straps on her bag. "Science."

3

Two weeks later.

"Jess." Josh is standing at her desk.

"I know, I know," she says, "I'm almost done with the capital stack, promise. I'm sending it . . . soon."

"No," he says, "it's not that."

She looks at him.

"I was actually just wondering if you wanted to get lunch."

They eat bagels on a bench in Rockefeller Park.

Josh says, "So what do you think of the LyfeCo. investment memorandum? I'm curious to hear your thoughts on how we've structured the document."

Jess drops her sandwich into her lap. "The investment memo? You asked me to lunch so we could talk about insurance?"

"Sure, yeah."

"Okay, well, I didn't know this was a working lunch. I would have prepared. Maybe brought some printouts."

"I'm only asking your opinion."

"Okay then. I think that LyfeCo. is basically a crime syndicate that exists solely to sponge profits off society's most vulnerable members." Jess knows she sounds like a hypocrite, but she figures the only thing worse than complicity is complete apathy.

"I was actually asking what you thought of the memo, not for a Marxist screed, but . . . okay." He pauses. "Do you think it makes sense to introduce the SWOT analysis so far ahead of the risk assessment when they're saying a lot of the same things?"

Jess shrugs and lifts the two halves of her bagel apart, rearranging lettuce and tomato.

He sighs. "Okay, what do you want to talk about then, Jess?"

She says, "I heard one of the managing directors is cheating on his wife with a PR intern. Someone saw them making out in the stairwell."

"Is that true?" Josh looks surprised. "Who?"

"I forget."

He sort of laughs. "Christ, you are so annoying."

He takes the last bite of his sandwich and wipes crumbs off his hands. He stretches his legs out in front of him and crosses one ankle over the other and Jess wonders if he pays to have his shoes shined.

He says, "Okay, here's one: Why do you hate Rich Golden so much?"

Jess considers saying something banal and untrue like *who, me?* but instead says, "Is it that obvious?"

"No."

"He's just so . . . mediocre."

"You know his father's on the board."

Jess nods. "I know. Everyone knows Dick Golden. I *get* it. It's just incredibly painful interacting with him. It's like trying to have a conversation with a sack of flour."

"He's certainly not the most inspired person I've ever met," Josh allows.

"I just find it frustrating that in five years he's probably going to be a VP and I'm still going to be taking coffee orders and printing out pitchbooks."

"He won't be a VP."

"What makes you so sure of that?"

"For what it's worth, I don't think what got him hired will get him especially far. I think Goldman does a good job of identifying and rewarding talent. The meritocratic ideal will win the day."

"You think Goldman's a meritocracy?"

"More or less, yeah."

"You would."

"Excuse me?"

"I said *you would*," Jess says, maybe slightly too loudly.

"I heard you," Josh says. "I'm asking what you meant by it."

"I mean you and all the Richs of the world would think that it's a perfect happy shiny meritocracy where all the smart, hardworking people are winners and everyone else is a loser."

"Me and all the Richs?"

"White people with penises."

"Okay, wow, I did think you were going to tap dance around that one a little bit longer," he says. "Anyway, Jess, I have nothing to do with Rich. He's a moron. I agree with you. But because we're both white, what? You have some kind of axe to grind?"

"I just think it's really unfair that by the time the crony capitalists are finished handing out favors to all the good old boys, there's nothing left for the rest of us."

"And how, exactly, does this affect you?"

"What do you mean?" Jess asks.

"You have everything."

"No, I don't. What are you talking about? You get staffed on more deals than I do. You get more recognition than I do. You get more calls from headhunters than I do. Should I go on?"

"That's not crony capitalism, Jess. That's because I'm better than you are."

"Better than me?"

"At my *job*."

"I'm not saying I'm the best analyst on the Street, but sometimes it would be nice to get the same special treatment that everyone else gets."

"What do you want me to say? I'm sorry you don't feel like the world rises to meet you in every single way. But we're in the same exact place, Jess. We had the same education. We have the same exact job. What else do you want?"

"I want the benefit of the fucking doubt! I want people to recognize something great inside me whether it's there or not, and to nurture and celebrate it. To tell me that I'm brilliant and wonderful and that they cherish my goddamn gifts to the world. I want people to say 'Jess is here too and she's amazing.' "

"Yeah, well," he says after a minute, "I don't think that's going to happen."

Jess tosses the rest of her bagel to a pair of pigeons flapping nearby. "Anyway, honestly?" she says.

"Yeah?" Josh asks.

"A rich guy named Rich? Really?"

"Well," Josh says, "maybe Little Dick was too on the nose."

•

In a bid to get promoted, Charles has begun pitching his own deals, has started winning his own business.

One of their biggest consumer clients—the world's "finest purveyor of cookies and cakes"—had been looking for an opportunity and Charles had identified a target. A family-run cracker company with strong fundamentals and a dominant position in the Upper Midwest market.

He called to gauge their interest.

After being passed around for several minutes he was finally put through to the CEO himself, the eighty-five-year-old paterfamilias who had run the company for fifty years.

Charles introduced himself.

"Charles Macmanus here, from Goldman Sachs."

A rheumy cough, and then a pause. "What's that, son? Speak up!"

"I'm calling from Goldman Sachs," Charles shouted into the phone.

"Who's it?" the old man croaked.

"Goldman Sachs," Charles repeated.

"Goldman Snacks?"

Jess relays this story to her father and waits for him to laugh.

"But Jessie," he says, "maybe he thought your friend was an investment *baker*."

And then instead of laughing at her joke, he laughs at his own.

Friday is quiet; the managing directors have all gone home for the weekend and so the analysts crowd into the bullpen taking turns playing a first-person-shooter game that someone illegally downloaded. Quarts of CGI blood spill in the streets and prostitutes scream in terror as stolen cars career recklessly onto sidewalks. Jess wanders over to the action and pretends to care that the abandoned warehouse is on fire.

Josh rolls his chair over to her. "You want to have a go?"

"Uh, no," Jess says, "I'm all set. I murdered a few innocent by-standers for breakfast. Still sated."

Other games they play: a complicated card game called Set. It starts with the traders. Because it is a game of logic, of quick wits and pattern recognition, it becomes for them a sort of shorthand, a way to identify winners and losers, in the game and in life. Set has a simple hierarchy: the better the trader, the more often he wins.

A palpable but unspoken tension exists between the bankers and the traders. The head of the trading desk is a guy who, born and raised in the Bronx, sold encyclopedias to put himself through City College and then worked his way up from the mail room. The head of the investment banking division is a Harvard-educated heir to a crayon fortune.

One afternoon, heady after a blowout earnings report, the entire floor finds itself in the midst of an impromptu tournament.

They play knockout style, so that with each progressive hand the winner is more likely to win, the loser more likely to lose. VP, associate, analyst, on down the line, until they are just watching one terrified first-year after another get pulverized by the champion. In this way the strongest devour the weakest. The traders are on top—their minds are agile and they are quick to calculate odds.

The bankers grumble.

But then Jess's managing director, Blaine, a dyed-in-the-wool banker with a British accent and an ascot, interrupts the traders' winning streak. In quick sets he stifles the hot hand of a long-tenured trader, an aggressive and brilliant risk-taker rumored to have lost $1 billion of the bank's money and won it back before anyone noticed.

The bankers slap each other on the back.

He wins and then wins some more. Analysts are summoned from other floors and then dispatched summarily. It is a bloodbath.

At some point it becomes Jess's turn. She demurs. Because Blaine hates her. She hoped it was her imagination, but when she mentioned it to Charles once, instead of reassuring her, he grimaced, "I suspect you're correct, Jones. I don't think he likes you one bit." Then, sensing Jess's dismay, he quickly added, "But everyone knows he's an insufferable prick."

At the point when she can no longer protest, she takes a seat in front of him.

They play the hand fast, faster than any other, and then one more and then another, until after five games in rapid succession, a stunned silence falls across the office.

There is defeat and then there is complete demolition and what they have witnessed is the latter.

When Jess looks up, slightly breathless, she sees in Blaine's eyes only one thing: murder.

Josh says, "Jesus, Rain Man, what the hell was that?"

Of course Blaine is a sore loser. Of course he thought she'd be an easy target. Of course no one thought she'd win. But what did they expect? For her to throw the game? Just to stroke his fragile ego?

"Do you think I should have lost on purpose?"

"No, of course not. Where's the integrity in that?" Josh pauses. "I just think you might have won more . . . effortfully."

Charles disagrees. "You fucked up, Jones."

Blaine has never liked Jess and now he likes her even less. He tells her that her work is sloppy or illegible or wrong, and he gives her junk assignments and asks her repeatedly where she went to school.

Something that has surprised Jess about working in a bank is that everyone works. Blaine plays golf and he has lunch and he has several assistants—pretty middle-aged secretaries who are never as dumb as they look—but he also works an enormous amount. He reviews every book that lands on his desk, with a red pen, like a rabid English teacher. And he pays attention.

*   *   *

"Why is this discount rate here 7.6 percent instead of 7.56 percent?" he asks Jess, combing through her model like it holds the secrets of the universe.

"Oh," she says, "rounding."

"No," he says, swiping his red pen across the page.

"It's 7.56 percent," Jess offers. "It just shows as 7.6 percent. I mean all the underlying numbers are calculated using 7.56 percent. I just thought it would be easier to read, I guess."

"It needs to *show* what it *is*," he says tersely. "Did you also round your GPA to one decimal place?"

He floods her work with comments of the most pedantic variety. The worst are the nits, the minor adjustments that he has her make back and forth, doing and undoing her work, as if he has no recollection of the demands he has previously made.

Nit: round to one decimal place.

Nit: *always* round to two decimal places.

Nit: right justify this header.

Nit: *always* center your header on the page.

Nit: too much white space in the margin.

Nit: margins are way too narrow.

Nit: catalo*gue* not catalog.

Nit.

Nit.

Nit.

Nit.

At one point he gets tired and draws a red line through the last seven pages of her deck and at the very end just writes "No."

Sometimes Jess feels like she is going to die here in this office.

Lydia calls.

"Earth to Jess," she says.

"I know, I know."

"Well, is it worth it?" Lydia asks, after Jess misses her birthday.

Is it?

Jess doesn't know.

There's the question of whether it's *worth it* worth it, in the existential sense. There are a million and one ways Jess could be spending her youth besides chained to a swivel chair in a windowless cubicle. But there's also the question of her literal worth, the difference between her liabilities and her assets, a number that she tracks in an app. This is something she had started recently, inspired by other analysts on the team. Though none of them are older than twenty-five, they are obsessed with retiring, the idea that they could have enough in the bank by the time they are thirty—forty at the outside—to do all the things they should be doing now but can't because they are working: taking trips, eating richly, seeking fulfillment.

And they all seem to have a number in mind. At which point they plan to ditch the nine-to-five to race catamarans in the Mediterranean. Or climb mountains. Dabble in venture capital. To them, money equals freedom. But to Jess it's more of a feeling. She didn't want a yacht or a private driver, necessarily.

Not that she doesn't like spending money. She can be wildly impractical—living alone in the most expensive city on the planet when everyone else has roommates, spending eleven dollars in delivery fees for an eight-dollar sandwich because she doesn't want to put on pants. And she likes nice things—a brand of French macarons that cost fifty dollars a box, a pair of three-hundred-dollar heels that made Lydia whistle.

This, despite the fact, or maybe because of the fact, that she hadn't grown up with lots of money. For her birthday every year, her father gave her an envelope with a twenty-dollar bill, which she genuinely believed he genuinely believed she would save for a rainy day. He had these old-timey notions about money that sometimes made Jess wonder if they were broke, even though he had a good job and a good salary. Benefits. Stability. Jess wanted that and more, of course, but that wasn't even it really.

More than luxury macarons or designer shoes, she wanted one thing: for people to take her seriously. If she had a million dollars—that was her number—maybe people would stop assuming, that she had nothing to offer or that she wasn't someone to be reckoned with or that she was a fucking secretary.

She was reluctant, initially, to work for a bank. Her dad worked for the local university, as the assistant dean of multicultural affairs, which meant that he championed diversity and enriched people's lives. It meant that no one stood outside his office with signs saying YOU ARE THE PROBLEM, which the Occupy Wall Street protestors did, in front of the banks where Jess went for job interviews and read their signs and registered their wrath and crossed her fingers and thought *I am not the problem . . . yet*. But her father. He helped people; he was on the right side of history; he didn't ravage America's economy with his greed.

And at school, the kids who wanted to make money, who signed up for classes about the stock market and who aspired to high-paying, soul-sucking jobs, were mocked and called pre-professional try-hards. Guys like Josh. So Jess had tried something different. The summer before senior year she'd gotten a job as a research assistant at a feminist magazine, which had nothing to do with her degree, because it seemed interesting. And it was—she researched everything from a college admissions scandal to troubling pornography trends—but the pay was a joke. Barely enough to rent a decent place in the city.

So she had rented an apartment that wasn't even really an apartment. And not not an apartment in the sense that Lydia's place—a big, bright one-bedroom in a glass tower in Midtown with a swimming pool on top—was not an apartment, because it was a pied-à-terre. Not an apartment in the sense that it was a Columbia dorm room with an extra-long twin bed, and a coed bathroom that she shared with strangers.

But it was cheap and close to the subway and it was literally all Jess could afford. She was always running out of cash. Holding her breath every time she checked her bank balance. Her debits and credits ships

passing in the night. Why had no one warned her how much everything would cost? What was she doing wrong?

Back on campus, in the fall, she figured it out. And then she felt silly.
She had been rummaging for a pen on Lydia's desk, picking through
a pile of change, a tangle of hair elastics, a tube of bright red lipstick
with a missing cap—Lydia had emptied her pockets—when Jess noticed the crumpled receipt. An account withdrawal: one hundred dollars plus a three-dollar fee, and a remaining balance of $97,432.66. At
that point Jess blacked out a little. Her life might have flashed before
her eyes. She recalled just the day before checking the price on a box
of tampons. Yet her roommate had a *hundred thousand dollars*? In
checking? She'd known that Lydia was rich, that she lived in a big
house and took expensive vacations and that she'd had a nanny to
peel her grapes and fluff her pillows until she was eighteen, but Jess
hadn't realized the extent of her wealth, hadn't realized just how naive
she'd been. There was no way Jess could work for a magazine. Who
was she kidding? She wasn't an art gallery girl. Josh was right. He was
right and she hated that. Plus, Jess had student loans.

By then Jess had received a full-time offer—if you could call it
that—from the feminist magazine. But instead of a six-figure salary
and a giant signing bonus, Jess would be paid hourly. There wasn't
even an HR department. On Jess's last day that summer, they had
handed her a check and asked her sheepishly if she wouldn't mind not
cashing it until the next week.

Going back after graduation wasn't an option. So, as the spring semester of her senior year rolled around, she resigned herself to a job in
finance. Anyway, the writing was on the wall. She was a math major,
which had an air of practicality, but how many job postings were
there for mathematicians? It seemed like all the other math majors
were doing one of two things: finance or academia. A fat paycheck in
a big city or chalk on her face and debt until she was thirty. It was a
no-brainer.

So she memorized the *Wall Street Journal* and wore a suit and said
smart things in her interviews. There were warnings—the hours, the

abuse, was she sure it was worth it? Of course she wasn't sure, but it was six figures, benefits, a big bonus. She didn't flinch.

And her father had been so proud. He'd flown up for her graduation, glowing. He kept wiping tears from his eyes, shaking his head, and saying things like "Where do the years go? Just yesterday you were in my lap crying over a skinned knee."

"It definitely wasn't yesterday, Dad."

He beamed. "And now look at you."

He placed both of his hands in hers, pulled her arms out to her sides, took her in, as if admiring a new dress she'd just tried on. "And now *look* at you. My little college graduate. Big-city girl."

"Da-ad." Two syllables. "I'm just graduating, not *dying*. It's not a big deal. I don't even have any honor cords, see?" She yanked on her lapels, the black gown draped inelegantly over her summer dress. "I'm nothing special."

At the baccalaureate service, the provost introduced the distinguished faculty speaker, who had won the university's teaching award for the past twelve years in a row.

Students clapped and cheered wildly.

Her father had leaned over and whispered, "What's he like, Jessie? Is he as good as they say?"

And Jess had had to explain that she had never seen this man before in her life, had had no idea he existed until this moment, although apparently he had been changing young lives since 1993.

And then on the graduation grass, before they handed out diplomas, her dad had pointed to a large group of students laughing and hugging under a magnolia tree—the Black Student Union—and asked Jess if she was going to introduce him to her friends. She had to explain, again, that she didn't know them.

Freshman year she had received countless flyers, brightly colored, emphatic, slipped under her door inviting her to fried chicken and waffle brunches and MLK volunteer days and, once, a lecture by Oprah, but she had ignored them all, so that her recycling bin was perpetually full of neon slips of paper.

The BSU members all marched across the stage in colorful Kente stoles and after the provost shook each of their hands someone in the audience beat on a steel drum.

Jess realized then that she had missed things and she felt briefly wistful.

But then they called her name and her father whooped and hollered. And in spite of herself, she smiled.

Everyone starts to accumulate deal toys, acrylic and Lucite trophies that look like elaborate paperweights, which are awarded to all the members of an M&A deal team when a transaction closes. The toys are lined up on desks like soldiers, like spoils of war. At some point, Josh runs out of room on his desk and has to start shoving them in his drawer.

Jess still doesn't have any.

But then the world's largest online retailer decides to acquire the world's fastest-growing online retailer, a company with the word *bitch* in the name that sells vintage clothing and lingerie to teenage girls. The CEO is a girl not much older than Jess who shows up at their office wearing stilettos and a leather jacket draped around her shoulders and who says "what's up?" instead of "hello." She demands a billion dollars for the company she built in her basement and refuses to do the deal without a woman in the room.

And so Jess finally gets staffed on a serious deal.

For her efforts Charles hands her a glass statue with a pair of thigh-high boots mounted to the base, her first deal toy, and says, "Pretty touch-and-go there with all that estrogen in the room, yeah?"

Jess comes into the office the next day to find all her computer cords pulled out of the wall like tentacles. Her monitor is blinking feebly, but nothing else is lit up. It's like a crime scene.

"What the fuck?"

Her keyboard, her power strip and her headset are all stacked on top of one another and shoved to the side. Her mouse pad is exactly where it's always been, but her mouse—the point-and-click—is gone, and in its place is an actual mouse—with eyes and ears and a long skinny tail. Her breath catches for a moment before she realizes that it isn't alive, that it's an incredibly lifelike reproduction.

She stomps over to the bullpen.

"Does anyone have a, uh, mouse I can borrow?"

Everyone is quiet, bent over their computers, but Jess senses a frisson, a thrum of barely contained laughter, and she can tell right away that she's the joke of the day.

"Charles?" She turns, her hands on her hips. "How am I supposed to get any work done without a *computer*?"

He shrugs. "You have a computer."

"You know what I mean. I don't have the appropriate *accessories* to use said computer."

"You have everything you need."

"Someone took my mouse."

"I don't think you heard me," Charles says, and he places his palms together like a sage. "You, young Jones, have everything you need. Yesterday you were but a girl and today you are a man."

"I heard you, but you're not making any sense."

Charles sighs. "You don't need a goddamn mouse, Jones. Do you see anyone else here using a mouse?"

She doesn't.

Their workstations all look like they have been stripped for parts. No one uses a mouse, and keyboard keys that are deemed useless—num locks, tildes, semicolons—are tossed in the trash. Her first week of work Jess had found an F4 key in the wastebasket and felt a pang for its fate.

She knows that returning your mouse to Facilities is an act of honor, like laying down your sword after a battle, but she has also come to know that none of this applies to her.

Or so she thought.

She has passed some unspoken test, crossed some invisible threshold. Even though it slows her down—she can barely open an email without her mouse—and even though the mouse mouse is still on her desk—she has to pretend away her peripheral vision and scoot her chair as far away from it as she can—for the first time since she has started working, she feels like she might be getting somewhere.

There is still the problem of the mouse on her desk. It is so lifelike, has such a pulsing, febrile energy that Jess knows she can't dispose of it. And so it sits there, making her hot and uncomfortable.

Josh comes over to her desk later that afternoon to ask about a leveraged buyout model they're working on. She sees him see the mouse, though he says nothing.

But then before he walks away, without a word, he takes the mouse off her desk and, as he crosses the room, drops it in the trash just outside the bullpen.

4

Josh is alone in the bullpen wearing giant headphones, like a deejay at a European dance club, and so he doesn't notice Jess standing behind him. He is pecking at his keyboard, navigating between tabs, a dozen open spreadsheets and pdf documents and work-in-progress presentations.

Jess watches as he taps the Enter key and a rainbow cascades across the spreadsheet, like a Lite-Brite: colors, numbers, charts and tables. Jess has no idea where they come from—they just appear. And then, more magic: borders and formatting and somehow, he has conjured an entire three-statement model out of thin air.

Jess says, "What the hell was that?"

He spins around, yanks his headphones down. "What are you doing here?"

"What was that?"

"How long have you been here?"

She narrows her eyes. "Long enough. What were you doing?"

He taps his keyboard twice more and all of the open windows disappear so that all Jess can see is his desktop. Most people have pictures of mountains or seascapes or puppies or personal pictures as their wallpaper, but his screen is just blue.

"Don't worry about it," he says. "Can I help you?"

"What just happened? Because that looked like pure sorcery. You literally just did two hours of work in eight seconds. Was that a macro?"

"Not a macro," he says. "A Python script. I wrote it."

"Can you send it to me?"

"No," he says.

"Why not?"

"It's not part of the shared library. I wrote it."

"So . . . you can't send it to me?"

He looks up at the ceiling, then at the floor, picks up a pen and taps it against the desk and finally says, "No."

"Why not!"

"Would you send a nuclear warhead to a fifth grader?"

"Oh, shut up. Are you really not going to send it to me? Why not?"

"You wouldn't know how to use it anyway."

"So this is your secret?"

"It's not a secret."

"Then why are you being so secretive?"

He sighs. "Because I don't want people like you bugging me all the time for shortcuts. I don't want to be the team's designated IT guy. I don't want anyone to know I illegally downloaded this IDE."

"Just send it to me."

"No."

"Please?"

"No."

"Send it to me or I'm going to tell everyone else about it. I'll totally blow your cover."

"Are you blackmailing me?"

Jess thinks about it. "Yes, yes I am."

At her desk, Jess pings him.

this file you sent, it's just a bunch of words in a text document

yes

where's the program or whatever

that's it

how does it work?

He doesn't answer and Jess forgets about it until much later, after she's spent the better part of an hour chasing forms around the internet for a loan commitment document. She pings Josh again.

what else can you automate?

anything

trading comps?

yeah

PIBs?
yeah
credit committee docs?
probably not that
why not? that's what I want to do
would be complicated
but not impossible?
I could do it
but I couldn't?
do you even know how to code?
can you teach me?
no
my friend Miky, she consumes so much weird shit on the internet,
and there's this guy she likes online, he makes these crazy cars, art cars,
and people buy them, like for a million dollars, and there's one he has,
it has two engines and maybe it runs on electricity? something like that,
and basically he built it from scratch, part by part
　　your point?
　　well, how he started was he taught himself to make a carburator
watching YouTube videos, so maybe I'll do that
　　Jess, it's spelled carburetor

It takes Jess forty, maybe fifty hours—she stops counting a couple of weeks in—and it doesn't work and it doesn't work and it doesn't work until it does.

She finds Josh.

"No way," he says. "You figured it out? Really?"

"Yeah," Jess says. "I told you I would rather stick hot pins in my eyes than spend another all-nighter on a credit comm doc, remember?"

"I remember," he says. "I guess it wasn't that complicated after all."

"Yeah," she rolls her eyes, "any moron could figure it out."

"That's not what I meant."

"Yeah, right."

"You learned Python?"

"Enough to be dangerous."

"So how did you resolve the cardinality issue?"

"Oh, yeah, that was annoying. I ended up using MapReduce to convert all the tickers to dummy numerical values so I could limit the number of dimensions." She looks at him. "What? What's wrong?"

"Nothing." He shakes his head. "That's actually very . . . elegant. Can you share it with me?"

And Jess says, "Nope."

"Play with me," Josh says the next day.

He's at Jess's desk with a Set deck, knocking the cards against his palm.

"You want to play cards?"

"I want to see how you do it."

"How I do what?"

"How you make the sets so fast. I want to understand how your mind works. Let's play."

"That was just once." Jess hasn't played Set at work again. Charles assured her it wouldn't be good for her career.

"So it was dumb luck?"

"I didn't say that."

"Good," he says, pulling a chair up. "Then let's play."

Jess rolls her eyes, but she lets him deal twelve cards on her desk. Before he's placed the seventh down she calls, "Set."

"No way," he says. But then she picks up three cards, a set, and he's forced to deal three more.

"Set," she says again, right away.

"So that's how you do it? You say 'set' and then you find the set? Like calling dibs?"

Jess shakes her head. "No. I see the set first. Otherwise, what if there were no sets?" She picks up three cards.

They play another hand and then she has three sets and he has none.

"So you pick a color? Or a shape? And then wait for the dealer to complete the set?"

"No." She sweeps three more cards off the table.

"You've memorized all the sets?"

"No."

"These aren't actually sets and you're just grabbing cards before anyone notices?"

"No."

"Then how do you do it?"

She looks at him. "Honestly? I don't know."

"Useless."

"Sorry I'm smarter than you are, but I can't explain why." She sticks out her tongue. "Sorry not sorry."

"You're not smarter than I am," he says, peering at the cards she has collected, stacked accusingly in piles of three, "but I am impressed."

They are tossing a rubber band ball back and forth, waiting for Charles's comments on a merger model when Josh asks Jess, "So did you take Linear Algebra?"

"In college?"

He nods, lobs the ball to her underhanded.

"Uh huh." She lets the ball bounce once and then catches it, throws it back. She can't help grinning when she adds, "I got an A."

"What else did you take?"

"Differential Equations. Number Theory. Combinatorics."

He seems impressed. "You could have been a math major."

"I was a math major."

Josh is about to send the ball back but stops midair. "Really?"

Jess bristles. "Yes *really*." She opens both palms, asking for the ball back. "What did you think I majored in? Sociology? Basket weaving?"

" 'Mathematics is the music of reason,' " Josh says and then throws the ball back. "So, what, you just love math?"

Jess nods. "Plus, if I'm honest, I feel like it was the only major where it didn't matter what the professor thought of you. You just took the tests, got everything right and then didn't have to argue with some stupid professor about your grade at the end of the semester."

She throws the ball high and wide and it bounces against the corkboard wall and then onto the desk behind Josh. "You know our Law and Society professor accused me of plagiarizing my final paper? On the basis of it was too good. He actually tried to fail me."

"Yeah." Josh picks up the ball and tosses it to himself, from one hand to the other. "Why do you think he did that?"

"Because he was a dick? Because he thought that, I don't know, I was from some shitty inner-city public school and so it would have been impossible for me to write a decent paper? Because he could? It was bullshit."

Josh is sympathetic. "That is bullshit, Jess."

The professor had called Jess into his office with "concerns" about her final paper. She'd researched an obscure Supreme Court ruling on the federal statute of limitations. It wasn't her best work, but she'd made some good points about the limits of congressional power. She had spell-checked it twice. But the professor had accused her of cheating and threatened to fail her.

Afterward, waiting for the elevator, Jess heard her name. She turned, and there was Josh. He was holding his final paper—he must have come to collect it from his student mailbox—and Jess could see the grade: a bright red A, and next to that, in the professor's handwriting, the words "Nice work!"

This drove her crazy.

She thought: *What a fucking surprise.*

She said, "What a fucking surprise."

Josh said, "Excuse me?"

The elevator doors slid open and they stepped inside.

Jess nodded at his paper. "Nice *work*," she said sarcastically.

"Smithson just called me into his office to accuse me of plagiarizing."
The elevator dinged to its final stop. Jess continued, "With zero evidence! I mean why would he ask me if I cheated?"

Josh stepped out of the elevator, but then turned and said, "Well,
did you?"

An article comes out in a reputable magazine saying that Goldman is
hostile to minorities. The journalist had interviewed several employees off-the-record, painting a picture of a firm that is biased at best,
blatantly sexist and racist at worst. Jess considers briefly that if she
had gone to work for the feminist magazine, she could be on the other
side of this story—they'd already published a blog post mentioning it:
Breaking, Goldman Sachs Employees Also Hate Goldman Sachs. She
thinks about how things might have turned out differently, sometimes,
but then she also thinks about being broke, living in New Jersey with
five roommates probably.

Even though the leadership team vehemently denies the article's allegations, a mandatory sensitivity training is scheduled. No one wants
to attend, including Jess. Everyone grumbles that it is going to be a
waste of time and since when do we pander to the press?

Worse, everyone on their floor looks at Jess like it's her fault.

Not because they think she's one of the unnamed sources—or, at
least, she hopes not—but because if she weren't there then none of
them would have to step away from their desks for an hour in the
middle of the day to be patronized to.

In the same auditorium where the secretary of the treasury recently
gave a lecture, a pair of very earnest facilitators tries to convince the
room that unconscious bias is real, while everyone stares at their
phones. Eventually they open it up for discussion and the conversation
unfolds so predictably that Jess wonders how many more times she
will be forced to sit in a room having her intelligence insulted.

She imagines having this conversation over and over again, forever,
until she dies. Sitting in her wheelchair, in the retirement home, sur-

rounded by people who will never stop asking why we must "lower the bar."

As if on cue someone stands and says, "This is a business, not a charity. Our responsibility is to our shareholders, not to try to create some utopia where everyone can be CEO. We need to hire the best and brightest, not lower the bar. That's how we stay competitive."

Murmurs of agreement ripple throughout the room.

Jess wants to say something, or at least stand on her chair and scream, but this isn't a college classroom—there are actual stakes, this is her livelihood—and so as much as she would like to be the voice of the marginalized, she would also not particularly like to shit where she eats.

Several rows in front of her, Josh stands to speak and Jess wishes he would sit down or jump off a bridge, so little does she want to revisit his opinions on this topic.

He starts, "Empirically, we know that intelligence follows a normal distribution—" and it's like déjà vu. Jess wishes she had a dart gun or a tomato, something to hurl across the room.

He continues, "But the problem is that success—money, power, opportunity—follows a power law distribution. So, there's an asymmetry. Systematic distortions—institutional sexism, racism, discrimination—that exaggerate the skewness. There's data to prove it. Researchers have done simulations that show the relationship between IQ and success is disproportionate and highly nonlinear. So, if you think we're lowering the bar . . . your math is wrong."

He pauses, takes a slow look around the room. "It's complicated, I get it, but you can't tell me it's not worth throwing a few coins at."

And then he sits down.

Jess can hardly believe the words coming out of his mouth, words that she agrees with. It doesn't make sense, she doesn't know what to think, except for *What the actual fuck?*

Later she confronts him.

Her hand is on her hip and she says, "Please explain."

He is at his workstation and he closes a file before he swivels in his seat to face her. "What exactly are you referring to?"

"The unconscious bias training. That whole point you made about the power law distribution of success being mathematically consistent with institutional racism?"

He leans back in his chair, crosses one leg over the other. "What about it?"

"Why did you say all that stuff?"

"I shouldn't have?"

"You don't believe any of it."

"I do."

"But that's not what you said in college. In class. Don't you remember—"

"Jess," he interrupts, "the hallmark of an agile intellect is the ability to continuously accommodate and integrate new information. To regularly and systematically update one's mental model of the world. It's the scientific method."

"So . . . you changed your mind?"

"Yes."

"Why?"

"Not one reason. But there have been a number of studies lately that kind of explicitly break down race and gender as being highly predictive of economic outcomes even when controlling for things like parental income and education. It's . . . compelling."

"So you read a research paper and now you're not racist?"

He looks at her. "Ha, well that's one way to frame it." He swivels back to face his computer. "But for the record, I was never racist."

The next week Jess is hunched over her desk fighting with a model when Charles slinks over. He raps his knuckles on her desk, then snaps a rubber band at her monitor, picks up a mechanical pencil and clicks it at her ear, making himself a pest. She ignores him, until he takes her chair by the arm and spins it around so that she's facing him.

"Can I help you?" she asks, all eyes and attitude.

"Such insolence," Charles says, mock-offended.

"What's up?"

He says, "You're famous." And then he leans over her and types "goldman sachs careers" into Google Search and *click-click-clicks* until the campus recruiting site appears on Jess's screen.

In large letters at the top of the screen it says *Our People Are Our Strength* and below that is a high-resolution image of Jess, looking serious in a suit, her hair pulled back, small gold hoops in her ears. Her head is tilted thoughtfully to the side and a pen hovers in her right hand just above a bright yellow legal pad. In the background men in blurred suits stand nearby.

She looks up at Charles. "What is this?"

"Well, Jones," he says slyly, "that's you."

She peers at her computer screen and says, "They can't do this!" She looks at Charles again. "How can they do this?"

He says, "What? Are you worried you look fat?"

Jess glares.

Charles shrugs and says, "Well, look on the bright side, Jones. As long as your face is plastered all over the website, they can't exactly fire you, can they, yeah?"

"This is so fucked up," Jess says to anyone who will listen.

"What's the big deal?" Josh asks.

"They're using my *likeness* for financial gain. How can they do that?"

"I repeat, what's the big deal?"

"Are you kidding me? You really don't get it? They think they can just slap my face on the website and suddenly two hundred years of institutional racism—the systematic denial of credit to Black people on the one hand and predatory lending on the other—just disappears? It's infuriating. First the sensitivity training and now this. But of course no one is actually going to do anything *real*."

"So you think this has something to do with that article?"

Jess gives him a look. "Um, yeah," she says, with as much sarcasm as she can muster, "I do."

"But recruitment and hiring are completely siloed from Media Relations. So I doubt it was some coordinated effort to exploit you. You're reading too much into it."

"You're not reading enough into it," Jess says. "It was one hundred percent coordinated."

"So you think it's some kind of conspiracy?"

"No, of course not. Do you see a tinfoil hat? I'm not saying this is the work of the Illuminati, just that I don't appreciate my good name being used to, like, absolve Goldman of its sins."

He says, "Are you familiar with Occam's razor?"

Jess says, "Yes, and?"

"Well," he explains anyway, "for each accepted explanation of a phenomenon, there could potentially be an infinite number of possible, more complex alternatives. So, the idea is that simpler theories are preferable to more complex ones because they are more testable."

"What's your point?"

"My point is that this applies here as well. There's probably a simple explanation."

"It is simple," Jess argues. "They're using me to curate a perception instead of actually changing the reality."

When he doesn't respond, she looks at him. "Okay, fine, Isaac Newton. What's a simpler explanation, then?"

"I don't know," he shrugs. "Maybe they just used your picture because you're pretty."

Jess doesn't know how to respond. He is so smug and annoying.

But, also, that word: pretty.

Once, in the bathroom at Avenue Tavern, two drunk girls had tapped Jess on the shoulder as she was washing her hands in front of the mirror. In the rear view, she had watched them debate whether to approach her, giggling and nervous, as if she were a celebrity that they were afraid to talk to.

Finally, one of them had said, "Excuse me."

And Jess had said, "Yes?"

And one of the drunk girls had said, "My friend and I, we just wanted to tell you that you're the prettiest Black girl we've ever seen."

And at first Jess had been flattered—the world was big, she was beautiful!

But then, a minute later, she thought, *Wait.*

In college Jess had dated a guy named Ivan and the disaster of their relationship was predicated on the fact that he thought she was pretty and she thought that was enough.

He had badgered Jess for months.

Out at night, at parties, in bars, he would find her, standing in line for the bathroom or bouncing quarters into red Solo cups with Lydia, and ask her to go home with him. She was wary—of being treated like garbage, of blistering STDs, of giving him the satisfaction—but also, she was flattered.

Though Jess knew better than to say so, Ivan was out of her league. He was rich and handsome and popular, could go out with anyone he wanted. And Jess knew there was a hierarchy: blondes, then brunettes and redheads, then everyone else.

In middle school, at a slumber party, Jess had reluctantly admitted to a crush on a classmate named Tom. Like Ivan, he was rich and handsome and popular; he rode a long skateboard with stickers on the bottom and had boy-band-perfect highlights. Jess's confession had not been especially interesting; every other girl in their class also liked Tom.

But the girls shook their heads. "I don't really see it, you and Tom."

"Why not?" Jess asked, though she already knew why.

"Because," they explained, "Tom has options. And when guys can pick any girl they want, they always go with the hottest. They go for blondes, then brunettes and redheads."

Jess had pointed out that she wasn't a blonde, a brunette or a redhead, and so they rolled their eyes and clarified: "Blondes, then brunettes and redheads. Then everyone else."

Jess had looked around at the other girls in their sleeping bags, pale-faced, fair-haired, from Northern European stock, and realized if they'd lined up in order of desirability—blondes, then brunettes and redheads—she wouldn't even be in the line.

But then there was Ivan. Girls (blondes, brunettes, redheads all) were constantly throwing themselves at him, but she—Jess—was at the top of his list. It was flattering. She was into it. So she played it cool.

"I always see you at the gym," he said to her one night at the Lantern, a smoky dive bar. "You look so hot in those little shorts." He leaned toward her, resting his palm on the wall behind her shoulder. She could feel his breath on her face when he said, "Like Beyoncé's sister or something."

"Like Solange?"

"What?" Ivan had leaned back slightly.

"Like Solange Knowles?" Jess asked, "Beyoncé's sister?"

"Who? No. I meant you look like you could be Beyoncé's sister. But prettier."

"So you think I'm prettier than someone who could theoretically be Beyoncé's sister?"

"Much prettier."

"So I actually don't look anything like Beyoncé's imaginary sister?" Jess teased.

Ivan didn't play along. He said, "Why are you giving me a hard time?"

According to her friends, he wasn't relationship material. He was a fuckboy and a flake. But that was precisely the attraction: he was hot and rich and cocky. Which created a force field around him. Standing next to him at the bar, Jess felt a part of it. When a random dude had bumped into her from behind, spilling her drink, she'd turned around expecting an apology, but it was like she was furniture. Until he noticed Ivan. Then suddenly he was so sorry. I'm an idiot. Let me buy you another drink. It was like Ivan proved that she mattered. Jess felt like she was stealing some of his power. It was a feeling she could bathe in.

She tried to explain this to her friends, but they were still skeptical.

"Fair enough," Miky said, "but do you really want to spend your Friday nights watching him snort cocaine off of his ab roller?"

*   *   *

Ivan's fraternity had thrown a Mardi Gras party: drinks in hurricane glasses and long strings of plastic beads draped all over the furniture. Jess found him on the staircase, scooping foam out of his beer.

"Hey." She batted her eyelashes.

"So are you ready to give me an answer?"

"To what question?"

He grinned. "What is it going to take to get your clothes off?"

And Jess said: "A date."

For their first date Ivan drove her into the city for dinner at an Italian bistro popular with mobsters and politicians. He picked Jess up in a sports car with blacked-out windows, like some kind of Bond villain. Jess knew she was meant to be impressed, and she was, mostly, but she had just paid her rent and had only twenty-three dollars in her checking account and so she was also, sort of, willfully unimpressed.

He showed up more than thirty minutes late, and instead of coming to the door he put the car in neutral and revved the engine. Jess slid into the passenger seat and, without a word, he stepped on the accelerator and the car flew forward at about a thousand miles per hour.

There was a stop sign at the end of the block.

"Is it safe for you to be driving this car?" Jess asked.

"Babe, if you want safe, I'm not the guy for you."

Jess made a big show of buckling her seat belt.

The next thing Ivan said, once they had merged onto the highway, was "You look hot."

"So do you."

He swerved suddenly onto the shoulder, stopped the car and turned on the hazards.

"What? What's wrong?"

He growled, an actual growl, like a wounded beast. "You make me so hard."

"Are you serious?"

"I can't drive like this."

"Like what?"

"With this giant erection."

"Would you like me to drive?"

"Ha! Nice try, babe," he said, as if Jess were the one whose genitals had just swung them across three lanes of traffic, "but do you know how many cylinders this car has?" He shook his head. "You'd be dust."

He angled himself toward her and spread his legs to expose the bulge between them. "What I'd like is for you to help me out with this." He raised one eyebrow and then the other, then lifted his pelvis toward Jess in case she'd missed his point.

She said, "Um."

Ivan waited for her to change her mind, and when she didn't, he just shrugged and put the car back in drive, as if it were nothing; *your loss, no hard feelings, just thought I'd ask.*

Jess was impressed by his equanimity, surprised he was such a good sport. It was, somehow, endearing.

And the truth was, though she didn't exactly want to give him a blow job on the side of the highway—in his ridiculous car, with the hazards flashing—she didn't not want to, either.

5

Everyone says that Josh is a rising star. In those words. After a year on the job, analysts have names and reputations. They're either crushing it or flaming out. And then there's Josh. People say he's "commercial," which is the highest compliment an analyst can be paid and means he gets the best deal flow and the most exposure and a never-ending stream of phone calls from hedge fund and private equity headhunters. It means that he is invited to play golf with the managing directors.

"You play golf with Blaine?" Jess asks.

"I don't *play* golf with him, I've *played* golf with him," Josh clarifies.

"That sentence makes me want to vomit."

"Which part?"

"The part where you're trying to hide your complicity in the old boys' capitalist club behind a past participle."

"You could learn to play golf." Josh pauses, grins. "You could have learned to play golf."

To make up for so many centuries of oppression, Josh buys Jess lunch.

And then, one day, because the guy at the kosher hot dog stand won't take his Amex, Jess buys Josh lunch.

And then Josh buys again because he bets Jess ten bucks that she can't spell *onomatopoeia*, but she can.

And then at some point they stop keeping score.

For lunch they usually circle the building, eating in a perimeter around West Street and North End Avenue. They discover falafel trucks and soup carts, sandwich shops and a place that sells only rice, in giant bowls sprinkled with sugar and cinnamon and honey.

"It's nice," Jess says as they stand in line for burritos, "going outside. Sometimes I can, like, feel my bones getting brittle, or like I'm turning into Quasimodo."

Josh says, "The hunchback of Notre Jess."

Sometimes, when it's very busy, instead of going out they have food delivered to their desks and eat it in an empty conference room.

"Any exciting plans for the weekend?" Jess asks one day, dipping a triangle of pita bread into hummus.

"Going home for the holiday."

"Easter?"

Josh nods.

"I thought you weren't religious," Jess says, chewing. She remembers an especially delightful diatribe he once delivered in class calling religion the foe of rationality. He'd quoted Nietzsche.

"So I should never have dinner with my family again?"

"Maybe you shouldn't. Maybe you should say: 'Mom, Dad, fuck you and the Popemobile you rode in on, 'cause I don't believe in motherfucking God.' Isn't that what any principled rational empiricist would do?"

He laughs. "You're insane, you know that? And my parents aren't even Catholic."

"What are they?"

"Nothing. Normal," he says. "Anyway, they're divorced. So it's just my mom this time."

"Then you'll just have to wait until Christmas to give your dad the finger," Jess says, smiling.

He picks up a chicken skewer. "So is that what holidays are like at your house? You telling your mother where she can shove things, throwing food, lighting the upholstery on fire."

"I don't have a mother."

He looks up.

"She died."

Josh doesn't say anything.

"When I was a baby, or, I mean, very small. I don't remember her, so, you know."

He reaches into the paper bag and pulls out a small square of puff pastry, honey and chopped nuts, folded in wax paper.

He hands it to Jess. "Here," he says, "for you."

Late the next Friday Josh stops by.

He half sits, half stands with his palms pressed against her desk.

"Working this weekend?" he asks.

"Probably not."

He nods.

But he doesn't say anything.

And she doesn't say anything.

But he doesn't get up to leave either.

And then at the same time as Jess says "So then—" Josh says, "My friend—"

"Your friend what?" she asks.

"My friend is having people over tomorrow afternoon. His parents are out of town."

Jess laughs. "So someone is going to score a six-pack and some weed and hopefully the neighbors won't call the cops?"

Josh laughs back. "I mean, he's got a nice place. His parents do."

"Yeah?"

"We used to hang out there all the time in high school."

"Yeah?"

"It's been a while since he had people over."

"Yeah?"

Josh picks up a pen, helicopters it between his pointer and middle fingers.

Finally, he says, "Do you want to come?"

Inside a giant brownstone with an iron gate a guy in pink shorts meets Jess at the door.

"I'm David." He's friendly. "Come in, come in," he says, and motions for Jess to follow him. He peers around the great room seeming momentarily lost, but then says, "You know what? Josh must be outside." He points with his beer can, then tips an imaginary hat and disappears into the room full of pale-haired people in polo shirts, drinking beer and taking shots. It makes her think of an old Abercrombie & Fitch ad. Or a Harvard-Yale tailgate. Or the kind of college party that used to make her cringe.

The most cringeworthy college party of them all: a mixer Ivan's fraternity once threw, an antebellum South–themed party with spiked lemonade in mason jars and girls dressed in puffy dresses carrying decorative parasols. For several weeks leading up to the party a Confederate flag had flown from one of the brothers' windows, right over the main quad, where it flapped menacingly in the winter wind every time Jess walked by, surprised each time she saw it to find that it was still there.

She thought it was racist. But no one else seemed to care or agree, the combination of southern pride—though Jess was pretty sure the flag belonged to a guy from DC—and free speech inoculating it from further scrutiny.

So Jess tried to ignore it. But it was hard to ignore the party, which she had been asked not only to attend but to "come dressed to impress." It felt like a slap in the face.

"Don't you think it's a little fucked up?" Jess had asked the friend who insisted that she come, that it would be fun, that the drinks would be strong. A friend who Jess hasn't spoken to since graduation. Her name was Gretchen.

"What's fucked up?" Gretchen asked.

"An *antebellum* party? The *Civil* War? The Con*fede*racy? Is this for real? Am I supposed to go dressed in my cotton picking best? And on top of everything, now there's that flag hanging outside their house? Is this happening? Am I on glue?"

Jess had been fired up.

"Relax! It's *southern* themed. Sweet tea and porch swings. Not slavery or whatever. Where on the invite does it say anything about the Confederacy? Don't be a spoilsport. Oh, *wait*." She was suddenly smug. "*I* know what this is about," she snorted. "Come on, Jess, are you really going to let him win? This whole thing"—she waved a hand in the air as if everything Jess had just said was gibberish—"it's about Ivan, isn't it?"

It wasn't about Ivan. Yes, they had broken up, just last week. And yes it had been ugly. Grisly, even. Humiliating, definitely. But it wasn't about Ivan. Or maybe it was a little. If they had still been together maybe Jess wouldn't have cared about the party. Maybe it wouldn't have bothered her. Maybe she wouldn't have noticed.

Gretchen had the invitation pulled up on her phone, and on it Jess could see the silhouette of a woman, puffy skirt and parasol, against the backdrop of a Georgian-style manor, which was obviously a plantation.

She would have noticed.

Still, Jess went—because it wasn't technically a Confederate party and because she wasn't going to let Ivan win. So she went and she became extremely drunk.

"You're going to barf if you don't stop," Lydia had warned her, prying a Solo cup from Jess's hands.

"Don't tell me what to do, Lydia," Jess slurred, so that *Lydia* sounded like *lithium*.

"You're wasted."

Jess shrugged.

"Ivan's not here," Lydia said.

"Ivan, *Schm*ivan." Jess flapped her arms around in an exaggerated *who cares?* dance, spilling her drink on herself and the floor. "You think I care?"

"Jess, you're really drunk, let's go home." Lydia took her arm. "Come on."

A girl walked by with lace gloves and a stupid pink hat. She laughed, and trilled in a southern accent, "Well, I do declare." It was too much.

Jess shook Lydia off and scrambled onto the pool table. "Hey, everyone," she shouted. "Hey! Listen to me!"

"Jess, please get down."

She started kicking billiard balls off the table.

"Jess, please. Stop."

"I have something to say," she announced, and when people turned, she shouted, "This party is fucked! Do you hear me? Fucked!"

"Fuck you," someone shouted back.

"Fuck *you*!" And then she pointed wildly around the room. "Fuck you. And you. And you too. *Fuck* everyone. Fuck this party. Fuck you, *ass*holes!"

It would only occur to Jess much later that she hadn't actually used the word *racist*. It seemed impossible that they wouldn't know, but then again it seemed impossible that such a party even existed at all, or that it was so packed that they were turning people away at the door. It was 2011! At a liberal East Coast university! There was a Black man in the White House! What the hell? So even though it was too late, and even though she was in a state, and even though it wasn't *technically* a Confederate party, and even though Jess herself was an attendee, in the end she felt compelled to Say Something. Although she was pretty sure this bit of blackout activism wasn't what her father had had in mind when he'd encouraged her to take up arms in the fight against injustice.

She heard someone say, "Ivan, you need to control your girl."

For the first time that night she saw him. On the other side of the room standing with a willowy blonde. His new girlfriend. Someone more beautiful than Jess. Blondes, brunettes, then redheads. Then everyone else.

"You!" Jess trained her finger, quavering, at him.

He shook his head and started to leave the room, the blonde's hand clasped in his.

"Don't walk away from me! Don't you dare!"

Jess wound up—she almost fell backward—and kicked the cue ball in his general direction. "You prick! I hate you!"

But she was way off, and instead the ball sailed straight ahead, right through a stained glass window, which it shattered with a surprisingly emphatic tintinnabulation.

Jess felt hands on her, someone dragging her off the pool table.

"Don't touch her!" Lydia said.

"She needs to leave."

"Give me a break. It's a party. She's wasted. Shocking."

"Take your friend home."

"Get away from her," Lydia said, pulling Jess toward her. "We're leaving your precious house right now, okay, *princess*?"

Outside Jess swayed with the trees.

"You're so drunk!" Lydia said.

Jess started to cry.

"Oh, sweetie, Ivan's not worth it. He's not."

Jess slumped to the ground.

"Poor Jess." Lydia crouched down, touched Jess's elbow tenderly. "Let's go home, okay? Can you stand?"

Lydia helped her to her feet. "It's okay, you're okay," she said, gripping Jess's arm.

She rested her head on Lydia's shoulder as they walked back to their apartment, until Jess suddenly stopped, shouted, "Wait!"

"What is it?" Lydia asked, concerned, startled.

"Assholes," Jess said, wagging her finger in the air as if the thought had just occurred to her. "Nothing but. A bunch. Of assholes."

"I know, I know," Lydia said. "But Jess. The next time you walk into a party and think 'Gee, these people are all assholes' maybe . . . don't?"

Jess follows the music into the party, then heads out the back door David had pointed to.

She finds Josh on the patio, and he smiles hello. "You made it."

"It was so hard to find," Jess says. "The smallest house on the block."

Josh laughs. His hair is messy and his face flushed; he isn't wearing shoes, though his shirt is still buttoned all the way to the top.

It is warm enough outside that it feels almost like summer. Josh leans against the stone wall that encloses the patio. He pulls a small tin of rolling papers from his back pocket and says, "Smoke?"

"Sure."

He cracks the ring off a half-drunk six-pack and tilts a can toward her. "Drink?"

"Sure." Jess takes the beer and looks at him sideways.

Jess watches as he expertly rolls one joint—he tongues the paper with amphibian-like precision—and then another. He puts the tip of both joints between his lips, flicks a lighter, blows smoke out the side of his mouth, and then hands her one.

The weed burns off the intensity in his eyes and when he looks up it activates something inside her; she feels—just for a moment—as if she is falling from a great height.

"I assumed you were a dork in high school," she blurts.

Through a mouthful of smoke he says, "Because you think I'm a dork now?"

"No!" Jess says quickly. "I just meant . . . no?"

He laughs. "What makes you think I wasn't a dork in high school?"

Inside someone turns the music up, and through the window Jess sees a girl with long hair shriek as someone sprays water from the faucet at her.

Jess says, "I mean I thought you were this goody-goody and now you're offering me drugs at a party and I'm a little surprised, that's all."

"Drugs?"

She holds up the joint. "Like, I didn't think you liked to party. You're so"—she uses her palms to make an imaginary box in the air—"you know . . . by the book."

He grins. "So you're saying you think I'm a square?"

Jess wasn't sure before—even when he's fuzzy and relaxed and shoeless he has such a serious demeanor—but now she's certain. He's flirting.

She flirts back. "Not completely, no . . . more like a squircle."

"You're funny," he says.

"Thank you."

"You're welcome," he says, and there it is again, that smile.

They blow smoke at each other in silence.

Finally, Jess says, "Where are David's parents? In, like, St. Barts?"

"Ha, no. London. His sister lives there. She has a kid."

"So this is where you had all your make-out parties in high school?"

"Pretty much, yeah. We would all sign out for the weekend and take the train down," he says. "You know the first time I was here? We got out of the taxi and I thought we were at a museum."

Jess smiles. "I did too. Or maybe one of those private family foundations, where all the art is pillaged from, like, lesser nations."

"You have a Marxist streak," Josh says. "It's charming."

"You know what's charming? When the means of production are communally owned."

Josh laughs.

He pops the tab on another beer, the last beer, and passes it to Jess.

"You don't want it?" she asks.

"We can share," he says.

"I'm wearing lip gloss."

"I can see that."

"I mean . . . you don't mind? Lip gloss on the can?"

"I don't mind."

So Jess takes a sip and leaves a sticky pink mouth print on the lip of the can. She hands it back to him.

He looks at her, puts his mouth to the can's mouth, over the lip gloss print, and tips his head back.

In that moment, despite everything, Jess decides she would kind of like to sleep with him.

They finish the beer and then they're out of beer. They finish the weed and then they're out of weed. The sun dips below the horizon and it starts to get cold. The music has stopped and Jess says, "Should we see what's going on inside?"

But when they slide open the patio doors, everyone is gone.

"Where are they?" Jess asks.

"Swimming, I think."

And Jess imagines everyone decamped to one of those designer hotels with a swimming pool on the roof.

But then Josh says, "Follow me."

He leads her down a long staircase, and at the bottom opens a door to an indoor swimming pool. And it's so over-the-top, so insanely gorgeous and impractical, that Jess laughs.

He laughs too. He says, "I know, I know."

Though Jess is pretty sure he doesn't know. She thinks, but is not drunk enough to say, *Tell me again about your middle-class upbringing.*

The walls of the pool room are teak, like a sauna, and the recessed lighting is low and ambient. A row of loungers is lined up along the pool and they look like they were custom-ordered from an endangered forest.

Jess spends all day thinking about money and talking about money and worrying about money, to the point that it has become something sinister and abstract. But standing at the edge of the pool deck she remembers how sexy money can be.

In the pool people are drinking beer from cans and playing keep-away with a sagging beach ball.

Jess turns to Josh. "I don't have a swimsuit."

"Follow me."

In a changing room he points to a drawer, three rows of bikini tops and bottoms, folded in neat stacks from small to large, the tags still on.

After he leaves she picks out a swimsuit embroidered with little pink and blue seahorses, string, with two tiny triangles on top.

Then she takes off her clothes.

On the pool deck she leans back in a lounger and Josh comes over and sits next to her on one edge.

Josh says, "Do you swim?"

"Are you asking because I'm Black?" Jess is teasing, but also not.

Josh raises an eyebrow. "I'm asking because you're not swimming."

"I'm just kidding," Jess says, then pauses. "But only sort of. Once? In, like, eighth or ninth grade there was this party? Kind of like this one, actually. Someone in my class had this aunt or something who was out of town. Or maybe she moved away, but she hadn't sold the house? Something like that. Anyway, the point is, the house was empty."

"Okay . . ."

"So everyone snuck into this house and we were, I don't know, doing teenage things, drinking light beer and eating Twizzlers, and this whole crew of guys—like the popular jocks—they all started jumping in the pool. But it was disgusting, you know? Maybe the pump had been broken, or turned off, and the water had been there for who knows how long, and maybe some squirrels had died in there and there were leaves and shit, floating on the surface. It was gross.

"Anyway, they started trying to get all the girls to jump in. I think they just wanted them to take off their tops. So, of course, no one did. But then this girl Cath, who was, like, whatever, God's gift to high school—"

"She's probably knocked up and working at Walmart right now," Josh offers.

Jess smiles. "I hope so! Anyway, she says to me, in this really bitchy way, 'You *can* swim, *can't* you?' And of course she didn't ask anyone else, and of course, the pool was about three feet deep anyway and filthy and disgusting, so it was irrelevant.

"But then one of her bitchy little friends leans over and fake-whispers—you know, loud enough so I could hear?—'It's probably because of her hair.' And then Cath goes, 'Oh, right, they have this thing about their hair. I've heard they don't even wash it.' She said *they*." Jess stops, makes a face. "So I jumped in."

"Jess, no."

"I did. It was so gross, like swimming in an oil slick. And then Cath says, 'You're right, see? She won't put her head under.' And so, of course, then I did."

Josh groans.

"And I ended up getting an eye infection."

"Christ," Josh says. "Well, at least you showed her. Fuck you, Kat."

"Cath."

"That one."

Jess shakes her head. "I didn't actually."

"What do you mean?"

"Show her! She was right! My hair did get messed up."

"What do you mean, 'messed up'?"

"Well, I mean it was straight, and then it was curly. Like this." She points to her head.

She used to straighten it, but then she stopped after she read an op-ed titled "To All My Sisters Out There Still Straightening Your Hair, The Time Is Now to Divest Yourself from Eurocentric Beauty Standards." Also, it took too much time in the morning. So now she just wears her curls naturally.

Jess says, "Like, I knew that Black women were supposed to be afraid to get their hair wet, but I thought it was a random stereotype, like . . . that Black people hate mayonnaise."

"Black people hate mayonnaise?"

"Well, no. I mean that's why it's a random stereotype." She pauses. "Actually, maybe it's that Black people love mayonnaise? I can never keep it straight."

"Do you like mayonnaise?"

Jess gives him a look.

"You hate mayonnaise?"

Jess stares.

"You . . . have no special relationship to mayonnaise?"

Jess grins. "Bingo. Anyway, there were so many things like that. Like, my dad didn't have a clue. He would buy me all these magazines, like *Ebony* and *Essence*, you know, for Black women? And he would leave them in my room, but he never mentioned it. I think he was hoping that somehow they could, I don't know, teach me how to use a tampon or whatever. I kind of felt bad for him. But anyway, my hair . . . When I showered, obviously, it got wet, but there was shampoo involved and a blow dryer and I guess . . . I didn't make the connection between being curly . . ." She turns her face away from his. "I don't know, it was really stupid. I literally had to get antibiotics for my eye. And the doctor was kind of a dick. He was all 'Why would you go in that water? What were you thinking? That wasn't a very responsible choice, young lady.' And I was like, 'You want to know why I went in? You really want to know? It's because my mother is dead, you moron.' "

Jess stops talking, feeling a little bit breathless and exposed.

But then Josh says, "Jesus, Jess. That is the saddest, funniest thing I've ever heard," and then: "I think your hair is pretty."

He reaches up as if to touch it, but lets his hand fall back down into his lap.

He is making good eye contact, looking at her with intent, and only occasionally down at her chest. Jess worries that he can hear the sound of her heart beating, or at least see the blood pumping in her throat. She keeps touching her tongue to her lips, she can't stop. His face is close, stubbly from a day without shaving, flushed from an afternoon drinking in the early spring air.

The triangles of fabric covering her breasts suddenly feel very thin. Josh asks, "Are you cold?"

"No," Jess admits.

She wants him to touch her, to acknowledge in some way the electricity coursing through her. She feels like one of those patients with an alcoholic anesthesiologist who gets the dosage wrong, so that even though they are meant to feel nothing, they end up feeling everything and can only lay in excruciating silence while their nerve endings erupt.

She glances through the door into the hall. David's house is full of endless hallways lined with doors that open into so many rooms. Jess wants to go with Josh into one of them and turn off the lights.

But then: "Hey, man." David is standing over them. "Abby thinks it's time for tequila."

From the pool a girl with dark blond hair in a long braid like Pocahontas—Abby, Jess assumes—screeches, "Tequila time!"

"Can you help me grab stuff upstairs?" David asks.

Josh looks at David then at Jess, seems momentarily unsure.

But then he gets up. "I'll be right back."

In the changing room Jess checks herself out. She makes a face in the mirror, pulls her hair up, then lets it down. She swirls a teaspoon of mouthwash from the medicine cabinet between her molars. She touches her neck and it's hot, then runs a finger along the underside of the bikini bottom waistband but stops. She hears voices.

She turns, but there's no one there.

The voices are coming through the air vent in the ceiling and after a minute Jess realizes that through some acoustical trick of the building's architecture that she's hearing David and Josh and someone else, whose voice she doesn't recognize, in the kitchen, their words faint.

She picks up only snippets.

Josh . . . hand me . . . Abby says . . . those . . . bottom shelf

She hears her name and stands perfectly still.

Jess . . . she . . . says David.

Yeah, she can barely hear Josh, *reminds me . . . she's . . .*

She's what? Jess wonders.

David says something else and they all laugh and then Jess hears glasses clinking and it sounds like they've stopped speaking, but then she hears her name again and one of them says, as clear as a bell, the words *jungle fever.*

Jess holds her breath.

Who said it?

She waits for someone to respond. Finally, Josh says something, though Jess can't hear what it is. Whatever he says it makes David laugh. Or maybe they all laugh. She can't tell.

One of them says, *Tenley . . . saw her . . . Jess?*

And Josh must have moved because the next thing he says, Jess can hear as if he's standing right next to her ear. What he says is *Tenley, she is not . . .*

The space between her legs goes cold.

She has no idea what that means or who Tenley is, but she is also pretty sure it's not a compliment.

Of course she wouldn't be his type, just like she wasn't—not really, not in the end—Ivan's.

It's not like she hadn't known. Though he had offered her veiled commitments—when she complained about Supreme Court Topics: "the next time Professor Fuckface tries to fuck with you, you let me know, and I'll fuck his fucking face up"—which seemed to emphasize his devotion to their ongoing partnership, he kept her at arm's length. It was clear from the beginning that she wasn't the kind of girl he saw a future with.

After they first started dating, even though she wanted to, Jess avoided having sex with him for as long as she could, like taming a wild beast by tying it to a fence. It had reassured her, how patiently he waited, though eventually, of course, his patience ran out. At which point he had pouted, then shouted, then called her a tease, until finally she relented.

The morning after, Jess returned to her apartment with smudged eye makeup and her underwear in her purse.

"Well?" Lydia greeted her. "How was it?"

"Good." Jess had flopped on the couch. "Fine? Good. It's just . . . he sort of did and said some things, and it made me wonder."

"What kind of things?" Miky asked.

"Made you wonder what?" Lydia asked.

"Like maybe if he has some kind of fetish. Like maybe I'm just, like, another notch in his United Colors of Benetton bedpost. Just another piece of 'exotic' pussy to brag to all his buddies about in the locker room. Not, you know, real relationship material."

"That's sort of a risk you run, isn't it though? Fucking with white dudes?"

"But Albie's not like that," Jess protested. "Is he? He doesn't, like, objectify you in a specifically Asian way. Does he?"

Miky had been hooking up with a graduate student named Albie Shumway, a Captain America from Salt Lake City. Jess had seen him hold a taxi door open to let Miky in and then walk around to the street side so that she didn't have to slide across the seat. As far as Jess could tell, he was swell.

"I mean, sometimes he reads Japanese manga porn."

"Really?"

"But," Miky added, "it's all very tasteful."

* * *

In the changing room at David's, her heart is still pounding. Jess finds the shelf with her clothes and pulls them on as fast as she possibly can. She wants to leave, right away. If she makes a quick turn at the top of the stairs, she can avoid them in the kitchen.

But she isn't quick enough and she runs into them on the stairs. They have bottles under their arms and stacks of small glasses in their hands.

Josh stops. "Hey!"

Josh turns to his friends and says, "I'll see you down there?"

To Josh, Jess says, "I have to go."

"What? Now?"

"Yeah." Jess doesn't look at him. "I forgot. I have . . . a thing."

"Oh," he says, frowning. "Well, let me walk you out."

"No!" Jess is almost to the top of the landing. "I mean, it's okay. Thanks for having me."

He makes a face. "Is everything all right?"

"Yeah. Everything's . . . fine. I just forgot I have . . . a thing."

He peers at her, puzzled. "Are you . . . ?"

He doesn't finish his sentence and she waits for him to say more.

But he doesn't and she doesn't either and then she leaves.

At work on Monday she ignores him.

He says, "Lunch?" but she is frosty. She says, "I can't."

Later in the week he asks again and she says, "Sorry, I'm busy," even though she's sitting at her desk looking at a website that sells shoes and is clearly not.

The next time he asks and the next time, Jess says she's busy.

Eventually, he says, "Jess, what's going on?"

"I just don't feel like having lunch."

"Why not?" he asks. "I don't understand."

"I just don't feel like it. I'm not hungry."

He looks at her for a minute, then shakes his head.

"Fine," he says, then walks away.

* * *

Someone has to work the "night shift," to stay late and process changes and check the printouts for a very important pitch deck for a very important deal, and Blaine volunteers Jess.

It is Friday night, the Wine Girls have procured VIP tickets to see Rihanna perform, and so Jess complains.

"Not tonight, Blaine, please?"

Blaine says, "Tell me, what could possibly be so important that it's worth wasting your breath?"

Jess hesitates. "I have tickets to a concert."

"A *concert*?"

"Rihanna," Jess says and immediately wishes she hadn't.

"Ri*hanna*?" Blaine says, and right away Jess feels silly. She doesn't even care about the concert, not really. But she's on thin ice with Lydia and Miky. She hasn't been able to hang out with them for weeks.

Blaine raises his voice, as if making an announcement: "I'm sorry, I just want to make sure I heard that correctly. Did anyone else catch that? Jess here would rather spend the evening jerking or twerking or whatever you call it at a Ri*hanna* concert than generating revenue for the firm."

Everyone within earshot looks up and Jess *really* wishes she hadn't said anything.

She sighs, "If it were any other night I wouldn't ask."

His voice sharpens. "This isn't a negotiation. The answer is no. This is a bank, not a Montessori kindergarten. Next time please don't bother asking."

Jess is grumbling at her desk when Josh drops by. "You're off the hook."

"What?"

"You can go. I told Blaine I would stay."

"Wait . . . really?"

Josh nods.

"Are you sure?"

"It's okay. You can owe me one."

She wants to hug him.

But she doesn't. Instead, she grabs her things before he can change his mind. At the door she says, "Thank you thank you thank you. You are being so, so nice."

He says, as if it's no big deal, "Don't sweat it."

And she says, "I take back all the terrible things I said about you."

And he laughs, but only a little, because it's Friday night and he will be in the office until 2 a.m.

The next week they have lunch again.

Over vegetarian samosas Jess says, "Sorry I stopped having lunch with you."

"Are you going to tell me why?"

"It doesn't matter."

Josh looks at her. "Well, anyway," he says, "I'm glad. That you've decided to have lunch with me again."

6

Another lunch.

At the salad bar Josh says, "You always get exactly one and a half strawberries. Why not just one, or two?"

Jess wonders if he remembers, in college, the strawberries. He probably doesn't. She doesn't ask. Instead, she says, coyly, "Are you trying to figure me out?"

"Maybe."

"Well, that's impossible because I'm unknowable."

"What's in a set of sets that don't contain themselves?"

"What?"

"Consider a set of sets that don't contain themselves. Call it S. Does S contain itself? If it does, then it shouldn't be in the set, but if it doesn't, then it should. So S is continually hopping in and out of itself. That's an actual unknowable thing. What's in those sets. You, like everyone else, are more predictable than you think."

Jess laughs. "Did you get your head stuck in the toilet a lot as a kid?"

He says, "A mind, Jess, is a terrible thing to waste," and then he scoops one and a half strawberries from the bowl and sets them on her plate.

Which makes her think that he remembers.

She and Ivan had just broken up. Jess was leaning against a brick wall behind the bike racks, crying.

Just standing there leaking, rubbing her eyes, trying to compose herself when someone bumped into her, hard, with a backpack.

A voice: "Oh shit, sorry." And then: "Jess?"

She looked up.

Josh.

He peered at her, "Are you crying?"

She shrugged.

"Are you okay?" he asked quickly. "Are you hurt?"

Jess shook her head "No," she said, but her voice was garbled. She was still crying. A lot. She couldn't stop.

Josh looked at her for a long time, then said, "Wait here, okay? Don't move." He started to walk away, then turned back and confirmed, "Okay?"

Jess nodded.

But as he disappeared around the corner, she wished she had walked away. She wiped her eyes and her face with her jacket and just stood there, like an idiot, crying, but trying not to, behind the goddamn bike racks.

She was fishing for a tissue in her pocket when he reappeared. It was cold and his breath came out in smoky puffs.

In one hand he was holding a banana and a plastic container of fruit and in the other was a pile of napkins, which he handed her.

She took the napkins, blew her nose, and then handed the whole snotty wad back to him. He hesitated but took it.

Jess said, "You got a . . . snack?"

"Oh." He looked down. "No."

Across the street was a popular fruit cart. When Jess went, she would get the mixed fruit plate, which was just melon and citrus, because even though they advertised exotic fruits—kiwis, mangos, papaya all year round—those cost more. But Jess could see that Josh had shelled out for summer berries, which were definitely out of season.

He held the container out to her. "This is for you."

"Strawberries?"

"They're my favorite." He smiled. And when Jess looked at him, confused, he added, "But I got them for you."

"How do you know I'm not allergic?" Jess asked.

Now he looked confused. "Are you?"

Jess shrugged. She actually was, just a little bit. Strawberries sometimes gave her hives, made her throat itch. But she ate them anyway—she'd read something once about exposure therapy—because they were her favorite, too.

"They're good, I promise." He shook them at her. "Here."

Jess took them.

They looked at each other. He was leaning too close to her and it made her think of Ivan, but not in a bad way, even though there were increasingly few not-bad ways to think of Ivan.

He smelled like wool and frost.

"Do you want me to eat them now?" she asked.

He laughed. "No. Whenever you want."

He smiled at her but she didn't smile back, even though she felt like she should. It was confusing. Just the other day in class he had been advancing the theory of the high heritability of IQ; Jess had said, "Funny, because even your precious founding fathers argued that all men are created equal," and he had said, "Well, actually, there are innate biological differences among all human populations." Then she'd called him a eugenicist and he'd called her irrational, anti-biology. Then the professor had told them both to knock it off.

She avoided his eyes.

"Hey," he said finally, "it's going to be okay."

And there it was.

He was so annoying, with his strawberries and his optimism.

She snapped, "How do you know?"

"Oh, Jess, come on—"

She interrupted, "Let me guess. You're going to tell me that whatever my problems are, they're nothing compared to, like, the heat death of the universe or, you know, that my concerns are but a pinprick on the cosmic calendar"—here she took a mocking tone—"*so why worry about any of it, bro.*"

He pressed his lips together, said nothing.

After a minute he said, "You're funny," and then Jess felt condescended to.

"You know what?" She wiped her nose on her jacket. "I have to go." She pushed away from the wall.

He nodded, stepped back to let her pass. "Look, I hope you feel better, okay?"

Still blinking away tears, she started to walk away.

"Hey," he said, and she turned to face him again, "you missed class."

Indeed, Jess had been skipping. It was the end of the semester, they had already turned in their final papers, she had nothing left to say.

He touched the sleeve of her jacket. "You should come back to class, okay?"

New York City broils again. A new class of analysts comes to save them, to suck up all the grunt work—status updates and pitchbooks and coffee runs—and to make them look good in front of the managing directors.

Things get quiet. VPs fly off to the Hamptons on Friday afternoons; Congress breaks for summer recess and the SEC investigators stop calling and, finally, Jess has a weekend off.

To celebrate they spend the long weekend upstate—Jess and Miky and Lydia and the Wine Girls—where Callie's family has a little place. It's thirty acres, on a lake, but the plumbing is finicky and the furniture is damp, so they call it a *cabin*.

"It's so quaint!" Lydia says.

"True-crime vibes!" Miky proclaims, as they drive through the woods.

"It'll be just like college!" Jess claps, unloading a grocery bag full of candy and alcohol.

The lake is green and scummy, but they ignore the No Swimming signs around it.

They bob on the lake in inner tubes, sipping beers and scooping algae from the surface. When their inner tubes bump up against each other, Noree tells Jess about a trip she took recently to Cambodia, where she stayed in a hotel room on stilts over the ocean and watched fish swim beneath the bathroom floor.

"Sounds amazing," Jess says.

"It was, but there was so much poverty. It was so sad."

Jess tuts in agreement, then they skim the surface in silence for a while until Noree adds, "You know what you should do, Jess? Investment banking bonuses are so outrageous. You should donate yours to a good cause."

Jess is planning to donate to charity, eventually. As soon as she opens the net worth app and doesn't see a screaming red number reminding her that she's still broke. As soon as the app stops pinging her whenever she buys anything except for groceries. ARE YOU SURE? YOU'RE STILL 4,381 DAYS AWAY FROM YOUR SAVINGS GOAL. Jess had looked up the cabin's property value, obviously, and even in its condition—"vintage lakefront, make it your own!"—it was enough to erase Jess's debt ten times over. More than her bonus last year or this year or the next five years combined.

"Yep," Noree repeats, "you should totally donate it."

Jess says, "Totally," but then pretends to get swept up by a lake current and turns and drifts away.

At work there is a sudden rash of dental emergencies, people disappearing from their desks for one and two hours at a time, as if a plague of gingivitis is spreading across the floor. They are sneaking away for interviews, gunning for coveted hedge fund and private equity gigs. Slipping out of the office with thin excuses and leather portfolios full of investment ideas.

Everyone is moving up or out, but Jess is happy to stand still. After the first year it's all been downhill; now she can reasonably survive on four hours of sleep and eat lunch in forty-five seconds. She is almost comfortable making eye contact with her dragon of a managing director and, most significantly, she has finally moved into the bullpen. When one of the second-years was promoted to associate, she assumed his desk and his distaste for first-years.

Why would she leave now?

Bonus season arrives. It has been a good year and the bank can afford to pay, but trickle-down economics are notoriously fickle and analysts notoriously overlooked, overworked, underpaid.

They are called into a conference room, with the glass walls papered over for privacy, and given their numbers one by one.

When it is Jess's turn, they hand her an envelope with her name printed on it. Her boss's boss smiles a tight smile, but otherwise is silent. She opens the envelope, poker-faced.

The number is lower than she expected, but still very, very high. When the check hits her bank account it will be the most she has ever had to her name, enough to buy a mid-priced luxury car, or an extremely expensive gold watch.

Though she does neither. Instead, she goes shopping. To one of those exclusive boutiques with $17,000 boots in the window, where the salespeople will ignore her, or steer her toward the sale rack. Jess walks in with her shoulders back. And while they aren't outright rude—it's New York City after all, there's a chance she could be somebody—it's clear that they don't think she is. They are politely dismissive and focus instead on the blonde and her friend who come in after Jess.

On a mission, Jess starts pulling things from racks until her arms are so full that one of the shopgirls is forced to attend to her. Through the fitting room door, they ask how it's going, if she needs any sizes, and when Jess says she doesn't, she can imagine them on the other side, giving each other looks like *I told you so*. And, in fact, when Jess steps back out onto the floor—clothes, shoes, bags, accessories in a disorganized jumble—and says, "I'll take it all," they seem stunned.

And that feeling of—gotcha!—*you think you know who I am but you're wrong* is one that Jess would pay a lot for, and indeed has. So now her bonus is gone, but she feels like a million dollars, even though her bonus is gone and she still doesn't have a million dollars.

In the bullpen Jess asks Josh, "So what'd you get? A car or a boat?"

But he shakes his head, "Not telling."

"What? Why not? I'm harmless," Jess says.

"No way."

"Come on! You show me yours I'll show you mine," Jess teases.

He laughs, raises an eyebrow. "Oh, yeah?"

"Hey," Jess says, pointing over his shoulder, "what's that?"

He turns, picks up a glass deal toy shaped like the letter L. "This?"

Jess frowns. "Where did you get that?"

"It's from the LyfeCo. deal," he shrugs. "Charles gave it to me last week."

"I didn't get one."

"No?"

"And I did half the modeling," Jess says, "more than half."

Josh doesn't disagree.

"And I handled all the due diligence calls."

"You did . . ."

"And the entire sensitivity analysis. And all the redlines. And the fetching of all the fucking drinks! So why would you get a deal toy when I didn't?"

"I don't know," he says, defensive. "Maybe they just haven't gotten around to it. Maybe you'll get one at the closing party."

"The closing party?" Jess's voice rises an octave. "When is the closing party?"

"Next Friday."

"Are you serious?"

"Come on, Jess. They probably just forgot, why don't—"

"I can't believe this! You get a deal toy. An invitation to the closing party. You probably got a bigger bonus than I did too!" She shakes her head. "Unbelievable."

What a convenient theory, that they'd simply forgotten about her. As if forgetting implied a lack of malice. Forgetting her hard work, her contributions, the fact that she exists. She almost wishes it were intentional and that they harbored some resentment, or somehow viewed her as a threat; that was better than being invisible, a nonentity. But none of this is worth explaining to Josh. No one ever forgets him.

She starts to leave.

"Jess, wait."

She turns.

"You should come."

"What?"

"To the closing party. You earned it. You're right," he says. "Come as my plus one."

Jess processes this, her expression cycling from mildly perplexed to slightly annoyed to really fucking mad.

"So you think," Jess says slowly, "that I should come . . . as your *plus one?*"

"As my date," he clarifies unhelpfully. And his face is so sincere, so hopeful, that Jess almost tricks herself into believing it's a good idea. She almost falls for it. But the deal toy, dangling from his hand, snaps her out of it.

"As your *date?*" she hisses.

He flinches, "I just thought—"

"What? That I would be happy to just tag along with you? Instead of being recognized along with everyone else who even laid a finger on that stupid deal? To just stand next to you like some kind of trophy bimbo banker girlfriend?"

"That's not what I meant. You deserve to be there. I agree with you. So I'm inviting you to come. I'm agreeing with you! And I'm trying to make it right."

She crosses her arms, "And that's the best you can do?"

"What do you want me to do?"

"Say something. Tell everyone that it's fucked up and unfair that I'm not getting credit for a deal we both worked on. Boycott the party! Throw the deal toy back in Charles's face."

"Come on, Jess," he sighs. "You know I'm not going to do that."

"Yeah, I know," she glares, then adds, "I'm not speaking to you."

And then she doesn't, even though it kind of sucks.

•

After a few weeks one of the other analysts says, "Did you hear about Josh?"

Apparently he has resigned. Has been poached by a cultish long-short equity fund run by a brilliant billionaire who is always responding to allegations of insider trading. According to everyone, Josh is going places.

Jess finds him at his desk packing a box.

She says, "You quit?" and he looks up.

"Yeah," he says, "I just resigned."

"You weren't going to say anything?"

"You're not speaking to me."

"So you're . . . leaving?"

He nods.

"Right now?"

He nods.

"What about two weeks' notice or whatever? I heard you were going to the buy-side."

"Yeah, well, they also have an advisory arm which means it's technically a competitor, so . . ." He shrugs in the direction of a security guard, hovering at the edge of the cube.

"So this is your last day?"

"My last hour."

Jess swallows. She feels something in her chest like panic. "But . . ."

Josh is looking at her, waiting.

She says, "I . . ." but doesn't finish the thought.

He reaches toward her and she blinks. Her corporate badge is hanging from a lanyard around her neck and he takes the cord between his fingers.

He says, "Hey," and Jess feels a slight tug on her neck as he pulls on it.

She feels her heartbeat in the back of her throat. The room is warm.

He holds the lanyard pointlessly, his fingers almost touching her blouse.

The security guard is still there.

Jess looks down at his hand. And then looks down and notices the contents of his box, notices the LyfeCo. deal toy poking out. Josh follows her eyes, sees her seeing the deal toy.

He sighs and lets go of the lanyard.

He says, "Oh, right."

And Jess says, "Right."

7

The fall passes slowly.

Bored and restless, Jess pesters her dad. She helps him set up an account on a video chat app and when he sees her face, he shakes his head, pleased. "You kids and your technology!"

"The future is now," Jess tells him.

Then he lowers his voice, jokily conspiratorial, "But now, Jessie, what if you had caught me on the toilet?"

And Jess reminds him, "You called me!"

At work Jess is staffed on different deals, but everything feels the same, as if she's running backward on a treadmill.

She reads a list online, thirty-five life hacks to try now, and teaches herself how to separate egg yolks with an empty water bottle, and how to light a candle with a stick of dry spaghetti, and then she rolls all her electric cords into toilet paper tubes, but still feels like she is getting nowhere.

One day at work she googles "quarter life crisis" and then "lack of sleep induced psychosis."

Over her shoulder Charles says, "A little inspiration for your suicide note?"

"That's private," Jess says, snapping her laptop shut.

"That's property of Goldman Sachs," he says. "Get back to work."

Then, in her in-box is an email from Josh. The subject is JESS JOSH MONTHLY DINNER, and when she clicks on it there is no message, just a calendar invitation.

They haven't spoken in more than a month.

Jess grins madly and clicks accept.

*   *   *

They meet at a Thai restaurant where the booths are made of old car seats and the waiters wear Hawaiian shirts and on Sundays they serve crickets.

"I've been wanting to try this place!" Jess says as soon as they are seated.

"It's on my way to work," he explains, "and whenever I walk by and look inside it makes me think of you."

She leans across the table and is only a little surprised how flirtatious she sounds when she says, "What else makes you think of me?"

He raises an eyebrow. "Clowns," he says, "puppet theater, bad improv."

Jess smiles. "It's nice to see you."

Josh smiles. "It's nice to see you too."

The waiter brings their entrées and Jess asks, "How's the new job? What are you working on?"

"Event-driven long-short equity mostly. It's great. I have a lot more autonomy. Goldman was great . . . but not forever."

"Goldman Sachs, Goldman Sucks," Jess replies.

He looks at her thoughtfully. "It's probably a long shot, we're not really hiring right now, but I could ask if you wanted. If you wanted to interview. Or talk to someone. About a job."

"I already have a job."

"Are you going to work on the sell-side forever?"

"As long as they're paying me the big bucks."

"I make more money than you."

"One dollar to my sixty-three cents, right?"

"That's not what I meant."

"I know what you meant. I just . . . Look, can we not talk about work? It's depressing."

"It doesn't have to be. You don't have to hate your job, you know, Jess. You should be doing work you love."

"No one loves their job."

"Not true. Anyway, I'm not suggesting you start designing handbags or launch a brand of diet vodka or something. I'm just saying that I don't think M&A finance is your destiny. I think there are other things you would be better at and enjoy more."

"Like, event-driven long-short equity?"

"Maybe."

"But isn't it, like, impossible to get a job at Gil Alperstein's fund?"

"There are lots of other funds."

"So what you're saying is, I couldn't get a job at Gil Alperstein's fund?"

"Like I said, we're not even hiring right now, so, yeah I'd say it's a long shot."

"Oh, *you're* not hiring right now? Are *you* on the hiring committee? Do you and Gil Alperstein get together every afternoon and, like, sip expensive cognac and play trash basketball with all the sad résumés you get from poorly paid sell-side analysts?"

"I wouldn't have mentioned it if I didn't think they would consider you. But since we're—*they're*—not hiring now it's probably a nonstarter. That's all I'm saying."

"Okay."

"Okay."

"Can we talk about something else?"

"Nuclear disarmament in the Middle East?"

They eat sticky rice and coconut curry, and Josh tells Jess how some physicists at Yale have come up with a hybrid system for ultra-high coherence between strongly coupled magnons and microwave photons.

"It's absolutely huge for quantum computing," he says, as if he is talking about sex or chocolate.

And when Jess stares at him blankly, he draws a series of circles and lines on a napkin, and then repeats, verbatim, everything he has just said. "Does that make sense?"

"No."

"Come on, Jess." He pushes the napkin in front of her. "You get it."

"There are only two types of people in the world: those who understand binary and those who don't," Jess says.

He leans back in his seat and folds his arms petulantly across his chest. He crumples the napkin and tosses it on the table. "Were you one of those girls who pretended to be dumb in high school so guys would like you?"

The waiter reappears. "Any interest in dessert?"

"No," Jess says.

"No, thanks," Josh says.

"No *thank you*," Jess says.

Josh rolls his eyes. "Just the check, please."

Outside the black curtain of winter has suddenly dropped on the city and it is dark and quiet, all the light and warmth from the restaurant dissolved into the night.

"I almost forgot how great we get along," Jess says sourly.

But Josh touches her elbow affectionately. "See you next month, okay, Jess?"

Josh messages her the next day.

A link to a pdf of a book called "Quantum Computing for Dummies," underneath which he's typed:

If your head starts to hurt, just look at the pictures.

•

At work, Charles is on a rampage. A big deal has completely imploded because the client has determined that the team is incompetent and it is, Jess understands, entirely her fault.

The deck shared with the client had included two extra pages, which Blaine never approved, and which were garbage. Worse, on each of those pages was a currency conversion error that misstated the company's value by an order of magnitude, nine zeroes where there should have been eight.

No one had noticed until it was too late, and the client was asking difficult questions. At that point Blaine had realized their mistake and asked the VP how he could be such a giant fucking idiot, who in turn had asked Charles how he could be such a giant fucking idiot, and now the shit has finally rolled all the way downhill and Charles is standing over Jess's desk, apoplectic, with a copy of the document held high above his head, splayed at the spine, like a crucifixion.

He tears out a single page and crushes it into a paper ball that he drops on the floor in front of Jess's desk.

"Do you find this fucking acceptable?" he shouts.

He tears out another page.

"Do you want to spread comps and make quals books for the rest of your career?" he shouts.

He tears out another page.

"Do you know how much money your mistakes cost the firm?" he shouts.

He tears out another page and then another, until every page in the book is crumpled at Jess's feet.

"Well, do you?" he says. "Do you?"

But something about his fury is so performative that Jess almost expects him to wink at her, to acknowledge that he is just putting on a show for Blaine. Which he is. Because even though technically Jess handled the deck last, was responsible for the final print and bind, she is not the one who fucked up. It was late and everything was finalized. Jess had been moving semicolons around the page for more than an hour and finally everything had been approved. Then Charles had sent her two more pages.

"Should I send these to Blaine?" Jess had asked.

And he was dismissive, cocky even, when he said, "Don't bother."

And so Jess hadn't bothered because Charles was smarter than Blaine anyway, and also because it was four in the morning.

But now Charles is stomping around like a madman, and it's as if that never happened.

The other analysts look on with a mixture of pity and schadenfreude and Jess just sits, blinking up at Charles, and takes her lumps.

*   *   *

Later Charles says, "Things got pretty ugly back there, yeah?"

That's not an apology, Jess thinks.

She says, "Did I fuck up?"

She wills him to say no, but he scrunches his face up, as if in pain, and then refuses to admit to anything.

"Jones," he finally says, "I'd say, best to always assume you've fucked up."

Josh stands her up for dinner.

Jess sits alone at a table for two dipping bread in oil and nursing an ice water while the maître d' glares at her from the front of the room.

"Maybe you'd be more comfortable at the bar," the waiter says with a tight smile.

When Jess calls Josh, he says, "Shit, I completely forgot."

"You *forgot*?"

"Sorry."

"Where are you? Are you out somewhere?"

"I'm at home."

"At *home*?"

"I'm sorry, Jess. I just . . . forgot."

Neither of them says anything for a long time.

Finally, Jess says, "Can I come over?"

Josh lives in a fifth-floor walk-up, on a cool little block downtown in what the Wine Girls describe as the last great neighborhood in Manhattan. Unlike Jess's neighborhood—walking distance to the office—which, according to them, is sterile, an overpriced concrete wasteland overrun with corporate automatons. Why didn't she move to Brooklyn, they were always asking, like they had. The vibes were better, the real estate more affordable, except not really when you lived in a big old brownstone with views of the water, which the Wine Girls did.

Josh's apartment is a surprise. Jess was certain he would live in an airless glass tower or a building with brochures in the lobby.

He buzzes her in and stands at the top of the staircase watching her climb each flight circling closer and closer until they are face-to-face on the top floor.

He sweeps his arm across the threshold and says, "Come on in."

Jess peers around, walks in a slow circle around the room. She looks up at the ceiling, really looks at it, as if it's painted, as if she's in a museum, and Josh says, "Okay, that's enough."

"It's different from what I thought it would be," Jess says.

"What did you expect?"

"I don't know . . . a bookshelf full of Ayn Rand? Maybe a framed copy of the Constitution. Piles of money in really neat stacks, so you can count them every night before bed. A hairless cat. Golf clubs? A Reagan-Bush '84 poster. *Posters.* Just covering every square inch of the wall. Human heads in the freezer."

He looks hurt.

"Sorry," Jess says. "That was a joke."

"You still think I'm an asshole."

"I don't."

"This whole thing"—he waves his hands around vaguely—"it's all getting to be a bit exhausting, don't you think?"

Jess wonders if he's going to ask her to leave, but he just says, "Do you want a drink?"

Jess nods and he points at the couch and says, "Sit. Take off your coat."

In the kitchen Jess watches him flick a burner on and fill a saucepan with water. He is opening cabinets, pulling out mugs, whiskey, tea.

He measures two fingers of Jack Daniel's, drops a tea bag into each mug and then tips the saucepan over and pours hot water over them. He cuts a cinnamon stick in two, which strikes Jess as both a lovely touch and completely ridiculous. When he's done he wipes the countertop with a cloth and then joins her on the couch.

He hands her a mug.

She takes a sip, burns her mouth. "Fuck, that's hot!"

"You *just* saw me pour boiling water in that cup."

She cradles the mug in her palm, blows ferociously. "Yeah, but I didn't think it would be so . . ."

"Hot?" he says, smiling.

When he smiles, Jess can see his dimple, a perfect divot at the corner of his mouth. She has a sudden, overwhelming desire to press her finger into it, like dipping a finger into a hot fudge sundae. But when she looks at him again, the dimple is gone.

They move to the floor, facing each other across his coffee table, and drink hot toddies until they are drunk. Josh teaches Jess how to play Texas Hold'em and they play hand after hand until Jess loses so many times in a row that she jumps up and stuffs a handful of playing cards in the garbage disposal.

Josh says, "Goddammit, Jess," but he is laughing and then instead of playing poker they watch a series of YouTube videos about the formation of the universe until Jess shouts "Boring!" and Josh says, "What is more fascinating than this?" and Jess says "This" and puts on a video of a cat plunging a toilet.

They play music and Jess dances and Josh doesn't. He says, "Please don't stand on the furniture," but he is still laughing and then he makes pasta but he forgets to strain it and instead dumps hot pasta and water into the sink, with the playing cards, and Jess spills olive oil on the hardwood floor and Josh says, "This is what a night with Jess is like, isn't it?"

And Jess says, "If you mean fucking awesome, then yes."

And Josh says, "I didn't mean that exactly, no."

They stare at each other moon-eyed, on opposite ends of his couch. Maybe it's minutes, maybe it's hours—suddenly her head is spinning and time is a flat circle—but the space between them closes. Inching closer, closer. But like a Ouija, Jess can't pinpoint a source. Is it him, is it her, is it some mysterious force? All she knows is that there were two cushions between them and now there is less than a foot. She can feel the static cling from his sweater, electricity on her bare arm.

"What are you thinking?" Josh asks.

She is thinking about sex.

Trying to remember if her bra hooks in the front or the back. Wondering if she smells like lemons and whiskey or if it's him.

"What are *you* thinking?" Jess deflects.

He makes a face like he's contemplating, touches his chin and says, "Hmm . . ."

"Actually, I know what you're thinking," Jess interrupts.

He smiles. "Oh, yeah? What?"

"You're probably calculating a third derivative," she teases, "or trying to solve some long-lost mathematical theorem that might be the secret to forecasting the price of soybeans."

He laughs. "You know, you're sort of right. I was thinking about a paradox of motion. You know Zeno's Dichotomy?"

Jess nods, but he explains it anyway.

"If I move an inch closer to you"—he does—"and then half an inch, a quarter inch, an eighth of an inch"—he does and does and does and Jess holds her breath—"I could move infinitely closer to you by halves, and the distance between us would always be greater than zero. In other words, we would never touch," he says, then pauses. "The dichotomy asserts that no finite distance can ever be traveled, which is to say that all motion is impossible. But that's demonstrably false, right? So how do you reconcile the paradox with the reality?"

Jess bats her eyelashes.

He holds her gaze. "Do you know how?"

Jess swallows. "No."

Her hands are on her knees, his hands are on his knees. Almost touching. Their knees, their hands, as close as possible without touching.

"This is how." He hooks his left pinky into her right, like pinky swearing. "If Zeno's paradox were unresolvable, could I do this?"

Jess laughs, because: it's such a line. But also because: finally, confirmation the feeling is mutual. And because: she's drunk and delirious and delighted! The smallest part of him, touching the smallest part of her, defying space and time. It feels so fucking right.

She smiles at him. "You say that to all the girls."

"No, I don't."

"You do." Jess can't stop smiling.

"I don't," he says, shaking his head. He lifts their hands, clasped, to his mouth. "Only to certain girls," he says, his breath spreading over her fingers. "Only to you. To girls like you."

Those words. Jess bristles. Almost involuntarily, she yanks her hand away.

"What?" Josh sits back. "What's wrong?"

Her hand is just hanging in the air, like a half-deflated balloon. She touches her temple, an afterthought.

"Are you okay?"

She shakes her head. She's not okay. Did he really just say that? *Girls like you.* He meant it as a compliment probably, but it wasn't. It only meant that he thought there were two kinds of girls: girls and girls like her. She doesn't want to do this again. She gets up.

"I'm not feeling well," she tries. "I mean, my head hurts. I have to wake up early. I think I might miss the last express train?"

"Really?" He looks concerned but doesn't otherwise protest.

"Sorry, yeah. I have to . . . I have to go." She doesn't wait for him to react, just grabs her things and flees. "Sorry, sorry, sorry," she says, slamming the door on his surprised face. And she is. Sorry that she didn't predict this most predictable thing.

In the hallway she takes a deep breath, his words echoing in her head. Girls like you, he said. *A girl like her.* What kind of girl was that, anyway?

Jess had discovered that Ivan was cheating on her in the most painfully mundane way. She would have liked to catch him in the act, in a dark corner, with his pants around his ankles, doing something disgusting, so that she could tell everyone what happened and they would have no choice but to agree that he was evil and depraved. Instead, it was in broad daylight, on the path in front of the library, and his parents were in tow. He had mentioned that they would be in town over the weekend and that he'd be busy, so when Jess ran into them on the walk, it felt like serendipity. His parents were fancy, she knew, and so she put on a little show: *It's such a pleasure . . . so wonderful . . . I've heard so much . . . Ivan is always . . . hahaha.*

It took a beat before she realized she was making everyone uncomfortable. She stopped talking. His father, in a sport coat, squinted down at her bemused. His mother, perhaps intuiting the situation, offered a tight smile. And Ivan, though Jess couldn't possibly imagine why, seemed to be looking at her with nothing short of contempt. It was then that Jess registered the girl. A waifish blonde at Ivan's elbow. She recognized her. A classmate. And suddenly it dawned on her. One of the girl's fingers was hooked through Ivan's belt loop. Had it been there the whole time? Jess had thought she was charming them, but she was just embarrassing herself. She suddenly felt like something scuzzy and vulgar: a carcass on the highway, sewer sludge on a clean street. How could Ivan be so cold? Before she could say anything else, his mother said, "Well," and then they all walked off, as if Jess were nothing more than a bit of debris to step around.

Later, she called Ivan but he didn't pick up. She called him again. And again.

She sent him a message:

pick up pickuppickuppickup PICK UP

And then another:

answer me

Another:

fuckface

In bed, with her hands balled up into fists, she seethed with humiliation and rage. When she could no longer bear it, she propelled herself out of bed, even though it was four in the morning.

The door to Ivan's fraternity house was unlocked and Jess let herself in. Tiptoed up the stairs and into his room. Relieved to find him in bed alone.

Asleep, his eyelids fluttered, and he seemed harmless. Vulnerable even. There was a part of Jess that still wanted to crawl into bed with him, which made her hate him even more.

She said his name.

Nothing.

Louder this time.

He shot up. "Jess?"

"I need to talk to you. The door was open."

He groaned and smashed a pillow over his face. His voice was muffled. "Jess, get the fuck out of here."

"No! You owe me an explanation. You haven't returned any of my calls!"

"Jess, really? Did you think I was going to fuck you forever?"

"So, what, you're with someone else now? And you didn't even think to mention it? Not even a courtesy fucking text? Hey, Jess, FYI, I'm cheating on you with a random slut."

"She's the slut?"

"So, I'm just someone to have sex with? Not to meet your parents?"

"My parents don't want to meet you."

"What? Why? Me specifically? They don't even know me!"

He stood up and leaned over her, his sour breath in her face. "Fine," he said. "Okay. I'm with someone new now. Happy? Get over it. And she didn't meet my parents. She knows them. Our families are friends." In his underwear, he crossed the room, and slammed the door open with his fist. Then through gritted teeth: "Will you leave now?"

But Jess didn't move. "Oh, cool. Your dads are golf buddies. You're members of the same club. She's a perfect flaxen-haired virgin who you would never defile with your penis. Just the kind of girl you take home to mother."

"Stop talking about my parents. And stop pretending I was ever going to introduce them to a girl like you."

"A girl like me? What's that supposed to mean?"

His eyes narrowed. "You know."

But she didn't.

Or maybe, deep down, she did.

"Ivan," she said, "listen to me—"

"No, you listen to me." He moved toward her and Jess flinched, stepped back.

He laughed a mean laugh. "Did you think I was going to hit you?" And then, sneering: "Get over yourself."

How quickly he had turned on her. Just last week he had told her that she was gorgeous and that her ass could launch a thousand ships and that fucking her was like its own religion.

It wasn't "Ode on a Grecian Urn," but it was something.

She said, "You know what, Ivan? That's rich coming from you. Do you know what people say about you? About your family? Your dad is a criminal." Jess spat. "A thief and a thug. And your mom is, like, some kind of mail-order bride. But *I'm* not the one you would introduce to *them*?"

"Get out." Bare-chested and heaving, he seemed ready to detonate.

"No! Everyone thinks you're a joke," Jess screamed. "It's so pathetic. You think your car is so special, but it's not! The only people who spend that much money on a car are limp-dicked middle-aged losers!"

"Get out!"

"Make me!"

And then he really did lunge toward her. He wrapped his giant hands around her neck, applied force. She tried to pry his fingers from her throat, but his grip was too tight. She tried to scream, but her voice came out garbled. She was surprised how much it hurt. It seemed that each and every one of her blood vessels would pop, and she was gasping, "Ivan stop stop stop."

She tried to push him off her, made fists with both hands and swung them, at his face and chest and arms. She felt a strange tingling sensation. Her thoughts became distant and fuzzy. And then, suddenly, he stopped. He pushed her backward and she stumbled and fell to the floor, coughing and sputtering.

She screamed, "What the fuck is wrong with you!" but her voice was hoarse. It sounded like nothing. Her throat would hurt for days afterward. Bruised and sore. And for weeks after that whenever she ate or drank, it would feel like swallowing stones.

*   *   *

The thing was, she should have known better. He was—Ivan was—exactly the kind of guy her father warned her about.

Sixth grade. Everyone had been passing around teen magazines and crushing on the prepubescent sitcom stars who graced their covers. In a fit of girlish industry, Jess had spent an afternoon poring over old issues of *Teen Vogue* and *Seventeen*, tearing out the pages with all the cutest boys. She had plastered an entire bedroom wall with them: handsome adolescent faces mugging for the camera, shirtless in the woods, sporting tuxedos on tarmacs.

At dinner her father had brought it up.

"You did some redecorating," he said, though it was obvious he wanted to say more.

"I guess," Jess said. She didn't want to talk about it—whatever "it" was—with her dad.

"Do you think those pictures are appropriate?" he asked.

"Yes! They're not even naked!" she protested. "Only some of them have their shirts off and that's not such a big deal." She wasn't sure that it *wasn't* a big deal. Her father didn't let her watch movies with sex or violence or "adult themes" but surely he wasn't this puritanical.

But he shook his head. "That's not what I mean."

Jess waited.

"All those young men are white."

Jess didn't know what to say. She didn't think that pointing out that one of them was half Japanese would be a helpful clarification, so she said nothing.

"It's not good to go chasing white boys. They'll never love you like their own." He paused. "And besides, how do you think a young man who's Black would feel walking into your room?"

Jess looked at her plate of spaghetti.

"Honey, answer me."

Hot shame burned in her throat. It hadn't even occurred to her, which made her feel worse.

"Jessie, answer me now."

"Not good," she mumbled.

"No, not good at all. Jessie, look at me."

Jess did as she was told.

"I just want you to think about the message you're sending with those pictures, okay?"

And Jess had. She had skulked back to her bedroom and considered her wall—the freckled faces, the pale skin and light eyes. Her shame had quickly turned to disgust.

What was wrong with her?

She tore down the photos in angry, careless sheets until there was nothing but a pile of torn, crumpled paper at her feet. She flopped into bed and felt a tiny bubble of rage start to form in her chest.

What was wrong with her *father*?

It wasn't like she was trying to hurt anyone's feelings. And more importantly, it wasn't like any boy, Black or otherwise, would ever see her room. None of the boys at school liked her. And there was only one Black boy in her entire class anyway, in the entire middle school, and did her father expect her to go gaga over fat Stevie Jenkins?

She knew what he didn't expect her to do: fail spectacularly to take what little advice he had offered, fall for the most uninspiring archetype of an alpha male, handsome, rich, oblivious, *white*.

At work Charles says, "You're late. Blaine was looking for you."

"Oh no."

"I told him you were on a coffee run."

"Oh, awesome. Thank you." Jess turns back to her computer.

Charles grabs the back of her chair and spins her seat around so that she's facing him. He sticks a Post-it Note to her forehead. Jess pulls it off. It says: *tall venti mocha, flat white with skim milk, double shot espresso, cappuccino.* He says, "I *told* him you were on a *coffee* run."

"Are you serious?" Jess actually has work to do.

Charles says, "I like my cappuccino extra dry, yeah?"

*   *   *

Josh texts:

> **I had fun last night.**
> **Thanks for stopping by.**

Jess starts to reply:

> . . .

> . . .

> . . .

She doesn't know whether to acknowledge that she made it weird and why. Whether to let it slide.

He sends another message:

> **Feeling better?**

It's fine, Jess thinks. Totally fine. He's not Ivan.

She texts back:

> **Yep**

And then on Sunday, crossing Fourth Avenue, Jess runs into Josh. She is on her way home from buying detergent and paper towels and coffee.

"Hey!" they say to one another, surprised, pleased.

They stand smiling dumbly at each other while tourists and NYU students brush past them, until Josh says, "Do you want to go somewhere? Get something to eat or drink?"

They walk, past the Big Kmart and the Strand and the AMC Theatre.

Jess points to the marquee. "Hey, I want to see that. Do you want to go?"

"Maybe. When?"

"Thursday?"

"That's Thanksgiving."

Jess shrugs.

"You're not going home for Thanksgiving?"

"Normally I would, but . . . it's kind of weird. My dad just called me, like, three weeks ago and told me that he's going on a wine tour with a friend," Jess explains. "Like, instead of Thanksgiving. Who goes on a wine tour for Thanksgiving? In South Africa? He's not the Prince of England."

Jess had been surprised, not just because he never traveled but because the only thing she'd ever seen him drink was sparkling cider on special occasions. But he'd sounded excited and, anyway, Thanksgiving for two was never her favorite.

They step into an Irish pub that smells like Guinness and french fries and sit in a booth in the back.

"What kind of friends go on a weeklong wine tour over Thanksgiving anyway?"

Josh looks over his beer. "The kind of friends that are banging."

"Ew! No! My dad isn't *banging* anyone. Gross. My dad doesn't bang," Jess says. "He's a kind and noble man."

Josh laughs. "So what will you do in the city by yourself?"

"I don't know. My friends are going to Cabo, but I can't, obviously, because of work. So I'll probably just eat Thai food in bed in my pajamas. Insist that they wrap it up in one of those foil swans, you know? To make it festive."

Josh says, "Just what the Pilgrims imagined."

They sip their beer.

Eventually Josh says, "Look, why don't you just come home with me for Thanksgiving?"

Jess forgets she has somewhere to be. Josh goes to the bar for more drinks and she calls Lydia, tells her to come meet them at this ale house on Third Avenue.

"My friend is coming," Jess tells Josh.

He looks at his watch. "I should go anyway."

"You can stay."

"Nah," he says. They finish their beers and he leaves.

Lydia shows up. She slides into the booth across from Jess and says, "Who was that guy? Leaving just now? Do I know him?"

Jess nods. "Remember Josh? From college."

"What were you talking about?"

"Nothing, why?"

"Because," Lydia says, and tips her head back, opens her mouth like she is laughing maniacally, although no sound comes out, "you were both like this."

"No, we weren't."

"You were."

"We were not."

"You were eating each other up with a spoon."

"Oh, shut up."

8

Josh borrows his friend David's car and they leave late Wednesday night to avoid the worst of the traffic.

"I'm glad you wanted to drive," Jess says. "It's been so long since I've been in the passenger seat of a car. I'm so used to taxis, you know?"

"So you're saying you'd prefer if someone smoked five packs of cigarettes and threw up in the back seat?"

"Very funny. I just meant it's nice. Out here on the open road. It just feels so, like, authentically American."

They pass a billboard advertising LIVE NUDE GIRLS and laugh.

"So how long is the drive?" Jess asks.

"Not too long," he says. "Greenwich is less than forty miles from the city."

"*Greenwich?*" Jess screeches. "You're from *Greenwich*? Con*nec*ticut?"

"What's that reaction?" Josh rubs his ear. "I don't think they heard you in New Jersey."

"I just mean"—Jess leans over the console—"how are you from Greenwich? I thought you said you were poor."

"I never said I was poor."

"But, like, if you're from Greenwich then you're rich."

He shakes his head. "There are a lot of rich people in Greenwich, that's correct, but my family isn't rich. Far from it."

"Right." Jess sits back, rests her feet on the dashboard. "You only had one pony when all the other kids had two. You wanted a Ferrari for your eighteenth birthday but your parents paid for your college education instead."

He says, "Just wait."

They drive through downtown Greenwich where the local stores, Hermes and Tiffany's and Brooks Brothers, are lit up in the dark like jewelry boxes—and Jess waits. They drive down one tree-lined boulevard and then another and another, past houses with gates and high hedges and Lamborghinis in the driveway—and Jess waits. They drive past a sailing club and a golf club and a private club otherwise unspecified—and Jess waits.

She is still waiting when Josh says, "Almost there," and by then the neighborhood does look different, everything smaller and less spread out, but it's still Greenwich and so Jess can't help but think, *Come on.*

He stops at the end of a street of neat little colonials, mid-priced sedans parked outside detached garages.

"Okay," Josh says, cutting the engine. "We're here."

Jess steps out of the car and looks around. It's a house like you'd see in a cartoon, a neat little rectangle with a triangle on top. Crooked blue shutters and a white picket fence.

"Not what you expected, right?" Josh takes their bags from the back seat. "Now do you see what I mean?"

And Jess shrugs, because while she will concede it is not a mansion, it otherwise strikes her as pretty fucking nice.

Inside, his mother, in a robe, whispers hello.

Josh says, "Mom, this is Jess. Jess, this is my mom." He crouches down and picks up a black-gray ball of fur. "And this ornery fellow here is Kachka."

The cat yawns lazily, licks a paw. He has blazing yellow eyes and when he trains them on Jess he seems to be asking *Who are you and what are you doing here?*

Josh's mother asks him to show Jess to her room, which is actually his room—he's sleeping on the pullout couch in the den—and then she pours them tea. They sit around the kitchen table, including Kachka, who perches in his own chair. He engages in a complicated form of cat yoga, one leg stuck straight up in the air, and licks his crotch aggressively while he glares at Jess.

"Look, Jess," Josh says, nodding in the cat's direction, "he likes you."

*   *   *

The lights are off by twelve. Jess brushes her teeth and changes into her pajamas in the dark, then slips under the covers into Josh's bed, narrow with a blue bedspread. It's strangely intimate, lying there surrounded by all his things. On the dresser is a lamp, a box of tissues, a mug full of pens and pencils, and a row of picture frames. Photos of Josh as a little boy. At an aquarium, blowing out candles, his feet dangling into a swimming pool. It occurs to Jess that he was a child once, that he didn't fall from the sky socially liberal and fiscally conservative. His father isn't in any of the photos. In the dark, Jess blinks at a picture of him in a Cub Scout uniform and feels a prickle of recognition. She was also a scout but hated it—all the mother-daughter movie nights and campouts and craft days.

Jess decides that she can't fall asleep—she feels compelled out of bed—and so she tiptoes downstairs, where the light in the den is still on.

She knocks.

"What's up?" Josh says. "Come in."

He is half lying down, half sitting up, on a big gray couch that has been folded out into a bed.

The cat is curled up in the crook of his arm and Josh is scratching his ears and head, absentminded, tender.

He looks so much like—and is, technically—a boy in a bed with his cat that Jess feels a sudden swell of affection.

She says, "Do you want to sleep upstairs?"

He raises an eyebrow.

"I mean, do you want to switch? I feel bad, forcing you down here. Don't you want to sleep in your own room?"

"Nah," he says, "it's fine."

Kachka suddenly stands up. He flicks his tail and then steps gingerly into Josh's lap. He purrs deliriously while Josh tickles him behind his ears and murmurs nonsense at him.

Jess is finding it impossible to reconcile him in this moment.

She says, half-serious, "Am I interrupting something here?"

Josh says, "Sit."

Jess remains standing and when Josh looks at her, she says, "Me? I thought you were talking to the cat."

She sits down on the edge of the bed.

Kachka nuzzles Josh's palm, and Josh says, "Who's a good kitty?" and "You's a good kitty," and Jess says, "Do you really think that Black people have lower IQs?"

He looks up.

"Jess, I think you're one of the smartest people I've ever met."

"Thank you. But that's not what I asked."

"No, Jess, I don't."

"I think about Law and Society sometimes," she says.

He sighs. "You shouldn't."

"I mean, I think I was just operating under the assumption that you were, like, I don't know, this heartless pink-pants Republican. But now—"

"You think I'm heartless?"

"No, I—"

"And when have I ever worn pink pants?"

"I meant that you used to. Or I used to think—"

"What do you think now?"

"I . . . sometimes . . . honestly, I don't know what to think."

Josh sits up and the cat complains, drops his tail and growls a little. Josh pushes him away and says, "I'm sorry, Jess." He touches her hand. "I'm sorry if I ever said anything that made you feel shitty. You're the opposite of shitty. You're . . . great."

He takes her hand and rubs his thumb lightly over her knuckles. It feels very, very nice. Jess thinks of Zeno's paradox. She remembers "girls like you."

She pulls her hand away. "You're sorry you said it and sorry I felt bad, but not because you don't believe what you said."

"What exactly are we talking about here?"

"All that stuff about class and race and like how affirmative action, or various forms of racial consideration are, like, racist against white people."

"I never said the words 'racist against white people.' "

"You know what I mean."

"I think, yes, I believed then and I still believe—though maybe now

I'd say it better, or differently—that the socioeconomic question is the more pressing one. I think the emphasis—on race, on ethnicity—of the current political discourse is misguided, pathological even, and misses a lot of opportunities to improve the economic situation for everyone, not just groups that we arbitrarily deem underrepresented or under-served, which, by the way, is always going to be a moving target and is always going to be a nonstarter in terms of garnering any meaningful bipartisan support."

"So you admit that Republicans are racist?"

"Are we having an adult conversation?"

"So you really think that being a poor Black person in America is an equivalent challenge to being a poor white person in America?"

"No, Jess, I've read a history book. I just think that there is a cer-tain irony in using racial preference to address racial preference. Es-pecially when there's a more obvious, elegant way to think about the problem."

"Yeah, right," Jess snorts, "because addressing systemic inequality is easy as one-two-three."

"Just listen. Why is racism bad? Because we want the world to be a hippie-dippie love fest where everyone treats one another with respect? Good luck with that, given the course of human history. But liberals would have you believe that's the end goal. A big fucking cir-cle jerk where we all celebrate one another's differences."

"You're not serious. You really—"

"Hear me out. Equality and justice are fundamentally economic problems and the more we get distracted by identity politicking and virtue signaling the less we actually accomplish in terms of addressing structural inequality. I honestly believe that most of the time liberals would rather be right than win. Their entire worldview is completely assailable, and I don't think it makes me a bad person to want to advocate for an approach that actually stands a chance of working."

He looks at Jess. "Does that make sense?"

"Yes."

"Do you disagree with me?"

"I don't know."

Neither of them says anything for a long time.

Eventually Josh says, "Do you want to watch a movie?" He points at the television with the remote.

"No." Jess shakes her head, stands up. "I'm going to bed."

"Headache?" he asks with a thin smile.

"I guess."

He nods. He picks up the cat's paw and makes a waving gesture with it. "Say 'Good night,' Kachka. Say good night to Jess."

The cat stretches indifferently and then lays down on his side.

"Good night, cat," Jess says. "Good night, Josh."

On Thanksgiving Day, over dinner, Josh's mother asks, "Now Jess, remind me, does your family celebrate Thanksgiving?"

"Mom, she's from Nebraska."

"These sweet potatoes are really good," Jess says.

"Does your mother make anything special for Thanksgiving?"

"Oh, hmm, no. No, I guess not."

She waits for more and so Jess is forced to say, "My mother died."

Jess wishes she could say this in a way that doesn't make people look at her like they've just stepped on her fingers.

But she can't and so Josh's mother does the whole thing. "Oh, dear, I'm so very sorry, so very, very sorry," she says.

"It's fine." Jess shakes her head and tries to change the subject. "These sweet potatoes are really good."

The table is quiet. And then, after a beat: "Were you adopted?"

"Jesus, Mom. She's not an orphan. Her dad is in South Africa."

He clarifies, "On *vacation*. She's not some adopted African baby, Mom. Her dad just happens to be traveling this week."

"Josh, honey, there's no need to get excited. I'm just making conversation." She turns to Jess. "I'm sorry if you feel I'm prying."

"You're not. It's fine, really. It's nice of you to have me." She stops and looks at Josh. "These sweet potatoes are really good."

* * *

"You put on quite a show there," Jess says later that night.

"Excuse me?"

"At dinner. You totally threw your mom under the bus. You basically accused her of being racist."

"Jess, she asked if you were adopted. Why? Because you have great diction? If I'd let her keep going she would have asked if you were born addicted to crack, or if your parents had AIDS."

"No, she wouldn't have."

"She would have."

Jess says, "You were trying to impress me."

"No, I wasn't."

"You were. I called you out on your questionable politics and you tried to prove me wrong by throwing your poor mom under the bus."

"That's not what happened."

"Oh, come on," Jess teases, "just admit it."

"I'm not admitting anything."

"Admit it."

"Jess," he says, "give me a break." But he is blushing.

Jess calls her dad to say Happy Thanksgiving, even though she assumes he is out of the coverage area, that he isn't going to pick up. But after a few seconds, she hears the flat pulse of a connection. She hears rustling and then a woman's voice.

Jess says, "Hello?"

"Yes?" the woman says.

Stupidly, Jess says, "Dad?" Even though her dad is not a woman.

She hears the woman call her dad's name and then he is on the line.

"Darling daughter!"

"Who was that?"

"Jessie?" he says. "What's . . . what did you say?"

He's not being coy, it truly is loud. Jess hears shouting, laughing, a megaphone?

"Dad, where are you! Can you hear me?"

"Oh, absolutely," he replies. "Just lovely. The most beautiful."

"What's beautiful, Dad? Where are you?"

A sound like rocks rolling around a canister, then static, then nothing.

On her phone, Jess taps END.

She thinks, *Weird.*

"So . . ." Jess says, the next morning, on their way out of town, "your house is pretty nice."

Josh turns out of the driveway, rolling over speed bumps and signs that say SLOW! CHILDREN AT PLAY.

"Yeah right." He gives her a look, because he knows exactly what she's suggesting. "Look out the window."

Jess does.

"I had to drive past this every day on the way to school."

"On your way to Choate?"

"No," he says, "when I went to day school. Before Choate." He peers out over the steering wheel through the windshield. "Every day."

Outside, as far as the eye can see, are mansions, or at least walls behind which are hidden mansions of the double-digit millions variety, which Jess knows because while she was pretending to read her email she was really looking up home prices.

She says, "In the land of the blind millionaire the one-eyed billionaire is king."

"You're not as funny as you think you are, you know that?" he says, laughing. "Here," he says, pulling over in front of a tall gate next to a security tower, "let me show you."

"Show me what?"

He nods toward the gate. "Let's look inside."

Jess laughs. "What? You mean like ring the bell and ask for a tour?"

"This is Gil's place."

"As in Gil, your boss? Gil, like the CEO of your fund?"

Josh nods.

"How do you know where his house is? And, what, we're just going to rock up to your boss's house the day after Thanksgiving and, like, ask him to host us for tea?"

But Josh is already pulling the car forward. He shakes his head. "Gil's not home. He's in Barbados."

He lowers the window and sticks an arm out to reach for the keypad.

"Are you going to talk to the security guard?" Jess asks, surprised. She leans close to the windshield, trying to see into the tower.

Josh says nothing, just punches a few buttons on the keypad and Jess watches, a little bit stunned, as the gate glides open.

"What the . . . How do you know the code?"

"I've been here before," he says, which doesn't really answer the question.

The driveway is long, comically so, and lined with high cypress trees, as if they are at fucking Versailles. The drive forks and Josh takes them right.

"What's that way?" Jess asks, pointing.

"Stables."

"Of course," Jess says. "Stables to the east, landing strip to the west."

"It's a helipad," Josh explains, "and it's actually behind the main house."

"It disturbs me," Jess says, "that you said that with a straight face."

The house—the houses—pop into view and Jess can't help it, she says, "Wow."

Three stone buildings, the largest of which looks like Wayne Manor. Jess says, "Does Gil fight crime at night?"

They circle around the property slowly. Horses and helicopters and swimming pools and water views, and after twenty minutes—it seriously takes twenty minutes to drive a car around Gil's property—Jess says, "So . . . this is what you want?"

Josh looks at her. "Don't you?"

Jess thinks about it. On the one hand, it's practically pathological chasing this much money. Probably pointless. A pipe dream. Though maybe not for Josh.

Growing up, whenever Jess was being a brat—demanding candy or clothes or a new cell phone—her father would say, "Don't confuse greed with needs," which seemed like an annoying dad thing to say, or like an after-school-special cliché. Jess wonders what he would think of her now. Chasing a number that's only a fraction of a fraction of what she sees here but is still certainly more than she needs. More than anyone needs.

Is it greed? Coveting all these terrible things? Things acquired through pillage and plunder and white-collar crime, on the back of corporate bailouts and the laboring class. But then, looking out over the estate with its wide lawn and the winding driveway, it's easy to ignore all that. It's all so private and pristine. But more than that, Gil is a really big deal. He lectures at Davos and has stacks of honorary degrees. When he walks into a room people stand at attention. People take him seriously. He just has to snap his fingers and write a check. That's what Jess wants.

So eventually she just says, "Yes, I guess I do too."

They sit on a stone bench by the swimming pool and Jess tips her face to the sun.

"So, that's the plan, huh?" she asks, looking at the sky. "You'll have a giant compound in Greenwich, with fountains and helicopters and Italian trees and you'll send your kids to boarding school?"

Next to her Josh says, "Maybe."

"And you'll have, like, a beautiful wife who makes the best pot roast and wins the tennis tournament at the club every year?"

He laughs. "Well, it won't be 1950, so probably not that, but high level? Sure. Maybe."

Jess nods. Then: "Who's Tenley?"

"Tenley? Cavendish?" He looks at her, spooked, his face going white. "Why? Wait, how do you know her?"

"I don't," Jess says. "I saw her in your yearbook. She wrote you a letter." Jess doesn't mention what she overheard at David's party.

"You *read* that?"

"Not really, no." And she hadn't, really.

In Josh's bedroom she had found his high school yearbook, on a low shelf underneath a stack of old textbooks. She had flipped through it, the pictures of the sailing team, student council, something called Garden Party, where the girls wore white dresses and flower crowns. At the very back, on one of the blank pages, was a letter, written in perfectly slanted cursive. It took up an entire page and it started *Hey, Josh!* but then quickly became more intimate, to the point that Jess had stopped reading. But before she closed the book she'd seen signed at the bottom of the page *Love you forever xo Tenley.*

Josh doesn't say anything, his eyes are on the horizon.

Jess presses, "So who was she?"

"A friend." He suddenly stands. "We haven't spoken in ages."

Jess stands too. "A girlfriend?"

Love you forever xo Tenley.

"Not really, no." He takes his phone out of his pocket. "Should we head back?"

Jess cocks her head, curious at his caginess, at his definition of *forever*, but just says, "Sure, let's do it."

9

Josh picks the restaurant for January. He waits outside on the corner for Jess to arrive and then holds the door open for her as they step inside.

"I feel like I'm in a sci-fi tiki bar," Jess says.

"Is that a good thing?"

"It's like if we were both restaurants and we had a baby, this is what it would look like."

"That's a weird thing to say," he says, looking around, "but I agree."

They are seated in a booth with bright blue upholstery and napkins printed with giant art deco flowers folded on silver plates.

"How's work?" Jess asks, peering at the cocktail list.

He frowns. "I've been worried I'm not doing enough for this tech platform I'm managing. Once you design the algorithm there's not much more creativity you can inject into the trading process, I recognize that. But I feel like I could be more out of the box with the models in the first place. You know?"

Jess stares at the menu, agonizing between a rum cocktail that comes in a coconut and a punch served in a skull. "Why don't you, like, mine cryptocurrency?"

"Mining cryptos? What do you know about that?"

"It's like digital money. It's encrypted to control reserves and you use a blockchain, like a distributed ledger, to keep track of all the asset transfers."

"I *know* what cryptocurrency is. I'm just wondering how you do," he says. "Are they doing a lot with cryptos at Goldman?"

Jess shrugs. "I don't know. No. Yes. Probably. The trading teams probably are? I'm not sure. I'm not exactly in the inner circle."

The waiter comes and asks them what they'd like to drink.

"Then how do you know about mining digital currency? It's so esoteric."

She looks at him. "That book you gave me."

"What book? I never gave you a book."

"The quantum computing one."

"You *read* that?"

"Jess. Know. How. Read," she grunts. "Ooga booga."

"I just didn't know you were interested in that kind of stuff."

"It was interesting. Not all of it, but some of it."

He lights up. "It *is* interesting. What did you find *most* interesting?"

"Well, professor," she says, folding her hands together and leaning across the table, "I thought all the stuff about the qubits and the particle spin states was pretty interesting. Like, using quantum superposition to make shit exponentially faster."

"Yes, exactly," he says. "Information storage patterns. That made sense to you? I mean you got it all?"

"God, Josh, the book had the word 'dummies' in the title. Yes, it made sense. Give me some credit."

"It's complex theory, that's all," he says. "So I'm surprised."

"Well, don't be."

"Well, I am."

"Well, don't be."

"You're surprising," he says, and then when she rolls her eyes, "It's not a bad thing, you know."

The waiter sets down their drinks and Jess takes a long sip from a colorful paper straw stuck in the head of a stainless steel skull.

"Well," she cracks a half smile, "that may be so, but tomorrow I'm still going to send you a pdf called 'How Not to Be a Patronizing Know-it-all for Dummies.' "

The next day Jess receives her performance review. It's good enough that she gets to keep her job, but not better than that.

Later, she catches Blaine in his office, holding a highlighter over a stack of documents.

She taps on the glass and when he looks up she says, "I know this is probably a longer conversation, but whenever you have a minute, I would really appreciate your thoughts on what I might do to have more impact. If there are any specific development areas I could focus on."

Truly, Jess doesn't give a fuck what Blaine thinks—it's like asking Vlad the Impaler for feedback—but he is master of her fate.

He stares.

"I can come back later . . ." Jess inches away.

"You know what you can do?" he finally says.

Jess waits.

"Learn the difference between a million and a billion."

Jess's dad calls.

"How are you doing, darling daughter?"

She sighs.

"Tell me about it."

So she does. She tells him about the million-billion fiasco: about Charles, and the disaster deck, and the angry client, and Blaine's rage and her skimpy bonus.

"They docked your pay?"

Jess is glad the video isn't on so that she doesn't have to see his face.

"You make it sound like I work on an assembly line. Bonuses are discretionary. They probably just needed an excuse not to pay me."

"Well, I don't like that one bit," he says.

"Me neither!"

"You need to say something."

"Like what?"

"You need to tell them that it wasn't your fault."

"Tell who, Dad?" Jess feels a prickle of irritation. What does he imagine she's going to accomplish? Who exactly is going to hear her complaints?

"Your manager. This what's-his-name, this Blaine fellow."

"That's not how it works."

"Jessie, you need to speak up."

"Dad, it's fine."

"Jessie," she can hear him shifting on the other end of the line, adjusting the phone, getting into lecture mode, "these folks aren't going to cut you any slack, you hear me? They'll find ten thousand reasons to doubt you and you want to give them ten thousand and one? And this is not just about you, Jessie. What about the next young sister who walks through the door? And the one after that?"

"Dad," she says, "I know."

Though if she'd known he was going to make a federal case out of it, she wouldn't have said anything.

Now he's going on and on about equal opportunity and the legacy of discrimination and the myth of Black inferiority.

This is why she can't tell him things.

She wants to ignore him, but it isn't that easy—he has a point! She was supposed to be blazing a trail, bending the arc of justice, not cowering in a conference room waiting for some yo-yo in a sport coat to shout her down about a few semicolons.

•

She has dinner with Josh at a Mexican restaurant behind the wall of a bodega, a speakeasy that serves burritos.

They sit down and Josh says, "I heard bonuses are out at Goldman."

Jess buries a chip in green salsa and doesn't respond.

"I heard they gave out bagels."

Jess chases a jalapeño around the bowl with a tortilla, ignores him.

But he just sips his water calmly until she finally relents. "Are you asking me if I'm in the bottom five percent of my analyst class?"

"Are you?"

"Wow, I almost don't want to dignify that with an answer. But no, I didn't get nothing. I mean, I'm probably not going to buy a Chanel purse this season either. But yeah, no. Thanks for the vote of confidence."

"So you're not going to stay?"

"I don't think I said that."

"But what's your plan? What are you doing next?"

"If you're asking if I'm going for PE or VC or B school, I'm not. I'm happy where I am."

"Yeah, right."

"What do you mean, 'yeah, right'? Why would I mess with a good thing? I mean I get it, everyone is sick of the hours and the abuse but . . . it's fine. I've figured it out. The devil you know and all that."

"You think you've figured it out?"

"Well, yeah. I mean, I'm not going to win analyst of the year, obviously, but I feel pretty okay about things. Maybe it didn't happen this cycle, but I'll definitely be promoted in the next one." She reconsiders. "Or the next one."

"You really believe that?"

"You're kind of being a dick right now."

"Well, do you?"

"Obviously, *you* don't. You've made that clear. Next topic."

"I'm just trying to understand what your plans are."

This is her plan. After almost two years of blood, sweat, tears and fetching coffee, Jess has no desire to start over. She's going to be promoted. It's just a matter of time. Probably. Maybe. She's not taking questions. "I don't have plans, okay?" she finally says. "What are *your* plans?"

"I've been promoted," he says easily, "and I'm going to be running my own trading desk."

"Well." Jess picks up her menu. "Congratu-fucking-lations."

"Jess. Don't be mean."

"Are you kidding me? You just finished telling me how shitty and pathetic I am and you want me to do cartwheels because you got promoted?"

"You're not shitty and pathetic. I'm not gloating. I mention it because I wonder if you would join my team."

"As in you would be my boss? Ha. Yeah, no."

"You're wasting your time at Goldman." Josh looks at her. "They don't appreciate you."

"And you do?"

"Yes," he says seriously, "I do."

"Since when?"

"Since . . . always."

Jess sighs at his earnestness. She touches the rim of her margarita glass and thinks. She rubs a large salt crystal between her fingers and finally says, "Okay, tell me."

He smiles. "It wouldn't be weird or hierarchical or anything, I swear. You'll technically just be a generalist member of the prop trading team, but you'll sit on my desk."

Jess considers this, imagines herself sitting, legs crossed, on his actual desk.

"Okay," she says. "I just have one question."

"Yes?"

"What do you actually do?"

He laughs. "Good question. Basically, we use machine learning to make faster trades and better bets. The idea is to use data and analytics to build a better trading model, and then to deploy those models to determine what, when, and how much to invest."

"So you build the models and the machines make the decisions?"

"Precisely."

"And Gil Alperstein is just going to give you a ton of money to, like, play the stock market?"

"That's one way to put it," he says, shrugging. "I'm good at what I do. And if I'm honest, it's also a bit of a marketing ploy. You know, boy genius runs AI-driven machine learning fund. People are seduced by the idea of a precocious intellect. You know, the wunderkind, the whiz kid."

"Boy genius?"

Josh half smiles. "I knew you would get stuck on that part."

"I just didn't realize I was sitting in the presence of greatness, that's all. When they invite you to the White House to get your award don't forget about us little people. The mediocre minds in opposition to your great spirit. The drooling disciples to your Jesus Christ superstar."

"Are you done?"

"The grubby autograph seekers to your Hollywood celebrity," Jess says. "Can you tell me more about the Church of Scientology?"

He waits.

"Okay, I'm done," she says. "So this is real? You're basically running your own fund and you're hiring people. And Gil Alperstein, *the* Gil Alperstein, is just letting you hire whoever you want?"

"Yes and no. I mean, you'd have to interview. This isn't the Wild West. But I'd help you prepare. Then you'd join my team."

"So what would I be doing while you—the boy genius—are writing all these algorithms, orchestrating the rise of our machine overlords?"

"You would be writing algorithms too."

"I'm sorry, I guess you didn't get the memo. I don't know how to write trading algorithms."

He shrugs. "You'll figure it out."

Jess doesn't look convinced.

"That's the thing about Gil's," Josh explains. "The entire place runs on pure intellectual horsepower. Not bullshit hierarchies and politics. Gil isn't as fixated on what you know as how fast you learn."

"Okay . . . but, I mean, are you sure? Why do you think I can do this?"

"You have the mind for it. You taught yourself Python. You play Set like a computer, and you're smart, Jess. You're really smart."

"But I mean, there are lots of smart people. Why me?"

"Because," he says, "you're here too, and you're amazing."

Part Two

10

"You're going to work for Josh?"

Jess and Lydia are in matching massage chairs having their nails painted at a crummy little storefront a block from her apartment. They used to go to a hotel spa—where you got champagne and a cheese plate with a mani-pedi—but now that Jess can afford it, she doesn't bother.

"I mean, maybe." Jess examines her nails. Bright red, which doesn't go with her Brooks Brothers, but which is also kind of the point. "According to him, no one at Goldman appreciates me and it's only a matter of time before they show me the door."

"So why would he want to hire you then?"

"That's what I asked him. He said it's because I'm smart. Or something."

Lydia looks at Jess. "It's probably because he wants to do it."

Jess laughs. "Shut up."

"Just watch yourself. At first it's all ratios and portfolios, and then next thing you know you're ass out on the photocopier while you're screaming his name"—she blows on her fingernails—"in pure ecstasy."

Jess goes into the office for a mock interview.

In the lobby Josh's secretary Elizabeth—he has his own secretary—greets her. She leads Jess through the office, where people pad around in shorts and hoodies, pulling bottles of flavored water and cold brew and one hundred percent fruit juice from the fridge.

Jess counts four games of chess underway. A guy in a Starfleet Academy T-shirt says, "Dude, your pawn structure is a mess." And the guy sitting across from him slumps in his beanbag chair, "Dude," he says, "I know."

Jess asks where the ball pit is, joking, and Elizabeth looks stricken. "I'm so sorry! It's actually booked right now."

Josh is waiting for her in his office—he has his own office—behind a giant frosted sliding glass door that Elizabeth heaves to one side as she shows Jess in. He's still wearing his usual button-down shirt and slacks.

Jess sits down, about to make a joke about the lack of peasants peeling grapes for employees in the kitchen, but Josh speaks first.

"We don't have much time, so let's get started." He pulls a legal pad from his desk drawer. "You have exactly one second to answer."

"Oh." Jess takes off her jacket and says, "Okay."

"What's one million minus eleven?"

"Oh, so, like, we're just, diving right in?"

"One second," he says.

"Nine hundred ninety-nine thousand nine hundred and ninety-nine," she says too quickly.

He raises an eyebrow and then makes an elaborate note on his pad.

"Actually, wait—" Jess starts, but he cuts her off.

He says, "What's fifty-four percent of one hundred and ten?"

He says, "How many tons does the ocean weigh?"

He says, "Make me a market on the temperature of this room."

He asks her to calculate the probability of pulling different color marbles out of a jar and the odds that a baseball series would go to game seven and how much she would pay to play a card game with a trick deck. She says twenty-five percent, five over sixteen, and nothing.

"Hmm," he says, "not bad."

Jess beams.

"Okay, last question," he says, "and it's the most important one."

Jess leans forward.

"Would you bet a trillion dollars on the sun rising tomorrow?"

Jess doesn't think about it. "Of course!"

"No, Jess," and the disappointment in his voice is palpable. "That's not a disciplined bet."

"But it's a guaranteed trillion dollars."

"And if the sun doesn't rise? You're wiped out. That's not how we trade. It's not just enough to know the math; you need to understand the strategy."

"If the sun doesn't rise, don't we have bigger problems than our P and L?"

He says, "Our P and L is always our biggest problem."

"I'll remember that when we're scavenging for protein cubes in the bunker."

"Jess," he says, "the jokes."

"Oh, come on. It'll be fine. You know why?"

He waits.

"Because I'm amazing." She sings the second syllable—ama*zi*ng.

He shakes his head and fights a smile. "I need to know that you're going to take this seriously."

"I will! That's why I'm here!"

"I need to know that you're going prepare."

"I will!"

"I need to know that you're not going to make me look like I have terrible judgment."

"I will!"

He frowns.

"I mean, I won't!"

He tears off several pages from the pad and shoves them at her. "Here. Study this."

Jess folds them carefully into her bag.

The phone on Josh's desk flashes red and Elizabeth says into the speaker, "I have your eleven o'clock on the line."

Jess stands. "I'm taking it seriously, I promise."

Josh doesn't say anything.

"Hey!" she says. "Don't make that face."

He says, "What face?"

"That I-feel-like-it-was-a-mistake-to-hire-Jess face."

"You're not hired yet."

She laughs. "Cool. Thank you. Reassuring."

"But Jess . . . that's the reason I think you'll be great."

"What is?"

His phone is lighting up.

"Your . . ."—he searches for the right word—"Jess-ness. You know? The way you can look at the same exact set of facts and come to a completely different conclusion."

"That sounds like a fancy way of saying I'm always wrong."

Elizabeth's voice on the speaker again saying, "Whenever you're ready!" Josh ignores it.

"It's my favorite thing about you," he says to Jess.

"That we disagree?"

"That you have a different take."

"What's your second favorite thing about me?"

She is expecting him to make a joke or shake his head or say something like "I don't have a list," but instead he says: "Your legs."

And then he picks up the phone and their meeting is over.

At a party later that night, Jess tells a guy standing over a bowl of salsa that she works at Gil's, and he is extraordinarily skeptical.

"You?" He says. "Really?"

And when Jess replies, "Yes. Me. Really," like she's spitting fire, he says, "Hey, no offense, I've just heard it's really hard to get into."

"Well," Jess explains levelly, "I'm a fucking genius."

"Sure." He shrugs. "Whatever." Then through a mouthful of tortilla chips, he says, "Hey, is it true that everyone plays chess between trades and that they fire the bottom ten percent of traders every half?"

And Jess is forced to admit that she doesn't technically work there. Not yet.

"You know, I'm not entirely sure," she says. "I haven't started. I'm still waiting for an offer."

"Oh, so you don't really work there at all." He seems as if order has been restored to his meager little universe. "Well, that makes much more sense then."

*   *   *

After that Jess studies.

She pores over the notes Josh wrote for her and dusts off a college textbook on probability and number theory, and when Miky texts, **plans this wknd? dranks and fuckery?** Jess ignores her.

Well, that makes much more sense then. The smug look on salsa guy's face, if Jess could bottle it, could power her through hours and hours of rage studying. It's all the motivation she needs. Although, there's also the money.

Josh had explained that their compensation was almost completely pay for performance, and that the upside was nearly unlimited. He'd told her how much she could make her first year, in theory, and it made Jess a little ill.

"That much money?" she asked him. "For pushing a few buttons?"

He said, "That's one way to look at it."

She could practically see the number in the app finally flashing green. Her dad always told her not to spend what she hadn't earned, even in her imagination, but it felt like winning the lottery: she could pay off her loans or buy a boat, donate to charity.

The night before the interview, Jess is all zeal and energy. Like the Kool-Aid Man, full of punch, ready to burst through a wall.

She texts Josh:

I AM READY FREDDY

He writes back:

Think you got the wrong number, this is Josh

Jess types:

OH YEAH

The interview questions are all about math and trading strategy—just like they practiced. Jess is given a stack of poker chips and asked by one interviewer after another to make bets and calculate all sorts of odds. It's like one of those poker tournaments on ESPN, where guys sit around in sweatsuits playing cards and it's somehow considered sports.

But at the end of the day she has more chips than when she started, and Josh calls a few days later to congratulate her on getting the job.

His friend David is having a party and Josh invites her to celebrate.

Jess says, "Are you sure we should be hanging out together, you know, now that you're my boss?"

"We'll keep it professional," he says, breezy. "It's just drinks, right? Not one of Berlusconi's bunga bunga parties."

But when they show up at the party—Jess brings Lydia—the house is jammed with bodies and the windows are steamed. They split up and fan out, a trick they learned in college, in order to maximize their chances of finding trouble: the good drugs, the hot boys, the best booze.

Jess is in the parlor inspecting liquor bottle labels when Lydia texts, **found Josh.**

In the kitchen Lydia is on her back on the countertop. Someone has poured a thimble of tequila into the flat of her stomach and it sloshes down her sides onto the marble. A guy has his tongue in her belly button and she is shrieking with delight.

Lydia looks up and says to no one, "Jess needs a shot!"

Jess asks, "Where's Josh?"

Instead, David appears with two shot glasses raised above his head. He shoves a box of English sea salt at her and says, "Here, put this on your neck."

Jess hesitates, but then takes the salt.

"Where's Josh?" she asks again.

David points with a shot glass and Jess turns and there he is.

And he's a mess. Wasted and sweaty. Hair plastered to his face. He says, "Hey, Jess," and to her he has never seemed sexier. Loose-limbed and glassy-eyed, licking his lips.

David says, "Put this in your mouth," and hands Jess a wedge of lime.

She doesn't take it right away and Lydia, still on her back, turns her head and screeches, "Do it!"

So, Jess tilts her head to one side and pours a little salt into her clavicle. She puts the lime between her teeth. David is standing in front of her grinning like an idiot and Lydia is clapping and Jess thinks, *Sure, this is totally fine.*

David hands the shot to Josh, and before Jess can react, Josh leans into her and she feels his mouth, wet and warm against her skin. His hair brushes against her face. He puts one hand on her waist, but applies no pressure, just lets it rest. And this gesture, the nothingness of it, his fingers just barely grazing her stomach, feels full of erotic possibility. Jess feels electricity between her legs.

Then: suction from his lips. He swirls his tongue aimlessly in the divot between her neck and shoulders, while she tries to control her breathing. It occurs to her that this is taking longer than it should, to lick an eighth of a teaspoon of salt off her shoulder. It occurs to her that they have veered into bunga bunga territory.

She feels like someone has turned the temperature up a thousand degrees. His fingers are still there, doing nothing. She imagines kissing them. Imagines him dipping them inside of her.

She closes her eyes.

But then he pulls away. Not completely. She can still feel his breath against her jaw, hot and even. But he lets his hand drop, then tips his head back and pours the tequila down his throat.

The last thing: the lime is still in her mouth. When he puts his mouth to hers, Jess thinks that it is entirely possible that she will come, right there in the kitchen. She holds her breath.

But he hesitates. Then, instead of using his mouth, he takes the lime from her lips with his fingers.

She exhales. Her heart pounds. Her crotch pulses.

He puts the lime to his own mouth and looks at her. He bites into the sour flesh, sucks the juice out of it, without breaking eye contact, and it isn't perfectly clear to Jess whether or not he knows what he's doing, whether he's being intentionally suggestive—he's so drunk, he's on another planet—but then he winks, and Jess's insides scream and she thinks, *Fuuuuuuuuuuuck*.

Definitely, though, keep it professional.

At work Jess walks past the photocopier and tries not to, but can't help thinking about sex. She imagines spreading her legs and sliding onto him. She would say, "Ruin me, Josh," and he would flip her over on the glass top, which would be cold initially, but then it would be warm and slick. She wouldn't care if they got caught. Thinking about it, she feels liquid between her legs. A sloppy blow job. A wet mess. A paper jam, probably.

But then something happens.

Jess is having dinner with Miky, at a cool little Spanish place that serves wine on tap, when she sees Josh. Seated across from him is a girl, catalog pretty with pearl studs in her earlobes and an olive-green waxed jacket hanging over the back of her chair.

It occurs to Jess that he's on a date. She tries not to stare.

Across the restaurant, Josh notices her. He smiles, surprised, and mouths *Hello*. The preppy girl turns to look. Josh nods in Jess's direction and makes a come-over-here face, but Jess shakes her head, embarrassed.

Miky says, "Who's that?"

"My boss. Josh."

"*The* Josh?" Miky cranes her neck to see. "Introduce me!"

Jess smacks her and says, "Hey, don't stare."

"You're not going to say hello?"

"He's clearly on a date."

"Maybe it's his sister."

"It's not." It's some girl who went to boarding school and knows how to sail. Some girl named Schuyler or Penelope . . . or Tenley.

Miky picks up her menu and asks casually, "Do you want me to go over there and throw water in her face?"

Jess plays dumb. "Why would I want you to do that?"

* * *

When Josh leaves the restaurant, he has his hand low on his date's waist and doesn't look back at Jess. Her throat tightens and she feels a strange mix of disappointment and relief.

What happened between her and Josh at David's party was nothing.

Nothing happened between them.

And nothing is going to happen between them.

She's not his type, for one.

And anyway, they agreed to keep it strictly professional.

And then something else happens.

At the end of her first week of new hire training, Jess receives a ping from Gil's secretary—one of his secretaries—asking if she can see him; he has a few minutes between meetings.

Jess rides one elevator down to the lobby and then another all the way to the top. His office is beautiful and looks like what Jess imagines a Scandinavian art museum might. Gray walls, blond wood, light pouring in at impossible angles. Jess has never seen a skylight in a high-rise building, but there it is.

Gil folds his hands together, leans forward over his desk, white composite with steel legs. He says, "I understand you used to work at Goldman Sachs."

"Oh," Jess says, surprised, "yes."

"I know some guys over there."

Jess wonders what he wants.

"We don't usually hire junior traders from the sell-side."

"You hired Josh from the sell-side."

"Josh is one of the most brilliant young traders in the game today."

"Well, maybe I will be too," Jess says, only half joking.

He leans back far enough that Jess can almost see up his nostrils.

"Given how successful Josh has been, given how much of an asset he's been to the firm, his hiring recommendations carry a lot of weight."

"Of course."

"But we maintain a very high bar and we pride ourselves on fostering a strong intellectual culture. The strongest. It's our sole competitive advantage. We have the best technology and the best traders. Period. Always have, always will."

Jess wonders if he's going to be the seventy-fifth person she's met at the fund who asks her to calculate a square root in her head.

"Do you understand me?"

In fact, Jess understands him perfectly, but she just tuts noncommittally.

Gil takes a different tack. "You met while in the analyst program at Goldman?"

By now she knows he already knows the answer to his question, but she plays along, corrects him politely, "Actually we met in undergrad."

"And you were . . . friends in college?"

"No."

"No?"

"We had a class together."

"And at Goldman?"

"We both worked on consumer products and insurance."

"You both worked on consumer products and insurance," he repeats back slowly.

"So, you know, he's familiar with my work."

"Is that all he's familiar with?"

Jess's eyes go wide.

Gil continues, "I need to be aware of any potential conflicts of interest."

"Are you talking about noncompetes?" Jess says, prim.

He narrows his eyes, sizing her up.

She stares. Thinks about the party, at David's, Josh's mouth, warm and electric, on her neck.

Eventually Gil says, "Well, I think we're finished here."

And Jess says, with a straight face, "Thank you so much for the warm welcome."

* * *

The new hire training program is called University; six weeks of classes in functional programming, finance and game theory. The classes have names like Convolutional Neural Networks and Reinforcement Learning in Finance, and it is like a boot camp. Not everyone has what it takes.

The instructor cold calls and one day he points to the guy to Jess's left, who responds "seventeen" even though the correct answer is "a nested Boolean operator." He is gone before the end of the week.

Jess thinks, *Look to your left, look to your right.*

They run simulated portfolios and for the most part her programs work. Another new hire, the guy on her right, asks her how it's going and she says, "Fine?"

He nods sympathetically. "It really doesn't help that this byte code compiler is so poorly optimized. I'm not saying it doesn't have its advantages—it has some really powerful abstraction capabilities—but everyone else is speaking Spanish and we're speaking Portuguese, you know what I mean?"

He introduces himself—his name is Paul and he used to work at Google. He offers her a stick of cinnamon gum and Jess is pretty sure that means they're friends.

Jess is assigned a desk. Six screens, a stack of Post-its, and a silver balloon tied to her seat. It is the first day of work—of work work—now that she has graduated from University.

The other junior traders are installed at faraway desks; Jess can only see one other silver balloon bobbing in the air above a desk three rows from her own. She leans over in her seat, looks past her monitors, and sees Paul, the Google engineer, sitting behind the other ballooned desk. He gives her a little wave.

Besides Josh there is one other senior trader on the immediate team, who Josh explains will be her mentor.

"What!" Jess cries, mock upset. "But I thought it was just you and me against the world."

Josh laughs. "Right now it's you versus your machine." He points at the tangle of cords under her desk. "Take the morning to get set up and after that he'll come find you."

He doesn't come find her and so in the afternoon, after she has downloaded all the software and set up her trading screens, she taps on the glass outside her mentor's door.

He calls, "Come in."

Jess steps inside.

"Hi," she says, cheerfully, "I'm Jess."

He looks confused. "A new admin?"

Jess actually looks over her shoulder, before realizing that he means her.

"Oh no. A new trader actually. On your team?"

"Bridge Intern?" he says, naming the program that places low-income college students in finance and banking internships.

Jess can't tell if it's a question or a statement, but either way, it makes her want to strangle him a little bit. "No actually." She smiles harder. "A new trader. On your team. Josh didn't mention it?"

"You're Jesse?" he says. "I thought you were a dude."

"It's Jess," she says, "actually. Like, short for Jessica. A female name."

He finally stands up.

Even though Daniel Murray is what's printed on the plaque out-side his door, he introduces himself as Dano, a nickname Jess guesses he picked up in some frat house.

"Well," he says, flatly, "welcome to the team," and then sits back down and looks at his computer.

Jess says, "So." Though what she means is *Teach me, Sensei.*

During University, a parade of execs, senior traders and desk heads had shuffled in and out, each with different bits of wisdom and advice—*be careful of correlated risk, never enter a position without a plan*—but they had all emphasized that the role of the junior trader was, above all, that of an apprentice. And even though this made Jess think of working in a coal mine, she got the idea. She would sit at

Josh's—or Dano's—shoulder and he would teach her things and they would make a billion dollars before breakfast.

Dano ignores her.

Jess says, "Josh said you were my mentor."

Distracted, he says, "Sorry, what?"

"I was just wondering," Jess says, "is there anything I can do?"

He finally looks up, says, "I could use a coffee."

•

In the team room Josh challenges Jess to a game of chess. "Want to play?" he asks, standing over the board.

Jess hesitates. Chess is big around here. They play as if it is a blood sport.

Jess doesn't know how to play, not really. During University she was invited to play in a chess tournament. She dropped a twenty-dollar bill into a Yankees cap with the full understanding that she would never see it again.

They played a convoluted version called bughouse, three chess-boards, six players, two chess clocks. They picked teams like in middle school gym class and Jess was picked last. She had never played chess before and every time she moved a piece she had to ask, "Is this allowed?" until finally her team lost and they surrendered the pot.

To Josh, she says, "I don't really know how."

"How can that be true?"

"I don't really feel like playing a brain game anyway. Can't we just hang out?"

"A 'brain game'? Would you rather play Connect Four? Do you want to arm wrestle? Grunt back and forth across the table at each other? Come on. This is part of your training. Sit," he says, and points to the seat opposite him. "If you don't sharpen your knives they get dull."

So Jess sits. They play and Josh wins quickly.

"Best out of three?" he offers and Jess nods.

She concentrates.

"Can I do this?" Jess asks, sliding a pawn across the board, her finger resting on its head.

"I wouldn't," Josh says.

They play in silence, until Jess cries, "I win!"

"Wait." Josh leans forward to inspect the board. "What?"

"Checkmate!"

"Are you serious?" Josh looks at the board, bemused.

"Look," Jess demonstrates with the various pieces, "when I put this guy here, I forced you to move that guy there, and then, this guy"— she holds up a rook—"got your king. See? I win!"

"Huh." Josh sits back and folds his arms. "I thought you said you'd never played."

"No, I did. That one time. I told you. During the new hire program?"

"And that's it?" Josh asks.

"Yes."

"Interesting," he says. "I should take you to Vegas with me sometime."

"To gamble?"

"Sure," he says, making eye contact over the chessboard. "We could start there."

And it sounds like he's suggesting something. And not a Celine Dion concert. Jess thinks of sex and drugs and the Strip. Vegas things.

Jess wonders if that's what he means. But then again: *keep it professional.*

Although the bar for professionalism in this office seems rather low. Dano, for example, has a mug on his desk that says NICE TITS with pictures of songbirds—chickadees and titmice—all over it. Jess had noticed it and said, "Bird lover?" and Dano had replied, "Yeah, right."

Did Josh mean it that way?

She looks at him.

He looks at her.

She changes the subject.

"So," Jess says, "Dano is kind of an asshole."

Josh, lining up a row of white pawns, half laughs. "Tell me how you really feel."

"He asked me if I was a diversity hire and then he made me get him coffee."

Josh looks up. "He said that?"

Jess nods. "Basically."

"I'm sorry," Josh says. "You're not."

Jess says nothing, pushes her queen to the center of the board.

"We hired you because you're smart, not because you're Black."

"Gee, thanks," Jess says, sarcastic.

Josh looks confused. "I'm agreeing with you. I just said—"

"I heard what you said, I just didn't like the way you said it. So like . . . defensive. Like you're dignifying his statement with a response. Like I actually was a diversity hire but you're trying to convince people I'm not."

"That's the exact opposite of what I said."

"It's just really fucking annoying," Jess says, rolling a knight between her fingers. "Like, clearly people don't get hired here just because they're Black. If that were the case there would actually *be* Black people working here"—Jess is the only Black trader on the floor—"yet somehow it's okay for people to imply that, I don't know, they're just handing out jobs to any Black person with a résumé and all you have to say is, 'Jess is smart'?"

"Sorry, I wasn't . . ." He shakes his head. "I get it. I'll talk to him."

"You will?"

"Yes, of course. It was a fucked-up thing to say. You're right. He was being an asshole."

"Okay," Jess says, looking at the board, "thanks."

Josh says, "Hey," and she looks up. "I'm really sorry."

"I know," she says. "It's fine."

"I want you to be happy here."

"I know," Jess says again. "It's fine." She doesn't actually like it when he gets all puppy-dog-eyed and apologetic. It makes her feel mean, like she's stealing his innocence.

*   *   *

Dano won't stop calling Jess "Jesse."

He says, "Hey, Jesse, can you help me out with these trade tickets?"

"Hey, Jesse, do you have those forex printouts for me?"

"Hey, Jesse, where'd the Nasdaq land after close?"

Hey, Jesse.

Hey, Jesse.

Hey, Jesse.

Like a taunt. She has no idea whether he's doing it on purpose or not—whether he knows her name and refuses to use it or whether he just doesn't care—and she's not even sure which is worse.

In the morning meeting one day she finally loses it. "For the five hundredth fucking time, it's *just* Jess."

Dano looks at her like she's crazy and says, "What did I say?"

And then everyone else looks at her like she's crazy and she realizes that he has won.

Later Jess says to Josh, "I can't stand that guy."

Josh says, "You don't say?"

"He's such a dick."

"He is kind of a dick, yeah," Josh admits, "but you shouldn't lose your cool over it. It just gives him ammunition . . . right, Jesse?"

"Don't call me that," she snaps.

"Sorry," he laughs and squeezes her shoulder. "Won't happen again, *just* Jess."

11

Once a week Gil descends.

He peacocks around the floor while everyone puts on a show.

When he steps out of the elevator, sometimes people literally clap. And then he sits on a high stool in the biggest conference room while everyone gathers round.

The room is always packed, standing room only, everyone rapt, while Gil shares with them his particular vision of the world. This is how Jess knows that the LIBOR spread is low this quarter, and that this administration's economic policy is a godforsaken mess, and that when it comes to prestige television there's no such thing as gratuitous sex (*ha ha ha*).

Jess thinks that Gil's opinions range from mildly obnoxious to majorly—the Wine Girls' favorite word—*problematic*, but no one else seems to agree. They all just stand there moon-eyed, nodding, taking notes, practically drooling, while Gil tells them what to think.

At the very end he invites questions, even though he usually talks so much that they run out of time. Even so, the whole spectacle is called Q&A.

During Q&A one day Paul finds Jess at the coffee maker, foaming a latte.

"You didn't want to kiss the ring?" he says.

"I had a really tall glass of Kool-Aid for lunch so, you know, I'm all set."

He laughs.

Jess offers him a mug and he takes it. "You know, people told me this place was a cult of personality before I joined, but"—she shakes her head—"it's real."

Gil's Six. That's what everyone calls Gil's time-honored musings on life, investing and leadership. Josh had shared them with her in a text right after she'd gotten the offer. Jess clicked a link to an article that had been shared over a million times with a headline that said: *Six Lessons on Leadership from a Billionaire who Knows.*

She read:

One: Buy when there's blood in the streets. In order to be successful you need to bet against consensus and you need to be right. Never do what the other guy is doing. Competition is for losers.

Two: Stay up late. If you work hard, success will come. If you don't, it won't.

Three: Be prepared to eat glass. If you're not prepared to suffer for your success then you don't deserve it.

Four: Keep death in mind. They say that the only constants are death and taxes, and taxes can be avoided. When you keep death in mind you live without fear and you die without regret.

Five: Pigs get slaughtered. Greed is good, but it makes people stupid. Manage your risk relentlessly, or you will lose.

Six: Excavate the rot. Abandon what isn't working as soon as you know it's not working; sooner if you can. Whether it's people or positions or entire lines of business, don't be afraid to let something go if it's not contributing to your bottom line.

Jess had read Gil's Six. Then read them again. Then she had shut her laptop and thought, *Gil Alperstein doesn't pay taxes?*

Jess had read Gil's Six to Miky and Lydia and the Wine Girls, rolling her eyes the entire time.

They were lying on their backs on Lydia's bed, their legs high above their heads, bottoms of their feet pressed against the wall, passing a small glass bowl packed with weed back and forth.

"Blood? Death? Slaughter?" Jess said, incredulous. "Did I just sign on to work at an MMA fight club?"

Lydia giggled.

"But, like," Miky sucked on the pipe thoughtfully, "if no one can talk about Fight Club, how do they recruit new members?"

"They're not even grammatically parallel!" Jess said, putting down her phone, "but everyone thinks they're brilliant, like they're the goddamn Ten Commandments."

Lydia inhaled. "So Jess, do you think Gil Alperstein is bare-chested in a basement somewhere beating the shit out of his associates?"

"Probably."

"You know what?" Noree said, sitting up. "You should totally write your own rules. Do we really need another rich old white man ejaculating his opinions all over the world? What do *you* have to say about leadership, Jess?"

"His post had, like, a million likes."

"Yeah, a million sheeple clicking blindly to perpetuate the ad-generated late-capitalist hegemony."

Miky passed the pipe to Jess and she took it. "So, what, I should just post a random list of rules online? Who would even read that? I'm just . . . a person."

"You could go into work early one day and pin them to all the office doors."

"Like Martin Luther?" Lydia laughed and twisted the cap off a water bottle.

"What would I even say?" Jess asked. "It's not like anyone would listen either way."

"I know what I would say," Miky said.

They looked at her.

"Okay, one," she said, keeping count on her fingers, "Queen Elizabeth is a cannibal. Fact."

Lydia snorted, spraying water out of her nose.

Jess said, "That's not a rule."

"Neither is kill pigs, or whatever."

Callie said, "You know, it wouldn't surprise me. Everyone knows the royal family is into some dark shit."

Miky went on: "Okay, two: Room temperature butter is the truth. Three: Karaoke isn't fun. Four: NASA knows about a second sun that they're not telling us about. Five: Bill Murray and Dan Ackroyd are the same person. Six: Fewer than three *ha*s in a *ha ha ha* text is rude."

"Did you just come up with those?" Lydia asked, impressed.

Miky nodded, tapping the pipe. With a straight face, she said, "I try to live my life with the utmost care and deliberation." But then, stoned and slightly unsteady, she let the pipe slip from her hand, spilling ash all over the duvet.

"Oops," she said, and they all laughed.

"So," Lydia asked lazily, impervious to the mess on her bed, "what does Josh think of Gil and his rules?"

"I think," Jess sighed, "that Josh thinks Gil is a genius."

Jess had shared Miky's list with Josh.

She sent him a message that said:

check it out, it's Miky's six, the queen is a cannibal, lololol

He wrote back:

I guess that was supposed to be funny

Jess said:

I mean . . . yeah?

Josh said:

Gil is an amazing guy, you know, and incredibly accomplished, we could all learn a lot from him

okay fine, Jess typed, *but you have to admit the list was a little ridiculous*

I mean . . . eat glass?

And then nothing.

Jess waited, but Josh didn't respond.

After half an hour she wrote:

anyway, it was just a joke

and then sent him an upside-down smiley face.

She stared at her phone.

Finally, he replied.

ha ha

●

Every week there is an Ideas Meeting, which is exactly what it sounds like. In the game room they sit in a circle on chairs wheeled in from offices or on the floor or on beanbags and they brainstorm ways to get rich. People shout and write things on the whiteboard and are definitely not shy.

Which is how Jess knows that all her ideas are terrible, horrible, no good, very bad ideas. And it's not just Dano who hates her but everyone else, too.

If Jess suggests they connect to the Twitter API, someone will argue that that introduces unnecessary overhead.

If she suggests that the fund should do more impact investing, someone will argue against it because they aren't in the business of making concessionary investments.

If she suggests that they should order bagels for next week's morning meeting, someone will argue that actually they should order pastries instead.

On the topic of whether it makes sense to strip their portfolios of companies with crude oil holdings, the conversation is heated, and Jess stands on a beanbag to make her point.

"Come on," Dano finally says, exasperated, "Josh?" Dano looks at Josh tapping away on his laptop, as if he is her tamer.

She steps off the beanbag.

Josh looks up, placid, and replies to Dano, "What?"

"Can you explain to her why throwing out half our portfolio would needlessly destroy our bottom line? This is an investment company, not a charity."

Josh looks at Jess. "Have you done the math?"

"Well, no," Jess admits, "not yet. But I thought . . . it's the Ideas Meeting. We're just brainstorming ideas."

"Then why not," Josh suggests, "have this argument again once someone has?"

Later Jess says to Josh, "Thanks for backing me up in there."

"It's not my job to back you up, you know."

He's right, probably, but it's still annoying.

They're standing in the doorway to his office, and Jess mutters something like *yeah, fine, whatever* and turns to go.

But he stops her. He takes her elbow and even though they're alone, and there's no one else in earshot, he lowers his voice. Almost whispering, he says, "But if it turns out the idea has legs"—and then, exaggeratedly, so there's no mistaking, he looks up and down, from the floor to her waist—"I'd be happy to support it."

Jess looks at his hand on her elbow, follows his eyes, along the length of her legs and then looks back up at his face. His face is the same as always, flat, professional—if anyone were to walk by it would look like they were talking about soybeans or the price of crude—but his mouth is dissolute. He's not licking his lips or anything, but he might as well be. He raises an eyebrow, like a question, and to Jess it feels like he's asked if he can bend her over his knee.

Is he giving her career advice or talking dirty? Or is he joking? Jess can't tell. What about the girl in the waxed jacket?

His hand is still on her elbow.

She feels caught off guard. She shakes his hand off, gently, tells him, "I'll, uh, keep that in mind."

Even later, in the micro-kitchen, Jess overhears a guy in a blue puffy vest say, "Josh needs to tell his girlfriend to chill out."

To which a guy in a black puffy vest responds, "She's not so bad."

Not so bad? Jess thinks. *Gee, thanks.*

And then she thinks, *Girlfriend?*

And then she feels bad, guilty about making trouble for Josh.

Leaving the micro-kitchen, they don't notice her.

Black Puffy adds, "She's actually a decent trader."

"Yeah," Blue Puffy says, unconvinced, "I guess there's that."

They know she's a decent trader because everyone knows she's a decent trader. Although *decent* is, she thinks, an understatement. And *actually* a most obnoxious qualifier. They know because there are leaderboards, giant flat-screens at either end of the floor, that rank every single employee on the trading team. Gil, or someone senior, designed an algorithm that accounts for the size of each trader's portfolio, the annualized returns and the absolute growth and then spits out a ranking, a number next to each trader's name. At first Jess was turned off by it—it seemed needlessly cutthroat—but as her rank rose she decided she liked it.

Because no matter how many eyes roll in the Ideas Meeting, or how many times Dano calls her by the wrong name, or how many people in the micro-kitchen stop to talk shit, it's how Jess knows she's good at her job.

Jess likes to work late—residual stamina from her banking days. When the market closed and everyone has gone home, she can really think. When the floor is dark and quiet, she tinkers with her portfolio and tunes her models. That's her favorite part about the job—the actual work.

Sometimes Paul joins her. About her long hours he says, "So that's how you do it: work harder not smarter?" And Jess says, "Har de har har."

When the office is empty they goof around. Paul turns all the lights off and holds his cell phone flashlight under his chin like a ghoul. Or they steal yoga balls from the break room and bounce around, laughing. Once, when Dano finds them, he says, "Very cute. But this is not Facebook or Google or whatever, so you might want to think about the level of professionalism, even after hours."

And that's her least favorite part of the job—her uptight colleagues.

The whole wearing jeans to the office thing is mostly a facade: underneath the casual clothing they're still garden-variety pompous jerks.

•

A month passes and Josh says ominously, "We need to talk."

They sit in his office with the door closed and Josh starts to speak but, freaked out, Jess interrupts: "Is it true that every half Gil fires, like, a million people?"

Josh looks up at the ceiling, inhales deeply, says nothing.

Alarmed, Jess says, "Wait, so it's true?"

She assumed it was just a rumor, water cooler talk. But then again, rule six: Excavate the rot. Which, according to the office chatter, means that every six months the fund makes significant staff cuts.

"I didn't say anything," Josh says.

"You said enough!" Jess feels her face getting hot. "Is that why we need to talk? Because I'm one of the people who's going to get cut?"

He doesn't answer immediately so Jess says, "Oh my god. Seriously? Is this you telling me I'm going to be fired?"

"Jess, relax. You're doing a great job. Your P and L is strong. I'm really impressed. You're picking it up quickly. It's just . . ." He pauses. "You're ruffling some feathers."

"Ruffling feathers? You mean Dano? Josh, that guy doesn't like me. At all."

"Is it that bad?"

"He's always re-reviewing my code, even after it's already been submitted."

"He's your mentor."

"And when I asked him to reschedule the Q3 strategy meeting because I had a conflict, he said I was being difficult."

"Dano can be tricky," Josh admits.

"I'm higher than he is on the leaderboard," Jess points out.

"I'm aware of that."

"So if anyone's going to be fired, shouldn't it be him? Just because he's more tenured and becau—"

"Relax. Please. No one's getting fired."

"Okay, but it sounds like Dano has a problem with me. And he talked to you about it? Why didn't he come to me directly?"

"He talked to me about you the same way you're talking to me about him. It's not a conspiracy. And anyway, it's not just Dano. This isn't even about Dano." He waves his hand in the air to dismiss the thought, to suggest they've gotten off track. "I've gotten other feedback."

"You have? Like what? From whom?"

"Like that you don't necessarily have a trader's temperament. Like maybe you're not a perfect culture fit. Like that you're . . . too familiar." He looks like he's in pain.

"Too fam*iliar*?" Jess wonders which of her colleagues said that. She feels a bubble of resentment build toward the Puffy Vests. Toward everyone who ever has worn or will wear a puffy vest. Jess doesn't have a puffy vest. When she'd asked for a puffy vest with the company logo, they told her that her size was on back order. And when she'd asked again, they told her to check back next quarter.

She continues: "What does 'too familiar' even mean? I should just sit in the corner like a grateful little bunny with my mouth shut? Is this about the Ideas Meeting? I have ideas. Why shouldn't I share them? Everyone else does."

"I'm not telling you not to share your ideas. You're just really new," Josh says, carefully. "It's not a great idea to show up and start stepping on toes. Right? Read the room. Pick your battles. Do you really think that a bunch of radical social investment ideas is going to win with this crowd?"

"You think impact investing is radical? I'm not asking you to set off pipe bombs at a police station."

He sighs, "This isn't complicated. Just sit back. Watch. Listen. Learn. Take this place for what it is and don't try to bend it to your will. You'll see, it's a great culture. It really is. How does that sound?"

"Fair enough, yeah, got it," Jess relents, then adds a little sadly, "I just really thought I was doing a good job. You even said my P and L is solid."

"You are. It is." He seems sincere. "All I'm asking is that you tread a little lighter. Not everything's about your portfolio."

"I thought our P and L was always our biggest problem."

"Ha. Touché."

He smiles and the tension dissipates.

Jess leans back. "So you're not going to fire me?"

"Stop asking that."

"So is that a no?"

He laughs, taps his pencil against the desk, "Just go back to your seat."

At the morning meeting there is a call for volunteers. A community service event in the office. Something with kids or a school or chess or something. Jess isn't really paying attention. She is fixated on her laptop screen, the overnight numbers from the European shift blinking hotly, as she counts her trades in dollars and euros.

Later, on her way from picking up a stack of printouts from Josh's office, Elizabeth passes by Jess's desk. "So can I sign you up?"

"For what?"

"The PS 318 event?" she says. "It's about a half-day commitment, in office. Minimal pre-work required. You'd just need to help with the agenda and some light setup."

"Oh, no, I think I'll pass. Thanks, though."

"No?" She taps the pile of papers against Jess's desk, straightening them out. "Really? You're sure?"

Jess is annoyed that she's even asking. Annoyed that Elizabeth is trying to sign her up for what amounts to office housework. Jess is sick of getting coffee and taking notes.

"I'm sure," Jess says. "I'll skip this one, but thank you."

"Well," Elizabeth says, collecting the neatened papers, "suit yourself. But let me know if you change your mind. They'll be here on the first of next month. Bright young minds. The future of the world and all that. I'm sure they'd love to hear from you."

But Jess doesn't care. She's a trader, not a babysitter.

* * *

"Can you play volleyball?" Paul asks one day, apropos of nothing.

Jess looks up. "Me?"

Paul looks around the office, there is no one else there. He says, "Yes."

"You mean, am I really good or, like, do I know the rules?"

"Either."

Jess thinks it over. "No."

The next day he stands behind her and dangles a flyer in front of her face. It says COED SOCIAL SPORTS LEAGUES.

Paul says, "We need a girl."

Jess takes the flyer and reads that social volleyball leagues are filling fast. "Ah, that old diversity chestnut," she says.

Paul shrugs. "We need a girl."

"And I'm the only girl you know?" Jess asks.

He says, "Basically."

•

One day, Josh doesn't show up for work. He isn't in the morning meeting and Jess watches, but she doesn't see him enter or exit his office. Eventually she pings Elizabeth.

Elizabeth replies: *Hosting the underprivileged kids! From the chess club!*

Jess remembers. Since Elizabeth first brought it up, she had asked two more times if Jess would volunteer to host. Elizabeth had never actually mentioned that they were underprivileged, just that they were really good at chess, that one of the middle schoolers in the club had actually won some sort of national competition, and that all Jess would really have to do was tell them a little bit about what working as a trader was like and play a little chess with them.

And Jess had imagined sitting across a chessboard from a brainy ten-year-old, some pint-size version of Josh, or worse, Dano, judging her for bringing her queen out too early, and then said no. And when Elizabeth asked again, Jess had said no again. Until finally she stopped asking.

Right before lunch Jess wanders into the micro-kitchen. As she is pulling a bottle of organic tea off the refrigerator shelf, she hears a crescendo of kid voices, arguing, excited. One of them says, "Wow, they got free soda!"

She turns and there they are, the underprivileged kids, in sneakers and sweatshirts, with pudgy faces and crooked little kid teeth. Their teacher, a youngish Teach for America type, smiles sheepishly at Jess. "You don't mind, do you? One of your colleagues told them they could grab drinks."

"Oh, yeah," Jess says, "of course." She gestures for them to go ahead.

The kids all rush the drink fridge, shoving and laughing and going gaga over the quantity and variety. They say "Wow!" and "Awesome!" and "The orange one is my favorite!" A boy in a Transformers T-shirt picks up a bottle of pure pomegranate juice and says, "This one looks like a butt!" and Jess smiles, because it *does* look like a butt.

"One each, please," their teacher warns.

A boy with bright eyes and braces turns to Jess. "We can have any one we want?"

Jess nods and he pumps a fist. "All right!"

The kids each take a drink and they are about to shuffle off when Jess says, "Hey," and then bends down and pulls out a giant drawer, hidden beneath the counter. It is stuffed with packages of gummy bears and jelly beans and candy bars and strawberry fruit leather and chocolate-covered nuts and yogurt-covered raisins and caramel corn and, Jess's favorite, pretzels dipped in peanut butter.

The kids look stunned, and Jess says magnanimously, "Help yourself."

"Wow! We can have some?"

"No wayyyyyy!"

They are so unabashedly, gleefully grateful that it breaks Jess's heart just a little bit, but at the same time she feels like, maybe, also just a little bit, in her own way, she has done her part to help enrich the lives of the underprivileged youth.

But then later she walks past the big glass conference room in the middle of the floor and sees Josh standing at one end of the conference table surrounded by kids. He is laughing, holding a chess piece in the air, and a little kid, also laughing—everyone is laughing—is jumping up and down swatting helplessly at it. Eventually Josh hands him the little marble pawn and the kid grins and takes a seat, shows the piece proudly to his friend, and for some reason in that exact moment Jess feels physically, profoundly guilty.

She wonders why the fuck Elizabeth didn't think it would have been useful to tell her that all the kids were Black.

She knows what her father would think. They'd talked about it. Not the volunteering, but the Charles Barkley controversy. He'd been in the news lately, a retired basketball player saying terrible things about Black people. Under a headline that read " 'Unintelligent' blacks 'brainwashed' to choose street cred over success" he'd claimed to reveal the "dirty, dark secret in the black community."

On the phone her dad ranted. This guy was definitely not helping the cause. What had possessed him? Don't Black folks put up with enough?

Jess agreed. The guy was an idiot. A racist. A proponent of respectability politics.

Her dad was perplexed. "What kind of Black folks don't support other Black folks?"

What kind indeed.

When Jess asks Josh about it, he says, "But Elizabeth said she asked you about ten times if you wanted to volunteer?"

"Well, she didn't mention that the kids were Black!" In hindsight, this makes perfect sense. Elizabeth is sheltered and skittish, afraid of the outer boroughs and Zika and food that's spicy, the kind of person who lowers her voice when she says *African American*.

"I didn't want you to think I was badgering you. Trying to use you to score diversity points. You specifically asked me not to do that. When Dano—"

"Okay, but that's different."

"I don't see the difference."

"The difference is that now all these kids think all traders are white and male and it would be nice for them to have a different kind of role model. Someone to look up to."

"Why can't they look up to me?"

Jess laughs. Josh doesn't.

"It sounds like you're saying white people can't be good role models for Black people."

"I'm saying it's *preferable*, given the woeful lack of representation in this industry, for them to see someone who looks like them."

"So, what, all your role models are Black women?"

"Well, no. Actually," Jess says, "none of them are."

"Oh," Josh says.

"Yeah."

He nods slowly and says, "For what it's worth, it did go well. I think they liked me."

"I'm sure they liked you." Jess likes him. He's fucking likable. That's the problem.

Later Jess is in Josh's office picking up printouts when she sees a Post-it on his desk with her name on it: a to-do list.

She picks it up.

It says *Nikkei numbers, lunch with Gil, check GTCs* and then in smaller, much messier print, as if written in a fit of frustration or rage or maybe just an afterthought: *the Jess problem.* A cryptic fragment. Her name and then the word *problem.* Preceded by the definite article—as none of the other items on his list were—that suggests a sort of grim specificity, something troubling and singular, a problem, *the* problem. With her.

Planning and performance season starts next week.

*　*　*

Paul insists that it's fine that Jess is terrible at volleyball, but it turns out it is not.

Everyone wears short shorts—which they call nut huggers—and numbered bibs pinned to the back of their shirts, or their shorts, if they're not wearing shirts.

Someone shouts "Sprints!" and they all run in sweaty circles around the court and then stop at the end to stretch.

Jess says, "I thought this was just for fun?" And one of her teammates windmills his arms dangerously, cracks his neck and says, "Baby, winning is fun."

They all have muscles and equipment and murder in their eyes and Jess is the only girl. She sits out the first set and the second and then the third, until they finally drag her from the sidelines: She has to play, it's the rules. So they stick her at the edge of the court where she can't really do much harm. But even so, on the first point, sensing weakness, the opponent's opening serve is spiked right in her face. A red welt blooms below her eye and then the ball drops petulantly to the sand.

They all point and hoot and yell, "Six-pack!" except for Paul's boyfriend, Dax, a graphic designer who wears prescription sport goggles, and who takes Jess gently by the elbow, saying, "Easy," and handing her a bottle of cold water to press against her face.

Jess asks, "What's 'six-pack'?" She flips up her T-shirt and palms her stomach, which is flat but without definition. "Is it fair to assume no one is shouting about my rock-hard abs?"

Sheepishly Dax explains, "A six-pack is when you get spiked in the face."

From the court someone cackles, "Hey, Six-Pack, nice tattoo!" and when Jess raises an eyebrow at Dax he explains again. "The imprint of the volleyball on your face," he gestures, "it's like a tattoo."

Jess stands on the edge of the court with Paul as he wipes sweat off his face with a bright blue bandana, like a cowboy.

Jess says, "This sucks."

He says, "Correction, you suck."

"Here I was hoping for some positive reinforcement and now you sound just like my boss."

"Josh?"

Jess nods.

"Josh doesn't think you suck."

"I'm not so sure. He keeps calling me into his office. To give me *feedback*."

"That doesn't sound so bad. Feedback is a gift, right?" Paul rolls his eyes. He sticks an index finger to the sky then draws quick little circles in the air with it, to put a point on his sarcasm, as if to say well, *whoop-de-doo*.

Feedback is a gift is what people say at Gil's when they want to justify saying something awful to someone's face.

"Anyway," Paul asks, "how's your P and L?"

"Fine," Jess says. "Good."

"Then what's the problem?"

"I don't know. Josh keeps talking about 'culture fit' and, like, how I should work harder to 'collaborate' more. It's just making me feel . . . insecure."

Paul says, "Culture fit?" He turns and grips her by both shoulders, as if she were a child about to step out into traffic. "Jess, that's bad. You need to do damage control around that. If you don't, it's going to affect your comp or, God forbid, you could be counseled out."

"What, no," Jess protests. "Gil only fires the bottom ten percent."

"Listen to me," Paul's grip tightens, "Gil fires whoever the hell he wants."

"Okay, but—"

"Have you talked to Josh?"

"Sort of?"

Paul shakes his head. "You need to have an explicit conversation with him. Demand answers. Do it now. Before your review."

"You're scaring me."

"You're the one who told me you were worried."

"But now I'm, like, actually worried."

"You should be."

"Paul! You just said that I didn't suck."

"It would be one thing if you'd lost a million dollars or, I don't know, spat in a client's face, but 'culture fit'?" He shakes his head. "You need to figure your shit out and you need to do it now."

Someone on the court shouts "Subs!" and Paul jogs back out onto the sand.

12

J ess finds Josh at his desk and asks, "Can we talk?"
He looks up. "Yeah, what's up?"
"Do you mind if we go somewhere?"
"Where?"
"Somewhere neutral."
"So this is a war?"
"I feel like you're mad at me."
He sighs, "I'm not mad at you."
"Okay," Jess pauses. "So can we talk?"

They go to a bar and are seated in the corner, at a booth that, if they were on a date, might feel cozy or intimate, but because they are not, feels uncomfortable and cramped.

They order whiskeys and when the waiter brings them, Josh immediately tips his drink back and then slides Jess's across the table and drinks that too.

She says, "All right, then."

The waiter brings another round, and then another, which they finish in sulking silence, until Josh wipes his mouth and says darkly, "You know this isn't exactly fun for me, either."

"I don't get it," Jess says. "What can I do?"

Josh starts to stay something then stops.

Jess says, "I'm trying." And she was. She'd set up a weekly one-on-one with Dano where she pretended to care what he had to say, and she and Paul had recently led a training on statistical memory profiling. She knows she isn't going to win a medal or anything, she's just hoping for a little acknowledgment.

But Josh says, "*Are* you trying?"

"Seriously? *Seriously?*" Jess asks, with ice between her teeth. She is buzzed and angry, like a stretched rubber band: precarious and full of energy. She can't help herself: "You're going to fire me, aren't you?"

He sighs and says, "Not necessarily," and Jess thinks *Not necessarily? Not fucking necessarily?*

She wants to slap him. Instead, she begins to cry.

She bites her lip and blinks very fast, but it's pointless, the tears fall. She wipes her eyes and takes small sips of water, but it's too late, she's coming undone.

He looks at her with sympathy and says, "Oh, Jess."

And she snaps, "That's all I fucking get? 'Not necessarily'? What kind of explanation is that?"

"Fit is only one factor," he tries.

"What are the other factors, Josh? The swimsuit competition? My plan to cure global poverty with puppies and rainbows? What about my actual performance, Josh? Why isn't that a factor?"

"Jess, come on."

"Don't talk to me like this. Like I'm just some fucking idiot assistant. Just some random person from your job."

"You're not a random person." He looks miserable. He says, "Please, Jess. Please don't cry."

"Why wouldn't I cry! You're telling me I'm going to lose my job!"

"I didn't say that."

"So I'm not going to lose my job?"

He hesitates. "No, Jess, no." He looks at her. "You know it's not completely my call, right? But I don't . . . please don't worry about losing your job. Please."

She is still crying and this makes her feel pathetic.

Outside the sky turns black and the waiter drops a candle on the table.

He says, "Please, Jess. Please don't cry."

She cries.

Then.

He touches her face, and his fingertips are warm.

She swallows, and then he reaches for her mouth, a finger resting on her lips.

Her heart beats in the back of her throat. She looks at him. He holds her gaze and she feels hot.

She says, "What's 'the Jess problem'?"

He pulls his hand back, seems surprised. "The what?"

"I saw it on your desk. You wrote a note. It said 'the Jess problem.' What does that mean? Like, I'm some kind of problem on your to-do list?"

He leans back, thinking. It takes him long enough to respond that Jess considers repeating herself, but finally he says, "You know in applied mathematics a problem isn't always bad. It can also describe a certain class of unknowns, an as yet unproven theory without a formal, or general, mathematical solution. Not so much a *problem*," he says carefully, "as an open question."

Jess says, "You just said nothing."

He sighs and then answers again as if she has asked him a hypothetical question. "I guess," he says slowly, "the Jess problem would be complex. Profound. Deterministic. Meaning the solution would be specific. Singular. Nongeneralizable. Just a beautiful, intractable problem, for which there exists no suitable generalization"—he is making intense eye contact—"yet."

Jess blinks.

And then they are kissing.

At first just a little bit: His lips on her lips, his hands on her face. And then they are making out spectacularly and Jess is breathless and liquefying, swinging a leg up over his waist. She straddles him in the booth, pressing herself so tightly against him that she can feel the buttons on the front of his shirt digging into the flesh between her rib cage.

He shifts slightly in his seat so that his mouth is only half on hers and Jess pulls him closer because she doesn't want him to stop. She wants to keep kissing him forever, wants to die here on top of him in this bar.

But he does stop, sort of. He kisses the side of her mouth and her face and her neck and wraps his hands around her midriff and her stomach flips and flips and flips.

Jess feels as if she has been sitting on top of an ancient volcano, with a thousand years of secrets and sediment buried inside.

His mouth is warm and she can taste whiskey, but also something essential to him, and the alchemy of it, her mouth and his mouth and the chemical interaction is new to Jess. It feels special. And his hands are hot on her skin, searing even, so that she feels like he is breathing fire into her.

Her mind is a synaptic mess, but she has one thought that rings clear, like a bell in her head: *Holy shit. Josh.*

They kiss and kiss and kiss until the waiter comes by to tell them to knock it off and they extract themselves from each other and sit stunned side by side in the booth.

Then Josh opens his wallet, drops several bills on the table, and says, "Let's get out of here."

They stand on the corner until an empty taxi materializes at the top of the street and Josh flags it down.

He opens the door for Jess and then gets in on the other side. He shuts the door but doesn't slide to the middle to meet her, just buckles up and says to the driver, "Two stops."

What?

To Jess, this feels like an abrupt end to the evening. Her lips are still swollen, and her shirt is still slightly twisted around her hips. Her face is still hot.

She would like to spend the night with him, would like to feel his body under hers, his hands warm under her shirt. But apparently the feeling is not mutual.

He stares out the window, placid, unspeaking, and Jess wishes that he weren't so uptight, so practical, so *professional*. It makes no sense to her. If he were feeling even a tenth of what she is feeling right now, he would be on the other side of the cab, sticking his tongue down her throat.

But he just sits there, calm as a spring afternoon, and the fact that Jess wants him desperately, has this sudden eruption of desire churning inside of her, doesn't seem to register. She looks over. There is nothing, clearly, churning inside of him.

He doesn't even look back.

She hates him right now. But she is also radiating a hot, unrequited lust. She could cry. Again.

The cab stops outside her apartment and Josh finally turns. He says, "Jess, I . . ." But he doesn't finish and Jess doesn't wait to see if he will. She gets out of the car, slamming the door.

She runs, practically, into her building without looking over her shoulder.

Jess enters her apartment noisily, kicking the door shut behind her. She feels hot and roiled and aroused and abandoned, like a kettle on a stove, removed from the flame just before the water boiled. She feels slightly feverish and the place where he touched her stomach is pulsing heat; she can feel the absence of his hand almost as strongly as when it was there. She feels certain that if she were to look, she would see five red-hot fingertips emblazoned on her skin. When she touches the spot between her hip bones she feels a jolt.

She considers, briefly, taking off all her clothes and touching herself, but the thought embarrasses her and so she thinks of baseball and spreadsheets and electric bills even though deep in her lizard brain she is thinking of him.

Her phone rings in her bag and it's Josh. She can guess why he is calling and so she doesn't pick up. She drinks a glass of water, turns off the lights and climbs into bed. On the nightstand the phone rings again.

Jess turns off the ringer and shuts her eyes.

She hears it buzz, once.

And then again, another time.

She picks it up.

A message from Josh lights up the screen.

I'm outside

*   *   *

When she opens the door he seems breathless, as if he has run. Which maybe he has.

He says, "Jess," and she says, "Josh," and then he steps toward her and pulls her close.

She's still agitated, keyed up, queasy with desire.

But then he kisses her again, and the panicked feeling in her chest falls away.

Fountains erupt, a choir of angels sings an aria, and Jess feels the earth tilt on its axis.

Pressed against the doorframe Jess kisses him back, one hand on his neck and the other clutching his back.

He grabs her hand and guides it toward his erection. She pulls her hand away, slightly, from the bulge in his pants, but his grip is firm around her wrist. She pulls away again and manages to slide her hand partway up his abdomen, but he nudges her hand back down between his legs. They've been kissing for approximately fifteen seconds. Why is he so insistent? And there it is: that prickle of panic. She worries that maybe he's a blow job missionary leave-as-soon-as-he-comes guy. Could he be?

She yanks her hand away again and places both palms on his shoulders, pushing him down to his knees. She waits for him to react. He doesn't complain, just glances up at her then takes her by the waist, slips his tongue into her underwear until her legs begin to shake.

In bed he positions himself on his knees between her ankles and enters her from behind. He has one hand on her hip, thrusting, and with the other he cups her breast and plays with her nipple. He is whispering filthy things in her ear—how wet she is, how tight she is, how bad she wants it—and Jess is gripping the headboard, cat-cowing her back, saying, "Oh, yeah, right there, yes," and it's all feeling a little bit porny, yes, but fine when Josh asks if he can pull her hair. Jess stops. She turns.

"You don't like it?" he asks.

"Why did you ask me that?"

Why did he ask her that?

He didn't ask permission when he put his tongue, or his fingers, or his penis in her vagina, or when he showed up at her door. Why was he asking now?

Did he read a manual? How to have sex with a Black girl? Don't touch her hair. Don't call her a Nubian princess. Don't be weird about her ass.

"Have you . . . done this before?" she asks.

He looks confused. "Done what?"

His hands are still on her hips; he is still inside her and she's twisted at a strange angle, trying to have a conversation.

It's awkward.

It's killing the mood.

She's killed the mood.

She rolls away, onto her back.

"What did I do?" He's on his knees above her, his erection practically vibrating.

Jess shakes her head, blinks up at the ceiling. "This feels . . . complicated."

He nods, then lies down facing her, propped on his elbow. "Can you relax?"

"No."

"Yes, you can." He pinches her cheek between his knuckles and grins. "I made you relax twice already."

"Ha, ha, very funny." She shakes her head to herself. "I think I'm . . . just . . ."

He touches her stomach and asks softly, "What do you like?"

She scrunches up her face. But there's not a specific thing—like feet or slutty lingerie or being called names. Also, it feels so personal. Telling him what she likes. She doesn't even know what she likes.

He says, "I know what you like."

Jess raises an eyebrow, skeptical.

"I know you," Josh declares.

He wraps his hand around her jaw and pulls her face gently toward his. "Jess?"

"What?"

"I love you."

"What?" Immediately her heart starts beating faster. "Since when?"

"Since . . . tonight," he says.

Jess swats him. "Shut up."

"I mean it," he says. He rolls onto his back and puts his hands behind his head, contemplating. "Or maybe since the first time I saw you, in a way."

"In Law and Society?"

"No, it was before that. At a party. There was this party. You and your friends showed up in these ridiculous outfits. They weren't even outfits really, more like underwear. Your friend Lydia? She had a stack of dollar bills she was carrying around all night. I don't know, maybe the theme was strippers or something? I'm not sure."

Anything for a dollar, Jess thinks. The point was to end up with the most dollar bills at the end of the night.

"Anyway, you basically had on just a bra and this little bikini thing," he says, then pauses. "And I used to think of you in that outfit all the time."

"Stop," Jess says. "I'm blushing."

Josh ignores her. "I mean it, Jess. I'd never been so attracted to anyone in my life. I would see you on campus and I would just feel . . . overcome."

"I always thought you hated me. I mean, why didn't you ever try?"

He shrugs. "I don't know. I guess we were always in class," he says. "It was never a good time. And besides, I did have you, in a way. I had this perfect image of you in my head. It was so visceral; I could just think of you in that bra and it would make me come."

"Josh," Jess says, and is now blushing for real.

"Jess."

"So you've been in love with me since freshman year of college?"

He thinks about this. "No . . . I mean, I loved your body, but I didn't know you. And then we had that class together."

"So since then?"

"No," he says. "I mean, I would still think of you when I was alone, when I was with other girls even, but I started to think of you as two different people. Your personality wasn't what I expected."

"What do you mean by that?"

"You were just"—he searches for the right word—"more three-dimensional."

"Than the picture in your head?"

"Than everyone."

"So you fell in love with my searing legal rhetoric?"

"Definitely not. Yeah, no. But that's when you became real to me. And then at Goldman I got to know you. We became friends and then, I guess, because I knew you, I didn't think of you the same way, not in that strictly sexual way. My mental model of you shifted. That person, my fantasy version of you, and the actual you were just completely different people to me. One wasn't real. And so I guess the more I got to know you the less urgently, physically attracted to you I became. Like this girl who I had done all these dirty things to in my head had nothing to do with the real girl I saw every day. This girl who was really smart and my friend and kind of silly and a little insecure but also sometimes really, really secure. A real person. You know?" He stops. "You're looking at me like I'm speaking Chinese."

"It just sounds like you're saying that once you got to know me you stopped being attracted to me?"

"I've always been attracted to you."

They stare at each other.

"What kind of dirty things?" Jess finally asks.

Josh smiles. "And then at the restaurant, when we kissed, it was like a switch flipped. You became both of those people to me. And the reality is even better than the fantasy." He lowers his voice an octave: "So much softer and wetter."

Jess giggles. "Shut up. Way to ruin the moment, you creepy loser."

She shoves him playfully, and he grabs her hand, holds it, rubbing his thumb in circles over her wrist.

There is a charged silence. Then Josh says, "I've never felt this way before. That's all I wanted to say."

Jess is melting.

"And I just . . ." He stops. "You're just so pretty."

Jess smiles. "How pretty? Am I the prettiest girl you've ever fucked?"

"Yes," he says automatically. Then leans over, trailing kisses down her jaw and shoulders.

"Am I the prettiest girl you've ever seen?" she asks into his neck.

"You are." He kisses her breasts.

"Am I—"

"Yes," he cuts her off. "Yes and yes." He moves his hands lower. "You're perfect."

Jess closes her eyes tight. She's wetter than she was before. Josh nudges her onto her side, slides his arm under her rib cage and pulls her close. Then they are spooning, her ass pressed against his erection, his breath hot in her ear. He slides his hand back between her legs and she bucks against him, dizzy with lust.

Eventually she climbs on top of him, butterflies her legs around his waist. They stare breathless at one another for a moment, until he touches her face and says, "You're amazing," and she is swooning and then there is that moment—neither of them is breathing—and she says *oh my god oh my god oh my god* and he says *Jess Jess Jess.*

•

At work doors are closed. Things are tense. According to Paul, an unabashed gossip, this is standard during planning and performance season: secret meetings and hushed conversations, whispered speculation about who or what is getting overhauled in the new fiscal year.

Jess is distracted. Anxious about her review. She keeps checking the leaderboard, because it makes her feel better, irrefutable evidence, displayed right there on the office wall, that she's a top performer—or a nearly top performer, or at least, better than Dano. But the bigger distraction is Josh. She can't stop thinking about him. Last night was like an earthquake and today she is still feeling aftershocks.

But he is nowhere to be found and when Jess asks Elizabeth when he'll be in, she just shrugs and says, "Meetings?" Which isn't really an explanation.

Jess pings Josh but he doesn't respond, and this makes her feel anxious, snubbed, and a little insecure. All day she just fusses with her positions and waits for him to appear.

Eventually Elizabeth drops by and says, "The big guy wants to see you."

Jess taps on Josh's door, while her heart beats wildly.

He says, "Come in," and explains, "Things have been really busy today."

Jess can't tell if this is an admission or an excuse. But then he gets up from behind his desk and stands close.

"I missed you," he says gravely. "I've been thinking about you all day."

Jess touches his wrist. "Really?"

He says, "Of course," and he smells so good and Jess's sense memory of last night is so strong that she wants to take off all her clothes right now.

She says, "Do you think we could get away with banging on your desk?"

He laughs, but says definitively, "We definitely could not," and then: "But what are you doing tonight?"

Josh has dinner with Gil and the other managers and doesn't show up at Jess's until late, after she has already fallen asleep. He lets himself in with the key code she texted him earlier and climbs into bed, smelling like steak and cigars.

He kisses her awake.

Jess nuzzles his shoulder and says, "You smell like a dirty old billionaire."

And he says, "You smell like roses."

13

But then on Monday morning, an afternoon meeting appears on her calendar. She's been invited alongside Josh and two representatives from HR, and the existence of this meeting, the inevitability of its outcome, is humiliating. Jess can't believe she let her guard down. She can't believe she bought all the talk about flat hierarchies and meritocracy. She can't believe she trusted the leaderboard. Why did she think that being good enough would be good enough? She feels foolish.

Jess tries to delete the meeting, which is stupid and irrational, but it doesn't work; she doesn't have edit rights.

Josh isn't in his office.

Jess panics. Rips half a pad of Post-its into tiny pieces of confetti, makes herself two cups of coffee, which she doesn't drink, then she does, sits at her desk, stares at her computer, stricken, while her heart pounds and blood rushes to her head. She considers leaving. Just packing up her Post-its and walking out the door, but she has never been the type. To quit while she's ahead, or even very, very far behind. She wants to know what happens, to see how it ends.

She texts him.

Josh

Then waits.

After an excruciating ninety-five seconds he almost responds:

. . .

She types:

are u there?

what's going on?

and then

I have a meeting from HR on my calendar

and later
what's happening?
Josh?
please
He doesn't respond.
can u please respond
please
please
please?

At her desk, instead of reading the morning reports, she googles. Death, divorce, discovery of being an adopted child. For perspective, Jess reads an inventory of life stressors in an attempt to properly contextualize her impending fate.

Dismissal from work, she discovers, is not as bad as acquiring a visible deformity, and only slightly less stressful than becoming addicted to drugs.

Jess checks her position on the leaderboard and discovers that her name is gone.

In the conference room the two representatives from HR are waiting. The blinds are shut for privacy even though everyone knows what's going on inside. Jess takes a small step in and one of the nameless HR reps says, "You'll want to close the door."

Jess does and then she sits down and then she is fired.

They explain that it was a difficult decision and that the firm is committed to helping her transition successfully into a new role, somewhere else, definitely not here, that will be a better fit for her skills and interests and *temperament*. They explain the terms of her at-will employment and the firm's exit policy, while blood rushes to her head and pounds in her ears. She feels thrown off-center, slightly dizzy, even though she knows she shouldn't be surprised.

They explain that she will have six weeks of "search time," during which she will continue to draw a paycheck and collect benefits, during which she may continue to use her corporate email and consult with a career counselor and use the gym on the first floor, though she will no longer be permitted to access proprietary or confidential information. She will be required to hand in her key card as soon as she walks out the door.

Jess doesn't register any of it. She is stuck on a single thought: "Where's Josh?" Jess asks loudly.

"Pardon?" the HR rep seems caught off guard by her sudden interjection.

"Josh? My manager? Where is he? How can I be fired without my manager present?"

One of the HR reps sighs, "These conversations can be difficult."

The other one says, "So we leave it to the manager's discretion whether they want to be in the room when their report is out-counseled."

"Wait." Jess sits up. "So you're telling me that Josh just . . . doesn't have to be here?"

The reps glance at each other.

"Is that what you're saying? Because that's not fucking okay."

One of them steps toward her, makes a gesture with her hand as if calming a frightened horse. Jess knows this is the point in the conversation in which they are considering calling security. Fine. Let them drag her kicking and screaming off the trading floor. Her heart is pounding pounding pounding.

"But I'm at the top of the leaderboard!"

"No," they say, taking her statement literally, "you're not. And, as you know, you're not only calibrated on performance but also on your community contributions. Collaboration. Community service. Volunteering. These sorts of things."

"You can't be serious." Jess would have volunteered! But because Elizabeth is afraid to say the word *Black* Jess is going to be fired. Unbelievable.

They remain impassive. "These were conversations you should have had with your manager."

She can't believe that Josh is too chickenshit to tell her this to her face. She hates him. She hates the firm. She hates Gil and these two goons from HR. She hates everyone and everything about finance. She hates corporations and prep school and elitism and smugness. She hates everything. She is furious.

They say, "We know this is difficult news."

Jess stands up. She can't listen to this anymore.

They say, "We're not done here."

Jess says, "I am."

They push a manila folder across the table toward her. "You'll need to sign some paperwork. It's for your protection."

Jess shoves the papers back toward them. "I'm not signing anything without my lawyer." She says this with the fervor of a suspect on an episode of *Law & Order* and then turns to leave, slamming the door to the conference room.

"Wait," they call after her, "someone needs to escort you out."

Jess doesn't turn around. She stalks back to her desk, colossally pissed off.

Inside her she feels a rage, vicious like bile, rising in her throat.

Betrayal. That's what the feeling is. It feels like Josh has led her to the precipice of vulnerability and then shoved her off the cliff onto the rocks without so much as a glance back. But what did she expect?

She texts Miky and Lydia to tell them that they are all going out tonight. Jess insists on a bridge-and-tunnel club in Midtown that Miky discovered two summers ago where they could "dance real trashy."

Jess has half a dozen shots and accepts drinks from strangers and drops her cell phone in the toilet and picks a fight with the bartender, until Lydia says "Jess, you are acting insane" and drags her off the dance floor.

Jess is sweaty and slurring her words and even though it's New York City, it's also a weeknight and so she is the wildest person there.

"What is up with you tonight?" Lydia asks, coaxing Jess into a sticky booth.

"Have you been roofied?" Miky asks.

Jess slumps in her seat and doesn't respond.

"Jess," Lydia is stern. "What's wrong?"

"I got fired," Jess admits.

"What!"

"Why didn't you tell us!"

Jess shakes her head miserably. "It's too pathetic. I'm too pathetic. I can't believe this."

"Oh, Jess, that really sucks. I'm sorry."

"You're too good for them anyway. Finance is for assholes."

Jess shakes her head and whimpers, "I can't believe this."

Lydia says, "Let's get you home."

In Jess's apartment Miky fills a water bottle, then sticks the straw in Jess's mouth. Lydia runs the shower on cold and makes Jess stick her head under it. They help her into a clean-ish T-shirt from a pile on the floor and then into bed. They lie on either side of her, and Lydia rubs Jess's back soothingly while Miky channels the Wine Girls, railing against the capitalist machine that has thrown Jess out in the cold.

Lydia says, "You didn't love your job anyway, right? Maybe this is a good thing."

"Yeah," Miky adds, "maybe you can just take some time off and travel or, I don't know, start a blog, like that girl who made three hundred sandwiches and got famous? It could be kind of awesome."

Jess scowls at them. "It's not *awesome*. I'm not going to fucking make lemons out of lemonade or whatever bumper sticker advice you're going to give me next. I was fired!"

"You can't take it personally," Lydia tells her. "I mean, it was probably just numbers. It sucks, it totally sucks, I'm not saying it doesn't, but Jess, you're awesome. It will be okay."

"It will, you're—"

"I fucked my boss!" Jess finally interrupts.

She can't take it anymore. She is pissed about being fired, furious even, but what's driven her to the edge is the thought that Josh knew it, knew that she was going to be fired, and pretended that he didn't.

"Your boss?" Lydia asks, surprised.

"Your boss?" Miky repeats, confused.

Jess nods miserably.

"The old guy? Gil What's-his-face? Jess, why!"

"Yeah, Jess, why!"

"Not him! Josh!"

"Oh." Lydia looks relieved. "That's good news then, right? You like him!"

"But he's my *boss*."

"But not really. I get that he hired you, but . . . you like him!"

"I like*d* him," Jess clarifies. "And I thought he liked me too. But now . . ." Jess presses the heels of her hands against her temples and makes a pathetic sound.

"Jess, what happened?"

She tells them. About the kiss and how he came over and how the next day at work he called her into his office just to tell her that he missed her. But also how he made it seem like she probably, most likely, wouldn't lose her job and then completely blew her off once she did.

"He tricked me!" she says. "He knew I would never speak to him again after he fired me, so he just . . . used me for sex. He had his chance and he took it, like a dirtbag *man*. And he didn't even have the balls to show up to the meeting when they fired me!" Jess's head is pounding and she feels like she might throw up, or cry, or both. She says, "My head hurts," and then curls into a ball and closes her eyes. She can't help it, she thinks of Ivan. How could she be so stupid? Why didn't she see this coming?

Lydia says, "Where do you keep your Advil?"

Without opening her eyes, Jess waves a hand toward the kitchen.

She hears Lydia get up, begin opening and closing cabinet doors. Next to her, Miky says, "Fuck that guy and fuck that job. You're better off without them."

From the kitchen, Lydia calls, "What are these?"

"What are what?" Jess asks into her pillow.

"These notes?"

"What notes?"

"By the sink. From Josh?"

Jess sits up, "What are you talking about?"

Still standing at the sink Lydia picks up a slip of paper and begins to read: "*Just Jess*"—she pauses—"is that what he calls you? Just Jess? Cute!" and then keeps reading: "*This isn't what it looks like: I tried to wake you up. But you sleep like you're dead. (Do you have a disorder? A reliable smoke detector?) I have meetings all day, but I'll see you in the afternoon. Can't wait.* Smiley face. Squiggle. *Josh.*" Lydia beams, "Jess, this is sweet. He's sweet!"

Miky shakes her head. "So fucking sweet."

"There's another one," Lydia says.

"What does it say?"

Lydia reads, "*Just Jess. You are so beautiful. See you at work.* Smiley face. Squiggle. *Josh.*"

She walks back to the bed and hands Jess the two notes and two Advil.

"Jess!" Lydia shakes her by the shoulders. "He's smitten! Do you really think he used you for sex?"

Jess doesn't reply.

"Come on, I don't think if he was a dirtbag who was just using you for random sex he would have written these," Lydia says gently. "I think it's just a shitty situation. It's terrible timing. But I think you should call him. Maybe this isn't all his fault, you know? Maybe there was nothing he could do. I think he cares about you, Jess."

"Well, I think," Jess says darkly, putting one pill on her tongue and then another, "that he's a giant prick."

The next day Josh calls and texts and calls and texts. Jess receives emails from him, and from HR, but she ignores them.

She's sure he has some excuse, but she doesn't want to hear it.

And she's sure as shit not interested in whatever parting words or waivers are coming from HR.

*   *   *

Jess mopes.

Her phone rings and rings—Miky and then Lydia and then a series of unknown numbers, which Jess assumes are Josh, or maybe it's just scammers hawking life insurance, trying to steal her social security number. She doesn't know and she doesn't care.

Her dad calls and she has the urge to answer. To let him cheer her up. To bask in the warmth of his abiding kindness.

But how would she explain her situation? *Hey, Dad, bad news: I got fired! But that's not totally surprising, because the CEO is a socio-path who fires people constantly. The surprising part? I slept with my boss after he promised he wouldn't fire me. But then he did anyway! Are you proud of me? Can I borrow some money?*

Jess is certain that even an abridged version would make him feel bad or sad, or disappointed.

When she was a little girl they used to play a game. It wasn't the safest—technically it was probably dangerous—but with her mother dead, there wasn't a woman around to tell him how to raise a child. Her dad would hang her upside down and hug her ankles, then spin her around in circles like a figure skater while she screamed with de-light. Almost daily, she begged him to play, until the day she thumped her head. They were too close to the doorway, or there was something off about the angle, or maybe she was in the middle of a growth spurt. Whatever it was, there was a crack—she heard it before she felt it— and then a big round knot began to form on her forehead. Her dad panicked. He reacted before she did. Cradling her head in his arms, pressing a frozen bag of peas against her forehead, apologizing pro-fusely.

She saw stars. She wanted to throw up. He wouldn't stop asking if she was okay. She could see her pain mirrored in his expression. Her lip quivered. His did too. She wanted to cry, but she could see that if she did, he would too. Her ears were ringing. But she swallowed her tears. Even worse than the throbbing in her head was seeing she could make her father this upset. She decided then that this was her least favorite feeling.

Jess puts her phone on silent. She opens the net worth app and stares at it bitterly, mourning the promise of so much money. She recalls what Josh said: if she did well, unlimited upside, and when she asked him what happened if she did poorly, he said *don't even think about it*. She's thinking about it now. She finally puts the phone down. It continues to light up and she grabs it, planning to turn it off completely when she sees the caller is Paul.

He calls again and again and Jess wonders if no one has ever heard of voice mail.

He finally texts, **Where are you?**

And Jess feels bad ignoring him, so she says: *at home.*

He writes back: **????????** to which Jess replies, *what? I feel shitty and depressed and I just want to be alone.*

But what about volleyball?

What about it?

You need to be here, approximately, now

Ugh, Paul, I can't, I feel like shit

You made a commitment darling

Are you serious? Are you really going to give me a hard time about this?

You're coming

I'm not

You have to

I can't

You don't mean that

I do

You have to come or you're a terrible person

At volleyball, the first thing Jess says to Paul is: "I don't want to talk about it."

He holds out his palms in a gesture of surrender, says, "I'm only here to play volleyball. I come in peace."

On the court Jess makes herself useless and eventually Paul says, "You have to admit though, that was a real deus ex machina." The ball sails past Jess's head, lands limply in the sand. Someone shouts, "Nice return, Six-Pack!"

Jess turns to Paul. "Stop distracting me."

He lobs the ball over the net to the opposing team's server. "All I'm saying," he says to Jess, "is that Josh didn't have to fall on his sword like that."

"Fall on his sword? Deus ex machina? Have you been getting into the medieval fantasy fiction again?" Jess swings wildly at the ball, but misses. Their right-side hitter lunges and makes the return. "Anyway," she says, wiping sweat from her face, "I wouldn't exactly call getting me fired falling on his sword. Unless I'm misunderstanding the metaphor."

Paul gives her a strange look.

Jess continues, "It just really, really sucks. Why does it have to be so fucking cutthroat. How could I let this happen? How could Josh? I am officially a person who gets fired. Someone who cannot thrive in capitalism."

Paul takes her by the arm and drags her off the court. He shouts, "Time out! Sorry!" and when people protest he just waggles a middle finger in their direction.

He looks at Jess gravely. "When was the last time you talked to Josh?"

"I *haven't* talked to Josh. He wasn't even fucking there when they fired me. Can you believe—"

Paul cuts her off. "Jess. Josh wasn't there because he was with Gil. Trying to persuade him not to fire you. This was upstairs so I didn't personally witness it, but I heard that Josh went absolutely batshit. Nuclear."

"That sounds crazy . . . no way."

"Jess. Yes, way. According to expert eyewitness testimony Josh found out they were going to fire you and he threw a hissy fit. This is common knowledge, Jess. He practically burned the office down. Everyone knows this," he pauses, "except for you, I guess."

"That sounds insane," Jess finally says.

"I agree. It is insane," Paul says, shaking his head. "His new fund is about to launch, he's Gil's golden boy. You're absolutely correct that it is an insane thing to do. No offense, but I personally wouldn't do it."

"Do what? I still don't even know exactly what you're trying to tell me!"

"I'm trying to tell you he threatened to quit."

"He threatened to quit?"

"He threatened to quit."

Jess considers this while Paul looks at her like she's just eaten a dirty shoe. "You need to talk to Josh," he says. "Now."

"But I mean," Jess says slowly, "why can't you just tell me? What happened?"

"What happened? Jess, he blew up every last shred of credibility he had with Gil, he went ballistic, exercised the nuclear option, all so that you could keep your job."

It finally sinks in.

And Jess says, "Keep my job?"

Part Three

14

J osh picks up on the first ring.
 He says, "Where have you been?"
Jess says, "We need to talk. What the fuck is going on?"
He says, "Do you really want to do this over the phone?"

The wait for the A train is excruciating, so Jess pushes back through the turnstile and hails a taxi. But traffic is at a standstill—it's a beautiful day—and so eight blocks from Josh's apartment she gets out and runs.

He buzzes her into the building and she runs up all five flights. When she gets to the top she is breathless and sweaty.

Josh also looks a little wild. His hair is uncombed and he isn't wearing shoes or socks. His button-down is wrinkled, his sleeves pushed all the way up.

They both wait for the other to speak. It is maybe four seconds, but it feels like an eternity. He looks irritated, which irritates Jess. They both can't be irritated. Why would he be irritated? There's no way what Paul told her is true. Paul had also told her, a few days ago, that a banana was a berry. He swore he wasn't joking, but Jess had forgotten to look it up. It didn't seem true. So maybe it wasn't true about Josh either. But Paul wouldn't joke about this. He wasn't a monster. Though maybe he wasn't joking. Maybe he had just gotten the details wrong. He said it himself, he hadn't been upstairs. And, even if it were true, being unfired is not much better than being fired. She was still fired. Fired! It was humiliating. Josh hadn't even been in the room.

She can't think straight. Josh is standing there, not saying anything. Not apologizing. Not explaining. Definitely not telling her that he saved her job. Just looking at her. As if she's the one who fucked up. She feels dizzy, disoriented. Her head is pounding and there's a feeling unspooling inside of her, a feeling specific to Josh, like her thoughts are being filtered through a hazy glass, like she can't trust herself completely. And then she is shouting.

"Tell me what's going on, Josh!"

"Why haven't you returned my phone calls?" he shouts back.

"How could you do this to me? Do you know how humiliating that was! You didn't even show your face! Where were you? They fired me!" Jess was at a seven, maybe, when she arrived, but now she's at an eleven and it's official, things have Escalated; they are Having a Fight.

"I was with Gil! Jess, listen to me, I was trying to—"

"This is just like at Goldman. With LyfeCo.! You're so fucking ruthless! The only person you care about is you! You said they wouldn't fire me! I believed you, Josh! We had sex!" This last word Jess screeches. They realize the front door has not been shut. A neighbor shuffling by, with two bags of groceries, looks up.

Josh kicks the door closed. It bangs. He folds his arms across his chest. "So, what," he says flatly, "you thought you would sleep with me and keep your job?"

"Are you kidding me?"

"Are *you* kidding *me*?"

They stand in his living room, glowering.

Finally, Jess says, "You're the one who fucked me right before I got fired, probably because you knew I would never speak to you again after pulling this shit. I was fired because I didn't fit in! How can that possibly be a thing? You used me, Josh."

"I used you? Way to turn this around! You just said that you were surprised you lost your job in the same sentence that you said we had sex. As if they're related. You said that."

"That's not what I meant! I wasn't thinking about . . . I wasn't thinking about that at all!"

"What then, Jess? What were you thinking about? You were thinking about all the ways you could save your job. Which, by the way, worked. Congratulations, you're welcome."

"No," she says, shaking her head quickly. "That's not it. I was thinking about . . ." She swallows. "I was thinking about how much I liked you."

His face falls. "Jess," he says quietly, "I'm sorry. I'm so sorry." He sits on the couch, rubs his head in his hands. "Fuck." He shakes his head, groaning. "Jess, I'm so sorry."

"I know." She takes a breath. "I know. I know. I'm just . . . upset."

"I swear, Jess," he looks up at her, pleading, "I didn't know until that morning. And then I did everything I could. It was almost impossible to get Gil in a room. I—"

"Did you really threaten to quit if Gil fired me?" she interrupts.

"Who told you that?"

"Paul. But he says everyone knows."

"Yeah, I did." He pauses, then bites back a smile. "I told him that his head was so far up his ass that maybe it was time for me to start thinking about my options. To go work for someone whose head wasn't so far up his ass."

"You told Gil his head was up his ass? Twice?" She is so mad, but she can't help it—she also smiles. "You really said that?"

Josh nods. "He said I was an ungrateful little shit."

"How did you know he would let me stay?"

"I didn't!"

"So, what, if he hadn't changed his mind you would have just . . . walked?"

"Of course. A threat is just a bluff unless you can back it up."

"Why would you do that?" She is standing over him, looking down. She sits. Looks at him. Waits.

"Jess," he says, "come on."

"Come on what."

He elbows her lightly. "You know why."

"No, why?" she asks, genuinely perplexed.

"Because . . . I love you."

Her heart pounds. "I thought maybe that was just a line."

"A line? Jess, are you out of your mind?"

Honestly, Jess thinks she might be.

He says, "Jess, I love you."

"You keep saying that."

"It bothers you."

"It doesn't bother me. I just don't believe you."

"Why not?"

"We just started . . . hooking up. You don't even know if you like me. What if I turn out to be a crazy bitch who, like, texts you twenty-seven times before you text me back. Or gets mad if you pee standing up. Or makes you hold my purse at concerts."

"I would still love you."

"Shut up."

"Jess, I see you every day. We've been friends for, what, two, three years? Enemies for a year before that?" He flicks her arm, grins, and says, "I know you, Jess. I like you. I love you."

"Okay, now you're just fishing."

"I don't need you to tell me you love me," Josh replies casually.

"What! Why not!" Jess is mock-offended. "Every man needs the love of a good woman. You don't want me to love you?"

"But you do."

"Oh, do I?"

He grabs her wrist, rests his thumb against the inside joint. He says, "Your heart rate is elevated"—he peers into her eyes—"and your pupils are dilated. And right now, look, you're mirroring my body language almost perfectly. It's just . . . completely obvious."

He kisses her fingertips before letting her hand go and Jess feels herself loosening.

"Wow, okay, thank you, Bill Nye, that was super romantic."

"Anyway," he says seriously, "what other word could possibly describe this?"

Jess swoons.

She scoots closer. "So if Gil hadn't caved, you would have given up your job? For real? Just like that? Even though it's everything you ever wanted?"

He nods. He takes her hand, rubs the pad of his thumb on the soft part of her wrist, the most vulnerable part. "The thing is, Jess," he says, "now I also want you."

Summer in New York. Butterfly weed, spiky and orange, blooms in Central Park. Cafés all over the city roll out their awnings and start serving cocktails on the sidewalk. Suddenly, baby socks dot the sidewalks, like Easter eggs, delicate and forgotten and pastel-colored.

They kiss on street corners and hold hands in museums and on the East Side ferry Jess makes Josh wrap his arms around her while river water sprays in her face and she shouts, "I'm king of the world."

They go to the orchid show at the botanical garden and Josh says, "Did you know that *orchidaceae* don't have an endosperm and so even the non-parasitic variety live in symbiosis during germination?"

In Brooklyn one Saturday they encounter a massive line snaking around a low cement warehouse and Jess proposes they wait on it.

"You just want to wait in a line? You have no idea what it's for?"

Jess thinks about it. "Yes?"

So they wait, and when they reach the front they are told they will each be permitted to purchase a maximum of six cans of a limited edition dry hopped triple IPA, a collaboration between two local microbreweries, which is, apparently, special enough that two hundred people have waited one hour to buy it. They get twelve cans then sit on a bench on the promenade sipping their beer.

After half a pale ale, Jess is tipsy. She says, "You make me so happy."

Josh says, "Happiness cannot come from without. It must come from within," and when Jess rolls her eyes he smiles and adds, "But, for what it's worth, you make me really happy too."

On Ninth Avenue they hold hands as they walk. Jess tells Josh, "My friend Miky? Her boyfriend? He always walks between her and the street, so he can protect her from, you know, oncoming traffic and, like, sewer rats."

Josh says, "Oh?" and starts to walk around to her other side.

But she grabs his arm and says, "Wait."

He stops. The sun is hot on the pavement and the sky is a bright aventurine blue. Girls in sundresses and open fire hydrants spraying water into the street. It's not quite a heat wave, but nearly. Air-conditioning units installed hastily in windows blowing cold air into stuffy apartments.

Jess looks up, eyeing a brick wall full of windows. "Actually? I feel like I'm always hearing about poorly installed AC units, you know"—she makes a splat gesture with her palms—"so maybe you should stay where you are."

"So you want an air conditioner to fall on my head?"

"When you say it like that it sounds really bad."

He walks back over to Jess's right shoulder, stands under a dripping air conditioner, says, "Who said chivalry was dead?"

•

Without a job or any serious prospects, Jess should be anxious or upset, but she is none of those things: She's in love. Nearing insolvency, but in love.

Jess has never considered herself especially proud, at least when it comes to her finances. She has no problem stooping down on street corners to pick up pennies, even though the Wine Girls are pretty sure that's how you got hepatitis. And she carefully tears coupons from the back of the Duane Reade circulars she finds folded into the Sunday paper, even though Josh never doesn't make the point that she is being irrational and that because of the time value of money it costs her more to use a coupon than to not—though now that she's unemployed, her time isn't all that valuable anyway.

She had fully intended to take her job at Gil's back. Decided that she definitely wasn't the kind of person who could take a year off to travel or to "figure it out" or write a blog about sandwiches. She was the kind of person who needed money, a salary, credibility.

She had gone back into the office to fill out some paperwork. When she walked across the floor it felt like everyone was looking at her, but then, it always felt like that. She met a lawyer in a conference room. He slid a stack of papers across the table.

She had every intention of keeping her job, despite the fine print. *Demotion . . . probation . . . qualified compensation . . .*

There was a line for her to sign on. They were waiting.

She fully intended to sign. But then. She frowned at the contract. She looked up at the lawyer, then back down at the document. Her name was spelled wrong. *Jerica* instead of Jessica. Something about it seemed vaguely racist. Insulting. She mentioned the error.

The lawyer just shrugged. "No problem," he told her. "Just cross it out, initial and sign."

He looked bored and his hair was slicked back.

Jess had the distinct thought, *What the fuck am I doing?* Swallowing a little pride for a paycheck was one thing, but abandoning all self-respect was another thing completely.

So she had walked.

And then told Josh. "Are you mad?"

He looked mad. His jaw was clenched so tightly it was almost vibrating. If she pressed the tip of her finger to his chin, it seemed as if it would shatter like glass.

But he just said, "I understand why you wouldn't accept the offer."

Jess felt terrible. "I'm sorry."

He repeated tonelessly, "I understand why you wouldn't accept the offer."

He was so mad!

But they never talked about it again. Why would they when they were in love?

Jess feels like she's living on a cloud or in a dream or in an old country love song, all sunshine and whiskey, butterflies and pretty brown eyes.

With a straight face, Jess attempts to explain this to Miky and Lydia when they stage an intervention.

They don't call before they arrive, just show up at her door, and shout into the intercom, "Remember us?"

"Where the fuck have you been?" Miky asks.

"Yeah," Lydia says, her hand on her hip. "Do you really want to be *that* girl?"

"What girl?"

"The girl who forgets all about her friends the minute she meets a magical penis."

"That's not true!"

"Okay, so where have you been?"

"I've been super busy," Jess says.

"With what exactly?"

"Why did you say it like that?"

Miky and Lydia exchange glances.

"What?" Jess asks, and when neither of them responds she huffs, "*What?*"

"That's the thing, Jess. We're happy for you that you have this new boyfriend. But isn't he also kind of the reason you don't have a job?"

Jess is still looking, though she doesn't have many leads. She tells them the same thing she told her dad the last time they spoke: "Everything's fine. Everything's under control."

"Really?"

"Yes! I even have an interview next week. For a sales role."

"*Sales*, Jess?"

"You work in sales!"

"I'm an art consultant," Lydia clarifies. "But Jess, this isn't about me. I *like* my job. We're just worried that you might be getting distracted. Like, Josh is great, I get it, but are you sure you're thinking straight?"

"I love him," Jess offers lamely.

"We know. We get it. We're happy for you. But . . ."

"Is this what you really want, Jess? To be unemployed and sleeping with your ex-boss?"

"You guys are being really mean."

"This hurts us more than it hurts you."

Lydia pats her shoulder reassuringly. "Yeah, Jess, sorry, but, you know, tough love."

"Not," Miky adds, raising an eyebrow, "to be confused with the hot, sweaty love that you've become accustomed to."

It's true though, Jess still very much doesn't have a job. Which was fine for a month, two months, even three—she was somewhat responsible, she had savings—but now she's running out of money. The cascade of bills—not to mention the taxis and the truffle burgers—are catching up to her. She'd almost forgotten what it's like to be broke: always checking the prices of things, paying late fines and overdraft fees, her debits and credits never quite where they should be. It had seemed cold-blooded to be let go right before the fund paid bonuses, but now, staring down the barrel of rent, student loan payments and credit card bills, it seems positively criminal. Jess has approximately one more month before she's going to have to start selling her things on Craigslist.

She contemplates panicking, but instead she goes online.

On the internet she looks at videos of cats and dogs and babies. She reads long-form articles about the earthquake that will destroy California, about the Ebola epidemic, about the rise of the Islamic State and the Brooklyn blogger mommy and designer clogs and cupcakes and the price of private kindergarten.

She reads about the shooting death of Eric Garner, another Black man murdered by the cops, and the rise of Black Lives Matter and her heart starts to race and she has to close the laptop.

When she opens it again, she searches for pictures of fire hydrants that look like people, she searches "should I go to grad school," "new freckles on the top of my feet dangerous," "new boyfriend how to keep." She searches "best place to buy a mini donut in New York City."

She looks at Instagram photos of friends and friends of friends and famous people at restaurants, on beaches, in bikinis, standing next to tall glasses of home-blended juices, posing in fields of wildflowers.

She looks at LinkedIn, all those résumés, perfectly curated and compressed, one perfect job after another, one beautiful degree after another, all the enthusiastic recommendations: *top ten percent of people I have ever worked with! Expert at financial analysis!*

She finds Charles. He no longer works at Goldman Sachs. He has moved on to a boutique firm controlled by a French and British banking family and has been promoted to vice president.

She sends him a message.

She writes, *Hi! I hope this email finds you well!*

He answers within an hour and sees right through her, replies: *Jones, do you need a job?*

Jess's dad calls, just to check in.

She doesn't tell him anything, because where to begin?

He says, "How is life treating you?"

"Great!" she says, pathologically. "Everything's fine!"

•

In bed, over the weekend, Jess says to Josh, "How about some pillow talk?"

Josh, with bedhead, in his underwear, says, "What?"

Jess says, "You know, like after we . . . do it. Wouldn't it be nice to, I don't know, talk? Whisper sweet nothings and private confessions. Share our hopes and dreams and fears. Isn't that what couples are supposed to do? I feel like every time we finish having sex—"

"We just have sex again?"

Jess laughs. She pats the pillow. "Pillow talk. Let's go."

Josh says, "Okay."

Neither of them says anything.

"Well," Jess finally says, "do you have any confessions?"

"This was your idea."

Jess turns around and unplugs her phone, lifts it from the windowsill where it is charging behind the bed. She says, "Okay, here we go."

She navigates to the Wikipedia entry for pillow talk and reads:

"Pillow talk is the relaxed, intimate conversation that often occurs

between two sexual partners, sometimes after sexual activity, usually accompanied by cuddling, caresses, kissing . . . hormone known as oxytocin . . . partners who orgasm are more likely to engage in the act of pillow talk versus partners who do not—"

Josh interrupts, "So I guess based on last night you should pillow talk three times."

Jess says, "Funny." She googles "pillow talk topics of conversation," and then announces, "Found something. Are you ready to take our relationship to a whole new level of intimacy?"

Josh says, "You know, some would argue that being in bed on your phone is the opposite of intimacy."

"Those people are old." Jess waves her phone at him. "Are you ready? 'Questions to ask to fall deeper in love.' First question: If you had a crystal ball that could tell you anything about your life or the future, what would you use it to predict?"

Immediately, Josh says, "The forex spot rate."

"This isn't word association. You don't have to answer so fast. *Think* about it."

Josh says, "Hmm, okay," and turns onto his back, rests his palm behind his head and looks up at the ceiling, thinking, and then finally pronounces, "My answer is unchanged."

Jess reads each of the questions aloud and they alternate responses.

She tells him that she regards the lowest depth of misery as being betrayed by someone you trust and in a close second place, having your face eaten by rats, which makes Josh smile and say, "How Orwellian."

He tells her that the person he admires most is Gil.

Jess says, "Really? Why?"

"He manufactured his own success out of essentially nothing. He started with nothing and built one of the most successful funds on the planet. How can you not admire that?"

Jess raises an eyebrow. "Nothing?" Jess recalls the Harvard pennant, hanging above Gil's desk.

"You know what I mean," Josh says, and even though Jess doesn't she lets it slide.

When Jess says that the one thing she would change about herself is that she wishes she liked Beyoncé more, Josh laughs. "That is not a real answer," he says.

"It is!" Jess insists. "Do you know what a big deal that is? For me to not get Beyoncé? She's everything. She's the most influential Black feminist on the planet. Not liking Beyoncé makes me feel like, I don't know, I'm missing out on some crucial component of Black womanhood. Like I'm a fraud or something."

Josh is still laughing. "Come on, Jess, you don't really believe that, do you? We're not talking about, I don't know, Malcolm X here, or even Malcolm Gladwell. She's a pop star! So you don't get excited about lowest common denominator pop culture. Why is that a bad thing?"

Jess is aghast. "Did you just call Queen Bey lowest common denominator?"

"You just said you don't like her!"

"Right, I don't love her music and I don't fully get the hype, I mean, like, emotionally, but *intellectually* I totally get that she's, you know, one of the most important artists of the twenty-first century, and definitely one of the most important voices in contemporary Black culture." She eyes him. "I hope you don't make statements like that in public, by the way."

"Jess, I think it's okay that you don't like Beyoncé. You don't have to like Beyoncé just because you're Black. She's got a decent voice, a good body, and a great publicist, and that's all."

"You sound like a horrible person right now." Jess is joking, but she also sort of isn't.

He puts up his hands in mock protest. "Hey, I'm not the one who hates Beyoncé."

"Ha, ha. Very funny," Jess says. "Okay, next one." Jess stares at her phone, taps the screen twice with a finger and then finally says, "Who was your first kiss?"

"That's not on the list." Josh leans over her shoulder to look at her phone.

She tilts it toward him. "Yes, it is. See?"

He squints at the phone. "Jess, that's a different list. That's *Man Repeller*, 'Ten cute questions to ask on a first date.' "

"Don't worry about it," she says, holding the phone protectively to her chest. "Just answer the question."

"Okay," he laughs. "It was freshman year of high school. A girl in my class."

"Was she cute?"

"Um . . . yeah."

"Where is she now?"

He shrugs. "Not sure. Lost to the annals of time. Or I don't know, in law school, maybe?"

"Wait," Jess says, sitting up. "Was it that girl?" She remembers his yearbook. The long letter. The words *xo forever*.

"What girl?" Josh asks.

"You know. *Tenley*." Jess says it self-consciously, like it's a word in a foreign language she's not quite sure how to pronounce.

"Where'd you come up with that?" He seems flustered, laughs uneasily.

It was a joke, Jess thought, but maybe not.

"Wait, was it?" Jess leans forward. She angles her torso so they're eye to eye.

"Who cares?"

"Was she your first love?"

"Ha!" He laughs again, but this time his discomfort seems real.

"I notice you're not answering the question." Jess peers at him.

"Because it was nobody. It was nothing. I was fourteen."

Jess says, "I see." And then quickly as if to catch him off guard: "What was her name?"

"Lindsey."

"Oh." Jess sits back, not completely satisfied. "Well."

"Sorry, Sherlock, case closed." Josh pinches her cheek playfully. "What about you?"

"It was nothing special. In college. Just some guy in the basement of a disgusting frat house."

Josh says, "Tawdry."

This makes her laugh. "Where were you, then? Under the eaves of some stately boarding school residence hall with the string section of the New York Philharmonic playing gently in the background."

He laughs. "No, it was here, actually. In the city, I mean. At David's."

Jess turns. "You've never kissed *me* at David's."

He looks at her with a serious expression on his face, an expression grave like life and death or war and peace.

He finally says, "I will"—he looks her in the eye—"I'll kiss you everywhere."

According to Miky, a great way to get STDs is by kissing on the subway. Nevertheless, Jess is doing exactly that, her tongue down Josh's throat, legs crossed over his lap, spread across three seats, as if they were alone. Which mostly they are. Riding an otherwise empty subway car from Josh's office on Seventh Ave to the World Trade Center, for a cocktail thing at one of the corporate restaurants downtown.

At West Fourth Street, the train rattles to a stop and a group of college-age students get on. One of them is carrying a pair of portable, all-weather speakers—bright orange, rubber—playing a song with a G-Funk bassline that Jess doesn't recognize. A girl with a piercing in her septum wears a T-shirt with a Black Power fist. They're all Black and Jess can equally imagine them on the cover of a college catalog, the picture of bright-eyed diversity, or in an advertisement for something cool, like limited edition sneakers or designer sunglasses or a hip-hop album.

Jess makes eye contact with the girl with the Black Power fist and the septum piercing. A look passes between them. But what is it? Jess can't quite place it. Recognition? Judgment? She feels vaguely that she should be setting a better example. Suddenly, she's self-conscious. Her hair pin-straight—they're on their way to a reception—Josh in a cable knit sweater the color of a macaron.

She swings her legs off his lap, takes her feet off the seat, places them on the floor. For reasons she can't articulate, she puts additional distance between them, sliding to the middle of her seat, folding her arms across her chest. Just two people sitting on the train in adjacent seats.

She feels bad, and she looks over at Josh, intending to issue a silent apology, but he just smiles back, none the wiser. At first Jess is surprised, and then relieved, and then annoyed, but eventually decides it's fine.

15

Jess finds what she thinks might be her dream job. An award-winning nonprofit news-magazine is launching a data-driven beat focused on race and politics and the economy and, according to a giant banner on their homepage, they're hiring like crazy. Jess is inspired.

"But there's good news and bad news," she tells Paul over brunch.

"What's the bad news?" he asks. "And what's the job?"

"I'm not qualified. Like, at all."

"Sounds promising. What's the job?"

She shakes her head, makes him wait. "First, ask me about the good news."

"What's the good news?"

"You're going to help me." She shoves her index finger into his shoulder, just to drive the point home.

"Am I? How?"

She opens the website on her phone and holds it up. A logo shaped like a fist above a slogan that says *We the People*. Provocative headlines about campaign finance, mass incarceration and the mysterious disappearance of Malaysia Flight 370.

There are links to a code of ethics and something called *The Nerd Blog*; instructions for how to send anonymous tips via their encrypted server and a mission statement in bold letters at the bottom: Advancing democracy through deeply researched and reported investigative journalism, powered by people, and by data.

"This is where I want to work."

He says, "Aha."

There are fifty employees, each with a photo and a profile, under a header that reads OUR STAFF, and Jess knows exactly one of them: Dax, Paul's boyfriend.

"I was wondering if maybe you could ask him about it. Help me get the inside track?"

"Of course," Paul says as he stirs his coffee. "He just started. But I'll ask. No problem."

The waiter takes their orders and Jess asks for avocado toast.

"What about the pay?" She looks at Paul. "Do you happen to know anything about that?"

She has been out of a job for five months and her very responsible rainy-day savings fund is about to run out. She should be eating ramen and looking for roommates, but instead she is having brunch. And ignoring the notifications from the net worth app that keep reminding her she's going broke. A chart on the app's homepage shows the trajectory of her net worth—money versus time—and instead of an arrow, up and to the right, it looks like a lopsided parabola, rising slowly and then falling fast. It feels like it's only a matter of time before the line dips below zero and the app starts serving her ads for casino openings and debt consolidation services.

"I'll ask Dax," Paul says, shaking his head, "but it's a news media nonprofit. So I'm pretty sure the pay is shit."

Jess wonders exactly how shit. They aren't that close, but Dax doesn't seem especially broke. Whenever Jess sees him he's wearing really nice clothes. If the pay were that bad, would he have Burberry sneakers? Jess thinks this must be one of life's great mysteries: how people afford things. But the bigger problem is that Jess isn't qualified for any of the openings. She scrolls through their jobs site looking for anything she could plausibly apply for. But she's not a reporter, she doesn't have a law degree, or a background in political economy, or even experience making photocopies. She doesn't have a degree in statistics or engineering or computer science, which is listed as a requirement for their data science team. But she ignores the requirements and holds her breath and applies. For relevant experience, she mentions the feminist magazine and tries not to think about the fact that it's taken her three years to come back to where she started.

And then at volleyball she pesters Dax for a referral.

"I thought you worked in finance."

"It's the same thing."

"Is it?"

"I was in trading. I can definitely wrangle the data and make all the complicated charts. It's, like, basically the same thing."

He looks skeptical. "I'm still pretty new myself," he says noncommittally.

Jess says, "I'm a go-getter. I'm dependable and action oriented. I have leadership skills. I'm proficient in French."

"You speak French?"

"I'm conversant in French."

"*Avez-vous étudié à l'étranger?*"

"Okay, I took French for a semester in college, but the rest of it is true!"

Jess desperately wants this. She can already imagine herself in a noisy newsroom, with a pencil tucked behind her ear, defender of democracy.

"Okay, okay," he relents. "Send me your résumé."

Instead of an interview, they give her a take-home test. They send Jess a million rows of government data and ask her to come up with a headline and craft a narrative, using only charts and graphs. They say: *the best visualizations create a synesthesia-like bridge between intuition and information.*

They give her three days to complete the exercise, and it takes her three days and an hour. She stays up all night working, it's like calisthenics for her brain—it's a little bit thrilling to use her powers for good—and when she is done with the analysis she sends back a headline that reads *It's Time to Talk About the Gender Pain Gap*, along with a series of interactive graphics that model the economic impact of excluding women from clinical research trials.

The email has barely left her out-box when a response flies back: We want you to come in and meet the team. We love your point of view.

Jess loves that they love her point of view. It is the first time she is buoyed by the thought of work in a long while. She is ready to wash the stink of finance off her.

When she goes into the office, everyone she meets has cool glasses and visible tattoos and they all have degrees in ethnic studies and investigative journalism and interned at places like The Hague and the ACLU.

She interviews with the editor of the policy and economics section and instead of asking Jess questions they talk about why the Supreme Court's recent Hobby Lobby decision was fucked up.

A few days later they make her a formal offer, and the pay is so incredibly, impossibly, unbelievably low that Jess actually cries.

Jess tells Josh about the data journalism job and he just kind of shrugs.

"What," Jess asks, "you don't think it would be a really cool job?"

They are eating dinner at a sushi bar, where they watch chefs press fish into rice and then place the nigiri directly on their plates.

"I thought you were waiting to hear back from some buy-side jobs?"

"I don't know," Jess sighs. "I'm not sure I want to do another grind-'em-up, spit-'em-out cogs-in-the-capitalist-apparatus thing. Maybe I want to work for, you know . . . a cause."

"A cause?"

"Yes," she says. "A cause."

As the chef slides a plate of tuna between them Josh says, "Jess, it's a magazine."

She can't imagine what he would think of the feminist magazine. Jess had played up her internship there during the interview and they had been impressed. Her byline had appeared on a single blog post the entire summer she was there, but it was a good one and had lent her significant credibility. The headline in its entirety had read: *End Fraternities.*

She says, "It's an award-winning investigative news-magazine."

He says, "Oh-kay."

She narrows her eyes.

"Okay, fine," he says, sighing.

He tells her that not only does he not think it's a cause, but he thinks it's barely a credible news source. And Jess is surprised he has such a strong opinion—he calls it radical and riddled with bias—surprised that he's even read their stuff.

She says, "Well, who died and made you the king of objectivity?"

"Jess, come on, I don't want to fight. You asked me what I thought."

Jess sighs into her plate. "Well, it doesn't matter anyway, because I can't afford to take the job."

He puts down his chopsticks and touches her arm. "You have a bulletproof résumé. I'm one hundred percent certain you'll find something way better in no time."

"Better than advancing democracy via the free press?"

"Right," he says, laughing. "Saving the Republic one tweet at a time."

He doesn't mean to be an asshole; he thinks she's joking but she's not. Still, it pisses her off. A waiter slides the check across the bar and Josh picks it up wordlessly, which twists the knife. He's started paying for everything, no questions asked, which is a relief, but also sort of humiliating.

Jess says, "You know what, Josh?"

"What?" He looks at her, oblivious, rice stuffed between his cheeks.

"Sometimes you make me really, really, really mad."

But other than that, he is perfect, they are perfect, she has never been more in love, everything's totally fine.

•

Josh is moving and his apartment is a mess, with bubble-wrapped furniture and boxes everywhere, so he spends the weekend with Jess. They lie under Jess's sheets watching recommended videos on her laptop and having lots of sex. They only leave the apartment once, for a late-night reservation at a secret bar, where they order craft cocktails and get giggly drunk.

On Sunday, to show him how much she cares, Jess makes Josh breakfast in bed, which is actually just bagels, cut unevenly with a dull knife and spread with chive cream cheese straight from the tub.

He says, "Aw, honey," but then: "Let me show you how it's done."

Apparently, Josh knows how to cook.

That afternoon, he goes to the organic grocery and buys pasta and long candles and wine.

They listen to a neo-soul album that always makes Jess want to take off her clothes, and they eat linguine and drink Sancerre, with the candles lit.

For dessert, Josh slices bright red strawberries and hand-whips a bowl of cream.

Jess bites a berry from its stem and says, "Wow, these are really good."

"I know," he says, pulling spoons from the drawer. "Elizabeth got them from Westchester. You know Stew Leonard's? In Yonkers?"

They demolish all the strawberries and then Josh looks at Jess licking whipped cream off her lips and then they are kissing and they are naked and Josh swipes a finger through the bowl and holds it up.

Jess takes a step back and says, "Don't."

"Don't what?" he asks.

She makes a circle with her palm, gesturing between her legs. "Don't put whipped cream in my you-know-what."

"Your you-know-what?" He laughs. "Jess, I'm trying to have sex with you, not give you a weird infection." He steps toward her. "I was thinking something more like this."

He runs his finger over her nipple and then pulls her by the small of her back into him and slowly licks her breast.

The whipped cream feels cool on her skin and his tongue feels hot. His tongue travels lower and lower along her rib cage and down her stomach, until his mouth is between her legs.

It feels so good, his mouth and her desire and she is so, so wet.

Her chest tightens and she is breathless, her entire body feels enflamed.

Everything is spinning, her vision is blurring and her legs shake.

She wants to whisper filthy things to him, but the words get caught in her throat.

She feels herself slipping and reaches for the table, toppling the bowl of whipped cream, which falls to the floor with a clatter.

Kneeling in front of her, Josh looks up. "What happened? Are you okay?"

She tries to say "yes" but it comes out more like a growl.

"Jess," he says, standing. "Are you okay?"

She says, "My . . . throat . . ."

He touches her lips and says, "Oh shit, oh shit," and everything is hazy and Jess wonders what's wrong, until she touches her face and, oh shit, it is so, so swollen.

"You need to get to a hospital." He is frantic. "Jess, hurry up, put on your clothes."

He has already pulled his jeans on over his erection. Jess paws around the floor for her underwear, and he shouts, "Jess, come on. We don't have time!"

On the street he flags down a cab and then bundles her into the back seat and she whimpers. Her throat is on fire, her head is throbbing and she's scared. She wonders if this is it, if she's going to die.

Josh holds her close and says, "It's okay, it's okay, it's okay."

And then he shouts at the driver that he would be insane to make a left turn at this hour.

The emergency room, just before midnight, is a shit show. People on gurneys, doctors running, Jess thinks she sees actual blood on the floor. A nurse in scrubs walks by and Josh shouts to get her attention. She indicates that they should stand in the intake line, but Josh pushes to the front and the woman manning the desk says, chiding, "Sir," but he ignores her and says, "She needs attention *now*," and the woman looks at Jess and frowns, but says anyway, "Please, sir, we'll be with you in just a moment. You can have a seat right there."

"This is bullshit," Josh says as he drags Jess away.

She slumps in a seat while he chews his fingernails.

He stands suddenly and says, "I'm calling Gil."

Gil? Jess wonders, and as if reading her thoughts, Josh says, "He gives a ton of money to Langone. This"—he waves a frustrated hand around the waiting room—"is not okay."

Josh's phone is at his ear and he's pacing angrily. Jess closes her eyes and hears him say, "Pick up, pick up, pick up."

"Gil!" Josh says, when he comes on the line.

Jess hears pieces of the conversation as Josh stomps back and forth. "My friend . . . Tisch . . . help . . . okay, okay, okay . . . thank you . . . no, yeah, my friend."

Even in her diminished state, that word rattles around in Jess's head: *Friend?*

Josh puts his phone in his pocket and says, "Jess, come on, we're leaving."

She starts to protest but he grabs her. "Come on, Jess, just next door."

He leads her back out through the big revolving door and pulls her, like a rag doll, across the street. She is feeling woozy and unsteady and her vision is getting worse.

He yanks her arm. "Come on, Jess, hurry up," and then when she barely cooperates he turns to her and says, "Jesus, Jess, your face! Can you even see?"

He looks so terrified that Jess begins to cry. The tears pool in her eyes and it stings it stings it stings.

He says, "Oh, Jess," and then sweeps her into his arms.

He carries her into the building like she is an injured war vet. She rests her head on his shoulder and closes her eyes, though maybe, she can't tell, they are swollen shut.

Everything is blurry and Josh is shouting a lot and then she is laid on a hospital bed. A doctor materializes and starts speaking to Josh.

Josh says, "We had linguine with clams. I think she's allergic to shellfish."

Through what's left of her vision Jess sees the doctor prep a long needle and flick it with a finger. He says to Josh, "Was this the first time?"

Josh says, "Yes."

In bed, Jess croaks, "No."

They both look down.

"Strawberries," Jess rasps, "I'm allergic. I get hives."

Josh says, "You do?"

"Yes." Her voice is garbled, and her vision is almost gone. "It's the strawberries. I have an allergy."

"You're kidding," Josh looks at her, bewildered.

She feels the needle go in and then she is out.

When Jess blinks awake the room is dark. Josh is sitting in a chair next to the bed, his head down, face illuminated by his phone.

"Josh," she says, hoarse, and he looks up.

He takes her hand in his and smiles. "Hey, sleeping beauty."

Jess feels like she's been hit by a truck. "How long was I asleep?"

"About half an hour? The doctor gave you a mild sedative in addition to the epinephrine."

"I feel like garbage," Jess says.

"Well, you look amazing."

"Are you joking?" Jess asks.

He shakes his head. "Your hair," he says, "it's kind of a mess. You look like you've just been ravaged."

She touches her face. "Am I still swollen?"

"No"—he shakes his head again—"your lips are a bit . . . but it's sexy."

Jess starts crying.

"Hey," Josh pats her hand, "everything's fine."

But she shakes her head and keeps crying.

"Really, Jess. The doctor said you would be fine. They'll give you an EpiPen to take home in case it happens again. Though obviously you can't ever eat strawberries again."

"It's not that," Jess says, wiping her eyes.

"Then what?"

"I can't pay for any of this. The hospital bill. I don't have insurance."

"You don't?"

"I don't have a job," Jess reminds him. "My insurance lapsed."

"I thought your dad worked at a university. Why aren't you on his plan?"

Quietly Jess says, "I haven't told him I lost my job."

"Oh, Jess," Josh says, squeezing her hand. "It'll be fine. We'll work it out. It'll be, what? A few grand? It'll be fine."

"I don't have a few grand," Jess sniffles into her lap. "I don't have any money. I'm basically broke. And if you ask me why I'm broke I'm going to strangle you." The Wine Girls hadn't seemed to comprehend that Jess could no longer afford things; at a recent dinner they wanted to split a hundred-dollar truffle burger and when Jess claimed that she didn't have the money, they asked what happened to all her hedge fund plunder and Jess had to explain that they stopped giving it to you when you stopped working for them. "Next month I don't know how I'm going to pay my rent or my student loans . . . I . . . I'm unemployed and have no money and I'm allergic to strawberries and my judgment is terrible, which is why I'm in this mess."

"Poor Jess," Josh says, stroking her face.

He climbs into the hospital bed and spoons her on top of the sheets. He rubs her shoulders and nuzzles her neck. He is, as ever, so solid, so warm. He kisses her face and she closes her eyes and it is quiet except for the sounds of the hospital.

Eventually he says, "I have an idea."

"What?"

"You could move in with me."

Jess rolls over onto her other side. "Wait . . . really?" she asks when they are face-to-face.

"You wouldn't have to pay rent," he says, his hand in her hair.

"But you haven't even really moved in yet. Don't you want to, I don't know, like, be a bachelor in his new bachelor pad for a while? You're this young guy. Why would you want some girl around all the time interfering?"

"Interfering?"

"Like, I don't know, always leaving bras and lipstick around the house."

"That sounds pretty great."

"We just started dating."

"It's been six months."

"I just . . . I don't know. Is it prudent?"

He laughs. " 'Is it prudent?' asks my broke, uninsured girlfriend."

"Hey," Jess warns.

"Sorry." He brushes his fingers across the side of her face. "I didn't mean that."

"But you did," Jess says. "I mean . . . you're right. I'm a liability. What if it takes me a really long time to find a job I can actually afford to take? What if I don't have any money for a while?"

"I have enough for the both of us. It's fine."

Jess sighs. "I guess I just really, really wanted that news-magazine job."

"Then why don't you take it?"

"I thought you said it wasn't a credible news source and that their reporting was super biased."

"Jess, don't listen to me. If you want the job, you should take it, who cares what I think?"

Jess pulls her arms to her chest, rests her chin on both fists. "I didn't turn it down because of you. It's just . . . don't you remember? The pay was crazy low. I couldn't afford it."

She'd done the math so many times—what if she refinanced her loans, or got a weird Craigslist roommate, or stopped buying lattes—but she could never make it work. Too many expenses and not enough income. It was like throwing pennies into a tornado. Plus, it was kind of a bummer. To think that, after everything—she'd worked one hundred hours a week at Goldman Sachs for God's sake—she'd be back clipping coupons for Duane Reade.

Josh says, "What if you weren't paying rent?"

"But . . . I mean, then it wouldn't be temporary. I might not be able to pay you back."

He says, "I told you it's fine. You can stay with me forever and you don't need to give me a cent."

"You would . . . do that for me?"

"Of course." He pulls her body closer to his, their pelvises pressed together. "But you know it's not just that. I love you. And I want to be with you all the time. I want to wake up next to you every morning. I want to come home to you every night." He stops, smiles. "I want to be the one to take you to the hospital when you go into anaphylactic shock in the middle of the night."

Jess laughs.

She says, "I love you too."

•

On the first day of work Dax appears at her shoulder.

"What's up?" Jess asks. "What's wrong?"

He says, "I'm here to help you."

"With what?"

"With everything."

Which he does. He introduces her to the team and shows her how to fill out a time sheet; how to use the coffee machine. He brings her a T-shirt with the company logo, and when it doesn't fit, he brings her another. He shows her how to export US census data and statistics to her hard drive and how to format her visualizations so that the numbers don't blur.

One day Jess says, "You make my life so much easier. You're amazing."

He brushes the compliment off. "You act like you've never worked on a team."

Jess brings Dax a card and a bar of Ethiopian chocolate and Tanzanian peaberry coffee.

"What is this?"

"To say thank you," Jess explains. "I know Paul likes coffee and I figured you would like African stuff, you know"—she leans close and stage whispers—"because you're Black."

Dax laughs and slides open the envelope with his thumb.

It says: *It's been great working together. So lucky to be your third.*

"Third?"

"It's a joke, because first Paul was my work husband and now you are. So, I'm your third."

He shakes his head. "Absolutely not the right usage."

"I just mean it's been so great here. Everyone's so great. So thanks for referring me."

"I didn't in the end."

"What?"

"By the time I sent your résumé they already had your application. So that was all you, kid."

Jess makes a face like she's going to cry.

He opens his arms and beckons her toward him. "Aw, come here."

It's the first time anyone has ever hugged Jess at work.

"We love having you on the team," Dax says, his arms around her shoulders.

"It's going to be so much harder when eventually I have to stab you in the back," Jess replies.

He squeezes her tighter. "Oh, Jess."

16

Jess and Dax work on the graphics for an article that goes viral. It is the summer before an election year and a race-baiting reality TV star is surging in the polls.

The headline says simply: *Blame racism, not the economy, for Donald Trump's rise.* For twenty-four hours people on the internet ping-pong back and forth on it and Jess almost feels famous. A friend of a friend posts the article on social media with a caption that just says: *This.* The writer, a guy named Michael from Wisconsin who was a Rhodes scholar and a Peace Corps volunteer, is invited to discuss the article on CNN.

Her dad calls, screaming-proud. "Atta girl," he says. "Never be afraid to speak truth to power." She had avoided his calls for a long time, jittery with anxiety every time she sent him to voice mail. She didn't want him to worry, or worse, ask hard questions. So she hid. And then, like a magic trick, the next thing she told him was that she had a new job, at the news-magazine. He'd whooped and hollered as if she'd won the lottery. And Jess got it.

Because she also felt it: that she was, finally, part of the solution, not the problem.

Josh's friend David invites them to dinner, and the article comes up.

Jess announces proudly to the table, "I wrote that!"

"Seriously?"

"Not the words," she explains, "but I did all the data analysis, and made all the charts."

"The chart with the bubbles? The ones that moved?"

"Yes," Jess nods, pleased. "I made that."

"Don't you think," David tilts his head at her, "it was kind of irresponsible?"

Jess tilts her head back at him. "What," she says with a not-so-subtle edge, "exactly was irresponsible?"

"Isn't it kind of ironic? To claim that Trump is stoking racial resentment by writing an article that . . . stokes racial resentment." David shrugs to indicate that he's not particularly invested in this argument and pours himself another glass of wine. "Though what do I know?"

Jess tries to make a face at Josh, but he looks away.

In the cab back to the loft, Jess says to Josh, "God, David . . . ugh."

When Josh doesn't respond, she says, again, "God, David . . . u—"

"I heard you," Josh says.

She punches him playfully. "Well, then, why aren't you agreeing with me? He said my article was *irresponsible*," Jess reminds him.

"You don't think it was?"

"Are you serious?"

"Jess, you made a very aggressive, very unsubstantiated claim. I'm not saying it was beyond the pale, but slightly irresponsible? Probably. Arguably. Don't you think?"

"No, I do not think! Are you kidding? Unsubstantiated? The whole *point* of what we do is that we do research. We use data and statistics to present an objective, and *substantiated*, point of view."

"Jess, that wasn't objective. You leveled a pretty pointed claim, and yes, there was data, but you cherry-picked specific data in service of your point."

"Why are you just bringing this up now? Why didn't you say anything before?"

"You brought it up."

"So, what, you've just been quietly judging me and you were never going to say anything even though you think I'm some kind of scumbag journalist trying to deliberately mislead the American public?"

"I just meant that your methodology was flawed."

"Oh, that's all? What are you even referring to?"

"The racism. It's a red herring. And I get it, it sells ad space or generates clicks or whatever, but Jess, it's just so reductive. It strikes me as incomplete, and yes, *irresponsible* to ignore the role of the economy. It's clearly a confounding variable."

"We didn't ignore it! The entire point of the article was that even though the economy may seem like the animating force behind Trump's popularity, it's not. That was the whole point! Meaningless tweaks to the methodology would not have yielded a different conclusion."

"So you really believe the explanation for Donald Trump is racism, full stop?"

"Yes! That's literally what the article said. Did you even read it?"

"Give me a break, of course I read it. I'm asking what *you* think. What you truly believe. Not the bullshit company talking points."

"I wouldn't have put my name on it if I didn't believe it. I do have a shred of integrity, Josh. That article represents my perspective. And I think, to the extent it's possible, it's an objective one. We did the research. I ran the numbers. I find it bizarre that you would rather engage in some kind of pedantic argument about confounding variables than actually grapple with the truth, which is that people who love Donald Trump are fucking racist. And yes, the economy. But more importantly: racism."

They get out of the cab.

In the elevator they don't speak.

The door slides open and Josh looks at Jess. He frowns. "I just don't understand why you're doing this."

"You mean, like, why I took this job?"

He nods. "It just seems like such a sharp turn."

"I guess," she thinks about it, "it's because . . . of my dad?"

"Your dad told you to take this job?"

She shakes her head. "No, not even." She sighs and plops down on the entryway bench, which Josh ordered from Denmark. "It's hard to articulate. It's more like . . . it's . . . I just feel bad. He raised me better than this."

"Raised you better than what?" Josh asks. "What exactly do you feel bad about?"

"I don't know!" Jess is frustrated, but also relieved; it would be nice if he just understood, but there is also catharsis in explaining it to him. "I guess the fact that I'm, like, fucking some white guy instead of, you know, fighting for civil rights or protesting police brutality, or whatever."

"Jess, what are you talking about? Protesting? You mean posting hot takes on social media?"

"No! Protesting. Like in Ferguson or Baltimore!"

"Jess, that's insane. What are you talking about? You want to protest? In the streets? That's not you."

"Well, maybe it should be! It's something, anyway. I feel bad enough as it is."

"For having a white boyfriend?"

"No. No, no, no. That's not it." She feels like it's all coming out wrong, even though on some level, it also feels right. She needs to explain herself. Her dad isn't a bigot. But he is principled. He definitely wouldn't like Josh's politics. But would he like Josh? That's harder to predict.

She says, "That's not what I meant. Sorry. I feel bad about the fact that I'm doing nothing at all to help the cause. You know? Mass incarceration and food deserts and the price of insulin and gentrification . . ."

"That's a lot," Josh blinks. "And I don't want to sound callous, but what does any of that have to do with you?"

She makes a face. "I'm Black. In case you haven't noticed."

"I'm aware."

"So I have a responsibility to, you know, do something."

"Why?"

"What do you mean?"

"Why is it your responsibility, specifically?"

"I don't understand."

"Jess, you don't owe anything to anyone. Yes, there are people suffering. But you don't know them. You don't have any unique obligation to help, you know that, right? Just because you're Black. Especially because you're Black."

"I just . . . I feel bad."

"Don't." He touches her arm.

"That's how I feel. I know it doesn't make sense, but it's like this . . . guilt. Or anxiety. Or shame, or something."

Josh says, "Oh, Jess," and then. "How often do you think about this?"

"Every day?"

"*Every* day?"

"I mean . . . yeah? Like especially now with Black Lives Matter, it all feels so immediate, and I feel so . . . detached. And like not only am I not contributing, but maybe I'm even undermining the whole thing. Like I'm part of the problem."

"Because you have a white boyfriend?"

"I don't know! I don't know what I'm saying."

"Why haven't you said anything before?" He looks sad.

"What was I supposed to say?"

"You're supposed to tell me what's on your mind. Tell me what's weighing on you. Be honest. Be open."

"But—"

"What? You didn't think I would get it?"

"Do you?"

"Honestly? I'm not sure. But I care about you. I'm trying to get it. But if you don't tell me things, I don't even have the opportunity to try. I'm on your side."

"Okay."

"Okay?"

"Okay."

She nods and he smiles.

He takes her hand, kisses it. She stands and leans against him and he rubs her back. Josh says, "I love you, you know that?" and Jess closes her eyes. She lets her head rest on his chest and they stand embracing for a long time. Eventually Jess tilts her head back so that they're eye to eye. He's still rubbing her back.

She says, "So you don't think the article was irresponsible?"

And Josh says, "I'm not saying that."

* * *

Josh's new apartment is a three-thousand-square-foot loft. Two bedrooms in an old book-binding factory, with original molding and hardwood floors and a special elevator that brings your car right up to your front door.

Josh had taken Jess to see it before he moved in and, without furniture or a coat of paint, the space was immense, unimaginably large. The guest bathroom was as big as a studio apartment and when they spoke to each other across the main room, their voices echoed. The light was spectacular, windows from wall-to-wall, and the views of the city made it feel like they were standing in a beautiful glass box on top of the world.

Oh, Jess had thought, *what money can buy.*

When Josh leaned over to kiss her, he slipped one hand under her shirt and with the other he touched his phone, and then all the window shades slid down with an expensive-sounding electronic hum. She had laughed into his mouth and said, "Okay, Iron Man."

And now they both live there.

On the day she moved in, Josh explained that all she needed to control everything from her own phone was to set up a secret six-digit code. Jess punched it in, but it threw an error. She tried again and then looked up at Josh and frowned.

"What is it?"

"It's not working." She typed in her six-digit code again, carefully.

He reached for her phone. "Let me see."

"No way," she said, holding the phone to her chest protectively, "it's secret."

"Give me a break." He shook his head, grinning. "What is it? Your birthday? I doubt it would take the NSA to crack it. Come on"—he gestured for her to let go—"hand it over."

She handed it over.

He tapped and swiped and tapped and then made a face.

"What?"

He started laughing.

"What?"

He said, "I figured out the problem."

"What?" Jess said.

"It needs to be a unique number." He slid his own phone from his back pocket. "Look."

He held up the screen and Jess could see that he had unhidden his password and it was exactly the same as hers: 1 1 2 3 5 8.

Jess said, "Your password is the Fibonacci sequence? Wow, Josh. That's so incredibly dorky."

"Yours is too!'

"Yeah," Jess said lightly, though her heart was exploding, "but it's cool when I do it."

Later, Josh had swung open the massive refrigerator door and said, "I have a surprise."

Jess looked at him, confused.

"Go on," he said, grinning so broadly that she half expected to find a diamond ring inside.

But there was nothing. Just a few cans of craft beer, a hunk of Gruyère and some leftover salad.

"I don't get it," Jess said.

Proud, he explained, "There are no strawberries. See? I threw them all out. This house," he shuts the fridge with ceremony, "is officially strawberry-free."

"But they're your favorite," Jess protested, and he just shrugged.

She was so touched; she felt like she might cry. "You do love me," she said, with emotion.

He laughed at her reaction and folded her into a hug. "I thought, you know what? I'm the kind of guy who'd prefer if his girlfriend didn't die."

It had occurred to Jess then that she wouldn't be able to video chat with her father from home anymore. If she did, he'd ask why she'd moved, and then she realized she'd have to reveal things. Like the fact that she had a boyfriend that she'd never mentioned, which made her feel guilty for hiding him, but not quite guilty enough to stop lying. Or the fact that she and said boyfriend had the loft professionally cleaned—Jess knew her dad would consider this an unfathomable extravagance—which also made her feel guilty, but not guilty enough to mop the floors or do the laundry. Or the fact that she'd been unemployed for almost half a year, which was what precipitated the whole moving in together thing, or that she'd blown through her savings and even dipped into her retirement fund, or that, since she'd left for college, she'd essentially been living frivolously, even though she knew better, and this too made her feel guilty, but not guilty enough to do anything differently.

✳

On Saturday morning Jess opens her eyes to see Josh in his nice shoes. He's wearing a button-down shirt and is freshly shaved.

"Hey," she calls, half-asleep, "where are you sneaking off to?"

He says, "Hey, beautiful," and crosses the room to kiss and cuddle her.

"Are you going to get breakfast? Will you get me a bagel? Ooh, and a babka, but make sure it's a crumbly one."

"Uh, no."

Jess blinks sleep out of her eyes and squints. "Where are you going? What time is it?"

"Work thing," he says breezily, "I'm just meeting Gil for a bit."

"You're going to the office?"

He shakes his head. "Um, no. Going to a restaurant."

Jess rubs her eyes. "Like . . . for brunch?"

"Sure," he says. "Yeah."

"Why?"

"It was the only time he was available this week," Josh shrugs. "We need to catch up. Are you . . . is that cool?"

Jess adjusts the pillow under her head and looks at him sideways. "It's fine. It's just funny to think of you and Gil gabbing over Bloody Marys."

"Actually, his wife will be there too." He is silent for a moment, then adds, "And, I'm not sure, maybe his niece?"

"His *niece*?" Jess sits up.

"Whoa, take it easy. And you haven't even had your Wheaties yet." He smiles, as if Jess will appreciate the joke.

"So Gil and his wife are having brunch and you're, like, going to babysit his niece?"

"Ha, no. She's not a little girl. She's a lawyer."

"Of course Gil's lawyer is his niece," Jess rolls her eyes. "Is his brother his consigliere?"

"Funny," Josh says, not laughing. He takes his wallet off the dresser and stuffs it in his back pocket. "Anyway, she's not *his* lawyer. She's *a* lawyer."

"Oh," Jess says. "Where does she work?"

"Look, Jess," he is rolling his phone over in his palm and shifting his weight from one leg to the other, "can we talk about this later?"

"Okay . . . well. It's just weird that you didn't mention it. You were just going to sneak out? What if I'd panicked and filed a missing person report?"

He laughs for real this time. "I'm sorry. You were sleeping. You looked so pretty and peaceful"—he leans over and kisses her shoulder—"and I didn't want to wake you."

"Well, why didn't you mention it yesterday?"

"Gil just asked me last night. He texted. After you were asleep."

"Oh."

"Yeah. Not a huge conspiracy. I'll be home in a couple of hours, we can get naked and have bagels then." He kisses her again, runs his fingers affectionately through her hair and says, "But right now, I have to go."

He is almost out the door when Jess says, "Wait!"

"What?"

"Can I come?"

He looks at his shoes, seems to consider it, but then says, "I'm already late. Some other time, okay? I promise."

And then he's gone.

* * *

Josh takes Jess out for pizza, an Italian bistro in the West Village, with plastic roses on every table. Outside they make out in kind of a gross way, all hands and tongues, as if they are alone, which they aren't— Bleecker Street on a weekend night.

When they come up for air, Josh says, "Oh shit." His face goes pale, a white sheet.

"What?" Jess looks up at him.

"Fuck," he says, staring straight ahead.

"What?" Jess asks again. She pulls her hand out from under his shirt and turns, but she doesn't see what he sees. "What's wrong?"

He runs a hand through his hair, "It's Gil."

Jess turns, "Is he lost?"

"Turn around, Jess," Josh hisses.

But before she does, Gil catches her eye. He gives them a bewildered look and then a strange little wave. Josh says, "Oh shit, do you think he saw us?"

Jess makes a face at him and says, "Um, yeah, definitely. Why, what's the big deal?"

"The big deal, Jess, is I told him nothing was going on."

"Well, there wasn't, but now there is. And that was ages ago. It's not like you lied. I don't even work there anymore," Jess reminds him. "Why should he care? Wait . . . is that why you said I was just your 'friend'? At the hospital?"

But Josh isn't listening. He is still peering over her shoulder, staring at the ghost of Gil on Sullivan Street.

"Don't you see how this looks?"

"How does it look?" Jess knows how it looks, in theory. But in practice Gil is a man who famously shorted the stock of his brother's failing company. Jess has a hard time believing, despite his prior warning, that something as quotidian as sex would offend his sense of morality.

Josh sighs.

"Okay, fine," Jess tries, annoyed that he's killed the mood. "If you're so worried about it, just tell him the truth. Or, you know, the half-truth."

"Obviously, I'm going to have to."

"And you think he'll be mad?"

"I don't know."

"Is he going to yell at you for hiring me?"

"I don't know."

"So what will you tell him?"

"I don't know."

"So what do you know?"

He gives her a look. "Honestly, Jess? I'm not sure anymore. I find myself abandoning all critical thinking and rational thought when it comes to you."

Jess smiles. "That's so romantic."

"No, Jess. No. It's not. It's really not."

•

And then it's June and love is love and volleyball is canceled and they paint rainbows on their faces and celebrate in the streets. The Wine Girls wear leis made of rainbow-colored flowers. Miky and Lydia wear T-shirts and carry flags.

"Where's Josh?" someone asks.

Josh? Jess looks around, the streets erupting, the sun blazing overhead, the city abuzz with people celebrating Pride.

"He's . . . at brunch." With the CEO of his fund, Jess doesn't add. It's almost every weekend now. Brunch, brunch, brunch. Josh comes home on Saturdays with the most precious confections—tiny éclairs filled with coffee cream, macarons flavored like lavender and orange olive oil—wrapped in the most precious boxes. Consolation pastries, Jess thinks, but doesn't say.

They find Paul and Dax and the guys from volleyball and they all kiss and cry and hug and Jess's heart swells, and everything is shimmering and everyone is best friends.

Until the following week when she misses a match point and

everyone groans and someone shouts, "Six-Pack, will you please get off the fucking sand."

•

Jess and Josh show up at the Wine Girls' Halloween party in matching outfits.

"What are you?" they ask.

Josh is wearing a T-shirt that says CORRELATION ≠ CAUSATION. He points two fingers at his chest: "The scariest thing of all: a logical fallacy."

"And I'm a lurking variable." Jess lifts her elbows and crosses her wrists, Wonder Woman–style. "X? Get it? The unknown variable?" She makes her hands into claws, lifts one knee slowly, and then the other, pantomimes an exaggerated tiptoe, "And I'm lurking! Get it?"

"A math joke?"

Jess and Josh beam at each other.

The Wine Girls walk away rolling their eyes. "You two need help."

•

After her dad's wine tour, they'd finally settled on a Thanksgiving tradition: skipping it. It was so close to Christmas, it just made sense to wait until December. So her dad is off to St. Louis for the weekend ("See you in a St. Louis second, Jessie!") and Jess goes home with Josh. They drive from the rental garage in Midtown to Greenwich. The moon is high and the leaves are at their riotous peak, bright reds and oranges that make Jess think of pumpkin pie.

Inside, when his mother hands him clean sheets for the pullout couch Josh says, "Actually, Mom, I think I'll sleep upstairs."

She doesn't immediately understand, and she starts to object, "Now honey, don't you think Jess would be more comfortable in a proper bed? If you're uncomfortable on the pullout—"

"I meant," Josh interrupts, "I'll sleep upstairs with Jess."

Confused, she says, "Oh," and then her eyes widen in surprise and connecting the dots she says, "Oh!"

They all stare at each other.

Until Josh says, "Yeah."

And Jess says, "Um, yeah."

And his mother says faux brightly, "Well, good night!"

Upstairs they take off all their clothes and get into bed.

The room is cold, and Jess pulls the flannel sheets up to her chin.

She says, "You made that *so* weird."

"What do you mean?"

"The sleeping arrangements," she says. "Your mom probably thinks we're up here, like, doing it."

He grins, a flash of white teeth in the dark, and pulls her toward him by the waist. "Well, that's not wrong then, is it?"

Jess ignores him and tries to scooch away and out of his grasp, but it's a twin bed and her back is already pressed against the wall.

"So you didn't tell your mother we were together? That I was your girlfriend? Your live-in girlfriend?"

"I'm pretty sure I just did."

"But, I mean, before? You didn't mention it." Jess wants to feel outrage, but the truth is, she's been coy with her dad too. When he asks, Jess says, *Nope, nothing new.* Which obviously isn't true. But it all feels like too much to explain. Where would she start? With the job she got fired from? Or the boyfriend who voted for Mitt Romney? It's just easier to spare him the details.

Josh says, "I may have mentioned I was seeing someone."

"But not me?"

"You know what, shoot," he smacks his palm against his forehead, "I knew there was something I forgot to tell her the last time we got matching mani-pedis at the salon."

"Sarcasm," Jess says, frowning.

"I just don't have that kind of relationship with my mom, Jess." He pulls her back into him, so their faces are close. "Does that surprise you? We don't sit around and gab about my life."

Jess says, "I guess."

Josh runs a finger lightly along her bottom lip. "You're so pretty," he says, "you know that?"

Jess smiles, "Don't change the subject."

"So, so pretty," he says, kissing her face.

"I'm not going to fall for this," Jess warns, though she already is. She closes her eyes and lets him pull her closer. Their legs are pretzeled together and their noses touch; his arms are looped, palms to elbows, all the way around her waist.

They kiss.

He says, "I'm happy you're my girlfriend. My live-in girlfriend."

And Jess says, "I forgive you."

But in the back of her head she's filing it away, in the same place she stores the memory of when he used the word *friend* to describe her.

Josh is in the shower when Jess finds his high school yearbook, exactly where she left it two years ago.

She flips right to the back, to Tenley's letter.

She starts to read it but stops at the same point she did last time. The part where it starts to sound like a nineties love song. It is so clearly private, this letter, Jess feels like a jerk reading it.

She shuts the book.

She isn't jealous of Tenley per se, or even the idea of her, it's something closer to curiosity, with only maybe a very small side of insecurity. She is curious who Josh would have picked if he hadn't picked her, who his first choice was, the first girl he kissed, the first girl he slept with. Jess wants to know what kind of girl starred in his high school dreams and she wants to know why, even though it's been so long, he's so cagey about her.

Jess wonders if he loved her.

She opens the book again.

In the back she finds the senior pages: each senior had an entire page to cover with personal photographs and messages and inside jokes.

She flips to Josh's page. It is sparse, just a photograph of him and his family, a close-up so she can't tell where it was taken, along with an Einstein quote about death.

Jess smiles.

She turns to Tenley's page.

A message at the bottom of the page says, "Love to Allie and Eliza for making these past four years so amazing and unforgettable. I love you Mom and Dad!" The rest is just photos, at least a dozen. Photos of her in swimsuits and on ski slopes, flanked by two other blondes, Allie and Eliza, Jess guesses. Photos of her in a lacrosse uniform, with a tennis racquet, in a scull on Lake Quonnipaug. Lots of photos of her with her parents and brothers and sisters, attractive WASPs who all wear watches.

One photo catches Jess's eye. A family photo: Tenley surrounded by smiling cousins and uncles and aunts all wearing summer linens and sitting around an outdoor dining table, in front of a bay.

She peers down at it.

She does a double take.

She says out loud, "No. Fucking. Way."

She brings the book right up to her face, just to make sure.

But she's sure.

The man in Tenley's family photo, with a hint of a sunburn and an avuncular arm around her shoulder, is none other than Gil Alperstein.

Josh comes out of the shower with a towel around his waist, shaking water out of his ears. For a moment Jess forgets herself—he smells like a mountain spring, damp and fresh-faced like someone from a deodorant commercial—but then he says, "Whatcha doing, Just Jess?" and she remembers the yearbook in her lap.

She looks up. "What the hell, Josh?"

"Excuse me?" Rubbing his hair dry with the towel, he stops, his head cocked.

She holds up the yearbook, shakes it at him. "Were you ever going to mention this?"

"Mention what?" he asks, confused.

She jabs at the open page, and then again and again, until she is attacking the yearbook with her pointer finger.

Josh crosses the room and bends over her. A single drop of water falls onto the page. "Oh," he says, "shit."

"Care to explain?" She is pissed off. It doesn't matter that his shoulders are smooth and muscled and that he smells like aftershave.

He sit-falls onto the bed. He looks up at the ceiling. "Yeah," he says, "that."

"That? *That?*"

"He's . . . Gil's wife is Tenley's mom's sister. He's her uncle."

"Are you for real? So you've been lying to me for what . . . two and a half years, and all you have to say for yourself is 'That'? What the ever-loving fuck, man? I don't . . . understand. Why didn't you ever . . . tell me that you and Gil had . . . a prior relationship?"

"I'm not sure."

"Tenley was your girlfriend, wasn't she?"

"It wasn't serious."

Jess rolls her eyes. "Why are you being weird about this girl you hooked up with in high school? Why do you think I care? Do you think I'm that insecure?"

The truth is, Jess thinks she might be that insecure. Tenley is clearly the perfect girl, clear-skinned and blond. The kind of girl, Jess assumes, he would properly introduce to his mom. A girl he could take sailing in the summers and whose father he would talk about the stock market with and call *sir*.

"Oh my god," Jess realizes suddenly. "Oh my *god*. All those brunches? You've been, like, *dating* her this whole time? You and Gil and his wife and *Tenley* going out together every weekend? And you were never going to tell me? You can't be serious."

"It's breakfast, not a nightclub. And we're definitely not dating. It's work. I didn't mention it because I didn't want it to be a . . . thing."

"You've got to be kidding me. You've literally been sneaking around with her for months!"

"With *them*. Gil and his wife and, yes, Tenley, but it's not like it's some kind of . . . tryst. And I wasn't sneaking."

"Then why didn't you mention it?"

"I told you, because I—"

"Right, right. Because you didn't want it to be a thing," Jess says, shaking her head. "This is so unbelievable. You've been lying to me for years! Do you realize that? Josh, this is shady as shit! Do you . . . are you . . . still into her?"

Jess thinks of that party at David's, all that time back: *Tenley, she is not.*

"No," he says quickly, "definitely not."

"Then I don't get it," Jess says. "Then why be so weird about it? Why . . . lie?"

He sighs.

"Why?"

"Because I thought you would give me a hard time about it." He looks at her and clarifies, "Not about Tenley, I don't care about Tenley, I swear. That was such a long time ago. But I thought you might give me a lecture about nepotism or white privilege or something and I guess, I don't know, I didn't want to hear it."

"A lecture? Because I'm always lecturing you? Because I'm a nag? Like some kind of sitcom wife who you have to hide from in the garage?"

"Jess, no. I didn't want to hear it because you'd be . . . right."

"So you thought that if I knew that I would, like, diminish you?"

"No. More like I thought it would be . . . revealing. That you would think it was all unfair and that I was untalented."

"I think you're so talented," she says.

But she also thinks it's unfair. He is smart and talented and hardworking, but still, most people don't get extra help from a supportive billionaire. But he is naked and chagrined and she loves him so she doesn't say any of this.

"I just can't believe you would hide this. I still don't even get it. You dated this girl in high school and now her uncle cares about your career? But it's a secret? Is that why you didn't want Gil to see us kissing? Because Gil is, like, your benefactor and you dated his niece? What, is he, like, grooming you to run his fund or whatever, so that one day you'll be worthy of his niece?"

"Jess, come on. This isn't the nineteenth century. We're not betrothed. I don't see her outside of brunch. We dated in high school. Briefly. That's it."

She eyes him, doesn't say anything.

He takes her face in his hands and presses his forehead to hers, so that she feels strands of his damp hair on her face. "I'm sorry," he says.

"It's not that," Jess says. "I don't care about Gil. Or I do, but it's the whole thing, with you and Tenley and all this history . . ." She can see it so clearly. Josh and Tenley, the perfect match. High school sweethearts that drifted apart. Supposedly. What if she's the one that got away?

Jess says, "It's just, you and I, we're so different."

He says softly, "But not in the important ways."

"I'm Black, you're white. I'm liberal, you're conservative . . ."

Said that way it almost sounds like poetry. Opposites attract. The best kind of love story. But that's not quite right. Or at least it's not what Jess means. They're not really opposites. More like two people playing for different teams.

But Josh disagrees. "Jess, my love," he kisses her knuckle, "you do know none of that matters?"

If none of that matters, how to explain war and politics and all of history?

But he's looking incredibly sorry and sincere, so Jess doesn't say that. She lets him pull her close, wrapping his arms around her shoulders for a moment.

"Besides," he says, standing, folding the towel around his stomach, "I'm a moderate."

Jess wonders if they are incompatible in some fundamental way. When she thinks about it she feels an existential knot twist tight in her stomach. Some days more than others. At a party the Saturday before, people were talking about an article that had been going around, about the rise of assortative mating, and how increasingly people only marry people just like them, so that everything is more polarized and stratified.

Someone had said, "So you're saying we should all marry our secretaries."

And someone else had said, "But isn't it kind of sad, how even now with technology, we can communicate across oceans, but we all somehow live in different worlds?"

"Jess is in love with a Republican," the Wine Girls had replied.

"Is that true?" someone else had asked.

And Jess was forced to admit that it was.

At dinner with Paul, Jess tells him about Tenley and all the attendant mythology.

For dessert they share an order of brûléed bananas foster with caramel sauce and mascarpone. It is so full of sugar it makes Jess's heart race.

She tells Paul about discovering the yearbook and that Gil is Tenley's uncle, that she and Josh were high school sweethearts and that she's the one who got away, probably, and about the fact that Josh lied. She tells him that Gil obviously wants Josh to marry Tenley, so that he can give him the fund when he retires, and Josh knows this, though he won't admit it, and he doesn't want to tell Gil that he and Jess are dating, which is . . . suspicious.

"Well," Paul chews on a banana, "that's quite a telenovela you've concocted."

"I'm not crazy," Jess says, eying him. "I mean, think about it. Why else would Gil take such an extraordinary interest in Josh? He completely favors him. He was there for less than a year when Gil made him a senior trader." Jess lowers her voice and leans over the table: "And do you know how much he pays him? He makes so much money! The loft cost"—she is whispering now—"four *million* dollars."

But Paul only shrugs. Her own reaction had been bigger. She'd been impressed and incredulous and a little bit jealous. She'd worked backward, guessing at the down payment and the mortgage, the price of money, and come to the conclusion that he must be earning at least five times her salary, which was annoying, but also unsurprising. Still!

He had so much money! He'd earned more in a few years than her father had in forty! Her father, who worked hard and paid taxes and gave a dollar to every homeless person he saw! She tried to reconcile the idea that her boyfriend was a twenty-five-year-old millionaire with the fact that she worked for a news-magazine with an entire beat dedicated to income inequality. Mostly she tried not to take it personally. Tried to ignore the fact that, lately, her own net worth had barely increased. At least the app had stopped sending her frantic notifications—HEADS UP! YOUR EXPENSES LAST MONTH EXCEEDED YOUR INCOME—but still.

"How else do you explain it?" Jess asks Paul.

Paul swirls a tiny spoon through his espresso. "Josh is a really good trader."

"But . . . that good?"

Paul nods. "Yes."

"Okay, fine, he's good." Jess kicks Paul's leg a little under the table, teasing, trying to provoke him. "But better than you?"

He nods again. "Yes."

Jess says, "Ugh, you're useless. Anyway, I'm not saying he's not. It just seems suspicious. That he never told me about his history with Gil. And Tenley. You don't think I should be worried?"

"Who knows?"

"Do you think he'll cheat on me?" That old voice in her head: blondes, brunettes, then redheads. Then everyone else.

"With this Tinfoil character?" Paul asks.

Jess nods.

"Eh," he shrugs. "No. Maybe? Probably not."

17

Jess is on the phone with her dad when Josh comes home.

In the bathroom with the door half-open she says, "I love you, I miss you, no, of course . . . yes, everything's fine."

When she hangs up, Josh is lying in bed, staring at his phone. Without looking up he says, "You taking secret phone calls in there again? You have another boyfriend you need to keep in touch with? A secret admirer?"

"Ha, ha," Jess says, shutting the bathroom door behind her. "*Dad-mirer.*" She slips into bed next to Josh, rests her head on his shoulder.

"How is he?" Josh asks.

Jess shrugs, "He's good."

"We should have dinner sometime."

"Who?"

"Jess, try to keep up. Your dad. Me. You. I'd like to meet him someday, you know."

"He lives in Lincoln," Jess says.

Josh laughs. "Yeah, Jess, I got that. I mean whenever he's in town next. Maybe we can invite him for a weekend or something. There's enough space. Don't you miss him?"

Jess nods. She does. But also, she can't imagine him here. What would she say? *Hey, Dad, why don't you come see me in New York? No need to book a hotel, you can stay with me and my boyfriend, who, oh, yeah, you didn't know existed. We live together in a two-bedroom apartment that cost four million dollars even though there aren't any walls, not really, but don't worry, I don't pay rent because my boyfriend feels guilty that he had to fire me from my last job, which, oh, yeah, didn't I mention that? By the way, my boyfriend? The one who I've never mentioned? He hates Barack Obama. How's the first week of April?*

They would go out to dinner and when he asked them about work

Josh would try to explain evolutionary computation over sixteen-dollar vodka cocktails. Her dad who wouldn't even buy a six pack of Coca-Cola at the grocery store if it wasn't on sale. "That's *sixty* cents a can, Jessie," he would say, shaking his head as if the world had gone mad.

Jess literally can't imagine.

Josh squeezes her shoulder. "So what do you say?"

And Jess doesn't say anything.

•

Jess overhears Josh making dinner plans.

She asks him, "So when's your hot date?"

Josh says, "Excuse me?"

He is sitting on the bed, putting on his shoes. He ties his laces like a first grader, two lopsided ovals folded into a bow. It reminds her of a song her father used to sing to her when she was a little girl, about a bunny who hops over, under, around and through. She thinks of this any time she sees Josh put on his shoes and it makes her simultaneously joyful and inarticulately sad.

"Are you having dinner with someone?"

He shakes his head. "Oh. No. I mean, yes. I'm going to Gil's. For Passover."

"Oh, really?"

"Yeah."

"When?"

"Passover."

"Ha, ha."

He smiles and clarifies, "It's Friday."

"What time?"

"All night, I think."

"Oh."

"Yeah." He stands up, crosses the room, places two hands on Jess's shoulders and kisses her cheek. "I'm going to Duane Reade, want anything?"

Jess says, "Can I come?"

"To Duane Reade?"

She looks at him.

He hesitates.

"Is it because you don't want me to meet Tenley? She's going to be there, right?"

"She might be," he shrugs.

"So, what? You're afraid I'm going to say something rude? Because I'm always 'rearing for a fight'?" He'd said this verbatim last week, when Jess had felt compelled to argue with David's girlfriend that no matter how warm it got in March, it was never okay to call it an Indian summer, even though Abby didn't mean anything by it, and did Jess really need to bring genocide into it.

He says nothing and Jess knows that's it.

"Do I embarrass you?" Jess asks. "Is that it?"

The truth is, sometimes he embarrasses her. Like the time he wore pink shorts with little sailboats on them to meet the Wine Girls for brunch, or at that same brunch, when he gave a ten-minute lecture on marginal conditional stochastic dominance, even though everyone's eyes were glazing over and the eggs were getting cold. But all that seems minor and avoidable. She doesn't want him to be a different person, just, sometimes, a slightly attenuated version of the person he is. But she worries that he does want her to be different. To be quieter. To be whiter. To fit in. To impress Gil.

"Jess, come on. That's not it"—he is touching his collar, lying, and Jess doesn't believe him, that's definitely it—"I'm surprised you want to come, that's all. It's not exactly . . . your crowd."

She looks at him. Doesn't blink.

He nods slowly. "Okay, fine."

Gil's dining room is surprisingly warm, given that it is the size of an airplane hangar. The table is set for twenty and Jess counts four crystal goblets at each setting, which means that there are eighty wine glasses in all.

She's seated about a half dozen place settings away from Josh. At the table she waves sadly to him and says, "Well, I guess this is goodbye," and he laughs and says, "So you'll meet someone new." But Jess is stuck between two very old people, neither of whom seems interested in talking to her, even as they lean across her lap to croak at each other.

She offers to switch seats, but for some reason, they decline.

Next to Jess, the man does that thing where he gets their cutlery all mixed up, stirring his coffee with her spoon, spearing lettuce leaves with her fork. But he is so old—one hundred? One hundred and sixty-five?—that Jess doesn't have the heart to correct him.

Plus, tonight Jess is intent on blending in. She will smile and acquiesce and if someone says something offensive, she will just breathe and count to ten. She is Making an Effort.

At the other end of the table Jess looks over at Josh, and her breath catches: Tenley. She is seated next to him and her head is turned toward him, smiling. She is absently running a polished finger along the rim of a wineglass, a gold bracelet hanging prettily from her slim wrist. Jess can see her only in profile, her neck lightly freckled, a low knot of blond hair. She is wearing a sleeveless silk top, her shoulders tanned and angular, practically erotic. The top looks plain, but Jess is certain that if she were to look it up online, it would be designer.

Of course, Jess thinks. She is the kind of girl who will make her feel sweaty and unkempt. The kind of girl who has her hair blown out three times a week, who has no fear of hot wax and whose nails are always perfectly manicured. The kind of girl who wears a white silk top to a seder, to drink red wine and eat beef brisket.

Gil says something and everyone laughs. Tenley's hand—five perfectly polished fingers—moves to rest on Josh's arm, the space between his bicep and his elbow, and Jess feels something inside her, vague and instinctual: panic. Besides Tenley's obvious prettiness, it is jarring how good she looks next to Josh. Like Barbie and Ken. Or Tom and Gisele.

It is much, much worse than Jess thought.

She texts Josh under the table.

Why aren't we sitting together

She looks up. His head is turned, listening to something Gil is saying.

She watches Josh's hands. He lifts his wineglass, spreads butter over matzoh with a small knife, uses a napkin to wipe his mouth. He doesn't respond.

But then:

normal at these things to separate couples

And indeed, Gil and his wife are sitting at opposite ends of the table, like royalty.

I want to sit next to you

I want to sit on your lap

Jess is bored.

I want to sit on your dick

I want your matzoh balls

Josh ignores her.

Gil is talking with his hands and everyone is laughing. Tenley says something to Josh, her hair loose now, brushing against Josh's arm when she leans toward him. He doesn't lean away.

Jess's heart drops.

Her phone buzzes.

An emoji from Josh: an eggplant.

Jess smiles.

Eventually Gil calls for a toast. He says "Welcome" and tells the story of Passover, the exodus of the Jews from Egypt. He says, "Chag Sameach!" and "L'chaim!" and everyone touches glasses and sips champagne.

"And now we're ready for the Ma Nishtana. Tenley?"

His wife explains to the group, "Our youngest guest, our niece, will now ask the Four Questions."

Someone who's had too much wine and thinks it's funny shouts across the room: "I thought you had to be Jewish for that!"

Gil gives the comedian a tepid smile, "She's an honorary member of the tribe," then turns back to the party, "Go ahead, Tenley."

But Tenley leans forward, makes eye contact with the table and, with a twinkle in her eye, counters, "In fact, I'm *not* the youngest guest." Her accent, which has a polished clip to it, reminds Jess of a European monarch, although Jess is pretty sure she's from Chicago. She continues, "Josh is actually younger than me."

Tenley turns to him and says, rather flirtatiously, Jess thinks, "He was born in August. I'm May."

Everyone turns to Gil, who chuckles at Tenley, "You can't argue with tradition."

His wife laughs and then everyone laughs as if he has made some fabulous joke.

Gil sweeps an arm in Josh's direction. "All right then, son," he says, "you know what to do."

Josh says, "Now wait a minute . . ." and everyone laughs again.

"Nope," Gil says, shaking his head amiably, "not going to shirk this responsibility."

Josh says, "The thing is," and he leans over the table, peers down a half a dozen profiles to look at Jess, "I happen to know that at least one person at this table is even younger than I am." He grins and points, "It's Jess."

Everyone stares. That fine line between feeling invisible and feeling the subject of ridicule.

"She's a whole year younger than I am," Josh explains. "She started kindergarten when she was four."

"Is that so?" Gil asks drily.

And Josh nods and grins, clueless.

"Don't embarrass her," Tenley says, touching Josh's arm.

And Jess says, too loudly, "I'm not embarrassed at all!"

Josh says, "The questions are on the place cards." He holds his up for her to see. "Here, Jess, this is what you say."

Gil scowls and Tenley says, "Josh . . ." and moves her hand higher on his arm, her fingers resting almost proprietarily on his bicep. Which drives Jess nuts. Her hair and her manicure and her poise—it is too much.

Jess snaps, "It's fine." She looks directly at Tenley and then starts, "Why is this night different from all other nights?"

Jess recites the questions clearly, with practiced confidence, and when she looks up, the other guests are looking on in bewildered amusement, probably wondering, among other things, who the hell she even is.

Except for Gil.

She catches his eye and he's definitely just pissed.

After the dinner plates are cleared, waiters come around offering coffee and dessert: matzoh cake with fresh strawberry compote served on real china. Jess rolls her eyes. Even if Gil doesn't know she's allergic, of course he would try to kill her. She is about to signal to a member of the waitstaff *no thanks*, when behind her someone says, "Miss?" She turns and at her elbow is a waiter.

He is holding a dessert plate that looks like it's levitating, his palm hidden Houdini-like underneath. Like the other waiters, he is in tails, a real professional.

Before Jess can object, he sets the plate in front of her, and when she looks down there is the matzoh cake, yes, but instead of strawberries, there are peaches. A special dessert just for her.

She looks at Josh.

When she catches his eye she points at her plate with her fork and raises an eyebrow.

He winks.

Her heart flutters.

After dessert: cocktails. Everyone shuffles into the library to mingle. Jess gets swept up into party circles like sea currents. She talks to a lawyer and a gastroenterologist and the ambassador to Peru; she makes an effort to avoid speaking with Gil; eventually, she finds herself standing next to Tenley.

They introduce themselves, formally, and Jess thinks of that game—what's it called? Ten Minutes with Mussolini? Ask Einstein Anything?—where the object is to come up with a single question to ask someone famous or someone dead or someone famous and dead to get to the bottom of things. This feels like that. Jess wants Tenley to reveal things, but she wants to be strategic.

They are holding their cocktails, smiling carefully at each other.

"So," Jess finally says, "you and Josh?" Not the most artful. Or subtle. But she's on the clock.

Tenley says, "Oh god. Ha. That was a million years ago. We were just kids. First kisses and all that."

First kiss? Had Josh lied? Why? Of course there was no Lindsey. Or was Tenley speaking in metaphor? Was that why she had used the plural? It's not like they'd had more than one first kiss. Although Tenley was probably the kind of girl who you could kiss for the first time more than once. She was just that sparkly and special.

Jess must look stricken because Tenley quickly adds, "He talks about you all the time."

Certainly that's not true. Why would she say that? Suddenly, it occurs to Jess: Tenley is trying to be nice. Jess wanted her to be bitchy, aloof, superior, beautiful. But pitying? That's so much worse. As if Jess is someone who needs to worry about her boyfriend. Who needs to be reassured.

Jess says, "You see him a lot."

Which . . . isn't even a question. Jess is skipping conversational beats. Exposing her insecurity. But she's running out of time. Already Gil's wife is moving through the room thanking people for coming.

Tenley is unflappable. "Josh is such a good sport," she laughs. "I'm sure a stuffy brunch uptown with my uncle is the last place he'd rather be."

But that's not true either, obviously.

Finally, it's time to leave. Jess is in the foyer, putting her jacket on, when Josh finds her. They are alone. He slips his hand into her jacket and under her sweater and kisses her wetly on the mouth.

"Tell me that thing again," he says, his hand wandering up her stomach, "what you said you wanted to do in your text."

"Hey." Jess swats him away. "Someone will see us." Though she doesn't mean it. She doesn't care.

"Well, then maybe we should give them a show." He pulls her closer, both hands clasped at her back.

Jess is giggling into his mouth when someone clears his throat behind them. Gil.

Josh turns. He takes his hands off her waist, puts them in his pockets.

Gil says, "May I speak to you in private?" He is looking at Jess.

She says, "Me?"

She looks at Josh but he just shrugs.

"Come this way," Gil says. "It will only be a minute." But then he leads her down one hallway and another and down a staircase until Jess thinks, *No one can hear you scream.*

In his office he looks her in the eye and says, "You and Josh have become quite close."

"Oh." Jess sits back, surprised, but also, not really.

"Do you remember a conversation we once had? When you joined the fund? Short though your tenure was, I imagine you remember this. When I expressed my concern about certain conflicts of interest?"

Jess takes off her jacket and says, "Is it hot?"

He leans forward, rests his elbows on the desk and folds his hands in front of him. "Do you recall that conversation?"

Jess really fucking hates this guy. "No," she says, and blinks innocently. "I can't say I do."

His face doesn't change, but his eyes go black. He says, "Look, young lady. I don't like to play games. Regardless of what you recall, I think it bears repeating that Josh's work requires focus. The fund is his priority and it needs to come first. You're proving yourself to be quite the distraction. And not for the first time, I might add." He leans back, then continues, "Josh can't tolerate any distractions right now. His future is too bright."

"I think he's really smart," Jess says, possibly agreeing.

"Well," Gil says, "that makes two of us. I'm glad we see eye to eye. My advice to you then would be to stop distracting him."

Her heart is racing. He wants her to break up with Josh, probably so he can be with Tenley, his beautiful blond niece. Then he can give Josh his fund without reservation and they can all get on with their perfect, tax-free lives.

Jess feels vindicated, but also a little bit freaked out. This is actually happening. Her life is a telenovela. She doesn't even blame Gil. Josh and Tenley make so much sense. She can imagine a particular kind of future unfurling before them: hedge fund dinners and a house in the Hamptons, an eight-digit bank balance, a wedding announcement in the *Times*; sons and daughters healthy and blond. They would never, ever argue. Even Jess can see it.

She says, "I think Josh would consider me a positive distraction."

"Is smearing his name on the internet positive? Calling the work he does criminal? Claiming some of the finest fund managers in the industry are paid through the nose for underperformance? You're lucky you don't get sued for libel."

Wow. Jess can't believe Gil has read her work. He is quoting from a recent piece about hedge fund profits. It had been popular, but she didn't think Gil would have read it.

She can't help it—she's flattered. Or she would be if that weren't completely beside the point. If he wasn't also threatening to sue her.

The piece was called *Follow the Money: How the Carried Interest Deduction Is Creating a New Kleptocracy*, and it had traced how funds flowed from hedge fund billionaires into political campaigns. As part of the story, Jess had created a diagram with circles you could click on to see how money moved from one rich person to another, from investor to hedge fund manager to industry lobbies, the vast sums of untaxed money lining the new kleptocracy's coffers.

The circles had looked just like bull's-eyes, with the richest political donors in the center and, naturally, Gil had been one of them.

"I mean, I get that he's not always thrilled about my work"—they had already fought about this exact article—"but we've always disagreed about this stuff. But, I mean, I love him and he loves me." She swallows. "I mean, overall I'm a positive uh . . . distraction."

"Is that so?"

"I mean . . . yes?" Jess wishes she said it with more conviction.

"No," Gil says, shaking his head.

"No?"

"A distraction is a distraction."

"So, what?"

"You're an intelligent young woman. I leave it to you to intuit my meaning."

"So . . . you're asking me to break up with him?"

Gil says, "I'm asking you to consider his future."

"But I'm part of his future."

He looks at her, and Jess can't tell if it's pity or disgust. He says, "Josh's future is much bigger than the two of you."

In the car home Jess is furious. "Gil shook me down," she says as soon as they shut the doors.

Josh looks across the seat, amused. "He shook you down?"

"Dressed me down, whatever."

"He dressed you down?"

"Yes," Jess says indignant, "he invited me into his study with the express purpose of undressing me."

"So, wait a minute, Gil extorted money from you?" It is dark, but she can hear the smile in his voice. "And then he took off your clothes?"

"Don't make fun of me, this isn't a joke."

"Then use your words, Jess. What exactly are you trying to tell me?"

"That Gil is an asshole!"

"On some level I think we both already knew that." He bites on a smile, but Jess's expression softens him. "So, what happened?"

"He told me I was a distraction. That I should leave you alone. That there was no point in dragging this all out since I'm clearly a Marilyn and you're going to end up with a Jackie. He wants you to marry Tenley. I was only ninety percent sure before but now I'm certain."

"He compared you to Marilyn Monroe?"

"Well, no, not in those words, but that was the subtext. Like I'm just someone frivolous, not good enough for his precious protégé, Josh." She makes a face. "Like I'm just some . . . tart from Trashtown trying to ride on your coattails to the penthouse suite."

"So in this analogy I'm . . . the president of the United States?"

"This isn't funny, Josh."

"You're extremely cute when you're mad, you know that?"

"Are you kidding me?"

"Like a feral bunny." He reaches across the seat and pinches her nose between his knuckles.

She slaps his hand away. "Well, I'm glad you think it's so fucking funny. I'm glad you and Gil think I'm such a big fucking joke." Her voice cracks.

"Come on, Jess, calm down." He grabs both of her hands and rubs his thumbs on her wrists. "Don't get so upset. Stop worrying about Tenley. It's making you crazy. I love you, you know that. You have to stop giving me a hard time. Besides, since when do you care what Gil thinks?"

"He thinks that I shouldn't be your girlfriend!"

"So?"

"That doesn't bother you?"

"Jess, no. Why would it?"

"But you value his opinion."

"Yeah, about work. Besides, I don't think he was saying what you think he was. I think he just got spooked about some of the stuff you've been writing. Either way, I don't exactly lose sleep over what he thinks about my personal life."

"Really?" Jess is skeptical. He'd done all sorts of calisthenics to make sure Gil didn't know they were together. What had changed? Jess isn't convinced by his conviction; she thinks it might just be the Manischewitz speaking.

Josh unbuckles his seat belt and scoots closer. He rubs her shoulder and kisses her hair and her face. He says, "Really."

She rests her head on his shoulder. "Well, then you should stand up for me. Tell him you hate him and you're quitting the fund unless he apologizes."

"Sure, Jess." He strokes her arm. "First thing Monday morning. First I'll demand the money and then I'll make him strip."

"Good."

Josh smiles. "Nobody messes with my Trashtown Marilyn and gets away with it."

18

Josh reads about an astronomical event, a satellite or a comet or something, that will be passing, for the first time or the only time or the last time, through the atmosphere. He makes Jess stay awake so that they can watch Pluto or Jupiter or whatever light up the night sky.

At three in the morning, they take the service stairs up to the roof.

Josh has a throw blanket draped over his shoulder and Jess is cradling what looks like a first-aid kit—a plastic box with a bright red cross emblazoned on it—but is actually where they keep the weed.

At the top of the stairs Josh heaves open a metal door and in front of them is the city. Lights are twinkling through the smog and when Josh takes her hand, it feels like the night before Christmas.

He shakes the blanket into the air, like a bullfighter. It flaps for a moment and then floats onto the roof, tar, soft as sand.

Jess opens the first-aid kit and pulls out a glass bowl, which they pass back and forth, smoking in silence, until Jess feels pleasantly high.

They lie on their backs, holding hands, staring up at the sky.

After a while, Jess says, "Hey, Josh."

He says, "Yeah?"

"Can you see anything?"

The sky is low and gray and hazy, and what looks like it might be a star or a planet or an asteroid on fire, upon closer inspection, is an aircraft light.

Josh laughs. "It is exceptionally cloudy."

"Wait"—Jess points at the sky—"do you see that constellation? The stars look like they're forming three points?" She traces it with a zigzagging finger. "See? It looks like a leaf?"

Josh nods.

"That's Cannabis Majoris. The ancient Greeks used it to chart their course in the night sky from one music festival to another."

Josh laughs. "But do you want me to tell you what that group of stars really is?"

"No."

He laughs again. "Okay."

She sits up and crosses her legs. Josh props himself up on his elbow and looks at Jess. She carefully presses weed into the bowl and they sit, smoking until everything is blurred around the edges.

"Where did you get this lighter?" Jess asks, flicking the cap on and off. "It looks like an heirloom. I like it."

"Gil gave it to me."

Jess says nothing.

"You really can't stand him."

"He fired me for no reason. He called me, a human, a person, sitting in front of him, a distraction. He thinks we should break up."

"Jess . . ." He looks sad.

"He thinks I'm nothing. They all do."

"They?"

"You know who," Jess says darkly. "The corporations-are-people-profit-motives-can-never-conflict-with-the-public-good-pull-yourself-up-by-your-bootstraps-discrimination-is-a-liberal-conspiracy-my-reality-is-the-objective-reality-so-can-everyone-just-shut-the-fuck-up-so-we-can-go-play-golf crowd."

Josh starts to say something then stops, then starts, then stops again. Eventually he settles on: "I'm sorry."

He sighs.

He rolls onto his back, closes his eyes, tips his chin toward the sky.

Eventually he says, "You know it doesn't matter, right? Do you ever look up at the stars"—he looks up at the stars—"or, I don't know, consider the universe, and think that's all it is? Bullshit? Pointless bullshit? None of it matters."

"It matters to me."

"But why? It's not . . . real."

"Josh?"

"What?"

"Is the next thing you're going to say 'there's only one race, the human race'? Because if it is, I'm going to strangle you."

He laughs. "Come on, Jess. Don't you know what I'm trying to say?"

"I don't know. Maybe."

"Look at it." He waves his free arm around. "It's all so vast. I mean . . . shit."

Jess looks up, again, and it's true. Through the clouds the sky is black, confettied with stars. Some are bright and some are faded, burning out. Jess thinks about planets and universes and galaxies and life and death and cells.

Josh takes the bowl, angling it from side to side. Finally, he says, "This is really bad for you, you know?"

"Well, it's a good thing nothing matters and we're all going to die." Jess flicks open the lighter and offers him the flame.

"That's not what I meant." He leans forward and accepts the light, blows smoke out the side of his mouth like a dragon. "I mean, that perspective can be a form of peace. Not that you're insignificant, but more like if you can see through all the layers of bullshit, even momentarily, then everything gets . . . easier." He pauses, taps on the pipe. "Also, I was referring to vapor. You should use a vaporizer. It's better for you. The effects of combustion from igniting dry herb can cause significant damage to the upper respiratory system."

"Sorry," Jess says, blinking. "Are we talking about metaphysics, or like, lung cancer?"

He laughs. "Both?" Then: "In all seriousness, though. I'm not trying to be an asshole or tell you how to . . . frame the world. I just thought a different way of looking at things could be useful."

"It isn't."

"Why not?"

"I don't need any more reasons to feel small."

"Oh, Jess." He looks at her sadly and reaches for her hand. "You're not small to me, you know that, right? To me, you're . . . everything."

He looks at her and she looks at him and then she laughs.

"What?"

"I don't know. You were just going on about the incontrovertible laws of nature and the effects of combustion on the upper respiratory tract and the meaninglessness of existence and then you, like . . . toss out this line. It's funny"—she forms her mouth into a half smile— "deep thoughts from yoga class."

Josh laughs. "You're right. That was lame. I was just trying to say that . . . I feel connected to you, on a level that feels cellular to me, I really do, but . . . it was lame. That was a lame thing to say." He rolls back over, face to the sky, hands folded behind his head. "I think I'm just really high."

Jess lies down too. Josh reaches for her and she scoots over into his outstretched arm, lets him scoop her body into his. Their noses are touching. "What do you think is going to happen next?" he asks.

"What do you mean?"

"What do you think the future holds? Where will we be in ten or thirty years?"

"Like, will we be together?"

He nods.

"I hope so."

"Me too."

Jess says, "If we ever break up I'm going to kill myself . . . and then I'll kill you."

"Thank you," he laughs. And then, "What do you think it would look like?"

"The murder scene?"

"No, us, when we're old . . . er."

"I don't know."

"We would get a dog," Josh finally pronounces, "and move to the suburbs and get fat and give up on life. Fight about the garbage a lot."

Jess smiles in the dark.

"Hey, Jess," Josh says, and his voice is serious, "we have fun together, don't we?"

He takes her hand, gives it a squeeze.

Jess squeezes back and says almost sadly, "We do."

Later, while Josh sleeps next to her, Jess considers things. How easy it is for him to compartmentalize. To divide the world into easy binaries: real and not real, important and trivial. Affects me and doesn't affect me. If he can't see it then it's not real, the empiricist in him. Jess stares at the ceiling and wonders what he sees when he sees her. How much of her he sees. Wonders if, to him, she's fully real. Wonders whether the aperture of his mind is wide enough to accommodate her in her entirety. Half-asleep, Josh mumbles, "Love you," then rolls over and drops a kiss on her shoulder. She kisses him back and then lets herself stop wondering.

•

Josh goes fly-fishing with David in Montana for a long weekend. While he's away, Miky and Lydia come over. They drink margaritas and play pop music in every room in the loft. In the bathroom they make a mess, giving themselves Korean face masks and manicures, spilling makeup and margaritas, while Miky screams, "Girls' night!"

Jess is scrubbing nail polish out of the tiles when Josh returns, smelling like canvas and lake water, with the beginning of a beard.

"Cleaning up the crime scene?"

"Josh!" She is so happy to see him. They hug and kiss and he smiles into her neck. "Hey, Just Jess."

"So," she says, leaning back in his arms, "what'd you bring me?"

"Just some Montana love for my love," he grins, smacking her butt, pulling her closer.

She laughs. "No, but really."

He laughs, pulls a small plastic gift bag from his pocket. "This."

Jess opens it to find a bag of chocolates meant to look like turds, Moose Droppings printed on the label.

She looks at him, laughs again. "Gross."

At work they watch the Republican primaries as if watching an automobile accident: unblinking, dismayed, slightly nauseated. When Donald Trump is officially pronounced the presidential nominee—his son casts the final votes for the New York delegation—the office emits a collective groan.

Jess turns to Dax on the other side of the cube. He stands suddenly, sticks his head into the metal cabinet above his desk, paws around for a minute, then emerges with a crumpled pack of cigarettes.

"Welp," he says, faux brightly, "I'd been waiting until the complete failure of the American experiment so that I could start smoking again." He taps the pack against his palm. "And here we find ourselves."

Then he is gone.

The editor materializes at Jess's desk. He appears to be in a mild form of pain—soda down the wrong pipe, a paper cut, a stubbed toe—and he says only, "I guess we'll have to update the maps."

"Yeah, of course," Jess says with a nod. He is referring to the interactive electoral maps that she has been building, a visual model of potential election outcomes, which up until this point had not included Donald Trump as a likely contender.

"I just can't believe he actually won, that he's, like, halfway to the presidency," Jess says, stunned.

"You and me both. That guy"—he shakes his head in disbelief—"gross."

The Wine Girls host a party. The signature drink is a tequila sunrise, three-parts tequila, one-part OJ, and everyone is obliterated within half an hour. Josh says, "Let's get out of here."

It is unseasonably cold and so everyone has brought sweaters and fleece jackets, and they are in a giant pile on someone's bed.

In the dark bedroom, they feel around for their jackets.

"Turn on the lights," Jess says, "I can't see."

Josh crosses the room, runs a hand along the far wall. "I can't find the switch."

In front of the bed he takes Jess by the waist. "Forget about your fleece. I know something else we can do in the dark."

He puts his palm against Jess's chest and pushes her backward.

She starfishes onto the jumble of coats, laughing. It's like a cloud, made of Patagonia down and winter weight cotton.

Josh climbs on top of her and they start making out, kissing and groping, on the pile of other people's clothes.

Jess is moaning and saying *oh oh oh* when the light snaps on.

They blink up to see someone standing in the doorway.

Josh has pulled Jess's top up and his palm is on her naked breast. No one moves.

The stranger snatches a coat from the pile.

He casts a withering glance at Josh and Jess. "Get a room," he says, closing the door. "Gross."

•

In the loft there is kind of a nook, between the kitchen and the dining room, where they keep unopened mail and menus from the Burmese delivery place, old editions of the *Financial Times* and piles of Canadian quarters, and where the cleaning lady drops household miscellany into a large cloth basket nestled against the wall.

Jess is rummaging through this basket, looking for a D battery, when a flash of red catches her eye. She leans over, peers into the basket. Inside: a blood-colored hat, white letters embroidered across the front. MAKE AMERICA GREAT AGAIN. She blinks twice, as if it were possible to unsee it. It is not.

She plucks it out of the basket, grasping it with just the tips of her fingers, like a dirty diaper.

"Hey, Josh," she calls. "Can you come here?"

"What is it?" he calls back from the bedroom.

"Just . . . come here!" Jess says, trying not to sound panicked. Obviously, he'll have a good explanation.

He appears behind her. "You called?"

Jess is crouched over the basket and she stands. She takes a pen, hangs the hat strap over it, turns and presents it to him, evidence.

"What is this?"

He sighs.

"David got them for us. It was a joke," he says. "Obviously."

That is not obvious.

"A *joke*?"

"Jess—"

"What kind of fucking joke is that? What is wrong with you!"

"Jess, please calm down. I know you hate Trump but it's just a hat," he says slowly, "it can't hurt you."

But it does hurt her.

He holds his hands up, like he's taming a wild cat. "It's just . . . a hat."

"Did you wear it?"

"What?"

"Have you worn it, Josh? Have you Put. It. On. Your. Head?"

He hesitates. "Briefly. It was silly." He shakes his head. "It was nothing. It's not like I'm wearing it around New York. It was for a dumb photo. David wanted—"

"For a *photo?* So you're telling me that not only was this . . . this . . ."—she jabs the pen and the hat at his chest—"this *hat* on your head, but there's a *photo* of you in it? Are you fucking serious?"

"Jess—"

"How could you bring this into our *home?*"

"Jess," he says, "come on—"

"Come on? Come *on?* What the fuck is wrong with you!"

The hat hangs in the air between them, practically vibrating, red-hot. Jess can barely look at it.

He says, "It's just a hat."

But it's not just a hat. It makes Jess think of racism and hatred and systemic inequality, and the Ku Klux Klan, and plantation-wedding Pinterest boards, and lynchings, and George Zimmerman, and the Central Park Five, and redlining, and gerrymandering and the Southern strategy, and decades of propaganda and Fox News and conservative radio, and rabid evangelicals, and rape and pillage and plunder and plutocracy and money in politics and the dumbing down of civil discourse and domestic terrorism and white nationalists and school shootings and the growing fear of a nonwhite, non-English-speaking majority and the slow death of the social safety net and conspiracy theory culture and the white working class and social atomism and reality television and fake news and the prison-industrial complex and celebrity culture and the girl in fourth grade who told Jess that since she—Jess—was "naturally unclean" she couldn't come over for birth-day cake, and executive compensation, and mediocre white men, and the guy in college who sent around an article about how people who listen to Radiohead are smarter than people who listen to Missy El-liott and when Jess said "That's racist" he said "No, it's not," and of bigotry and small pox blankets and gross guys grabbing your butt on the subway, and slave auctions and Confederate monuments and Jim Crow and fire hoses and separate but equal and racist jokes that aren't funny and internet trolls and incels and golf courses that ban women and voter suppression and police brutality and crony capitalism and corporate corruption and innocent children, so many innocent chil-dren, and the Tea Party and Sarah Palin and birthers and flat-earthers and states' rights and disgusting porn and the prosperity gospel and the drunk football fans who made monkey sounds at Jess outside Memorial Stadium, even though it was her thirteenth birthday, and Josh—now it makes her think of Josh.

He says, "It's just a hat."

"It's not just a fucking hat!"

"I don't say anything when you wear that Black Lives Matter shirt," he says.

He is calm.

It is infuriating.

"Are you kidding me? Are you *fucking* kidding me? That's not at all the same!"

"It's political rhetoric," he says blandly.

"So you're telling me that fighting for justice and equality is the same . . . as calling Mexicans rapists?"

"No, of course not. But that's a false equivalence and you know it. You always do this. On its face, neither statement is problematic. Don't try to suggest that I don't think Black lives matter. That's dis-ingenuous. But your point, which I *agree* with, is that it's not just the words themselves, it's the rhetoric around the words, all the ideas and judgments animating it, that can be 'problematic,' "—he uses air quotes and it makes Jess want to do something violent—"but if you're going to call out one, then you need to call out the other. Black Lives

Matter is a political statement. Make America Great Again is a political statement. Both statements deserve to be interrogated."

"So you're telling me that Black Lives Matter is equivalent to Make America Great Again? I'm just repeating that back, so you can confirm that that is actually what you're saying."

"Not equivalent, no. You're putting words in my mouth."

"Then what?"

She can see him picking his words carefully. "Close cousins."

Not carefully enough.

"Are you fu—"

"My point is"—he puts up a hand to stop Jess from interrupting—"when you wear your politics on your chest, I don't say anything. I don't get mad. I don't ask you what the fuck is wrong with you, I just . . . let it go."

"So I'm supposed to let *racism* go? When my boyfriend brings home racist paraphernalia I'm just supposed to go about my business?"

His jaw clenches. "It's not racist paraphernalia."

"It is! It's—"

"Donald Trump is the Republican nominee, Jess!" Josh is finally angry. "What do you expect? Every single Republican is not racist, Jess. Voting the party line is not a fucking crime. It doesn't make you racist."

"Yes, it does! Just because no one's literally claiming the mantle of racism—although honestly the way things are going I wouldn't be surprised if they started wearing T-shirts that said *I heart racism*—just because no one's beating their chest and shouting 'I'm a racist' doesn't mean they're not racist! They're voting to perpetuate a racist system. It's the literal definition of racism! How can you say that's not racist? And what about the fact that the Republican Party is ninety percent white? Ninety percent! A whole party just for white people! A party whose entire platform is just one loud dog whistle. Immigration and tax cuts and states' rights and the working class. It's all racist bullshit!"

"So what are you saying, then? Are you saying that I'm a racist? Am I racist, Jess?"

She thinks about it. She chews on her lip and closes her eyes and really, really thinks about it. Finally, she says, "Um."

He shakes his head at the ceiling. "You can't be serious. How could *I* be racist?"

"What's *that* supposed to mean? Like, why not? Because you have a Black girlfriend? Like you think that inoculates you?"

"You can't be serious."

"I am! I'm not a get-out-of-racism-jail-free card, Josh. Just because you have a Black girlfriend?"

"That's one more Black friend than you have," he spits, as if throwing a spear.

Jess leans back, as if hit. "What are you talking about?"

His mouth gets small. "What do you think I'm talking about?" He shakes his head, fuming, royally pissed. If they weren't fighting before, they're fighting now.

"Dax is my friend!" Jess can hear that she sounds defensive. Shrill. Guilty.

Josh says, "Who the hell is Dax?"

"My friend!" Josh is making her feel like a liar. "Paul's boyfriend. You've *met* him."

"Okay, fine. That's one. We're tied."

Jess racks her brain, scrolls through the names and faces of all the Black people she knows, has ever known. All the Black names in her phone. Besides Dax: A guy she met on an app and went on one date with. Someone from college. Her father. The list is not long. Josh is right, technically—what's fucking new?—but he's also wrong. So wrong.

Jess says, "My point is that just because you have a Black girlfriend doesn't mean you're not racist." She stops, recalibrates. "Just because *one* has a Black girlfriend doesn't mean *one* isn't racist."

"You're unbelievable, you know that?" He hasn't stopped shaking his head. "One, I never said it did. And two, for the record, the reason I can't be racist is because I'm not racist. I give money to all your charities, I volunteer, what do you want me to do? Proffer myself at the feet of every Black person in America? What would make you think

I'm not racist? Nothing, that's what. Because you're so married to this narrative you've created in your mind that everything and everyone is racist and that shouting about it on social media is somehow constructive. And you're wrong."

"I'm *wrong*? I thought you were on my side! All those times you were like, 'Yeah, Jess, it's so fucked up, Jess. It sucks, Jess. I'm so sorry, Jess,' you were, what, rolling your eyes behind my back?" She shakes her head. "I really thought you had changed."

"Changed?"

"I thought you had grown as a person. Evolved. Developed a deeper sense of empathy. Woken up!"

"You mean you thought I was"—he scoffs—"*woke*? Jess, I'm the same person I've always been. *You're* the one who's changed. And not for the better, frankly. Ever since you got this new job all you do is post these bullshit articles and spout this bullshit left-wing propaganda."

"*Bull*shit? So, what? When we were on the roof and you told me none of it was real you didn't mean in the cosmic sense you meant in the real sense? You think I'm full of shit?"

He dodges the question. "We've always disagreed, Jess! And you've always been okay with it. This is what you signed up for! Now all of a sudden you're this rabid, I don't know . . . social justice warrior with a permanent axe to grind. You've lost your mind. Where did my cool, fun girlfriend go? Why are you suddenly so . . . fixated on all of this?"

"I've always cared."

"You've always *said* you cared. You sure said a lot, but you never did anything."

"Now I'm doing something and you're accusing me of being crazy!"

"You're not doing anything! You're posting inflammatory shit on the internet! And then you think I'm a bad person because, what, I'm white? Because I think supply-side economics is a smart bet? Like all of a sudden I'm not good enough because I don't subscribe to some narrow bullshit worldview."

"You're the one who doesn't think I'm good enough! You didn't even want Gil to know we were dating. You were so fucking terrified to tell him because he's your meal ticket, and he doesn't like me because I'm not his perfect fucking niece, and you know what? I think that sometimes you think that too. You wish that I were different because I don't fit into your perfect image of what you dreamed your life would be like growing up on the wrong side of Greenwich fucking Connecticut! All you care about is being rich and having money and fuck everyone else!"

"You're such a hypocrite."

"Sorry, what?"

"You post your little articles about how Gil is this robber baron, crony capitalist enemy of democracy but it's a lie, Jess. You're a liar and a hypocrite."

"I'm a hypocrite because I correctly point out that concentrated wealth is antithetical to a functional republic?"

"You're not exactly a monk, Jess! You want all of this too! You can't have it both ways. You're a hypocrite because this is what you want too, Jess. All of this"—he gestures at the gleaming marble, the windows, the view, the floors, all of it, and Jess feels sick.

He lunges past her to the refrigerator, swings it open. "This"— he picks up a package of sliced *jamón ibérico*, examines it haphazardly—"you spend twenty dollars on five fucking slices of ham!—"

"I did not!"

He lifts the package and peers underneath it. "Oh, excuse me, *seventeen ninety-nine*. My mistake," his voice drips with arsenic. "Wow Jess, you're a real working-class hero." He sticks his head back in the fridge. "How about this?" He takes a bottle of organic juice out of the door. "It's carrots and water and you paid twelve dollars for this!" He is shouting now. "Oh, sorry, actually, *I* paid twelve dollars for this, with money that I earned from working for Gil goddamn Alperstein. I didn't hear you complaining about income inequality when you bought this fucking juice." He shakes it at her, then slams the refrigerator door.

Then he lowers his voice and says, "You know what, Jess?" He waits until she looks him in the eye to say: "We're exactly the same. We wouldn't be having this conversation if you were in my position. You don't have a problem with the system, just your place in it."

Jess blinks. She starts to speak, but her voice wobbles. She swallows. Finally, she says, almost a whisper, "I can't do this anymore."

And then she starts crying.

His face falls.

"Jess, I'm sorry. I didn't mean that. I hate fighting with you, I'm sorry." He stares out the window. "You called me a racist and I just . . . I'm sorry."

"That's it?"

"I'm sorry."

"What exactly are you sorry about?"

"About . . . everything."

Jess doesn't buy his apology. He's the one who's always telling her to use her words, asking her to articulate her feelings more clearly. Which, thinking about it now, only pisses Jess off more. It's easy enough for Josh to argue with impassivity—after all, it's all a game to him. He said it himself on the roof: Nothing is real. But it's real to Jess. It's too real.

The hat is still on the floor where Jess dropped it. She picks it up and flings it hard at his chest. He is momentarily startled but catches it. And then—and this will haunt Jess—he takes it by the brim and smacks it twice against his thigh, shaking away dust. Such a casual gesture. He then sets it on the desk as if it's something he's planning to pick up again. As if it's any old thing to leave around the house. As if the past twenty minutes never happened. As if her feelings don't matter.

He doesn't even notice. His hand is resting on the hat, absentmindedly. He is looking at her, apologetically. She can't stand it.

He says, "I'm sorry."

"You don't even know what you're sorry about!"

"I—"

She stomps around the loft throwing things—clothes, face wash, laptop—into a duffel bag while Josh trails after her saying, "Jess, please, come on."

She ignores him and instead jabs at the elevator button, impatient and fuming, tears running down her face.

Josh reaches for the duffel bag, but she yanks it back. He says, "This is crazy. Where are you going? Please stay."

He reaches for her again but she pushes him away. "Please nothing! Now I know what you really think! You think I'm a money-grubbing hypocrite and a liar!"

"Jess, come on, please. I don't think that! I didn't mean it. I was upset."

But it doesn't matter if he doesn't mean it, because he is not completely wrong, which is maybe worse than if he were.

She has surrounded herself with beautiful things and bad people and she can't even slam the door when she walks out. Instead, she just stands there, furious, until the elevator glides to a stop at their door, sliding soundlessly open and then soundlessly closed—the drive system is hydraulic, expensive, state-of-the-art—and then she is gone.

Outside her phone buzzes immediately.

I'm so sorry, please come back

I didn't mean it, I was upset

I love you

Don't go

Jess shows up at Lydia's breathless. "I think me and Josh are over."

"*What?*" In the kitchen, Lydia pours tequila into a tumbler. "Why?"

Jess flings herself on the couch. "I think he's racist. Or something."

Lydia sits down. "Here." She hands Jess the drink, folds her legs under her. "Since when?"

"I don't know. Since always, maybe." Jess rubs her face. "He's going to vote for Donald Trump!"

Lydia frowns. "I'm sorry."

Jess starts crying.

Miky and the Wine Girls come over with a roasted chicken and more tequila.

Lydia says, "Maybe he won't vote."

"Or maybe he'll vote for Rand Paul," Miky says. "Finance bros love that libertarian shit."

"What am I supposed to do?" Jess wails.

The Wine Girls tut. "We hate to say it, Jess, but at this point is it even ethical to be dating him?"

Paul says, "Girl, get a grip."

"Even though my boyfriend is everything that's wrong with America?"

"You forget I'm from bumfuck Tennessee?" Paul asks.

"And what? Everyone there is a Trump supporter? So you're going to tell me it's fine because they're poor or they work in coal mines or whatever the fuck."

"Forget about Trump." Paul waves a hand in the air, dismissive. "My parents. They go to church eight days a week. Total pray-the-gay-away types."

Jess frowns. "But I thought your parents were cool. Weren't they here in April? I thought you took them to Carbone."

"They are cool," he says. "In some ways. In others? Not at all."

"I'm sorry."

"Don't be sorry." Paul flicks her on the forehead. "Just learn how to compartmentalize."

"Or don't," Dax chimes in. "Josh is who he is."

Jess asks, "What does that even mean?"

"Well, he's a white dude from . . . ?"

"From Connecticut. Greenwich."

Dax opens his palm as if to say *I rest my case.*

"So you're saying it's fine?"

"What's fine?" Dax asks.

"That Josh is kind of, like, I don't know, a product of his environment? This archetypal conservative guy? Like he is who he is and that's it?"

"It's . . . not surprising." Dax is gentle, but Jess can read between the lines. What he's really saying is: *What did you expect?*

What *did* she expect?

That her willful naivete would never catch up with her?

That beneath his pink polo was a heart beating with empathy?

That love and understanding were the same thing?

Josh is who he is.

What did she expect?

If she'd asked her dad, she was certain he would say the same thing. He would be nice about it, obviously, but the point remained. Josh was who he was and Jess couldn't change it. She could pretend it away, maybe, for a while, but not forever. It was a form of denial, she knew. Of avoidance. Whenever her dad caught her pretending—not hoping or dreaming, but inventing a convenient reality—he'd say, "Are you wishing or are you thinking?" and ninety percent of the time she'd be forced to admit that she was not, in fact, using her brain.

Jess stays with Lydia, ignoring Josh's texts and phone calls. She buys a pack of underwear from Duane Reade and says, "Well, I guess we're roommates now."

Lydia raises an eyebrow. "You know you have to speak to him eventually."

Dax texts to check in.

how's it going? he asks.

Jess replies, *I don't know*

Dax types:

just wanted to say sorry didn't mean to be flip the other day

only met Josh a couple times

but Paul says he's all right

We still haven't spoken, Jess admits.

really?

I mean . . . it got pretty ugly

I called him racist

really?

Yeah

and what did he say?

Nothing! He was just like, well, you don't have any Black friends

why would he say that?

Because I don't

:(

Have any Black friends

Present company excluded

why not?

No good reason

I didn't grow up with any other Black kids

And then in college it didn't seem important

Or I guess more like it wasn't a priority

And then, I don't know, it was too late, everybody already had friends

. . .

That's bad though, right? That I don't have any Black friends?

Dax doesn't write back. Seconds pass, then minutes, then several long hours: No answer. Which is kind of an answer in itself. Jess wishes she hadn't said anything. Because now she's revealed an uncomfortable truth. She's invited him to appraise her private failings. She's made it weird.

Later that night though, Dax replies.

sorry Paul made fajitas, it was a WHOLE thing

He sends a photo of a steaming skillet, Paul smiling behind it.

neways

to your question: not good or bad, I reject that binary

but

I will say

I do think it's healthy for a soul to have some relationships where there's no need to explain anything

Jess thinks about that.

Do you have to explain things to Paul?

not really no

Jess isn't sure if this makes her feel better or worse.

She asks, *Do you think it's because he's gay? Like, solidarity, marginality, etc. etc.*

Dax says, **either that or because he's a Virgo**

Jess types *lololol* but her heart's not in it.

Jess knows Lydia is right, that she eventually has to return to the loft, but she's still mad or sad or something.

She is debating exactly when—should she give it another day, or maybe three?—when she receives a strange call.

A woman who Jess doesn't know, who identifies herself only as Barbara, calls her at work.

"Your daddy is very sick," she says. "You need to come home."

Panicked, Jess gets in touch with her dad.

"Dad!" she cries when he picks up. "What's going on? Someone named Barbara called me. She said you were sick."

He chuckles into the phone and Jess is surprised.

"I don't understand. What's going on?"

"Oh no, Jessie, please don't fret. Barbara is just worrying over me when she needn't be."

"But . . . what? I don't understand. Who's Barbara?"

"She's a friend," he says, "but don't worry about what she said. I'm all right."

"So you're not sick? I don't need to come home?"

On the other end, Jess gets no response. "Dad? Are you still there?"

"Jessie," he says, "everything's fine."

But then the Barbara woman texts:

You need to come now

Part Four

19

At home everything is smaller than she remembers. Jess used to ride her tricycle in the house, and she remembers the corridor as an infinite runway. But now it seems so small.

Smaller still, because of Barbara. Barbara, who Jess didn't know existed until forty-eight hours ago, but who acts as if she has always been there: folding towels and pressing buttons on the dishwasher and answering the fucking phone whenever someone calls. Barbara, who has giant breasts and is wearing too much perfume and who is clearly her father's girlfriend, though he never said a word about her. Barbara, who let Jess in when she arrived, and when Jess asked "Where's my dad?" replied, "Baby, he's dozing. Why don't you put away your things and I'll make you a cup of tea?"

Baby? Jess thinks. *Dozing?*

She wants to tell this Barbara person that she didn't fly all the way from New York for a cup of fucking tea. She wants to see her dad.

But Barbara is already in the kitchen fussing over the kettle, so instead Jess sulks while Barbara boils water for chamomile.

Barbara, who hums to herself while she opens and closes cupboards and drawers. Barbara, who, apparently, thinks her father would rather doze than see his own daughter.

Barbara, who Jess has known for all of twenty minutes but already can't stand.

It's true, Jess never asked. When he was in South Africa she let it slide. And then it just seemed easier to ignore it. An imaginary pact between father and daughter, perhaps, to avoid discussing their secret loves. Jess had been curious, of course, but she knew that if she started asking questions, he would too. And what was she going to do, lie?

* * *

Eventually, her dad emerges.

Barbara says, "Now I know you're not out here on this tile with no socks on," and Jess rolls her eyes, because even though it is dinnertime and his hair isn't combed and he's wearing pajamas, he seems fine.

He opens his arms to Jess and smiles wide. "Darling daughter, what a wonderful surprise," then he turns to Barbara and says theatrically, "Gracing us with her presence, all the way from New York City."

Jess hugs her dad and tries not to cry; she'd seen him at Christmas, but it feels much longer. She thinks she must be the worst daughter in the world. He squeezes her tightly then takes a step back.

"So . . . what'd you bring me?" he teases, a twinkle in his eye.

See, Barbara? Jess thinks. *Everything's fine.*

She rummages through her bag until she finds his gift. It's a stupid T-shirt that says NEW YAWK FRIGGING CITY in big letters on the front. Jess got it at the airport; she was hoping he would laugh.

But then he tries the shirt on and it hangs loose, like a big burlap sack, and Jess can see that he's lost a lot of weight.

"How are you feeling, Dad?" Jess says. "I mean . . . you're okay, right?"

"Yes, yes," he assures her. "Now that you're here, I'm just fine."

Jess finally messages Josh:

> **had to go to Lincoln for a bit, talk when I get back?**
> **What? Why? Is everything okay?**

Is everything okay? Jess isn't really sure. Her finger hovers a millimeter above her phone as she tries to think of what to say.

Josh texts again:

> **How long?**

Again, Jess isn't really sure. She writes back:

> **a few days?**

He says:

> **I miss you Just Jess**

She wants to type **me too** but instead she says:

> **Okay**

* * *

"Baby, why don't you clean up a bit in here?" Barbara asks the next day, standing in the doorway of Jess's bedroom. For a split second Jess has an almost uncontrollable urge to shout *You're not my real mom!* but, of course, that would be ridiculous.

Why is Barbara even here? Wiping down counters like she lives here and fawning over her father as if he were a child. It strikes Jess as melodramatic and excessive. But Barbara keeps cleaning and her father keeps sleeping and Jess starts to wonder why *she's* here. Her father isn't feeling well, she can see that, but it's not like he's dying.

Barbara invites Jess to go grocery shopping.

Her head is in the refrigerator when she says to Jess, "Baby, let's go to the market. You've been inside all day."

Her father is in bed sleeping. And Jess is in the living room, one leg thrown over the back of the couch, her computer in her lap, pretending to do work, while Barbara makes noise in the kitchen, doing God knows what, cabinets opening and closing, pots and pans rattling.

At Hy-Vee Barbara pulls a cart from the stack lined up at the front. It has a wobbly wheel so Barbara takes a flyer from a pile, folds it into a neat little square, then bends down and slides it into the caster. Like a middle-aged goddamn Girl Scout. She even has an alphabetized list. She reads to herself: aspirin, bread, cantaloupe, diet soda.

Barbara navigates the supermarket, brisk and efficient, while Jess follows her through the aisles feeling useless.

In the produce section Jess spots a mound of cantaloupe and finds a way to make herself useful. She squeezes one and then another and then another, selects two perfect cantaloupes, and drops them into the cart.

"Look," she points, "two for five."

Barbara frowns. "Are those organic?"

"They are," Jess says proudly.

Barbara shakes her head. "Baby, those aren't on sale." She nods in the direction of the inorganic produce, where cantaloupe and honeydew are on sale for thirty-nine cents a pound. But at least she leaves them in the cart. Jess feels like she must be the most profligate grocery shopper in the world; first Josh and now Barbara. It confirms for Jess that, yes, she is the worst kind of person. Not only the kind of person who buys eighteen-dollar *jamón*, not only the kind of person who buys eighteen-dollar *jamón* and *can't afford* eighteen-dollar *jamón*, but the kind of person who buys eighteen-dollar *jamón* and can't afford eighteen-dollar *jamón* and pays for eighteen-dollar *jamón* with her boyfriend's money—his hedge fund plunder, as the Wine Girls would call it. The kind of person who buys eighteen-dollar *jamón* while writing her name under headlines like *How Income Inequality Is Destroying Society*. The kind of person who wants a million dollars—an obscene sum of money—just to be seen.

She's no better than Josh. The only difference between them is that when she buys eighteen-dollar *jamón* she at least feels guilty. But that feels like something. A wave of fresh indignation grips her. Josh may have been right about some things, but not everything. Not even close. And at the end of the day, better to be a hypocrite than an unrepentant free market enthusiast. Right?

She removes both cantaloupes from the cart.

In the bakery they pass the bread and boxed pastries and, standing in front of the donut case, Jess says, "Hey, Barbara. We should get a couple of these for my dad, he loves them." The house special donuts are jelly filled and sugar dusted.

"Oh, baby," Barbara says sadly, "your dad isn't feeling too well."

"I know." Does Barbara think she's blind? Jess opens the glass case, wraps her hand around a filmy sheet of wax paper like a claw. "He'll have them when he's feeling better. Or ready for a treat."

But Barbara shakes her head and says, "No, I don't think so."

"It's fine." Jess puts a donut in the cart. "It's just a couple of donuts. No need to freak out."

This time Barbara takes them out. "Oh, baby," she says, "don't you know? It's cancer. Stage four."

* * *

Jess decides to clean up her room.

It is clear that Barbara is pathologically tidy—she scrubs pots and mops floors and sorts mail all day long—but also, she is not wrong. The room is a mess.

Jess gets on her knees and reaches under the bed. She finds: a broken alarm clock, a *Where's Waldo?* puzzle book, an old pair of tennis shoes. Also, a plastic box full of CDs. She extracts a jewel case: Destiny's Child.

It had been a gift. In middle school, they celebrated birthdays once a month and in Jess's month, September, there had been three birthdays and they each received a CD. For the boy who always wore black eyeliner, Metallica. For the girl who carried a pink purse instead of a backpack, the latest hit album from a reality TV star slash country singer with blond hair and a baby voice.

And for Jess, *Survivor* by Destiny's Child.

On the playground that day, Cath, who was the queen bee, said half-bitchy, half-sweet, "We thought you'd like it, because it's so ghetto fabulous."

After that, Jess was sure she'd thrown the CD in the trash, but now here it is. She cracks the plastic case open and slides it into her old CD player.

"Bootylicious" comes on and she laughs.

She turns the volume up.

Cath was an asshole, one hundred percent, but the song is definitely not subtle.

Next: In the back of her closet, Jess finds gel pens and sticker books, a bag of stuffed animals and old Barbie dolls. She pulls the Barbies from the bag one by one. She empties the bag until they're all in a jumble on the floor, then holds two dolls up in front of her, one Black and one white.

Yep. They all have shiny hair and slutty outfits, but the Black dolls have sluttier outfits. Shorter skirts, higher heels, slashes of bright pink makeup across their faces. One is wearing a shirt that says *hott!* For a moment she contemplates outrage but decides she can't be bothered. She tosses the dolls back in the closet.

As the music rings in her head, she looks around for more. More what? Evidence of her past, maybe, of the person she used to be, for whatever remains beneath the piles of old clothes and the stacks of notebooks and paper-clipped essays.

Her desk is a mess. She pulls a metal chain attached to a lamp and the bulb pops and then dies. She tries to open the desk drawer but it's stuck. She slides her arm as far back as it will go, her ear pressed against the desk, hand groping for the source of the jam. She extracts a crumpled sheet of paper: one of her hot-guy magazine tear-outs. The blond curls, the pretty pecs; she remembers them so clearly.

She remembers how her father felt about them.

She thinks of Ivan.

And then Josh.

Josh.

She flips open an old birthday card and a two-dollar bill from her father flutters out. She smiles.

Her father was such a good father, *is* such a good father. He has done everything for her, has given everything to her. And how has she repaid him? By leaving and never coming back. By keeping secrets. But he held her to such a high standard! Jess still feels like she might never live up to it.

How can it be cancer?

Barbara taps lightly on the door. "Baby," she says, her voice muffled from the hallway, "how about some tea?"

"What?" Jess doesn't hear her. Her ears are ringing a little bit and the music is still on. The room was a mess before, but now it is a disaster.

Barbara taps on the door again and then pushes it open slightly.

She surveys the mess, but then her eyes land on Jess, who is surrounded by all the things she has ever owned, crying. Barbara says, "Oh, oh my."

Jess can't sleep. She roams up and down the hall until she hears a light in her father's room switch on. And then, into the stillness of the house, she hears him call.

She steps through his bedroom door and says, "Dad?"

He is sitting on the edge of the bed with both palms on the mattress, his frame just visible in the dark. Jess thinks he needs help getting up so she walks over to stand in front of him. The balls of his feet just skim the floor and in this moment he looks incredibly young.

"Are you okay?" Jess asks. "Is there anything you need?"

But he shakes his head and pats the bed next to his left leg. Jess takes a seat, hopping up on the bed.

He says, "It's good to have you home."

"Oh, Dad," Jess says, her voice clipped, on the verge of tears.

They sit in silence, the entire house quiet.

Jess speaks first. "Why didn't you tell me you were . . . that it was . . . that it was this bad?" She had looked up his prognosis online: he is dying. "I could have come sooner."

He shakes his head. "I didn't want you to come sooner. I didn't want to disrupt your life."

"But Dad—"

"You're here now. And I'm glad."

After more silence, Jess asks, "Are you scared?"

He shakes his head slowly. "I'm not."

This makes Jess feel unbearably, existentially sad.

As if reading her mind, he says, "But Jessie, I know you, you'll be fine."

She nods. "Why didn't you tell me about Barbara?"

Quietly, he laughs. "You're full of questions tonight."

"When did . . . I mean, how long—"

"Since you left."

"Wow. Why didn't you ever . . . introduce us?"

He looks at his hands. "Barbara is married."

"You're married?" Jess asks, shocked.

He looks at her like she's younger than she is. It's not that she doesn't understand what he's saying, more that her specific idea of him can't quite accommodate this information.

He says slowly, "Barbara is married. To another man. Separated now, but they weren't when we met."

"That's . . . wow." Jess doesn't know how to respond. She looks at her dad. "But I mean, that's why we never met? Because you thought I would judge you or something? I like Barbara"—as Jess says this she realizes that it's true—"life is . . . complicated. I get it. I would never judge you."

He pats her knee. "I know you wouldn't, darling. You're a much wiser soul than I." He gives her a sad smile. "There is no judgment in love. You know that. But it took me longer to understand that. I was, I felt I was doing something wrong. I still feel that way. I didn't want to disappoint you. But I've learned, Jessie, that sometimes it's better to be happy than right."

Jess feels tears welling behind her eyes. She blinks them back. "Dad, you could have said something. You could never disappoint me."

"You were in New York," he says. "At first there was shame, yes. But then after that wore off a year had passed and then another and it seemed strange to mention it when I hadn't before. It wasn't my intention to be dishonest. But I wasn't forthcoming, and I apologize."

Jess shakes her head. She's not trying to give him a hard time.

She gets it, this feeling, that there are things you'd like to share but that it's too late.

She'd like to tell him things too, but then that refrain in her head says *It's too late, it's too late, it's too late.*

It's like that time she had spent a long weekend with the Wine Girls upstate. The showerhead in the bathroom was complicated. Jess had gotten undressed and stepped into the shower, then fiddled with the spigot for way too long. She twisted, she pulled, she pressed and pinched, but no water came out. By then someone was knocking on the door, yelling at her for hogging the shower. Jess knew she should have asked for help sooner, but fifteen minutes later, naked and dry, it was too late to do anything without embarrassing herself. Her window of opportunity had closed. All she could do was splash herself with water from the sink and get the hell out of there.

Why hasn't she talked to him? Why did she wait until it was too late? Why hasn't she told him things? What was she afraid of?

"I have a boyfriend," Jess admits.

"Is that so?" her father smiles.

She nods.

"And why didn't you mention him?"

Jess makes a face, shakes her head. "I don't know. I guess, I was also . . . I was worried that you would think he wasn't a good person. Sometimes I'm not even sure."

"Oh, Jessie, how could that be? Does he treat you right? Is he decent?"

"I . . . don't know."

He frowns.

"I mean, he's nice to me. But I don't know if he's decent." She stops, thinks. "The thing is, I don't even know if I'm decent."

"Now why would you say that?"

She shrugs.

"Oh, Jessie."

She says, "I'm so sorry that I just left."

"Left?"

"Here. Lincoln. Home. I'm sorry I never came back."

"Oh, darling, don't you feel bad about that. You weren't supposed to stay here forever. What kind of father would I be if I expected that? I'm so happy you have your own life. That's exactly as it should be."

"But I've missed you, Dad."

"And I've missed you too. But I knew you would never stay. Ever since you've been a tiny little thing"—he lets his palm hover three feet above the floor—"you had one foot out the door. I knew this place was never going to be home. It served us well, but I'd have been fooling myself if I expected you to stay. Hell, if I had been twenty-two I would have gone too."

"Wait, really? But I thought—" Jess's head is spinning. "So if . . . if Mom hadn't died, do you think we would have left?" Jess is imagining the possibilities, even as the familiar guilt sets in. He had given her everything, and she still wanted more.

"Well, no." He thinks about it. "I'm not sure about that. We both wanted the same things."

Jess waits for him to say what.

"A safe place for you to grow up. A good school, a nice neighborhood."

"But what about Chicago?" Jess's mother had grown up in Chicago.

"Well, you know, we both had complicated relationships with our families. Your mother's parents"—he looks at her—"your grandparents, by the time you were born, they had died. She took care of them for a long time. And her brother, he had problems. And you know my own family was also demanding. There was so much . . ."—he rubs his chin, searching for the right word—"baggage. We didn't want you to have to carry any of that. We wanted a fresh start, for you to grow up free."

But Jess had often wished for a compass. Instructions passed down for how to be and what to value. When she was younger and had asked about their extended family, all he had revealed was that it was complicated. That families weren't always what you dreamed they'd be. But what a bitter irony. He wanted to free her from the demands of family, and now she is practically an orphan. The worst kind of freedom, to be sure.

"Did you ever feel lonely though?" she asks. "With no family? Without my mom? Here in Lincoln?"

"Sometimes, yes. But I had you"—he squeezes her knee—"and then it wasn't so bad."

"I'm so sorry, Dad. I'm so sorry I never came back."

Again, he waves his hand in the air, like it's nothing. "You have your own life. I never wanted to interfere."

Jess thinks of her friends' parents who absolutely interfere. Lydia, who talks to her mother three times a day, and Miky, whose parents visit all the way from Korea every six months.

"I'm proud of you. All that you've accomplished."

She shakes her head. "I feel like I do a lot of things I'm not proud of."

He leaves space for her to tell him, but Jess doesn't know where to start: the friends, the jobs, the boyfriend, the choices that were all so wrong, but all of it boiling down to one simple thing: wanting to be someone different, rejecting all the things he'd given her. And for what? Just so she could feel bigger? So people would listen? So she could prove that whatever people assumed about her was wrong? It hadn't even made a difference. Now it all seems so silly, but she doesn't say any of it and, ever delicate with her, he doesn't force the issue.

He takes her hand. "Oh, Jessie, you're young. You have so much time. There's nothing you've done that can't be undone. I raised you right, didn't I?"

She nods into her lap.

"Jessie, look at me. You're a smart, talented young lady. And it's not always easy, I know that, but I know you'll make good choices."

But has she? Has she? She thinks of Josh, how he called her a hypocrite. He was right. Her father has the wrong impression. He thinks that everything she does is good and nice. But he doesn't fully know her, knows only the outline of her life. Even now, she has the feeling that they are somehow talking past each other.

"I . . ." Jess's voice cracks, she's trying not to cry. "I just wish I were a better person. I wish I were more like you."

"Come on now. None of that," he says. "Now give your old dad a hug."

She does. He rubs her back, in soft circles like when she was a little girl.

It is comforting.

She holds him tighter, until she can feel his spine, each and every vertebra poking through his shirt, like a skeleton, and finally she cries.

•

Josh calls every day, multiple times a day, but it is never a good time, so Jess doesn't answer.

It has been almost two weeks. She hasn't told him that her dad is sick, or why she went away.

He keeps calling and leaving messages, until her mailbox is full, and still Jess can't bring herself to answer. She misses him, but he also feels far away, and in some ways completely irrelevant to this moment; to sitting at her father's bedside watching daytime television, to chopping vegetables to puree for shakes—her father is officially on a liquid diet now—to falling asleep in her clothes on the couch at odd hours, being tapped awake by Barbara at four, five, six in the morning to relieve her of her watch.

Jess tells herself that she will call him tomorrow. She doesn't want to talk, but she does want to hear his voice. She doesn't want to know what's going on in New York, or tell him what's going on here at home, but she does want to tell him that she loves him.

Tomorrow, she promises, she will call him tomorrow.

She doesn't call him the next day.

But he calls her.

She is in the kitchen with Barbara when her phone lights up. Josh's face, his lips puckered, a photo taken after Jess had taught him duckface, flashes on the screen.

Barbara is drying cutlery on the other side of the table. As the phone vibrates between them, she leans over to look at the screen.

She smiles. "That your man?"

Jess says, "Yeah, I guess it is."

"He's handsome," Barbara winks.

Jess says, "Yeah, I guess he is."

"Well, you going to answer him or what?"

Or what.

But he doesn't stop calling. In rapid succession Jess ignores eight calls, and then he texts.

I'm here

She doesn't know what that means. She doesn't respond.

In Lincoln

Send me your address

Jess?

Jess sends him a message, the first one in two weeks:

what do you mean?

I'm in Lincoln, we need to talk

are you serious?

In Jess's hand her phone buzzes; he's calling.

She doesn't pick up. She texts:

I can't talk rn

But she is thinking, *What the fuck what the fuck. Here?* In the news-magazine, they'd once published an explainer on impaired decision-making. It talked about the difference between hot and cold cognition, how the warmer the emotion, the harder it was to think straight. There were examples of what they called hot and cold function tasks. Cold: sorting laundry, reading textbooks, doing math. Hot: any activity associated with arousal, having sex, debating politics, discussing money.

It had occurred to Jess that her whole relationship with Josh was one long hot function task. When she's with him, she can't see clearly. Even with thirteen hundred miles between them, she's . . . confused. How can she see him *here* when she doesn't know what she wants?

He calls again. Jess doesn't answer.

You have to talk to me

This is crazy!

Are you okay?

I'm sorry, you know that right?

Jess, this is really unfair

I'm in Lincoln!

Jess starts to reply:

. . .

. . .

. . .

Eventually she settles on:

I need a break

It feels like she hasn't even tapped SEND when he writes back:

WTF

I need some time

Jess, we haven't spoken for two weeks!

can we talk when I get back

?

He says:

When's that?

She takes a long time replying and finally:

I'm not sure

Jess tries to imagine him in Lincoln and it doesn't quite fit. Tries to imagine him in her living room and she can't conjure the image. Tries to imagine him standing at her father's bedside, what exactly that would look like.

He calls again. She taps Decline. Her heart is pounding and her mouth is dry. Josh in Lincoln. In her living room. In her father's bedroom.

He tries another time and Jess lets her finger hover over the Accept Call button. Closes her eyes and tries to imagine. Josh here. In Lincoln. In her living room. In her father's bedroom. But then it occurs to her that she's never not doing this, accommodating Josh. She's constructed a whole complicated scaffolding around him and their relationship and what has it achieved? A life she doesn't quite recognize and a father who doesn't know who she really is.

She places the phone on the table facedown.

It buzzes twice in rapid succession, a message or a voice mail.

Jess flips it over.

She has one new message:

Jess this is really fucked up

20

Two guys in scrubs with plastic badges around their necks from the medical equipment company appear. They have brought a hospital bed, a giant motorized mattress attached to a metal frame with wheels.

Barbara says, "Sweetheart, move out of the way," as they haul the old bed to the side—the bed where Jess used to sleep when she was little and had nightmares.

One of the guys says, "On the count of three," and then with an efficiency that Jess finds heartbreaking they lift the sheets under her sleeping father and transfer him from one bed to the other. Jess tries unsuccessfully to block out the realization that this is the bed he will die in. This bed with a remote control and plastic railings attached.

Barbara says, "Nobody should die in a hospital." And Jess has the childish thought that no one should die at all.

They are losing him. He is all angles and bones, skinny and brittle. His eyes have gone black, like stones, glassy and inert.

He is on so much pain medication that he is barely lucid. At first it just made him quiet and a little bit dopey, but now he is confused, in and out of consciousness, and Jess can't believe this is happening, that it happened so fast. She is not ready.

Another week passes and then Jess has been in Lincoln for a month. At some point her dad stops talking altogether. He has morphine dreams and sometimes he smiles at Jess through a faraway fog, but every day death comes nearer.

Barbara insists that they never leave him alone. They operate in shifts: four hours on, four hours off. In the evening Jess takes the late shift, Barbara tapping her awake just after midnight. Jess crawls out of the fold-out bed and takes up watch in her father's bedroom as he sleeps. She sits in an old brown easy chair—Barbara got it from who knows where and dragged it into the bedroom one day—and watches television until she's numb

Even though he probably doesn't notice either way, Jess keeps the volume off and becomes accustomed to reading the captions.

She watches television judges call people idiots and settle small claims. She watches old legal procedurals set in big cities. She watches game shows and cartoons for kids and infomercials selling all kinds of junk. She watches political news, the endless talk cycles around the upcoming election. The commentary has reached a fever pitch, and the coverage is almost nonstop. Pundits and prognosticators shouting back and forth in front of city skylines projected onto green screens about whether the American electorate is falling asleep at the wheel or is finally waking up.

A talking head who Jess can't stand says, "If it's between reality TV and the Clinton machine, I can tell you exactly where I stand . . ."

And another one adds, "Now if not for the emails, she might be all right . . ."

And Jess thinks, *The world is burning but at least ad sales are fine.*

Jess wishes she could turn off the television, but she can't, because there is her father. She can't bear to be near him, but she also can't bear to be far. And so the gray chatter of the television allows her to be both present and at the same time apart.

Eventually the vigils begin. Morose friends and colleagues with Tupperware and glass dishes sealed with tinfoil, in and out every day to pay their respects.

"How is he?" they ask, and Jess wants to scream, "Can't you see!"

"How are you?" they ask next, and Jess can never say anything real.

She says, "Thank you for coming. He knows you're here. It means the world to us both that you're here."

She says, "Dad, you have guests. They've come to say hi."

What she means is *Please Dad, don't die.*

* * *

Jess hasn't checked her email in weeks. At work they kept sending her articles, said that it was no problem at all for her to work remotely, but after a while, she asked them to stop, removed her work email from her phone. She said she was dealing with a family emergency and she got a nice email from the editor saying, *I'm so sorry to hear that, take all the time you need.*

She retrieves her computer from its neoprene sleeve, where she left it, idle. She has a routine now, completely divorced from the life she led with this laptop.

She decides she will send a few emails or ask her editor for something small to do—she misses the news-magazine, misses the office, misses coffee with Dax. Or maybe she'll heart some posts on social media, maybe even reach out to Josh.

She flips open the top and taps at the keys, but the laptop doesn't hum to life. She looks for her charger and then realizes, after turning her bag inside out, that she left it in New York. Jess could go to Hy-Vee—grab one of the cheap plastic USB cables all lined up alongside the checkout—or maybe Barbara has a charger she can borrow.

But instead she just sighs. Leans the laptop lid down. Decides she will worry about it all at some other time.

A hospice worker shows up. She is dressed like a nurse, almost comically so, as if she is on her way to a costume party: white shift with a matching hat, pantyhose and hideous shoes.

She consults a clipboard, and then says, "A sixty-three-year-old man. Jones?"

"My father," Jess says, and leads her to his room.

She comes out unsmiling.

And when Jess says, "Well?" she nods and says, "I'm very sorry," and leaves behind a pamphlet about how to cope when a loved one is dying.

*   *   *

The next night, her father dies.

Jess makes phone calls from her father's landline, shares the news with a long list of people printed neatly in her father's address book. She is numb.

She faintly recalls placing a call to Lydia, who doesn't recognize the number but—bless her—picks up anyway, with a curt "Lydia speaking," and then the surprised cry "Jess!" when she identifies herself.

Lydia says, "We miss you! How are you? How's your dad?"

And all Jess can reply is "Gone," and then stands crying into the phone.

Barbara organizes the memorial according to Jess's father's instructions and even though she asks everyone to send donations instead of flowers, people still send flowers.

The house is filled with zinnias, peonies, chrysanthemums and casseroles. The sweet musky fragrance of flowers, and death.

One arrangement in particular, orchids, four feet tall, all white, in full bloom, looks to Jess like it cost a grand at least. In its extravagance it doesn't fit in with the rest.

She returns to the orchids during the long series of days that mark her father's death. The day they carry his body out of the house, in a black bag, just like that. The day well-meaning friends and distant family—an uncle, a third cousin once removed, swarm the house and smother her in their pitying embrace. The day he is interred, his body becoming dirt. The day it all ends, when there is nothing left to do or say, but to grieve, alone, lonely, orphaned, and figure out how to live her life a different way.

Through it all, the orchids give her comfort, somehow. They touch a specific place in her heart, in her broken psyche. They remind her of New York.

At some point she notices a tag.

She tears it off, opens it up.

It says: *Jess, I'm so very sorry. Thinking of you. Love, Josh.*

Jess checks her voice mail.

She scrolls JOSH JOSH JOSH. There are other messages too—from Lydia, from one of her father's doctors, a robocaller asking for donations—but she skips over those.

She scrolls to the middle of the list, picks a random voice mail dated from about a week after she left.

"Just Jess," he says, and his voice has the quality of being transmitted over a great distance, faint, otherworldly, "I miss you." About fifteen seconds of silence and then, "I guess that's all."

She listens to another one, from earlier.

"Jess," he says, and she can hear shuffling in the background. He covers the phone and says something to someone. "Look, I'm at work. Call me later. Or I'll try you later. Either way"—more shuffling—"regards to your dad."

And then one from later, much later, near the end. "Jess, where are you? Are you okay? Talk to me," and Jess hears a sigh so profound, the weight of which reaches through time and space, such that she knows it's not going to be okay, that the damage she's done is most likely permanent. "I'm worried about you. I haven't heard from you. It's just," he sighs again and then the line goes dead.

•

Jess follows her life in New York on social media. She scrolls through photos of Miky and Lydia at restaurants and parties, in the Hamptons and, one weekend, at a famous golf tournament on Long Island wearing ridiculous hats and smiling wild-eyed into the camera with gray-haired men in polo shirts lurking behind them. Josh isn't active on social media, a blessing and a curse.

She likes and comments and Miky and Lydia always write back:

miss u jess xoxo

and

wish u were here :(:(:(:(

The photos are intoxicating and Jess feels like she's missing out. Jess misses the city but can't imagine going back.

She keeps scrolling and scrolling, it's impossible to stop.

David posts a bunch of party pics, and one day there is Josh. He is smiling, with a drink, and when she sees it she starts to cry.

It is a series of photos from the party and Jess clicks through them one by one. Her breath catches at a photo of Tenley, who was at the party too. She is photogenic as ever, beautiful in a gray and blue top, with her blond hair glistening and her freckles perfect little dots. Jess zooms on the photos and follows her eyes. She is smiling, or laughing, at someone just outside the frame. Jess knows instinctively that that person is Josh, knows it deep in her bones, and at this understanding she feels a deep ache with no name. She feels her pulse quicken and grief well up in her chest, a sadness so heavy that she has to lie down. This keeps happening. It comes in waves. As if she's swimming in the sea while a tsunami rises. Everything calm and then a giant wave slams her sideways: her dad. Gone forever. She thinks of him dead and she cries or screams or kicks things. And then as soon as she catches her breath, comes up to the surface for some air, there's another wave crashing behind it: Josh. It doesn't feel like hyperbole to say that she's lost everything. Has anyone ever been this lonely?

But Josh is in New York living his life. Still going to work and to parties, like everything is all right. While Jess hurts almost physically, and with no end in sight. She wishes she'd never met him, but she also misses him so much she could die. Sometimes she wishes she could talk to him again, somehow give it another try.

She composes message after message, but never taps SEND.

hi . . .

hey, Josh

Josh, hey

I'm sorry

I forgive you, okay?

I love you

I miss you

I hate you

can we talk?

She takes off her shirt and types a message that is just a photo of her naked top.

Even though she tries not to, she still thinks of him this way. Alone at night in bed, in the dark, she slips her hand into her underpants and whispers his name. It's embarrassing and pointless, but she can't make herself stop.

She begins to follow David obsessively, but there are no more pictures of Josh. Instead, he posts mildly offensive hot takes as the presidential election draws nearer.

Dems' soak-the-rich policies sure to backfire.

Stop complaining about too-low taxes: Americans are world's most charitable, top 1% provide 1/3rd of donations.

Democrats a big socialist joke.

We can't just make health care "free": here's why.

Between Trump and a 90% tax rate, guess what Americans will choose and why?

And

What it would be like living in Hillary's tax fantasy, which garners one hundred and seventy-two likes, one of which comes from Josh.

Eventually Jess gives up, closes her eyes and turns off the lights. Flattened by an anvil of grief sitting on her chest. She stops listening to the internet chatter, and even mutes her friends online. It is easier this way, she figures, to just pretend that everything is fine.

Jess spends hours, days, years staring at her phone. Opening and closing apps. Scrolling mindlessly. Playing stupid games. She is presiding over the residents of her Candy Kingdom when it buzzes with a notification. From her photo app: REMEMBER THIS DAY. She taps the screen and a photo of her and Josh appears. The Wine Girls' Halloween party: Josh and Jess in their matching math costumes, bodies and mouths pressed together, making out. Lydia had shared the photo and captioned it *OMG THESE TWO* and Jess had hearted it and then wrote *looooove*. Miky had added *nerd sex!* and, below that, from one of the Wine Girls, a yellow emoji puking its guts out.

Jess stares at the photo until her screen locks. And then for three more minutes until the screen dims again and again and again. She is typing in her passcode for the fifth, sixth, seven hundredth time when finally she sits up. She scrolls her recent calls, down almost to the bottom and, trembling, taps his name and calls Josh. He doesn't pick up. But it doesn't go straight to voice mail and it doesn't ring through either. He's screening. A kick in the teeth.

She navigates to David's profile, expecting nothing, but it's worse. Much worse. A series of pictures from a trip. At a restaurant called the Rusty Anchor, the sun shining like it's July. In the background, champagne bottles and a fondue pot. A long weekend in Nantucket. Fine. Okay. But then a single photo that makes Jess's heart stop. A foursome, smiling on a sailboat: David and his girlfriend, Abby. And Josh. And Tenley. Her worst fears, finally, confirmed.

It occurs to Jess that she's been asking herself whether she's done with Josh. She hasn't considered that he's done with her.

21

The house in Lincoln is empty.

Jess wakes up late and the only reason she gets up is to close the drapes. She doesn't get up the next day or the next day or the next, until the days and nights begin to pass in one unbroken blur. She doesn't change her clothes, doesn't shower, doesn't read, doesn't sleep, doesn't even really eat—she draws down slowly on a sleeve of saltines that she keeps on the pillow next to her, like a lover. She just stares up at the ceiling, while her sheets go stale and life goes on outside.

At some point she finds her father's pills—the narcotic-strength painkillers that Barbara was supposed to destroy upon his death but apparently forgot to. Jess takes one and then another and then another until she feels cotton in her mouth and few thoughts in her head. Then, feeling sick, she drinks a liter of water and eats a stack of saltines, makes herself throw up a little bit. She doesn't want to die, she just wants to disappear.

And it works. She disappears into a fog, a dreamless fugue state, taking pills and drinking water and setting an alarm to go off every two hours to make sure her heart is still beating and in this way days, maybe a week, pass. Jess, alone, bathing in her grief, ignoring everyone and everything, the outside world, the ringing phone.

She is sick, and a little delirious—the combination of profound loneliness and pills is a potent one—when she hears the front door open.

"Dad?" Jess sits up a little, wondering if maybe this has all been a nightmare.

She hears movement in the kitchen, but no one answers.

Without getting up she calls, "Who's there?"

Barbara appears in the living room, with a confused look on her face.

"Jess?" she asks, startled, and then seeing her, a mess, stuck to the sofa: "Your hair! How long have you been lying here, just wasting away in here? When was the last time you took a comb to it? It's going to get matted. What on earth are you doing here?"

Under a blanket, Jess replies moodily, "I live here."

"Why aren't you in New York? What's going on?"

And in this Barbara has touched a nerve. Jess is angry, annoyed, but also still thick with pills and so she slurs, "Why are you even here, Barbara? This is my house now. My dad gave it to me. It's in the will. So you shouldn't even be here."

"Somebody needs to look after this place, young lady. I don't see you taking on that responsibility"—she gestures at the mess around the sofa bed, and then she notices the pills. They are strewn like trash all over the floor, where they'd spilled after Jess fought with the safety cap, and where she plucks them directly off the carpet whenever she needs more. Barbara's face flashes disdain. She bends down and picks up an empty bottle. "And what exactly do you think you're doing here?" she says, shaking the bottle at Jess. "Are these your *daddy's* pills? You're in here getting high and God knows what all. You think your daddy left you this house so you could trash it? Trash yourself? You ungrateful—"

Jess says, "Fuck off, Barbara. Get out of my house."

Barbara does no such thing. She stalks toward the sofa bed and yanks the pillow from under Jess's head, throws back the blanket and attempts to pull Jess off the couch.

Jess says, "What the fuck!"

Barbara says, "You need to get your act together, missy. Your daddy would be rolling in his grave."

"Barbara, get the fuck out of my house."

"Your language!"

She gives the blanket, which is damp with Jess's sweat and caked with cracker crumbs, a final tug, flinging both it and Jess to the floor.

Jess screams, "What the fuck is wrong with you!"

She flails underneath the comforter on the floor, pouting like a petulant child.

Barbara says, "Get up."

Jess says, "Make me."

Barbara turns to leave and Jess feels deflated—she was ready for a fight.

But Barbara stops in the hallway. She still has on her coat and the thin arches of her eyebrows flare in anger. She points a finger at Jess and says sharply, "Get up. Take a shower. I do not have time for this foolishness. I'll be back in an hour," and then she leaves, the screen door banging behind her.

Barbara is back in less than an hour, plastic bags swinging from her arms. Jess is still on the floor, out of spite or despondence, she can't actually say. But Barbara's temper has cooled and she coos, "Come on baby, get up." She takes Jess gently by the elbow, coaxes her off the floor and onto her feet.

She gives her a light shove into the bathroom and then steps in behind her, finds a clean towel in the linen cupboard and turns on the tap.

She says, "Get in. You need to shower."

Jess stands under the hot water for what feels like hours and only steps out when the water starts to cool. She puts on a robe and pads into the kitchen, where Barbara has busied herself.

Barbara turns and smiles when Jess walks in. "Now doesn't that feel better?" she asks, and Jess has to admit that it does. "I made you a sandwich," she says, and slides half a bagel across the table.

Jess shakes her head. "I'm not hungry."

But Barbara says, "Well, baby, you have to eat."

Jess sits at the table and takes a tiny bite. She takes one and then another and then another until the entire turkey sandwich is done.

Jess realizes she was in fact hungry. Very hungry.

Barbara takes her plate away and puts it in the sink, seemingly satisfied.

She claps her hands together. "Now, what are we going to do about your hair?"

Jess's hair is a riot of curls, dry and tangled, with a large indent on one side where she has rested it against the pillow for days on end. In the shower she used a detangling, moisturizing shampoo and worked her fingers, slowly, painfully through the knots, but it still looks unkempt, like it hasn't been combed for ages, which, in fact, it hasn't been.

Barbara pulls four long rectangular packs of synthetic hair out of a bag that says BEAUTY SUPPLY WAREHOUSE on the side.

"Come," she says, and takes a chair from the kitchen table into the living room, the packs of hair tucked under her arm. "Sit. I'm going to put some braids in your hair. Or do you want twists?"

No one's ever braided—or twisted—Jess's hair. Her father tried his best, but his best was tying her hair up in lopsided bows. And he's not here anymore to do even that.

Jess sits and Barbara tugs her shoulders back.

She separates the strands of synthetic hair and lays them on the couch arm, a long uneven row of horse tails. She picks up a piece and holds it against Jess's head.

"One-B," she says proudly. "Perfect match."

She gets to work.

Jess feels a pinch and twist on her scalp as Barbara begins to braid tiny sections of her hair, threading Jess's own hair with the strands she has set out on the couch. The tension becomes lighter and lighter until only a faint pressure remains and Barbara lets go. A single braid falls over Jess's shoulder. Jess picks it up and rolls it between her fingers. It is tight, neat and long.

It reaches her waist.

Jess tells Barbara, "I've never had my hair braided before."

Barbara stops what she's doing for a moment and leans over, surprised. "Never? Your girlfriends never did your hair?"

Jess almost laughs trying to imagine Miky or Lydia with hair oil between her fingers, a pack of acrylic hair draped across her lap.

Once, at a bar, Jess had noticed a girl with hot-pink cornrows. She'd turned to her friends and asked, half-serious, "Do you think those would look good on me?" and Callie had wrinkled her nose and said, "Cultural appropriation much?" And then when Jess had given her a look, she'd laughed and said, "Just kidding. I totally forgot who I was talking to."

Jess had contemplated braids, but there were too many reasons not to. Work, for one. It wasn't 1980, she could wear her hair however she wanted, she knew that. But. Once she'd worn gold hoop earrings to the office instead of the little studs she normally wore, and somehow everyone had noticed. Charles said, "Jones, you look like a rapper's girlfriend," and she'd never worn them again, or anything remotely big, or blingy, or interesting, and even then, she had a bracelet with red, blue and green gemstones—it was from Tiffany's—and someone had still asked if it was "African."

But the real reason Jess has never had braids, really, is because every time she considers it, she feels like a bit of a fraud. Like somehow she needs permission. An invitation. Some sort of formal initiation.

Barbara stands behind her, with bobby pins between her lips.

Barbara continues, pinch and twist, pressure and release, until a clump of braids, long and straight, falls down Jess's back. Jess reaches up every now and again to touch the unbraided portion of her hair until Barbara says, "Baby, we're not even close, you know it's going to be a while. Why don't you turn on the television?"

Jess does as she is told. She flips through channels until she sees Beyoncé, singing in a striped dress on a police car submerged in water. Jess pauses, intrigued.

Barbara says approvingly, "Beyoncé is my girl."

They watch as she changes outfits, locations, hairstyles—at one point she is in twists, just like the ones Barbara is installing in Jess's hair at this very moment—she sings, she dances, she is Saying Something. It is not a music video, it's a visual album, and while Barbara swishes her hips and hums along, Jess stares at the screen, rapt. She has never seen anything like it. As much as she's argued about her, she's never actually paid much attention to Queen Bey and her loyal subjects. Though maybe she should have.

Watching it feels almost spiritual. Beyoncé sings about Jay-Z's betrayal and tears form in Jess's eyes.

Barbara notices and leans down, her face in front of Jess's face. "You tender-headed, baby?" she asks.

Jess shakes her head. She says quietly, "My boyfriend."

Barbara frowns. "He cheating?"

Jess says, "Something like that."

This isn't true, but it feels like it is. How can she describe what he's done to her, the weight of it, with the truth? It would sound thin. It would sound silly. It would implicate Jess.

Barbara shakes her head. "Men can be dogs." Then she leans close, so Jess can smell her perfume, and adds in a low voice, "She white?"

And Jess almost laughs at Barbara's intuition.

Jess feels her shoulders go slack, feels some tension in her body release, the relief of being cared for, of not quite being understood, but not needing to be. She feels, for the first time in weeks, lighter, like maybe—not now, but someday, eventually—things will get better.

She nods. "Yes," she says to Barbara. "Yes, she is."

Eventually Barbara thwacks a towel against Jess's shoulders and says, "All done."

They stand in the mirror.

Jess touches her head. "Wow."

Barbara seems pleased. "It suits you."

Jess feels pretty. She piles the braids on top of her head and then lets them fall. She twirls one long braid around a finger and then another. She tips her face to the ceiling, feels the *swish-swish* of the hair against her back. And she ignores the fact that she could have looked like this the whole time.

In bed later Jess can't sleep. Her thoughts race and she closes her eyes and takes deep breaths. She tries not to think about Josh, but she can't not. She thinks about how he made her feel seen, but also, so many times, like she was invisible. She thinks about how he made her feel cared for and defended, at Goldman, with Gil, but how on some level that also made her feel helpless and insecure. She tosses these contradictions around in her head as she tries to fall asleep, unsure of how to reconcile it all. She loves him. She loves him not. He loves her. He loves her not.

Jess can't stop thinking about him. About the ways they fit together and the ways they didn't. But also about Tenley.

It isn't cheating to have an ex and still keep in touch.

Even if she is the feminine platonic ideal.

It isn't cheating to lie about the nature of said relationship or to benefit professionally, financially, psychically, from her family's largesse.

It isn't cheating to want a life that can't quite accommodate the person you love.

And it isn't cheating to want that person to be somebody else.

Not technically, it's not.

Isn't it?

She loves him. She loves him not. He loves her. He loves her not.

She keeps her eyes closed.

Takes deep breaths.

Jess feels her thoughts growing gauzy. Josh, Josh, Josh, she thinks, but everything is muted, pressing down on her in dull gray instead of shocking technicolor.

In the space between asleep and awake, her thoughts turn to Beyoncé. The lyrics from earlier mixing with her memories.

Josh, I'm so sorry.

Sorry, I ain't sorry

Sorry, I ain't sorry

She tries to let him go.

I ain't thinking 'bout you

I ain't thinking 'bout you

Her thoughts become more tangled. She is dreaming, she is awake. He is taking up space in her brain. She is Beyoncé in a fur coat. She is sorry, he is sorry, she ain't thinking 'bout him.

She is angry, sad, hurt, filled with love, despair, regret.

She wants to tell him again: fuck him.

Middle fingers up

Boy, bye

She thinks of Tenley and her pale skin and her flaxen hair, and she tosses and turns and wishes he were here or that she were there.

But also, somehow, it feels right that she isn't.

* * *

The next day Jess makes two phone calls. The first, to her editor, to ask for more time. The second, to Lydia, to tell her that she's leaving New York. Lydia doesn't pick up, so Jess sends her a message.

Probably not a surprise but I'm leaving NYC, I've decided. It's final.

:(

Things I'll miss most: Momofuku Milk Bar, mani-pedis at Kabuko, and you!!!!!!!!!!

Lydia replies fifteen minutes later.

Waaaaaaah I'm at work, can't talk, but I hate u!!

I need a chnage . . .

*change

I know, I know, but selfishly I'm going to miss u

Later Jess's phone rings. Lydia. Jess picks up.

Lydia's face appears on the screen and she says, "Surprise! It's me."

"A video chat!" Jess says. "So sneaky!"

"Flip the camera over!" Lydia shouts. "All I can see is your door."

Jess does as she's told and for a second Lydia stares. She exclaims, "Oh my god, Jess, your hair!"

"Do you like it?"

"It looks so good! You look like a new woman!"

Jess laughs, she says, "I know, right?"

22

Barbara is the only person Jess talks to anymore. She comes over several times a week, with dinner or groceries or, once, a new steam mop. They discover that they both love marmalade sandwiches and a show deep in the cable television lineup called *The Ultimate Scam*.

Over coffee and buttered muffins one morning, Jess finally asks, "Did my dad ask you to take care of me or something?"

"Of course not," Barbara says, matter-of-fact. Then she stands and puts the dishes in the sink. She wipes crumbs off the counter and then transfers the contents of her mug to a portable cup.

Jess sips her coffee and her insides warm.

Before Barbara leaves, she gives Jess a little squeeze on the shoulder. She says, "Now don't let these dishes sit here all day," and then she is out the door.

•

Later, everything changes. Jess is outside on a street corner, waiting for the light to change, when her phone buzzes with a notification. She pulls it from her pocket and holds it to her face. A pop-up from the net worth app saying CONGRATULATIONS. At first, she doesn't register what's happened, but then it dawns on her and she feels lightheaded, a little unsteady on her feet.

She remembers a lawyer's office, the oversized desk covered with stacks of paper. Framed credentials on the walls, a tufted leather chair with loose stuffing. Paperwork. Retirement funds. Insurance. A mortgage paid in full. Condolences. Her father had left her everything. Of course. But Jess hadn't been paying attention. Why should she? He clipped coupons. He was a college administrator. But he was also responsible and astute. He was her dad. And apparently a savvy investor. Or he would have been if he hadn't died. If he had lived long and retired. But now it's all hers, his sole heir. The app says HOORAY! YOU MADE A LOT OF MONEY TODAY! and Jess counts the figures, yes, there are six next to her name. It's not everything, but it's enough—enough to pay off all her debt and keep her job and rent an apartment and maybe donate a little to charity. Jess has been waiting for this day. And yet.

Jess looks up from her phone. She surveys the street. It's an ordinary day. Mild weather, slightly cloudy. A pedestrian crosses on yellow and a car horn honks. Someone exits the drugstore and the bells over the door jingle. A woman pushing a stroller says, "Excuse me," but otherwise people mind their own business. What did she think would happen? Something. A lightning crack maybe, or confetti. Something.

But nothing has changed. There's no fanfare. Just the app blinking its alert, insisting on congratulations.

Jess texts Dax. Ostensibly to check in on work, to see what assignments she might do remotely, but then he messages her back immediately— so nice to hear from you, here if you need to talk—and Jess realizes she does and so they do, one long text conversation that unfurls over days and then weeks.

In New York, he's an hour ahead and so Jess wakes up to his messages, which are about the weather (which is only ever *shit* or *gorgeous*) or the particular flavor of coffee he and Paul are enjoying (*boy loves his beans*) or with a link to some awful headline that he's pretty confident will upset her, which it invariably does, but which, on some level, she also pines for, like picking at a scab or eating food that's way too spicy.

Jess appreciates the fact that they are outraged by all the same things, for all the same reasons, which increasingly seems like a strong foundation for a friendship. They are annoyed by, yet permissive of, all the same things. A white lady pretending to be Black: acceptable, because of her commitment to the grift. The apologist memoir by the family values conservative masquerading as a liberal: the worst, even though no one else agreed. Eddie Murphy memes, definitely.

Lately, they've been going back and forth on the breathless coverage of the white-working class in the media. Photographs of down-and-out Rust Belt factory workers on the front page of every major newspaper, the silent majority and the face of a nation, or just a bunch of racist assholes, depending on who you ask. (The Wine Girls on social media: *We need to start a national conversation about why half of Americans are willing to vote against their own self-interest. Medicare for All now!* David on social media: *Tell me again the last time interventionist trade policy led anywhere good.*)

According to Dax it's lazy journalism, at best. At worst, it's pandering to a complacent coastal elite that would rather blame class than race on the country's problems. It's just easier. Jess agrees. She texted Dax: *All these, like, "profiles" are literally just 2,000 words on how to say "I'm racist" in the most oblique way possible.*

Now Jess will wake up to a text that just says: I'm a hardworking American.

And she'll read the latest headlines and then parry one back that says: *Why can't they just do it legally?*

Sometimes if the headline is especially annoying Dax won't send any commentary, just an eye-roll emoji and a single word: wypipo.

Jess wonders if maybe they should . . . stop.

But Dax says, nah, remember, gotta read across the entire political spectrum

This was something that was emphasized again and again at the news-magazine. In order to understand the world they had to engage with it. An echo chamber was the most dangerous place to be.

Jess says, *It's funny how we call it a spectrum, which implies a line, with two ends, when really it's more like a circle*

say more

Jess sits up in bed, types a paragraph and then another, explaining her theory of American politics, which is that fundamentally it's all utterly predictable.

Basically, she texts, *the only difference between a right-wing nut job*

*and a left-wing nut job is, like, the weather in the zip code where they
were born*

    lol

    fair

    really miss your point of view

    it's not the same here without you

    I'm sure it's totally fine

    we have a temp covering for you, but he's no good, way too slow

    everyone wants you to come back

    Really?

    for sure

    everyone loves you

    your work is so solid

    we all miss you

On the other end of the phone Jess is blushing.

    you know what everyone thinks was especially cool about you?

Jess can't help but take the bait. She writes back: **???**

    we all thought it was incredibly dope how you never used a mouse

Jess has been waiting for an excuse to ask Michael, her boss, if she can send him a few pitches. He says, "Are you sure you're up for it?" and Jess assures him she is. And then she sends him ideas, one after the other, until she's monopolized the top of his in-box and he pings her to say, *No pressure, feel free to ease back into things*, though she knows he doesn't mean it, because he's a rabid workaholic who regularly spends the night under his desk.

But Jess has a lot to say, suddenly. Things she wants to get off her chest. She's been biting her tongue for too long. Michael approves her stories—all but one, about how there is data to suggest that serial killers are more likely to identify as conservative politically, to which he responds, "Hmm, maybe a touch incendiary?"—and Jess gets started. And then instead of being bored and restless, she's working.

Inspired by their conversation Jess proposes she and Dax collaborate. The headline: *How One Number Predicts Your Past, Present and Future*. The analysis: how the zip code someone was born in is almost perfectly predictive of a person's worldview, as defined by the General Social Survey. Dax does the design and Jess creates the charts. Deep in the data, she thinks of Josh. How they had so much in common but not enough. There had been so much to explain. And according to Dax that was unhealthy for a soul, and Jess agrees. Their fundamental incompatibility borne out by the facts of the analysis.

When she shared the initial data with Dax, he said, "Well, that's depressing. Fascinating, but depressing," and it was, a little, the idea that people weren't agents, fully, of their own destinies, that the world chose for them, before they were even born. But Jess saw it differently. It was satisfyingly explanatory. The answer to a question that had been weighing on her. The perfectly rational reason why an entire relationship could unravel under the weight of a simple asymmetry. Love conquers all, except geography, and history, and contemporary sociopolitical reality. Dax found their conclusions depressing, but to Jess it was all strangely cathartic.

Eventually one of Jess's pieces hits the website's list of top ten trafficked, and her Twitter account is hacked.

"Congrats," Dax tells her.

"Congrats?"

"You know what it means when you get hacked, right?"

"What?"

"You're a big deal."

Jess keeps banging out articles, tagged under racism and politics and the economy, and then before she knows it, it's November.

•

And then one evening she wakes up to the sound of her phone ringing. She picks it up, groggy, thinking it might be Barbara or one of the kind telemarketers from the local library asking her if she'd like to make a contribution this holiday season.

But no.

"Josh?" Her voice is heavy with sleep, so she hopes that it doesn't betray her, doesn't lay bare her surprise, but more than that: her relief.

"Hey," he says.

She says nothing.

"Are you still there?"

"Yes."

"How are you?" he asks.

"It's late," she says, rubbing her eyes.

"It's later in New York," he says, and then after a pause, "I thought you would be awake." Another pause. "Because of the election."

The previous evening Donald J. Trump was elected president. People on the internet were already screaming about how 2016 was the worst year ever, and it's true, as soon as the returns from Florida were in, Jess felt her heart sink; she felt a sense of loss that was much more than losing—more than losing the election the presidency the country—instead, it was the feeling that half the nation, even if it was the smaller half, had stood in a line sixty million people long to spit in her face and say: *people like you don't matter*. And then Jess had felt herself falling back into the same black black as she had when her father died, when she broke up with Josh.

There were watch parties, Jess was aware of this. Lydia had told her about them, restaurants with champagne towers, female guests in pantsuits, ready to usher in the dawn of a new era: first a Black president, then a woman. Though, of course, they were all wrong.

Barbara, resignedly apolitical—"Baby, I don't trust none of 'em, you hear?"—had committed to watching CNN until ten, until it was "time for her to retire."

"It won't change a lick if I stay up late, but I *will* be tired tomorrow."

So Jess had been at home alone, ready for it all to be over, for Trump to get the fuck off the stage. And, without really being able not to, she had thought about Josh.

It wasn't even eleven, the election hadn't even technically been called, but unable to watch as the country slid into chaos, Jess had gone to bed anyway. She had tossed and turned, embracing the black black, feeling pitiful and alone, until eventually she fell asleep.

And then the phone rang.

"Because of the election," Jess repeats slowly. Then adds bitterly, "Oh, yeah, just that."

He says, "Jess," and hearing his voice, she feels a little bit overcome.

She doesn't know what to say. She rubs her finger over her sleep-sticky teeth, combs her hair with her fingers. Even though he can't see her, she would like, somehow, to seem less disheveled and vulnerable.

He says, "How are you holding up?"

The concern in his voice touches a nerve. She begins to cry audibly. Through the rising tide of tears, she can barely manage any words, "I don't know."

He says, "Oh, Jess. Don't take it personally. I know you. There's the worst-case scenario, which I'm one hundred percent certain you're turning over in your head right now, which is this narrative that there's a line of sixty million people who just spit in your face. And then there's reality, which is a lot more nuanced."

"You voted for him, didn't you?" Jess interrupts.

He says only, "Jess."

They breathe into the phone.

Finally, Josh says, "I just don't want you to be upset."

"Why wouldn't I be upset!"

"I just think it might help to frame it differently. With the economy—"

She interrupts, "Why are you defending this?"

"I'm not," he says, "I'm trying to help reframe things for you. I'm trying to help."

"You're trying to help? Why don't you go help your racist, xenophobic, misogynistic piece-of-shit coal miner friends? According to you they need it. They're the ones crying out for it. Oh, boo-hoo, my perfect white supremacist vision of the world is dying. If only those wily marginalized Black and brown people weren't getting so many darn opportunities, to get shot by the cops, to have their humanity denied—"

"Jess, please stop."

Jess stops.

She says, "Is that why you called? To condescend to me about politics?"

He says, "No, it's not."

"Then why?" she asks quietly, giving in.

He says, "I called you because I miss you and I love you and . . . and not being with you isn't working for me."

Jess holds her breath.

He continues, "Jess, I called because I can't live without you in my life."

She misses him. She does. Sometimes so much it hurts. But then she remembers. And that hurts too.

She calls him a week later.

It rings and rings and she holds her breath. But then he picks up. He says, "Hello, beautiful," and she feels it happening, something tight in her chest unraveling, not forgiveness, or acceptance, but something closer to recklessness. A champagne bubble of excitement blooming in her chest. A feeling, a memory maybe, of warmth, of pleasure.

She has been so sad, so despondent. And now, she's certain, she'd rather be happy than right. Besides, it's not like they're getting back together, it's just talking.

She calls him on the landline and she sits on the carpet twirling the telephone cord around her finger like a lovestruck teenager.

He picks up right away. "Hey, Jess."

"How'd you know it was me?" Her house phone is not one he would recognize.

He says, "You're the only one who calls."

She says, "You're the only one I call."

"Oh, yeah?"

"Well, I hate talking on the phone," Jess explains.

"Doesn't everyone hate talking on the phone?" but then: "I don't hate talking on the phone with you."

He sends her messages and she sends him messages, memes, think pieces about the nearing singularity, videos of cats. Sometimes they are sweet and sometimes they are serious. Sometimes they are short and sometimes they are long, emails she has to scroll through with paragraphs and punctuation. He addresses them: "Dear Jess."

Every day, multiple times a day, messages between them ping-pong back and forth. Jess doesn't put her phone down. It buzzes and she stops what she's doing, smiles dreamily at the screen.

Barbara raises an eyebrow, says, "Now who's that on the other end?"

Jess insists, "It's no one," but she knows that Barbara can tell she is lying.

•

Jess asks Barbara how you know if something is meant to be. "Like, in a relationship. Boyfriend, girlfriend."

Barbara looks at Jess. "Are we talking about this Mr. Cheating Boyfriend character?"

"Well . . ." Jess hesitates, "it's complicated."

Barbara nods. "You have to ask yourself: 'Is this person capable of change?' You can't change people. Whoo boy! Now that's a fool's errand to be sure. Believe me, I know. But. People do change. So, you ask yourself: 'Is this person on a path of personal growth or are they fighting change?' And baby? That's the best you can do."

Jess thinks about this.

Barbara gives her a smile and a pat on the knee. "The most important thing to remember?"

"What?"

"You're still young. So whatever mistakes you make there's time to unmake them."

Jess says, "I see."

Josh calls with a funny story. A wedding he attended where the groom got fall-over drunk and passed out on the cake. The panicked bride tried to catch him but slipped. By the time a member of the waitstaff rushed over with a roll of paper towels half the bridal party was on the floor.

It makes Jess sad to think of Josh going to parties without her, but she laughs anyway. She says, "And you're sure this was a wedding and not an *SNL* sketch?"

"It happened, I swear."

He sends her a link to the photos.

Jess laughs. "So no one had cake?"

"This was after they cut it."

"Was it good?"

"I didn't try it."

"Why not? Watching your figure?"

"No, you can't see from the pictures, but the whole top tier was strawberry."

"So?" she asks.

"Strawberries give you hives."

"So?"

"Jess, you can't be serious. Remember our little visit to the emergency room, and you—"

"So *you* stopped eating strawberries because of *me*? Even though we're not . . ."

He waits for her to finish her thought, but she doesn't.

He says, "No, you're right. It's not strictly logical. I didn't wake up one day and say 'I'm never eating another strawberry.' More like . . . we stopped eating them at home and then gradually I stopped eating them everywhere. I don't think it's something I did consciously."

Jess says, "I see."

23

One day Josh calls and turns the video on, and they are staring face-to-face for the first time in six months.

Josh says, almost stunned, "You're so pretty."

And Jess laughs. "Nice of you to forget about me so fast."

But he is serious when he replies, "Jess, I think about you all the time."

She touches the screen as if caressing his face.

"I miss you," Josh admits.

"I miss you too," Jess agrees.

"No," he says seriously, "I mean, I miss you, the physical presence of you." His voice gets low. "I miss seeing you every day, the way you smell and your sweet little ass and you in my bed, I miss . . . you."

Surprised, Jess says, "Oh."

And then they have phone sex. And it is sexy but also unsatisfying and leaves Jess wanting more.

Later Jess says, "Okay, that's enough of that."

Josh seems hurt. "What do you mean?"

She says, "I need to come back to New York." She hadn't quite realized how true it was until she said it.

Jess would fly out the next day if she could, but she knows that's crazy. But she is desperate to see him, to be close again. Through the fog of grief and loneliness and of the flat Lincoln winter it's almost hard to remember why she ever doubted him.

She says, with a tentativeness that belies her excitement, "Maybe I'll come for a week."

He says, "Come for a day, come for forever. Just come soon. Okay?"

"How soon is soon? Like the long weekend in February?"

"February?" he says, "No way." A pause: "What are you doing this weekend?"

*   *   *

Jess says goodbye to Barbara.

She lets herself be smooshed against Barbara's breasts, inhales her perfume. In a store recently Jess had recognized the scent and surprised herself by spraying it on her wrists.

"I'll be back soon," she tells Barbara.

Barbara smiles like Jess has said something half-funny. She says, "Okay, baby."

At the airport Josh is waiting for her as soon as she lands, among the military families and limo drivers with signs. She sees him right away and her stomach immediately flips. They run toward each other, a tangle of arms and hands and lips.

He says into her ear, "I've missed you so fucking much, Just Jess. I'm so happy you're home."

They hug and kiss and make such a fuss that by the time they schlep back to baggage claim all the luggage from Nebraska has stopped spinning around and Jess's bag has been set next to the carousel.

In the taxi they can't stop touching. Josh is kissing her face and neck and Jess is giggling and tingly and she says *it's felt like an eternity* and he says *one hundred and eighty days* and she says *the cube root of five million eight hundred and thirty-two thousand days* and, laughing, he says *my sexy savant.* Then he pulls away.

"What?" Jess leans back against the plastic seat of the cab.

He looks at her, chewing the inside of his cheek. Jess recognizes this look. He's perplexed. Why is the price of money up when the economy is contracting. Why an otherwise sane person would stand in line for an hour for a cupcake.

Jess says, "What?"

He takes a braid, one long lock, between his thumb and index finger. He lifts the braid away from her head, stretches it across almost the full length of the back seat.

"Your hair," he says. "It's really long. Much longer than it looked on video."

"Oh. I mean"—Jess takes the braid back, smooths her hair—"I like it."

"It was kind of short and now . . . it's really long."

"So you're saying you hate it?" Jess says as if issuing a dare.

She watches his eyes, follows them from the top of her head to the middle of her waist, to the place where her hair, belly button length, stops, and his face still looks like he's solving a puzzle, but then he laughs. Kisses her again. And again. And again. He says, "There's nothing about you I hate."

They have dinner at a restaurant, waiters gliding by with chilled bottles of wine, and for dessert they share an incredibly rich mousse. Jess remembers New York nights with Josh, but also something about this feels new. He leans across the table to kiss her, and they hold hands until he signs the check.

Later, when they are lying in bed, he says, "Hey, Jess," and she says, "Yes?"

He rolls over and blinks at her in the dark. "Please don't ever leave again."

Jess decides that she won't.

Half her clothes are still in the closet. She swipes through hangers, fingering the fabric of shirts and sweaters that she forgot. Josh stands behind her.

He says, "It made me sad to see your clothes every day, while you were gone."

Jess turns to face him. "Then why didn't you send them to me?"

He shrugs. "Because that would have been sadder."

She hugs him.

*   *   *

At home, they watch every single season of *Planet Earth*. They watch the ice shelves break apart in super slow motion and big cats swallow crocodiles and fish the size of school buses bury themselves deep in the ocean floor.

Jess's favorites are the birds of paradise. They are, with their technicolor feathers, ridiculous creatures, delightfully fastidious, singing and dancing, flapping their technicolor wings and tapping their feet, to attract a mate.

"Now that's what a woman wants," Jess says, wagging her finger at the television screen.

"Is it? A burlesque feather-fan dancer that sounds like a car alarm?"

"*Romance.*"

Later she hears Josh singing in the shower, an old rock and roll song, hitting all the high notes.

"I couldn't help but overhear your birdsong," Jess says, sliding the shower door open. Josh has shampoo in his hair and it forms a peak on the top of his head, like a mohawk.

He turns away from the nozzle and grins, then throws his elbows out and does a little tap dance, pantomiming a mating dance.

Jess laughs. "Is there room in the nest for one more? I mean"—she raises her eyebrows suggestively—"is this twig taken?"

"Always room for one more," he says, and then following Jess's eyes adds, "Hey, I'm up here. Though, to be frank, you wouldn't be the first lady besotted by my, ahem, plumage."

"Nice feathers," she says, pulling her shirt over her head. "Want to pluck?"

At Duane Reade, in front of the soda display, Jess begins to weep. Josh flies to her side.

"What's wrong?" A basket full of toiletries hangs on his arm; mouthwash and deodorant and a foaming face wash formulated for men.

He rubs her back and waits for her to compose herself, but when people start to stop and stare, he leads her out of the building, across the street, abandoning the basket.

"What's wrong?"

"It's my dad," Jess shakes her head, through tears, "thinking about him. It makes me sad."

Josh nods. "Tell me about him."

"What do you want to know?" Jess wipes her face.

Josh says, "Anything. What were his favorite things? What made him tick? What do you miss most about him?"

"Well," Jess says, "he loved Coke"—she gestures toward the Duane Reade—"obviously. But he would only ever buy it on sale. Like, that was a line he absolutely would not cross."

Josh laughs. "What else?"

Jess tells him about her dad: that he always cheered for the little guy, he was all about justice and equity ("Sounds like somebody else I know," Josh says, and Jess says, "But he really *meant* it."), he was always helping people, doing the right thing, although, it occurs to her, in the end, he was more complicated than she realized. ("Who isn't?") Jess explains that when she was little, he used to let her ride her tricycle in the house and that made her feel like the luckiest girl in the world. He made jokes, bad ones, dad ones. He was funny.

Jess says, "This is probably going to sound like a cliché, but he really loved me. He believed in me. Thought I could do anything I set my mind to." Jess looks at Josh. "It's nice to have someone who's one hundred percent, no questions asked, totally behind you, you know what I mean?"

Josh nods. "I wish I could have met him."

Jess stands, she feels a little bit better.

Josh puts his arm around her shoulder and they head back across the street. "Well, he sounds like an amazing guy. Discerning." Josh elbows her jokily, "I'm sure he would have thought I was a cool dude. That you had impeccable taste. Don't you think?"

Jess laughs, "Ha!" but she doesn't answer the question.

*   *   *

Later, she calls Barbara just to say hello. She tells her, "I cried today thinking of my dad in front of the soda display. It was on sale." Barbara sniffles, "Oh, sweet girl." Then she clears her throat and laughs deeply. "Here I thought I was the only one at the supermarket crying over cans of Coca-Cola."

•

Work is busy. Everyone is worried about the new administration, anxious about the next four years. Although no one wants to say so—it feels gross, like they're war profiteers—it all makes good copy. The tweets, the outrage, the insanity. There's an almost frantic quality to the work. A sense of panic, but also purpose. The feeling that they're on the right side of history.

They publish something on Russian troll farms and right-wing conspiracy theories and there's so much traffic, the website briefly crashes.

There's always something new on the tip line and whenever Jess arrives at the office, instead of saying "Good morning," now Dax says "Buckle up."

A winter storm warning goes into effect. "Stay inside," the local news station blares as snow begins to dump. Jess lights candles and shakes out a pair of wool blankets. "I got a text message from the power company," she explains, "saying to expect intermittent outages."

It's bright outside, the moon high, everything white. Quiet. The only street noise is the damp tread of car tires on snow. In the loft, by candlelight, they eat pizza straight from the box.

Josh says, "This is nice."

"So what should we do now?" Jess asks.

He raises an eyebrow, suggestive. Jess laughs.

They decide to play strip poker, but they can't find a deck of cards. They rummage through their junk drawers until Josh says, "Aha!"

"You found them?"

"Something better," he says. "Strip Set?"

Jess says, "You might as well just take off all your clothes now."

"You don't always win," Josh says.

"I do."

"You don't."

She does.

And then Josh is sitting naked on the hardwood, stripped of even his socks. Jess is fully clothed, still wearing a sweater, even.

"You forget that I'm a Set savant," Jess teases.

"You know," Josh says, reorganizing the cards into a clean stack, "there's a real mathematical elegance to this game that's pretty compelling."

Jess agrees.

"I like the simplicity. Just shapes and colors and shading." He knocks the cards against his palm. "Easy."

Jess agrees.

"And I like that even though there is something like seven hundred thousand layouts in which no set can be taken, that on a finite four-dimensional space, they all reduce to essentially one set."

Jess nods, *Me too.*

He is shuffling and reshuffling so that the cards go *thwyp thwyp thwyp*. "And there's a certain harmony to the game, everything different or everything the same. I like the idea that there are more winning combinations when all the cards are different than when they're the same." He looks up. "Do you know what I mean?"

"Yes," Jess says, "I do."

She does she does she does. He is naked and they are in love and it's simple. Beauty, harmony. They sit together in the moment and everything feels easy.

Suddenly, Josh smiles. "Remember Blaine? I still remember his face when you beat him. I thought he was going to bring the wrath of Hades down on you."

The memory is distant enough that Jess also smiles.

"They were all so terrified of you," Josh says.

"What? That's not true."

"It is," he says. "Your bullshit tolerance back then was exactly zero."

"And now it's not?"

"No," he shakes his head, "I mean you're still opinionated, obvi-ously. Some might even say strident"—he looks at her sideways, gaug-ing her reaction—"but you've mellowed out."

"Hmm. Okay."

"It's a good thing."

"That I tolerate more bullshit?"

"More *nuance*."

Jess makes a face. Coming from him, she knows it's a compli-ment, but it sounds wrong. Like there's a bullshit threshold and hers is getting lower. Like she's less principled, or less interested, or less convincing.

She says, "Hmm. Okay."

"It's a good thing," he insists. "You're evolving."

One day Jess finds a bright bunch of flowers on the table, zinnias and roses and Stargazer lilies. There is a note stuck to the vase and Jess reads it and smiles. It says: *I love you, lots.*

Jess finds Josh in the bedroom.

She holds up the note, grinning madly. "Are you cheating on me or something?" she jokes.

Josh looks Jess right in the eye and says solemnly, "Oh, baby, I'm all yours."

The Wine Girls host a party to welcome Jess back to town. Dinner and drinks at their place. At the table they pass around bowls of salad and bottles of California wine, which the Wine Girls have shipped from the Napa Valley in boxes, and stack in the pantry as if preparing for the end times. They chitchat about traffic and weather and a brand of flavored water that's become popular. But then the conversation turns. Someone asks if they've seen the story, the one that came out recently; the mayor is running for reelection, and a snarky *Post* reporter has cataloged de Blasio's meager achievements. At the top of the list: the repeal of the city's long-standing ferret ban. Somehow this starts an argument.

The Wine Girls think it's actually a powerful legacy, whereas Josh thinks it's silly. They wonder what exactly he has against ferrets. And Josh tells them that he's got nothing against ferrets particularly, he just doesn't think they need an entire lobby. And Noree informs him that, well, sorry, the mayor disagrees, and is, in fact, a public advocate for ferrets' rights. Which makes Josh laugh and say that that doesn't surprise him—just another feckless liberal dicking around on the tax-payers' dime, you know? And he says this so cheerfully, spearing his salad greens so affably, that it's obvious he's not trying to start shit. Yet shit he starts.

The Wine Girls go, *wow wow wow wow*. And even though Miky interrupts with a joke—a ferret walks into a bar—and it's funny and everyone laughs, the Wine Girls aren't ready to move on. Just the opposite. They tie their waist-length hair up in a knot, as if preparing for battle, and repeat: "Feckless liberal?" Josh tells them he didn't mean anything by it—no harm, sorry, just, ha ha, you know, if the mayor has his way, he'll turn the city into some kind of socialist utopia where everything is rent controlled and the tax rate is seventy percent, ha ha, you know?—and even though he is some version of apologetic, Jess thinks, *Noooooooo*.

But somehow the Wine Girls are still smiling, or maybe they're baring their teeth. They ask Josh prettily what objections there could possibly be to rent control. Are you saying that the poor, the infirm, the elderly aren't entitled to live affordably?

And Josh tells them, not exactly, and he's mostly commenting on the fact that subsidies are notoriously inefficient. It's literally supply and demand.

The Wine Girls say, Oh, supply and demand is it, and they no longer sound pretty. Supply and demand? That's it? Because we also took Econ 101. And it's not that easy.

Lydia asks then if everyone could please not fight—isn't the chicken beautiful!—and Miky says, We're fighting? Should I get the inflatable pool and the Jell-O?

And the Wine Girls insist that no one's fighting, everyone's fine, but then they lean forward.

They want to know what Jess thinks. But Jess is not getting involved. Jess, they say, you of all people! And Jess resents being dragged into this, resents the assumption that, for unspoken reasons, she can provide moral clarity.

Don't tell us you agree with him, they say, and it feels like a dare. So Jess tells them, actually, it's something in between. She tells them that rent control is a nice idea, but not if it isn't means-tested. She tells them, Otherwise, you just end up with a bunch of random old man sculptors paying two hundred dollars a month to live in ten-thousand-square-foot lofts. She tells them, You know what, actually, it's kind of fucked up.

It's not fucked up, they tell her. Artists are the lifeblood of New York City!

They explain that the city is sliding toward inexorable decline, devolving into a late-capitalist hegemony run by Russian robber barons and Chinese billionaires, with their shell companies and Gucci handbags and spoiled children, buying up all the real property. They buy whole buildings at a time just to launder their dirty money, and these buildings, they don't ever occupy them. It's killing the culture of the city. It's sapping the life out of it.

Jess thinks, *Russian robber barons and Chinese billionaires, did they forget to mention the California trust fund kids?*

Josh says, New York is hardly a ghost town.

They say, New York shouldn't be for sale to the highest bidder.

And Josh says, Then who should it be for sale to?

In the kitchen later, scraping plates, Jess and the Wine Girls get into it. The problem is that Josh thinks the Wine Girls are idiots and the Wine Girls think Josh is an idiot and Jess thinks maybe everyone she knows is an idiot.

Noree says, "He's toxic."

Jess says, "He's not."

Callie says, "He was completely out of line."

Jess says, "It's fine."

In the middle of all this Josh wanders in, looking lost. By now more people have arrived, and the party has devolved into low-grade chaos. In the living room, someone has turned the music all the way up, and the neighbors are banging on the ceiling. One of the Wine Girls' yoga buddies is literally standing on her head. A guy that Jess has never met is smoking weed out of an apple.

Noree says to Josh, "Can we help you?"

"Do you have any milk?"

She rolls her eyes, but points to the fridge. "There's Oatly in there, probably."

"But, cow's milk?"

"What?"

"Or a can of tuna?"

"Sorry?"

Jess wants to tell Josh that he's being weird, but by the time she turns to say something he's disappeared.

The Wine Girls pick up where they left off. They say, "Honestly, Jess? We think you're compromised."

Jess says, "Compromised?"

They explain: "*Dick*-whipped."

Jess goes to find Josh. He's on the patio, crouched in the far corner, and Jess wonders if he's sick. If maybe he's hurled in one of the planters, which would be gross, but also would show the Wine Girls.

Jess slides the glass door open and when Josh turns he doesn't look sick at all, he's actually smiling, a goofy, lopsided smile. He stands and in the dark Jess can see he's cradling something in his arms.

He says, "Hey, Jess, look what I found."

She steps out onto the patio, and in the moonlight she can just make it out: a ball of fur, gray stripes, a tail curled up in a little circle. It's a cat.

"A baby cat?" Jess asks.

"A kitten."

"It's a stray?"

Josh nods, pulls the cat closer to his chest. He murmurs sweetly into its ear, "I found you wandering around all alone out here, didn't I?"

"Should you be touching it like that?" Jess asks. "Aren't you, like, worried you're going to get hepatitis or something?"

"There's only really evidence of protozoal infections passing from felines to humans," he says, not looking up, "and even that's pretty unlikely." He's bouncing the cat in his arms like a baby, scratching it behind its ears.

"Well, that cat is super tiny, it probably needs shots," Jess says. "Maybe you should be worried *it's* going to get hepatitis."

Josh laughs. "Which one of us has hepatitis in this scenario?" He tilts his head, beckoning her over. "Come on, come say hi."

He gestures for Jess to join him until she crouches down next to him. The cat is between them, dipping its tongue in and out of a little saucer. Purring softly while Josh tickles its belly. The cat stretches its little torso forward and rubs its face against the back of Josh's hand. It's mewling, a sound like a miniature dinner bell or a tiny toy trumpet, and suddenly Jess feels overcome.

It's a feeling she doesn't completely recognize, maybe it's nirvana or a higher power breathing through her or maybe it's just the salad dressing.

Josh notices. "What's wrong?"

"I just don't understand . . ."—Jess sticks her arm out to indicate the cat—"*this*. You."

"What are you talking about?"

"Why would you say that New York City should evict poor people?" Jess asks, hiccupping.

"When did I say that?"

"At dinner! Inside. When we were talking about rent control and—"

"My point was that rent control leads to market disequilibrium and creates deadweight loss in the economy."

"Okay, but we weren't talking about supply and demand curves and, like, economic theory."

"Jess, that's exactly what we were talking about!"

"No, we were—" Jess cuts herself off. "Ow, ow, ow," she cries.

"What?" Josh leans toward her, "What is it?"

"The cat," Jess says, "it's scratching me. Ow." The cat is on its hind legs, two front paws clutching at Jess's knee.

"She's not scratching. That's kneading. It means she likes you." Josh smiles and then says to the cat, "We like Jess, don't we. Yes we do. The purest heart. I know it and you know it too." He turns back to Jess. "Look. She's completely smitten. A smitten kitten."

Jess looks and what he's saying seems true. Because even though they've just met, the cat is staring up at Jess with big marigold eyes, blinking slowly, its little face completely open, its little beating heart completely exposed. Jess looks over at Josh and he is making the same face, looking at her the same way. Jess can't take it.

She loses her balance a little bit, reaching for him. She pulls his face toward hers and kisses him. He immediately kisses her back, palms starfished across each other's faces, wrist over wrist. Inside, someone screams, a glass breaks, but they keep kissing. Another crash from inside and Miky yelling, "You break it, you bought it!" Then everything gets quiet. As if there is a hermetic seal around them. It always surprises Jess, this softness in him. She could stay here forever, until—

"Found them out back! Making out again."

They stop kissing.

They stand and Jess shields her eyes with her hand as if staring into a bright light.

The cat is in Josh's palm, pressed to his chest, rubbing his thumb over its neck. It lets out a little screech.

One of the silhouettes in the doorway says, "What's . . . happening? What is that?"

"It's a baby cat," Jess explains.

"A kitten," Josh clarifies.

Jess's eyes adjust to the light and she sees her friends in the doorway. To their confused faces, Jess proclaims, "Josh saved her from a burning building!"

Miky steps forward. "Oh my god, *Jo-osh*," she coos.

The Wine Girls roll their eyes.

Lydia makes a picture frame with her hands. "I love this tableau. Stay there, I'm taking a photo!"

Jess beams. She missed this. Everything feels exactly the same. Except for one thing: her. She feels different—smarter, sadder, more sure—and that's why it's okay.

Jess tells her friends that she's staying, it's official.

Paul says, "You're back!"

"I'm back."

"Well," he says, folding her into a hug, "you owe me approximately one thousand espressos. But I got the next one."

Miky and Lydia take her out to celebrate over dim sum.

Miky makes a toast to Jess and to BFFs and to steamed dumplings, and they clink their Tsingtaos together.

And the Wine Girls, who sent Jess dozens of messages while she was away, saying *we're there for you* and *sending you positive energy* and *we hope you're okay*, say darkly, "Impeccable timing."

The inauguration is on Friday. On Saturday they will go to Trump Tower to protest. They have pink hats and posters with slogans: THE FUTURE IS FEMALE and DIE NAZI SCUM and MAR-A-LAGO FUCK YOURSELF. They take Jess to Duane Reade where they buy poster board and thick markers.

Josh raises an eyebrow.

Jess says, "Our democracy is under attack."

"And this is how you fight back?"

Jess loves him she loves him she loves him so, so much.

She thinks: There is no judgment in love.

She says, "Let's not talk about it."

Other things they don't talk about: Tenley, Jess's most recent article

(*Visualizing Lies: Analysis of 1,000 Political Speeches Shows Conservatives 10x More Likely to Bend the Truth*), money, that hat.

Jess is on her way to work, almost out the door, when Josh stops her. He has his hands behind his back; he's grinning like a maniac.

"Bodega run? So early?" Jess asks. "What are you hiding?"

"This," he replies, and whips out a bouquet of flowers.

Jess presses them to her nose. "They're beautiful."

He smiles. "Just like you."

She smiles back.

"What's in your other hand?"

He laughs. "Can't get anything past you." He hands her a small plastic gift bag and says, "Here."

Jess takes it and reads the letters printed on the side. "You went to the Intrepid Museum? When?"

"Just the gift shop," he says. "Open it."

It is a key ring with a single key attached.

"The key to your heart?" Jess asks.

"To the loft. Since you can't find yours . . . I wanted to get you something to say welcome back. Do you know what it is?"

It looks like an old-timey model airplane with an open cockpit and stacked wings. It's about four inches long. Bright red with a little blue propeller.

Jess says, "An airplane?"

"A World War II fighter plane."

"Okay . . ."

"Have you heard of Abraham Wald?"

"Like a Wald statistic?"

"Exactly! Same guy. Brilliant statistician. So during World War II he was part of a classified program of elite mathematicians. The Statistical Research Group. Are you familiar with it?"

Jess shakes her head.

"They worked on a bunch of different things but one of the main ones was figuring out how to armor fighter planes. You can't armor the entire plane because it gets too heavy. You need to be strategic. So the navy asks Wald to analyze all the planes coming back from combat to figure out where most of the bullets are hitting. And when he looks at the data, the pattern is clear. Way more bullet holes in the fuselage than the engine. In pretty much every case, the body of the plane is Swiss cheese, but the engine is pristine. So where does Wald recommend they install the armor?"

"Is this a trick question?"

Josh nods. "Yes. It's a paradox."

Jess thinks about it. "The engine."

"Exactly! Why?"

"Because you said this was a paradox and that's the opposite of my intuition."

"Ha, okay right. That's right though. It seems obvious to install the armor over the fuselage because that's where the planes are getting shot. Right? But it's the exact opposite. The *reason* that the fuselage is so damaged is because it can withstand it. Planes that get shot in the engine don't even make it back. So . . . what I'm saying is that I think people tend to confuse the fuselage with the engine, so to speak, to mix up the part that's weak with the part that's strong. And I guess I was hoping that this"—he points to the little plane—"would remind you that there's . . . this thing between us that keeps getting tested, but it's not the fragile part. You know? I'm sure there's a better way to say it, but there's only so much you can express with a key ring." He pauses, waits for her reaction. "So what do you think?"

"So this is . . . a metaphor?"

"Correct."

"For our relationship?"

"That's right."

"Wald's . . . paradox."

"Am I making sense?"

Jess nods. "I think it's . . . really romantic."

He smiles. "I thought you would like it."

Jess slides the key ring over her middle finger so the belly of the plane rests against her palm. She closes her fist over it.

"Thank you," she says. "I love it."

He kisses her, and she kisses him back.

He says, "I love you," and she says it back.

She folds her arms around his shoulders, and he folds his arms around her waist. They are kissing and saying *I love you I love you I love you* back and forth, until Josh kicks something over and they stop.

They look down.

It is one of Jess's posters, which she has lined up next to the door.

One is facedown on the floor and the other is still propped against the wall. It says DUMP TRUMP.

Josh looks at the poster, then looks at Jess, then at the ceiling, then at the floor.

He says nothing.

Neither does she.

They just stand blinking at each other until the silence becomes unbearable.

Josh touches his collar.

With her fingernail, Jess flicks the wisp of a propeller—it has the texture of thin cardboard—around and around in lopsided circles and contemplates the war metaphor.

Finally, after about a thousand years, Josh says very carefully, "The inauguration is today."

"I'm aware."

"Where are you watching?"

Jess shakes her head. "I'm not. I can't."

Josh looks confused. He angles his head toward the posters. "I thought you were going to the march tomorrow."

"I am."

"So you're going to protest a democratically elected leader and . . . you don't even know what you're protesting?"

"I know what I'm protesting. Racism and xenophobia and misogyny and—"

"It won't be that bad. Campaign rhetoric is not the same as administrative policy."

"Yeah right."

"Watch it with me," he says.

Jess looks at him like he has ten heads.

"I just want you to see. It won't be that bad."

"I have work." Jess gestures to her bag, her coat.

"So work from home."

"Don't *you* have work?"

"It's Friday," Josh shrugs, "no meetings." And then: "Seriously. I know you're worried, but you don't need to be." He smiles at her like he means it. "You'll see."

Jess hesitates.

Then she hangs up her bag. "Okay, fine."

They work on opposite sides of the apartment, Josh, in the bedroom, tap-tapping on his laptop—nothing short of nuclear apocalypse would hamper his productivity—while, in the kitchen, distracted and queasy, Jess can only stare at her phone.

At eleven-thirty Josh calls, "It's time."

Jess calls back, "I've changed my mind."

But he's already emerged from the bedroom and is walking toward the TV. "You can't just bury your head in the sand for the next four to eight years."

"*Eight* years?" Jess shudders.

"Come on," Josh says, picking up the remote. "It's your civic duty. Whatever you're imagining will be much worse. I promise." He beckons her over. "Come here. Come on."

Jess doesn't move.

"Come here." He waves his hand.

Jess joins him on the couch.

He has the remote in one hand and he offers Jess the other. He laces his fingers through hers and squeezes.

He finds the live telecast on their streaming service and taps Play.

On-screen, the motorcade arrives, a long line of limousines with blacked-out windows studded with American flags.

The day: completely gray.

The president-elect's face: somehow both mean and vacant, in a bright red tie, his suit jacket open.

Mike Pence behind him: what a fucking asshole.

The crowd gathered on the Mall: white people wrapped in blankets, cheering in red hats.

Barack Obama: dressed for a funeral, utterly inscrutable, while Michelle stands beside him, looking—and maybe Jess is projecting—absolutely terrified.

Then Anderson Cooper: in the CNN studio, intelligent and somber.

All of this seems to happen in a matter of seconds and Jess's heart beats wildly with something primal. Dread and resentment laced with anxiety.

Finally, Donald Trump is sworn into office over a Bible, and when he stands at the lectern Josh looks at Jess and says, "Ready?"

The new president starts speaking and, yes, Jess has to admit, he is atypically coherent. His subjects and verbs are in agreement, and the words he is saying, they are all in the dictionary. He is reading, verbatim, from the teleprompter.

But.

But but but. Surely that can't be enough.

Jess messages her group chat with Miky and Lydia and the Wine Girls.

Are you watching the inauguration?

omg yes

On the CNN live feed a commentator writes, *So far, this may be his best speech yet.*

On her phone, the group chat says, **this guy is completely fucking insane.**

immigrants are ravaging America??

no ragged edges . . . the address is feeling absolutely presidential

Next to her Josh says, "See?"

stop the carnage??

. . . sober and unifying . . .

this country is fucking doomed

Americans everywhere will be wondering what comes next . . .

I'm moving to Canada

. . . and the message here today from both the incoming and outgoing administrations . . .

"Hey," Josh pokes her, "you're not paying attention."

. . . is that the time for disunity is over . . .

the Cheeto-in-chief thinks he's the new führer

America first??

wtf is wrong with him?

the blood of patriots??

And then the speech is over and the talking heads act relieved. They admit that perhaps the gravity of the office has tempered his rhetoric. They admit they've all overreacted.

Heartening to see that the transition will be handled peacefully . . .

Miky joins the conversation late. She sends a poop emoji and writes Sad!

. . . and that this country will be okay.

The coverage cuts to a commercial, a middle-aged couple on bicycles, advertising a drug that lowers LDL-C.

Josh points the remote at the television and turns it off.

"Well?" he asks. "How was that?"

Jess is numb.

"Not exactly Hitler in the Sportpalast, was it?"

Jess shakes her head slowly, can't quite reply.

"See?" He pulls her closer, squeezes her shoulder. "Everything's fine."

ACKNOWLEDGMENTS

But for these two people this book would not be in your hands today: Hilary D. Jay and Andrea Blatt. Hiljay, every creative person deserves as fierce and fervent a fan as you and every person deserves a friend like you. Andrea, thank you for always seeing what this story was, is, and could be, and for always being able to articulate it beautifully. And for, quite simply, being the best agent ever.

To my smart, wonderful, sharp-eyed editors: Carina Guiterman and Lashanda Anakwah at S&S and Sophie Jonathan, Roshani Moorjani, and Anne Meadows at Picador. Thank you for your care, enthusiasm, and patience. I used to wonder about people who gave their editors too much credit—like, who actually wrote the book here!—but now I get it. Thank you. And thanks to everyone else at S&S and Picador for your full-throttled support. I am endlessly grateful.

To everyone at WME: Andrea Blatt (again), Caitlin Mahony, Fiona Baird, Olivia Burgher, and Flora Hackett, thank you for seeing and believing. I can't sing your praises highly enough.

And to all the writers and creatives I've met along the way who helped shape this book in some way: Laura Bridgeman, Michelle Brower, Vanessa Chan, Jennifer Close, Anna Furman, Meng Jin, Olga Jobe, Rachel Khong, Lydia Kiesling, Danya Kukafka, Heather Lazare, Mitzi Miller, Rina Mimoun, Sarah Schechter, Emily Storms—thank you for engaging seriously and generously with my work, even when (especially when) it wasn't quite a book yet. And especially thank you to Madeline Stevens, whose sparkling insight helped me shake the manuscript up just when it needed shaking up the most.

To my friends and family: Julie Bramowitz, Katy Dybwad, Rose-Marie Maliekel, thank you for your friendship, and Jasmine Kingsley, thank you for inviting me to Lincoln! Nico Fritsch, thank you for supporting me in both my day job and my side hustle. To the Marrs and Sullivan and Dybwad families, thank you for taking me seriously when I said I was "working on a novel" . . . for three years. And to my family, thank you for loving and supporting me from the beginning. To Michael Rabess who, after a lot of handwringing encouraged me to "just send it out," and to Margaret Rabess who always loved a good (or a bad) romance.

And to my mother, who taught me to read and to write and to love books. Thank you for everything.

And to Alex, thank you for always seeing the true nature of things and for scraping me off the floor when and as needed. And thank you for our perfect, beautiful children, without whom I would still have the time management skills of a peanut.

And finally, thank you for reading.

ABOUT THE AUTHOR

Cecilia Rabess is a writer and data scientist in San Francisco. Her work has been featured in *McSweeney's*, *FiveThirtyEight*, *Fast Company*, and *FlowingData*, among other places. *Everything's Fine* is her debut novel.